DR. GULLY'S STORY

DR. GULLY'S STORY

ELIZABETH JENKINS

COWARD, McCANN & GEOGHEGAN, INC.
NEW YORK

Where I will heal me of my grievous wound
—TENNYSON: "The Passing of Arthur"

Introduction

Though I first felt the fascination of the Bravo case many years ago, ever since I got to know about him, its chief attraction to me has been the personality of Dr. Gully.

Most writers about the case have treated him as a peripheral figure of dubious respectability, whose only claims to interest were that at the age of sixty-two he inspired an extraordinary infatuation in Florence Ricardo, a beautiful young woman of twenty-five—an infatuation that ultimately resulted in a scandal that shook Victorian London to its foundations.

In fact, Dr. Gully was a man of outstanding ability and personal magnetism, and his career as a doctor, which he gave up at sixty-three to go away with Florence Ricardo, was one of the most original in nineteenth-century medicine.

With his partner, Dr. Wilson, he established the water cure at Malvern in Worcestershire—their answer to the sensational development of drug medicine which has led us in this century to the horror of thalidomide babies.

Whatever theories he professed, Dr. Gully was a born doctor; his practice was enormous, so was his success. Tennyson and Carlyle were grateful patients; Charles Darwin called him "my beloved Dr. Gully"; Florence Nightingale said he had genius.

He was in many ways more attuned to our age than to his own, and he suffered then as one feels he would not now.

In my view, Dr. Gully's personality is so absorbing that the famous case itself is interesting chiefly for its tragic consequences to him. I would have liked to make this book a biography but the idea presented too many difficulties. I have, however, worked on all the biographical material I could find (though some of this had to be omitted for reasons of space) and I have tried to represent the story as truly as though it were a biography. Though I have ascribed thoughts and feelings to the characters and invented scenes and conversations so that the book cannot claim to be anything but a period novel, I would like to say that all references to public characters—*i.e.*, Tennyson, George Eliot, Sir Percy and Lady Shelley, William Crookes and Daniel Dunglas Home—are factual; all medical opinions ascribed to Dr. Gully are taken from his works; and all the evidence given in my account of the inquest is taken from the contemporary reports in the *Daily Telegraph*.

I have told the story from Dr. Gully's point of view, and in my account of the crisis I have excluded almost everything which he would not have known. A valuable source of information on family details is the brief and incomplete memoir, unpublished, left by Dr. Gully's son, William Gully, who afterward became the Speaker of the House of Commons.

The pearl necklace and the gold repeater watch with "Florence" enameled on the back, which Florence gave to her godchild, William Gully's daughter, are in the possession of the latter's granddaughter, Mary Ryde. For showing me diaries, letters, pictures, photographs and relics of Dr. Gully, I am most grateful to the following members of his family: the dowager Lady Mowbray and Stourton, Mrs. Marie-Louise Harrison, Mrs. Gladys Paul, Mrs. Mary Ryde, Mrs. David Yorke, the Honorable Luke Asquith, and David Jeffcock.

My warm thanks are also due to Mrs. Leslie Hammond, the owner of The Priory, Balham, for her great kindness in allowing my numerous visits to the house; to Lady Mander, for two invaluable references; to Robin Price of the Wellcome Historical Medical Library, who kindly corrected the erroneous statements published elsewhere as to the treatment of Dr. Gully by the medical profession; to Mrs. Geoffrey Goodwin for identifying from ordinance maps the houses originally called Hillside and Stokefield in the Leigham Court Road; to Mrs. J. B. Rustomjee and Gerald Morrice for guiding me to houses in Malvern; to the Tennyson Society for its sympathetic assistance; and to the College of Psychic Studies for the unique facilities which have been available to me.

DR. GULLY'S STORY

Chapter 1

᯽

I⊤ was the first of May, 1870. In a large first-floor bedroom in
Malvern House, whose windows commanded a view across the
county into Wales, Florence Ricardo was sitting at the dressing
table, while her maid, Laundon, unfastened her hair to brush
and put it up again. Florence had told Laundon to do this, but
she could scarcely sit still while it was done. Restlessness and
fatigue were wearing her almost to desperation. She had asked
peevishly why her tea wasn't there, and when the second maid
brought it, she had let it grow stone-cold at her elbow. Laundon
quickly fastened up the chestnut hair, saying: "Perhaps that
will do for now, ma'am, as you don't want to be troubled."
Florence seemed about to make a reply, but before the words
came, her eyes had flooded with tears and she held out her
hand with a blind gesture; Laundon put a handkerchief into it.

Florence had wound herself up to the effort of explaining to
Dr. Gully how ill she was, which up till now no one had properly
understood. If she couldn't make Dr. Gully understand, her last
chance was gone. She was frantic with the need for help, but
when she was asked what was the matter, her mind was a
blank. Bracing herself for the interview, she had struggled for
hours not to give way to the collapse that threatened, every
time she made an effort of any kind. A cab drew up at Malvern

House at quarter to six; wretched, with drowned eyes and unsteady from want of sleep, she got into it, followed by Laundon.

The May evening was overcast. The room into which she was shown was lofty and hushed. In the grate under the marble chimneypiece a handful of red-gold fire was lying. The ring of glass cups on the gasolier was not lighted but on the massive desk at the far end of the room a lamp with a moonlike globe burned with a soft, intense radiance. Behind it, Dr. Gully got up, came around the desk and walked toward her. For an instant his keenly intelligent blue eyes scanned her face; then he smiled. He said something kind and welcoming but she hardly knew what it was; she found herself sitting in a chair at one side of the desk while he resumed his seat at the other. He said kindly: "Your mother is a very old friend of mine, though we haven't met for many years. She tells me that your husband is very poorly and has been causing you a great deal of anxiety."

"Yes," she said in quavering tones, her large blue eyes the larger and bluer for being underwater.

"That is grievous," he said, "but now we must think about taking care of *you*. You are feeling very unwell, aren't you? Can you tell me where the trouble is?"

She had nerved herself for this moment; now that it had come, she was incapable. A long shudder went through her and she pressed the handkerchief to her mouth; over it she looked at him in despair and terror; but Dr. Gully did not seem at all impatient or at a loss.

"How is your appetite?" he asked gently. She looked as though she had not understood the question.

At last she said, "I don't know." He came around to where she sat, picked up her wrist and with one movement found the pulse. With his disengaged hand he drew out his gold watch and flicked open the cover; he looked at the dial while the story she was too exhausted to give, continued itself under his fingertips. Then he snapped back the cover and returned the watch to his waistcoat pocket.

"How do you sleep?" he asked.

"I can't sleep unless I take chloral. But that makes me feel worse. It makes my head ache."

"Does your head ache now?"

"Yes." She gave a strangled sob and the long shudder went through her again. He came to the back of her chair and withdrew the pins from her small, forward-tilted hat, lifting it from her head. The mass of chestnut hair was bunched on her neck. He pushed his fingers underneath it and began a slow, rhythmic friction, up and down the back of the neck from the nape to the base of the skull. He spoke again but Florence could not understand him, her head was beginning to swim with sleepiness. She just made out that he was saying: ". . . more comfortable on the sofa."

He seated her at the head of it, then stooped, raised her heels and stretched her out at full length. Waves of sleep were engulfing her; she forced her eyes open and saw his face and bald forehead under the lamp, bent over something that he was writing. Her last thought was: "If I have to go out of this room, I shall die. Let me stay here for ever and ever."

Dr. Gully rang the bell at the side of the fireplace, then he went to the door and stood outside. "Pritchard," he said, when the butler appeared, "bring Mrs. Ricardo's maid here, and you had better dismiss that cab." When Laundon came into the hall, he said: "Mrs. Ricardo appears quite exhausted. She's fallen asleep. Of course she must have her sleep out. My butler and cook will make you comfortable for an hour or two, but first I would like you to tell me as much as you can about Mrs. Ricardo's state of health." He led her into the library, leaving both doors ajar. He motioned her to a chair and sat down at the writing desk.

Laundon was a neat, smart young woman. She had a pair of sharp eyes, but her manner was respectful and she seemed truly anxious. A small reservation about her crossed his mind, lost sight of as he questioned her.

"Now," he said, "how would you describe this illness?" Laundon searched her mind.

"She's always crying," she said, "not exactly crying, but with her eyes full of tears. And sometimes so restless she won't lie down when her mama and sister want her to, but other times it's just the opposite; if you tell her it's time for luncheon, she'll say she can't get up out of her chair—she'll be frightened and say her limbs have failed her."

He made a few notes, then said: "Can you remember anything else?"

"I don't know that I can, sir, except that she can't make up her mind. So different from what she'd used to be! The other day she was to go out with her sister, Mrs. Chalmers. She was so long coming downstairs they came up to see after her. But I couldn't do anything with her. She'd got all her brooches laid out and she was crying because she couldn't decide which to put on."

The doctor was silent. Then he said: "And what has been done for her, so far?"

"Well, she's taking some tonics, and the chloral to make her sleep; but there wasn't anything else anybody *could* do. It wasn't as if she was really ill."

"Not really ill!" Dr. Gully repeated.

"Well, not to stop in bed."

He said: "I'm afraid people can be very ill, even if they don't stop in bed. Mrs. Ricardo is very ill now, but we must set about curing her."

"I'm sure I shall be thankful!" the young woman exclaimed.

"I'm sure you will. Now, about her husband. How long has he been drinking like this?"

"Two years at least and getting worse all the time."

"Is he violent?"

"Oh, *yes,* something shocking. When it's at its worst no one can go near him except his man; he'd brain anybody. Then he'll be all worn out and so dazed-looking, he says what a miserable wretch he is and begs her pardon. At first it made her cry over him and try to help him. But it went on too long for her, you understand."

"I think I do."

"Now she can hardly bear to be in the same room with him, though he's to come up here in a week or two. Even when he wants to be good to her, she can't bear it. And then, it's the sickness. Ladies don't complain of home nursing, whoever they are. But this! The smell, it's never out of the house, not once you get near his rooms. We came back in the carriage to Lowndes Square—all the family was in London. The carriage stopped at the door. But Mrs. Ricardo didn't get out. The footman, he looked at me but I couldn't help him. She just sat there. 'I *can't* go in,' she said, white as a sheet. Then they brought the old mistress out. 'Come along, my love,' she says, and we got her onto the pavement. The butler came down the steps, worried because of the people passing in the square. We all tried to hide her. But she gave a terrible loud wail and said: 'Let me stay in the open air, Mama, or I shall be sick myself.'"

The doctor was looking down at the table; he said impassively: "Of course it's extremely trying and disgusting; but it's often a result of drunkenness."

"I think it'll drive her mad if she has much more of it, I do indeed."

"Well!" said Dr. Gully, getting up. "We must see what can be done for her. If she is still asleep, Pritchard will take you downstairs and I'll send for you as soon as she is awake." They went quietly into the consulting room and found Florence fast asleep on the sofa, one hand trailing on the floor. Dr. Gully stooped, raised it and laid it by her side. Having sent away Laundon in Pritchard's care, he with great precaution lifted a lump of coal and settled it noiselessly in the glowing bed of the fire. Then he lit a pair of candles and turned down the lamp. He had been working at the desk—he did not know how long—when Pritchard's head appeared in the opening of the door; when Dr. Gully went to him, he asked below his breath if the doctor wouldn't have some dinner, it being now past eight o'clock. "Not yet," Dr. Gully answered. After another half hour, Florence stretched herself with a great sigh, opened her eyes and then lay still, gazing tranquilly at him as he came and stood over the sofa.

"You feel better now, I hope?" he said.

"Yes," she said, moving her head about, and gradually remembering where she was. Dr. Gully turned up the lamp and rang the bell. When Pritchard and Laundon appeared, he told the former to have the carriage put to; then he asked Florence if she would like some tea or soup.

"Tea," Florence said, and in a few minutes Pritchard came back with a cup of tea on a salver.

Dr. Gully's objection to hot drinks as injurious to the digestive tract was so well known that tea in his house, as a matter of course, was served as a cool, fragrant, refreshing drink rather than a hot, stimulating one. Florence, now sitting up, took the cup and saucer, Dr. Gully meanwhile speaking to Laundon in low tones as they stood on the hearth. A moment later Florence said, in imperious tones, "I'm afraid this tea is cold." She was sitting erect, beautifully flushed, her eyelids heavy and swollen but her round blue eyes starry. Dr. Gully did not think the occasion one for a lecture. "Pritchard," he said, "please bring a small pot as Mrs. Ricardo wants hot tea."

Pritchard retired at once. He could not avoid the idea that people who were so fortunate as to enjoy the doctor's personal supervision should take their tea as the doctor thought fit, but not a trace of this appeared in the correct bearing of the manservant when he presented Florence with a small silver tea equipage. She drank a cup thirstily while Dr. Gully watched her. He said to Laundon: "Perhaps Mrs. Ricardo would like some soup or a milk pudding when she gets back to Malvern House. After that, I think she should go straight to bed."

"Really," said Florence, stretching herself. "I am very sleepy."

"That is excellent," said Dr. Gully. "We must hope that Malvern is beginning to do you good already. Will you try tonight to go to sleep without chloral?"

"I'll *try*," she said.

He appeared satisfied. She leaned back against the head of the sofa. She heard him say to Laundon: "I will be at Malvern House tomorrow morning at eleven o'clock. I should like Mrs. Ricardo to have her first packing then. I will arrange for a bath attendant. She had better stay in bed; it will tire her to get dressed and undressed again." Laundon replied. Florence did not mind what they were saying; she was luxuriating in heedlessness and serenity. Then the front doorbell pealed twice.

"That is the carriage," Dr. Gully said. He and Laundon took her each by an elbow and set her on her feet. She staggered in her first attempt to walk but the sense of well-being did not leave her. They guided her across the hall to where wheels were visible at the open door and horses' heads were tossing and jingling out of sight.

"I think you had better get in first, Miss Laundon," the doctor said, "then you can help Mrs. Ricardo in." Laundon jumped in nimbly, turned around and held out her hands. Dr. Gully put both his hands at Florence's waist and with what seemed no effort, lifted her to the step. With a rustle of draperies, half-falling into Laundon's hands, she was seated. He shut the door and said: "Malvern House, Griffith," and she was driven away into the spring darkness.

Over his solitary dinner—for it was a rule of the household that when detained, he was not waited for—he thought deeply about this case. Continuous mental suffering had brought on a physical collapse; the state of the body increased the mental suffering. As he had written of this type of nervous ailment: "Morbid impressions commencing in the brain are reverberated on the visceral ganglionic system, exciting in the viscera sensations and movements. Abnormal sensations and movements in the viscera are reflected in the brain."

Well, they had, it seemed, a fortnight before this deplorable husband reappeared to interrupt her recovery. In that time, he expected some actual benefit from the treatment, but, still more important, that he would have established her confidence in the curative routine, so that she would continue it of her own free will, let the husband's condition be what it might.

He was reasonably optimistic; for one thing, the result of two hours' natural sleep had shown him that she had considerable resilience, that, taken in time, the mischief might be conquered. He had felt obliged to leave the chloral bottle within her reach for one more night, in case she felt she needed it; cold sitz baths and spinal washings would, he was confident, soon do away with her dependence on it. Moral as well as physical treatment would be necessary and some protective influence to ensure that her domestic circumstances didn't destroy any improvement as fast as it was made. A young married woman was sometimes more helpless, more vulnerable than a girl; the latter might have the protection of loving, capable parents; in the last resort, the wife was at the husband's mercy, the father and mother were often forced to stand aside. But in this case, the parents would have his assistance to reckon on.

Chapter 2

THE time of year was a piercing reminder of the spring of 1842, when he and his friend, Wilson, had left their London practices and established themselves here, in a Malvern that was then a little hillside town of scarcely two thousand inhabitants. They were both in revolt against fashionable drug medication, whose immediate results were so startling and whose long-term effects often so disastrous. Wilson while on a tour in Bavaria had found a peasant called Priessnitz achieving extraordinary cures by hydropathy, and his acute medical insight had convinced him that the system had a scientific basis: that, since all chronic disease arose from the viscera's being starved of blood or engorged with it, cold water applied to the skin by various methods, by stimulating the circulation would cure the morbid condition or check and relieve it. His enthusiasm inspired Dr. Gully at the moment when the latter was prepared to make a momentous change.

He had been born in Jamaica, the son of a well-to-do coffee planter; brought to England at one year old, he remembered nothing of the beautiful island, but its name, Xaymaca, the land of springs, called up in his mind a network of sparkling waters. As a medical student he had shown uncommon gifts and his early years in practice had proved that he was what patients call "a born doctor."

He had lost his young wife in 1838, and his two sisters, affectionate and sensible young women, lived with him and took care of his children, Susanna and William; his youngest child, his darling, the two-year-old Fanny, had died of croup. He meanwhile was making a name as a physician and a writer of medical tracts; a successful future seemed, ultimately, to be assured; then, in 1841, he made the mistake of his life.

A Mrs. Kibble, a widow of ample fortune, living in one of the beautiful houses on Park Square East, fifty years old to his thirty-three, made it plain that she admired the vigorous, magnetic doctor. Driving ambition told him that her money was the one element he lacked for success, and blinded him into believing that the marriage could be advantageous to them both. At the very start, it was unpromising; Mrs. Kibble refused to have his sisters and the children living in her house, so he established them as near as he could, around the corner in Albany Street.

The marriage broke down almost at once; the domineering, vindictive temper she had concealed while she was eager to marry him showed itself when the dedicated doctor put the claims of his profession before a perpetual attendance on her. At the end of eighteen months, the misery was so acute that Wilson's vehement desire to carry him off to Malvern met with no opposition from her. A legal separation was effected and Mrs. Gully retired with a companion housekeeper and a staff of servants to a handsome house in Brighton. He had never seen her again, but she was there still, hale as ever at seventy-eight.

He had transplanted his sisters and the children to Malvern in the Worcestershire hills, the place chosen by Wilson and himself as offering the pure air of the heights and copious water, exquisitely clear. Their immediate success had astonished even themselves. Within five years Dr. Wilson had built a spa and a large hotel next it, Malvern House, that catered for invalids. Dr. Gully had acquired two houses side by side under the lee of the great hill on whose side Saint Anne's Well poured out its diamond water; he had at first lived in part of one of them but had soon been obliged to give up all the accommodation to patients, and had bought The Priory House at the end of the town for himself and his family. This was of Regency Gothic, with crocketed gables; behind it, a large lawn, sprinkled with evergreen trees, sloped down to an ornamental water like dark-green glass. Above, the great circle of the hills seemed to be hanging in the sky; at their foot, the Priory Church was half hidden in trees.

The air and the water were aids to a healthy regime but the actual water treatment was an elaborate system, based on a daily examination of the patient at which one form of hydropathy or another was prescribed, varying, often from day to day; the process was at first uncomfortable; its ultimate success was bringing patients from all over England.

In 1847 and again in 1848, Dr. Gully received one of his most interesting cases: Alfred Tennyson, aged thirty-eight, a year younger than himself, tall, gaunt, with dark hair always rough and dark, visionary eyes. He was suffering from morbid depression, a classic instance of Dr. Gully's saying: "The brain thinks but as the viscera dictate." Packing in sheets wrung out of cold water caused Tennyson to exclaim with gloomy energy that he had been "half cured, half destroyed" by the treatment.

One day, standing in the drawing room of The Priory House, he took a piece of paper out of his pocket and gave it to the doctor. It was a copy of a poem of three verses, beginning "Come not when I am dead," and the last verse ran:

Child, if it were thine error or thy crime
I care no longer, being all unblest;
Wed whom thou wilt, for I am sick of time,
And I desire to rest.

Dr. Gully read the painful lines with admiration and a secret compassion for the desperate-looking creature who had put them into his hand.

"Mr. Tennyson," he said, "I value this greatly. It will be something to leave to my children."

Tennyson was only one in a range of celebrated patients, who, among crowds of humbler sufferers, came to him over the years. Ironically, the split with Wilson had come about through their phenomenal success. Their practice had resulted in a great and continuous expansion of the town: Hotels, houses, shops sprang up; in 1861 the railway reached Malvern in a beautiful little station decorated with the local ironwork—cast-iron wreaths of plants around the capitals of the pillars on the platform and ironwork lace on the roof, spiking up against the sky. The railway led to a further increase of the population, and it was inevitable that the civic appointments should be bestowed on Dr. Gully, urbane and with a strong grasp of practical affairs, rather than on Dr. Wilson, speaking seven languages and sometimes to be found in the street bareheaded because he'd forgotten at which house he'd left his hat.

The publication of Dr. Gully's book, *The Water Cure in Chronic Disease,* which, since it was made up from his casebooks, conveyed a picture of himself, authoritative from experience and success, further eclipsed Wilson's image in the public mind. They had separated long since, each taking another partner. Wilson's death in 1867 brought back painful memories of the time when they'd been inseparable colleagues, wild about medicine and music. Nowadays when he went to the Royal

Opera House—for opera was still his passion—he wore a satin-lined cloak and sat in a stall. He would turn and gaze up at the vast prospect of the theater, picking out the tier where the two impecunious young men had sat.

But the life of an extremely busy doctor did not leave much time for thinking about the past. He was not only concerned with orthodox medicine; he said it was the duty of the physician to use any method that would help the patient, and he used mesmerism to induce sleep and a clairvoyant to help him diagnose internal conditions. The famous medium Daniel Home had been his patient, suffering from hemorrhage of the lungs which the water treatment had checked, and Home's extraordinary powers had been exercised in The Priory House itself. That the doctor's child, Fanny, should be heard speaking to him—that, perhaps, was merely the telepathic communication of a darling wish; but the sliding about of furniture, raps on the shutters and the door, the bookcase wall concealed by a sheet of silver against which figures moved, while all the time the medium sat with his eyes shut, his pale face illumined by a wreath of starry lights—none of this could be accounted for by any merely common-sense explanation.

Dr. Gully had been present in Mrs. Milner Gibson's drawing room in Hyde Park Place when, on an evening in August, 1860, Home had performed his amazing feat of levitation: rising into the air and floating across the room. The report of this affair, published in the *Cornhill*, aroused such animosity in those who hadn't seen it that finally Dr. Gully wrote a letter to the press, giving his testimony that the event had actually occurred, though he offered no explanation of it. "Who shall say," he wrote, "that we know all the powers of nature?"

In this circle he had met Sir Percy Shelley and his wife, the poet's son and daughter-in-law. Shelley was his favorite poet, and he was delighted to meet the son who had his father's

large eyes, though without the light in them. Lady Shelley, energetic and radiant, had given him one of his treasures: a print
of a portrait of the poet, with a signature cut from a letter,
under the glass. He often visited them at Boscombe Manor outside Bournemouth. The railway took him as far as Poole, and
the Shelleys' carriage then conveyed him five miles through the
fragrant darkness, the wheels and hooves sometimes muffled
by the thick carpet of pine needles. These visits always had a
great charm for him, and they held one exceptional interest.
Lady Shelley's adopted niece, a child of twelve, began in 1865
to make a series of automatic drawings. She threw them off with
great rapidity and then seemed to be as much puzzled by them
as anybody else. They were obviously the work of a child but
inspired to an unearthly degree with airiness and joy. They illustrated the spirit leaving the body at death and rising toward
angels, who stooped down over it, their foreheads and shoulders
scintillating with crystals and stars. These beings took care of
the spirit, explaining to it where it was and helping it adjust
to its new sphere of life. The drawings had a quality which
delighted and awed him, and the child's unconscious manner
of producing them, he thought, gave them an extraordinary
significance.

His visiting and entertaining, his civic appearances, his yearly
travels on the continent, his crowded, famous professional life
—though the fact of a separated wife was known—all this made
most people assume that what they saw of his existence was
all that there was to see. Some few believed a rumor that he performed abortions; even they did not suggest that he did so
merely as a means of making money; they only said, guardedly,
how sad it was that humane and liberal ideas should lead to
the encouragement of vice.

Liberal and humane he was known to be, but very few were
aware that on matters of sexual morality he shared the beliefs

of the most advanced thinkers. In the locked bookcase in his dressing room he had a copy of Dr. Drysdale's book, *Prostitution, Poverty and Celibacy*. Drysdale claimed that if some sexual intercourse were available to all women, it would prevent "sexual morbidity and repressed sexual desires," and their effects in cases of chlorosis, hysteria and diseases of menstruation. This, Dr. Gully believed, was medically sound, but impossible to apply in the present state of society. Drysdale added: "It is absolutely impossible to have a free, sincere and dignified sexual morality as long as marriage continues to be the only honourable provision for union of the sexes and as long as the marriage bond is so indissoluble as at present."

His own situation brought the words home to his very soul. He never went near Brighton but he kept in touch with the establishment at 42 Brunswick Square through his wife's solicitors who sent him a report four times a year when her quarterly income was received. They assured him that Mrs. Gully enjoyed her meals and drives and was wonderfully well.

He was now sixty-two, Ann fifty-five and Ellen fifty-two. Of his children the beautiful and self-contained Susanna had married eligibly, but she had been left a widow with four small children, to whom he was a kind grandfather. His son, William, was doing very well at the bar; of the qualities that make for success, he had the quieter ones: a cool head, a sound memory and outstanding integrity. He had made a delightfully happy marriage; his young wife, ingenuous and intelligent, was an enchanting mixture of candor and sweetness; and when Dr. Gully went to London, he thoroughly enjoyed his visits to their house in Queensborough Terrace. They already had three children, two boys and now a girl, Gertrude, whom her grandfather called Gi-gi. She was his favorite, but no child had ever taken Fanny's place. He had had a bust made from her death mask; it stood upright, but had the closed eyes and the sideways turn of the head as it had lain on the pillow. The hair was copied in reeded curls that he had last seen like damp feathers on the bluish-white temples. He had been alone with her for a few minutes before the final paroxysm. Her blue eyes were open but glazed and he thought she had gone beyond the point where she could recognize anybody; then, for a second, the life came back; she put up her little hand and stroked his face. He had never been able to tell anyone that, not even his sisters who had nursed her so devotedly. He kept the bust in his dressing room.

Though so many of his trains of thought were unrevealed, they played their part when he studied a patient. His skill in diagnosis had got to a point where it was felt to be uncanny. A worn-down sufferer would sometimes break off his dismal tale to say: "But I believe you know how I feel better than I can tell you." But now, the success which was so eminent and of such long standing was becoming a little flat; though he was at the height of his intellectual powers and though his physical ones were very little diminished, he was conscious now of a very slight but perpetual fatigue. He supposed it would grow on him till at last it dulled every faculty of enjoyment; that what he had missed in life so far, he would now never find.

The spring was always a disturbing time. It came late in the Malvern hills, but now at the beginning of May, it was just about to burst into heat and scent. On the morning of May 2, the day after he had seen Florence Ricardo, he woke when his gold repeater told him it was only quarter to five. He lay looking at the faint light behind the cedar boughs, and as he listened to a few half-uttered, brief notes, they began to swell in number and volume and he realized suddenly that for once he was hearing the dawn chorus, fluting, whistling, warbling, singing, a whole orchestra of sweet, ringing sounds. As the light grew stronger the music died down and in a pause, all by itself, he heard a cuckoo's unearthly cry. When the noise had sunk to the sporadic bird-notes he was accustomed to hear in his waking moments, he lay with his head turned to the wide-open window, the sensation caused by that miraculous burst of song still in his blood.

Chapter 3

PROMPTLY at eleven the next morning Dr. Gully was shown into Mrs. Ricardo's bedroom at Malvern House. The door of the dressing room was open and he saw Laundon and the other maid within. He gave one glance at the figure in its white draperies propped against the heaped white pillows, then went to the window, which was almost closed, and lowered the sash. Freshness from the vast height of sunlit air poured into the room. Having brought in the aid of one of his most powerful helpers he came up to the bedside and said "Good morning" as he took her pulse. He looked at her but did not ask her how she was. As he stood with his fingers on her wrist, she gazed up at him, so fresh and spruce, so impressive and so impersonal, and felt that this was very different from the impression she had gained the night before. Laying down her hand, he inquired about bowel movement, looked at her tongue and then said: "And how did you sleep?"

"I had *some* sleep," she said. He would ask, she thought, about the chloral; she was considering whether to give him the answer he wanted to hear; Laundon, she knew, would not contradict her. But before she could commit herself to a damaging lie, he raised one of her eyelids and examined the pupil.

Then, dismissing the matter, he said: "Mrs. Rideout is here.

She is one of our very best bath attendants. You couldn't be in better hands. She'll give you your first wet sheet packing now. You'll find it a little shivery for the first few moments. Then, I promise you, it'll be extremely comfortable. I should like you to have another in the late afternoon, but I'll look in before that."

She saw his bald head and his erect back disappearing through the door before she could collect herself to say—what did she want to say? She turned restlessly. Laundon and her fellow maid, Rogers, spoke in undertones in the dressing room. It was a relief to be told that the mistress was really ill, though she hadn't fever or pains or a rash. Taking care of her in her bed was much easier than having her up, dragging about and crying and you not knowing what to do for her.

Mrs. Rideout was a small, thin woman in cap, apron, print dress, all of immaculate cleanness, with a large gunmetal watch in her bib pocket. Her chiseled features and clear eyes belonged to an interesting type of face, but her manner was completely unself-conscious, cheerful, dedicated to service.

She said, "Good morning, ma'am," and Florence, who had been waited on all her life and had a discriminating eye for good servants, liked her immediately.

Malvern House supplied the essentials for the water treatment, and there had been carried down the corridor after Mrs. Rideout, and were now brought into the room, a small camp bed with a mattress and clean blankets, a shallow hip bath and two tall jugs of water. Mrs. Rideout herself carried a large bowl; in this a sheet that had been dipped in cold water and wrung out by twisting was lying coiled like a rope.

Mrs. Rideout, helped by Rogers, spread the mattress on the camp bed and covered it with a blanket; on this she spread the damp sheet. Then she said to Laundon: "Now, if you'll help the lady to take off her dressing gown and nightgown?"

Florence, divested by Laundon, crossed the floor naked. Hesitant, cautious, she lay down on her back and gave a sharp exclamation as Mrs. Rideout laid the two sides of the sheet across her, then covered her with another blanket and tucked it firmly in, and drew the large watch out of her pocket.

For a few seconds Florence was odiously uncomfortable from cold and damp; then she began to feel merely uncomfortable, not cold but clammy. In another minute the disagreeableness had departed, a warmth was invading her, a soporific warmth. Before she knew it she had fallen into a doze, and ten minutes later she awakened to peevish annoyance at being roused and stripped of her hot, moist covering.

Laundon and Mrs. Rideout guided her into the hip bath and when she was sitting in it, Mrs. Rideout poured tepid water over her back: "So you don't take cold, ma'am," she said. "Now, will you please get out?" Florence stood on a folded towel, and Mrs. Rideout enveloped her in another, larger one, rubbing her with a brisk, all-over movement such as she had never experienced. After a brief spell of this, Mrs. Rideout said in her pleasant, courteous tones: "If you wish to be dressed, now, ma'am, that is all the doctor has ordered at present."

While Laundon brought a pile of underclothes from the dressing room, and began putting them on her, Mrs. Rideout with Rogers' help cleared the bedroom. They carried the bedstead and the hip bath into the dressing room and stood the jugs outside the bedroom door to be refilled. Mrs. Rideout piled the sheet into the bowl and saying with her earnest pleasantness, "I wish you good morning, ma'am," left the room.

Laundon went on rapidly lacing the corset over Florence's chemise. When the white petticoats had been tied around her waist, Florence said she would not be dressed any further, and Laundon put over them a white cambric peignoir trimmed with a quantity of lace. When Florence had had her luncheon, sitting in the window, which she had told Laundon to close because the breeze was a little strong, the latter asked if she would like to order a carriage. Florence, with a return of irritability, said no. She had a novel on her lap from the Malvern House Library for the Use of Visitors; but it did not hold her attention. She moved impatiently and wondered at what time Dr. Gully would come again. Her little gold repeater watch, in a nest of the coiled links of its gold chain, lay winking in the light. It was a pretty little thing; on the back was engraved a flourishing R, and across it went a ribbon of crimson enamel with "Florence" in white letters. It had been one of Alexander's presents. She pushed it away from her. She would be obliged very soon to give her mind to a whole, inner scene of troubles, fears, oppression and abhorrence. She would have to exert herself to find a furnished house for them all—that was what she was expected to do, and what she had come to Malvern to do—but in twelve hours after consulting Dr. Gully, she had been gently, firmly, made to assume the status of an invalid herself. She was no longer to be looked upon, for the present, as someone capable of ordinary existence. She had not been able to explain to anyone how ill she was, but Dr. Gully had seen it at once without any explanation.

As she was thinking of this Rogers came into the room with a large bunch of lilies of the valley. Florence's eyes brightened and she took them, breathing in the rich, exquisite scent. A woman below was selling them and had sent up to know if the lady would buy any. Rogers had asked, "How much?" and the woman had said, "Anything the lady liked to give." Florence told the girl to give her half a crown and to say that she might bring more; with lilies of the valley, you gained the best effect by a lavish use.

Florence had brought with her a boxful of things to supplement or replace those of Malvern House. Her own sheets were now on the bed and her own pillow cases, monogrammed and edged with deep borders of crochet lace. In the bottom of the trunk a set of tea china had been carefully packed, and from this layer Rogers disinterred two glass vases, one green, one rose color, both heavily enameled in white.

"Put them in the green one," Florence said. She was lying on a cane chaise longue, with the flowers close to her head, when Dr. Gully came in at four o'clock.

"And how did you feel during the packing?" he asked. "It wasn't too uncomfortable, was it?"

She had been meaning to say that though the experience had not been so very uncomfortable after the first few minutes, it *had* been rather wearying and that she did not feel inclined to have another dose of it that day; but with Dr. Gully standing there, it did not seem very easy to say this. She sighed. "No, not really," she said.

"I think you'll find it becomes more and more soothing as you persevere with it." She noticed that he said, "as you persevere," not "if." She wanted to make a petulant remark, but he went on: "And did you feel comfortable with Mrs. Rideout?"

"Yes, I did."

"You would like to keep her as your bath attendant?"

"Yes, I should."

"Well, she will come to you again at five o'clock, and after your second packing I think you should find it easier to sleep tonight. I want you to give up this chloral as soon as possible. It's very bad for you."

"Yes. It makes me feel wretched. But I can't lie awake."

"I don't want you to. That's why I haven't forbidden it for the present. But there are parts of this treatment specially useful in procuring natural sleep: cold sitz baths and spinal washings. We will try them and then you'll find you don't need chloral or any other opiates." He went to the dressing room where the two maids stood up as he appeared at the door. Before he needed to ask for it, he saw the ribbed, dark-blue glass bottle on a chest of drawers with a medicine glass and a silver spoon beside it.

"How much does Mrs. Ricardo take of this?" he said. Laundon approached and touched the side of the glass.

"That is a very strong dose," said Dr. Gully in a low voice.

"Well, sir, nothing less has seemed to do her any good."

"I hope she won't ask for it tonight. If she does, give her half that quantity."

Laundon said, "Yes, sir," but he did not entirely trust her. If she were not trustworthy, even taking the bottle away would be useless; she could buy more in the town. His only sure method was to establish such an influence over the patient that she would reject for herself anything he had forbidden. He returned to the bedroom. Florence was inhaling the scent of the lilies as she lay; she could not smell it with every breath she drew, it numbed the sense; she realized it only in intermittent breathings.

Dr. Gully said pleasantly: "That is a very fine bunch but it's too near your nose. The flowers are interfering with your supply of oxygen." He picked up the vase and carried it to the table near the window. Then he said to Laundon: "Leave them there during the day and put them outside the room at night; and keep this window open," he added. He lifted the sash.

"I had it shut," Florence said, "because the breeze was too strong."

"Then you must sit away from the window."

"But I do so enjoy this view."

"Naturally you do. But fresh air is very important for you. Getting well is a task, you know. We have to work at it and give up some of the things we enjoy while we're engaged on it." He took her hand in his firm hold. As she looked up at him her eyes were wistful but they were no longer under standing pools of tears. He felt great satisfaction at having established her in the protected situation of an invalid, removing the burden of daily existence from her worn young mind. He gave the smile that she already found so charming, so reassuring.

"Mrs. Rideout will be here at five o'clock," he said. "And I will see you before she comes tomorrow morning. And now, I hope you'll have a better night with some natural sleep." She watched him leave the room and lay with her eyes turned toward the door long after he had disappeared through it.

She was beginning to feel herself surrounded by healthful, soothing influences, and when Mrs. Rideout appeared, carrying her great bowl with, this time, two coils of sheet in it, Florence felt that the pleasant, quiet briskness gave her the confidence she had needed for a very long time.

This evening, Mrs. Rideout said, the doctor had ordered twenty minutes' packing with a change of sheet halfway through. The preparations were made and Florence, with the usual gasps, surrendered herself to the cold clasp. She remained awake in spite of the stealing warmth; then came the discomfort of being peeled of the warm moist coverings and having to encounter the chill linen again; but this time warmth passed into drowsiness and then into a blessed nothing. Even the tepid sponging and the all-over friction did not thoroughly rouse her, and when she was in her nightgown lying among the pillows she had only a hazy idea of Mrs. Rideout's leaving her. Some time later a basin of arrowroot was before her and Laundon's encouraging words in her ear, but when she had eaten a spoonful or two, sleep overpowered her and Laundon caught the basin before it was upset on the bed.

As the sky darkened, the maids lit the lamp in the dressing room and with the door open, alert for any sound, they settled to an evening of crochet, and of low-voiced conversation; most of this was on their own affairs and some of it about Field, the master's valet—he was called a valet, but in the sinister phrase of the servants' hall, he "couldn't be done without"—and they agreed it was a cruel thing, that "he" should come to Malvern, and throw her back in the first improvement she'd shown for months.

Florence slept soundly till six the next morning, and asked for her breakfast as soon as the maids came to her. Rogers went downstairs to fetch the tea and toast and she was called down again at what was still quite an early hour; the woman had come with another great bunch of lilies of the valley, morning gathered. When Rogers brought them in, cold with dew, Florence told her to arrange them in the second vase; she would have both vases on her bedside table. Laundon began gently to say what the doctor had said, but Florence repeated her order impatiently.

Now that the power to sleep was coming back, it surprised her at unexpected moments. Though she had slept so well already, she fell asleep when her tray was removed, then woke, and was asleep again when Dr. Gully came into the room.

He noted this time that the window was wide open behind the white curtains that stirred in the current of air, but he also saw the lilies of the valley standing on the marble-topped cupboard beside her head, and not one bouquet but two. He said to Laundon: "I asked you to move those flowers."

"I did, sir, but Mrs. Ricardo would have them back, she enjoys the scent."

Dr. Gully said: "A few in a wineglass will give her the scent." He took the two great bunches and put them firmly on the round table. While Laundon stood respectfully apart, he approached the bed again and looked at the sleeper.

She was lying with her head on one side. The nightgown with its bishop's sleeves, its mass of tucks and frills, was crumpled but spotless; in the shaded light it had a marble whiteness. She was breathing very quietly. He took the hand nearest to him and felt the pulse, then felt her forehead with the backs of his fingers. After that, he stood with his hands behind his back, looking down at her.

At last he came over to the door and said to Laundon: "I won't order any packing this morning. It's much better that Mrs. Ricardo should sleep. Of course don't wake her. Let her sleep as long as she can."

When he came in the afternoon, Florence was sitting up in an armchair, still in her white dressing gown, but her hair had been drawn up, curving like a great wave behind her head—a process which, before, she had been too tired to undergo. She was pale with shadows around the eyes, but though she looked weak, she no longer seemed on the verge of collapse.

She said with a taking graciousness: "I'm sorry I was asleep when you came this morning. Why didn't you wake me up?"

He said: "Because I preferred that you should sleep." He sat down and saw that the flowers were still where he had put them.

"You had those lilies put back beside your bed after I had said they must be moved."

"Yes, I do so love the scent."

"If you must have the scent, it's a simple matter. Call in a doctor who'll let you do as you like, whether it's good for you or not." He spoke so lightly and pleasantly, it was not till a moment afterward that she realized he meant what he said. Then, resentment and self-pity nearly choked her. It was very hard to be spoken to in this unfeeling way when she was so ill. Her eyes, though the lids were red and heavy, had been dry for thirty-six hours. Now they filled with tears again, but natural, smarting tears called up by anger and shock.

"My dear Mrs. Ricardo," Dr. Gully said, "I don't want to be harsh, I only want to make you well; but if my instructions aren't followed, I can't go on with the case."

"Just because I wanted some flowers by my bed—"

"Not *just* that, I think. After all, if you won't take my advice in one particular, how can I be sure that you will in another?"

Florence was now crying unrestrainedly.

"Come," he said, "don't cry. You'll make me feel quite unkind."

"So you are," she said brokenly. "How can you suggest that I should call in somebody else?" He did not find it necessary to answer, but picked up a handkerchief which lay with her watch on the small table and handed it to her. She held it to her eyes and he noticed a letter, pushed half back into its envelope.

"I see you have a letter from Mrs. Campbell," he said, to cause a diversion in her thoughts. "I daresay she is anxious for news of you."

"Yes, I suppose she is."

"Would you like me to write to her?"

"Yes, very much, if you will be so kind. But"—and a haunted look came over her face—"she wants to know if I have found a house."

He said at once: "You can't look for a house at present, but if you tell my sister, Ann, the sort of house you require, she will inquire of an agent in the town what houses are available. Then you can take a carriage and go to see them."

"Oh, *yes!*" Florence breathed, smiling through the tears, with a quick recovery like a child's that touched and moved him.

Chapter 4

❦❧

WHEN, by her brother's arrangement, Miss Gully called on Mrs. Ricardo to offer help in finding a furnished house, her appearance pleased Florence at once: plain but agreeable, intelligent, her gray linen dress simple but correct in outline with all its fullness gathered at the back, of a ladylike quietness that avoided the dowdy as well as the fashionable.

Florence, now strong enough to be completely dressed after her morning's packing, was beautiful in sky-blue muslin in which she took up three times as much room as Ann Gully. Though Malvern now had its share of fashion, Ann had never seen clothes so elaborate and impractical as these; she recognized at once the need for the two maids in the background.

In spite of being well enough to undergo this dressing, Florence still looked fragile and pale, which made the color of her hair and eyes the more remarkable. Ann hoped that she would soon be feeling much better and Florence said: "If you'd seen me when I came, you'd know how much better I am already. It's so refreshing to have natural sleep. Oh! How like Dr. Gully you are when you smile!"

They got on famously, and Ann set off to inquire at the letting office for a house that would accommodate a master and mistress who needed not only dressing rooms but a separate bedroom each.

It was the beginning of the summer season and the most commodious and charming houses were already taken, but after a good deal of going about and much close inspection of water closets, sinks and larders, as well as mattresses, sofas, cupboards and wardrobes, Ann recommended Orwell Lodge, a house on the outskirts of the town at the corner of two roads. It was foursquare and painted white; its front door opened almost onto the pavement, but a wedge of garden lay to the right of it and the back windows commanded a view of the plain.

The first floor was allotted in two sets of rooms to Florence and her husband, with a room for Field; the other servants were to sleep on the top floor, though if Florence wished it a bed for Laundon could be put up in her dressing room. There were living rooms on the ground floor and the rest of the premises were retained by the landlady who would act as housekeeper. Florence was by now driving out in a hired carriage every afternoon, and Dr. Gully had begun to speak of her walking up to Saint Anne's Well. The carriage conveyed her and Ann Gully to Orwell Lodge a few days later; Florence inspected it with a sharp eye and said that it would do, but wearily, as though the matter were one in which she took no pleasure.

Dr. Gully had never been inside Orwell Lodge and he suggested that on one of Florence's afternoon drives he should accompany her so far, and when they had viewed the house, the carriage should take her on her usual airing and he should walk back.

"Won't that be inconvenient for you?" she asked.

"My dear Mrs. Ricardo," he said with his bright look, "Orwell Lodge cannot be more than ten minutes' walk from my own house!"

"Not more than ten minutes?" said Florence, wondering.

"Not more than ten minutes of *my* walking," Dr. Gully said.

There had been rain in the morning but by early afternoon the sky was clear as glass. Florence in a cloak of dove-colored silk, a bonnet on the back of her head scarcely large enough to support its wreath of dark, iridescent cock's feathers, sat beside Dr. Gully in the carriage while Laundon occupied the seat behind. The wheels made a smooth, hissing noise on the graveled road while the horses' hooves kept a rhythmic hollow-sounding beat; rain had left a sparkle everywhere and a fresh, exquisite smell. Florence had not enjoyed carriage exercise so much for a very long time. Dr. Gully beside her was debonair and attentive; in a dark-gray morning coat cut to show a starched linen waistcoat, a top hat of woven straw and washleather gloves, he was dressed formally but in summer terms. She thought how very well turned out he was.

The carriage came to the end of Southfield Road where Orwell Lodge stood at the corner. Dr. Gully descended and held out his arm for Florence to lean on as she got out. Laundon was not told to get out, so remained seated. Dr. Gully naturally did not withdraw his arm but waited for Florence to remove hers; Florence, however, remained linked with him; as an invalid, she felt entitled to his support. He took off his hat and they went into the hall where the landlady curtsied and hoped that Mrs. Ricardo would find everything comfortable. She knew Dr. Gully well by sight and was gratified to see him under her roof. Dr. Gully said briefly but graciously that he was sure she would give Mrs. Ricardo every attention.

Since Florence was, in effect, the mistress of the house already, the woman did not accompany them; she remained in the hall and as she watched the couple slowly mounting the stairs, she could see what care of the lady the doctor was taking.

When they were in the large first-floor bedroom where the

windows commanded a vast view, he looked about him and said: "This seems fairly comfortable; I hope you will find it so."

She said, "Oh, yes, I daresay."

He opened the door of the spacious dressing room and said: "By the way, when you leave Malvern House, you'll need some appliances as this good lady doesn't supply them. Sparkes in Church Street hires out everything of the kind. Shall I tell him to deliver here what I want you to have?"

"Oh, yes, please do!"

"And Mrs. Rideout of course will come to you here just the same."

A fleeting look of alarm crossed her face. "Oh, *yes,* I couldn't give up the treatment when I come here—"

"Give it up!" said Dr. Gully with a severity which was reassuring to her. "No, you certainly mustn't give it up till you are a great deal stronger."

The ordeal that lay ahead of Florence, which she had managed quite often not to think about, could not but loom, as she stood in the house that had been hired so that her husband might come there and molest her with his presence; but even here, Dr. Gully's firm assumption that she herself was an invalid requiring care gave her a sense of protection. She crossed the landing and opened the door of another large bedroom. "This is the room for my husband," she said. Dr. Gully gave scant attention to the room itself; he was taken up with noticing how near it was to the other.

"Since your husband has been so ill, he has had a separate set of rooms, I think? Quite separate from yours?"

"Yes. In Lowndes Square they are on the ground floor."

He said nothing but went back to her room and turned the key in the lock, to and fro. The key was well oiled and the lock strong.

"You must meet my husband when he comes," Florence was

saying tonelessly. He replied that he would indeed hope to meet Captain Ricardo. To himself he said that the man he wanted to see was Field.

A fortnight of wet-sheet packing, Malvern air and the influence of Dr. Gully had made a remarkable improvement in Florence's condition and though she was still easily tired and would sometimes collapse in trembling and tears, this happened rarely. To herself, the most encouraging thing about the cure was that she now slept naturally for several hours every night. To wake up feeling refreshed, to drink her tea with relish and look forward to the day, instead of merely regaining a consciousness of misery with a head aching from the effects of chloral, was a delight that was still new.

It therefore disappointed her almost beyond bearing that after the visit to Orwell Lodge, she had a thoroughly bad night. She did not suffer the hours of wakefulness that used to torment her; but she kept waking up all through the night and by the morning she was exhausted and distressed and almost crying. She fell into a disturbed sleep after breakfast and at ten o'clock awoke to find Dr. Gully standing over her bed. He had come earlier than usual.

As soon as she realized his presence, she poured out the tale of her wretched night. "I don't want to take chloral again," she wound up, "but I'll have to if I can't sleep naturally. I *can't* go back to having sleepless nights—even chloral would be better than that." He sat down beside the bed and said, "We must get you to sleep again without chloral."

"I hate it, but you don't know how dreadful—" She was silent, biting the edge of her handkerchief and looking at him with round blue eyes welling over.

"I think I do," he said. "I also know that you are troubled at the idea of living again with your household. It's natural when you've suffered so much already. But we can't allow it to impede your return to health. When you move to Orwell Lodge you will have still to be regarded as an invalid, undergoing regular treatment. Nothing can be allowed to interfere with that." Her gaze became calmer, she listened with a hungry, thirsty attention that was being satisfied.

"Meantime, I do not think one bad night, undesirable as it is, will have done much harm."

"It frightened me so, I thought I was slipping back, to be ill again in that dreadful way—"

"Of course, and I am so sorry; but you need have no fears of that sort. However, it mustn't be repeated. I want you to have a cold sitz bath and spinal washing this morning and again before you go to bed. These treatments are very successful in inducing natural sleep."

He saw that the tenseness had left her frame, that as she listened, she was lying in languid comfort. He could repair the damage while she was here, completely under his control, but when she was at Orwell Lodge, exposed to the suffering that had destroyed her nervous health before, could he protect her even though she was still his patient? He sat a moment in silence, his fingers on her wrist, determining that he would protect her, against her husband, against her family, against society itself if any attempt were made to put her so-called duty to a drunken lunatic before the needs of her own health and sanity.

When Mrs. Rideout's thin, pleasant face appeared at the bedroom door, she was followed by two Malvern House attendants who carried in a sitz bath and spreading a large towel underneath it, filled it with cold water. To this Mrs. Rideout added hot water from a small jug, measuring the temperature by a large, wood-encased thermometer. "Now, ma'am, if you'll please to sit in the bath?" she said.

Florence rose, pulled her nightdress over her head and dropped it on the floor for Laundon to retrieve, then walked

lightly toward the sitz bath. She showed no caution or reluctance
now. The sitz bath was something like a very large coal scuttle
without a lid, made of spotless enamel, speckled gray on the
outside, inside a pure milk-white. Mrs. Rideout supported her
by the elbows as she sat down in it. The chill water rose to
her waist. She gasped, and quivered like a fish but made no
protest. Almost at once the sharpness of the cold disappeared
and she was encircled by a strong, cool sensation. Mrs. Rideout
wrapped a clean blanket around her shoulders and stood with
the gunmetal watch in her hand.

"How long?" Florence asked.

"Five minutes, ma'am."

Florence's naked legs and feet were stretched out in front of
her, sloping down from the rim of the sitz bath which was under
the backs of her knees. Her feet were very delicate, the toes
almost as unblemished as a child's. She shifted her position
slightly once or twice and each time an increase of coldness
swept around her waist and thighs, then disappeared again.

Meantime Laundon and Rogers swiftly stripped the bed, beating up the pillows. The mattress was a flock, for it was known
all over Malvern that Dr. Gully disapproved of feather beds. Dr.
Wilson, the builder of Malvern House, had disapproved of
them too, but it was Dr. Gully's opinion that was quoted. The
maids shook out the sheets and blankets between them and
remade the bed firmly and neatly.

Mrs. Rideout was now helping Florence to her feet and wrap-
ping her in a large towel. She said: "Would you like to rest a
little, ma'am, before you have the spinal washing?"

"No," Florence said, "I am not at all tired." The sensations
she already had were so soothing and refreshing, she was eager
to see what spinal washing meant.

Mrs. Rideout produced a board which she put over the sitz
bath, to one side of it, and unwrapping Florence from the towel,

asked her to sit on the board, leaning a little forward. Then, using the water in the bath, she poured it from a jug down Florence's spine, tilting the jug at the nape of the neck so that the water ran all down the spine, over and over again. After several minutes this induced a dreamy state and she was unprepared to hear Mrs. Rideout say: "That is all for the present, ma'am. Now, if you would like to lie down on the bed, I'll give you the friction."

Florence had always enjoyed Mrs. Rideout's skillful rubbing, but this, applied only up and down the spine as she lay on her face, sent a sensation of well-being into some deep region of the consciousness. The instructions which Dr. Gully gave the bath attendants while they were learning their art always contained the warning: "Rubbing after the spinal washing must not be too vigorous; the most sensitive and the largest nerve structure is here, immediately beneath the hands of the rubber." Mrs. Rideout, without book knowledge of physiology, not only carried out his orders but had an instinctive understanding of them.

The treatment, repeated in the evening, had the result Dr. Gully had encouraged her to expect; Florence slept soundly for six hours. Rogers, who had been in her service a few months only, was taken by surprise when she brought her breakfast tray.

"Really quite what you'd call a beauty, isn't she?" she said to Laundon afterward.

"Pity she's got to—" Here they both became silent.

A few days later, Florence said eagerly: "When I go to Orwell Lodge, I *must* go on seeing you. You've done so much for me, I can't, I *can't* give it all up—" Her energy had brought her to her feet. Dr. Gully took her hand between both his own.

"My dear Mrs. Ricardo," he said impressively, "so long as you wish to remain under my care, I shall keep you under my care. Your being at another house won't prevent my visits, or my carrying out any treatment that I find does you good. You go to Orwell Lodge on the twenty-eighth, I believe. I shall call about six o'clock on that evening, and we will arrange for you to resume the treatments on the following day." The hand between his hands clung to his fingers with a grip like a drowning creature's.

Chapter 5

AT six o'clock on the evening of May 28 Dr. Gully arrived at Orwell Lodge. He did not announce himself at the front door because he saw Florence on the lawn and went to join her. The westering sun made the garden a vivid green; she was walking beside a border with bent head. Dr. Gully came toward her, hat in hand; she stood quite still, then started forward to meet him.

When he had hoped that the move from Malvern House had been accomplished smoothly, he said: "And how is Captain Ricardo?"

Florence was walking by his side down the border and had stopped beside a Bourbon rose. She touched it, wanting to speak about the scent and color, but he went on: "He has arrived, I presume?"

"Yes, he came at teatime."

"And how is he?"

She shrugged. He persevered.

"Does the vomiting continue?"

"Not so far, not at present."

"I'm glad. Would he be willing to see me, do you think?"

"Oh, I daresay. Only he can't keep his mind on anything for long."

"That must be expected, but perhaps we might have just a word." He touched her elbow to steer her toward the house. As they passed slowly up the lawn, he looked at her. "And you," he said, "I am very anxious that you shouldn't have a disturbed night. I think that Mrs. Rideout had better come and give you a spinal washing and sitz bath just before you go to bed. Shall you be dining with your husband?"

"Oh, dear, no. Alexander is not equal to anything of that kind, not at present."

"We must hope that he may be before he leaves Malvern but I will send Mrs. Rideout to you, say, between nine and half past."

"Yes, thank you—"

"Sparkes has sent all the things I ordered?"

"Yes, they're all in my dressing room. I found them here this morning. I *shall* be glad to have a spinal washing tonight. I was dreading going to bed without one and having to lie awake all night as a result. Why do you smile?"

"I was thinking you showed very little confidence in my power to take care of you."

"That would be very silly of me, and very ungrateful too. I'm glad you're only smiling about it."

The smiling pair reached the porch, then gravity overcame them. Florence said: "If you will go into the drawing room, Doctor, I will see where my husband is."

Dr. Gully stood in the drawing-room window, his hands behind his back. He wondered in what trim the fellow really was; a few minutes should show. A small man, fair and light-eyed, appeared at the door. He gave a sharp glance, then said respectfully: "Dr. Gully, sir?"

"Yes. Are you Field?"

"That's so, sir. The captain will be with you in a moment."

"Thank you. And could I presently have a word with *you*, I wonder?"

"Certainly, sir. I shall be on hand."

After a few moments a light, shuffling step was heard crossing the hall. A tall, slight young man appeared in the open doorway, where he stopped, running his fingers up and down the doorpost, uncertainly, like a blind man, before he got his bearings sufficiently to allow him to enter the room. Once inside, he made for an armchair and collapsed rather than sat down in it.

"Sit, sit, won't you?" he said.

Dr. Gully bowed and said, "Captain Ricardo? I am Dr. Gully, an old friend of your mother-in-law's."

"A fine old girl," Captain Ricardo said, "but I'm afraid, Doctor, you won't be able to do *me* any good." His manner was the remains of something that had once been excellent. His expensive clothes were clean because his man saw to it that they were; for the same reason his hair was smoothly brushed, his nails clean and trimmed, his boots polished, but his whole appearance was one of hopeless downfall. His face was pale with patches of broken veins over the nose, his eyes were bloodshot and glazed, his hands shook and trembled ceaselessly.

Dr. Gully said with straightforward kindness, "I wish someone could be found who *would* do you good, Captain Ricardo." The young man cocked his head on one side; for an instant, the intelligence that had been driven into hiding looked out of the ruin of his face.

"Yes, it's hard on my wife, isn't it?"

Dr. Gully replied in stong tones: "It is hard on your wife. It's also very hard on you. You are a young man, Captain Ricardo, in my eyes a very young man, and I'm deeply concerned to see you like this."

"But there's nothing you can do about it"; the young man spoke in almost a triumphant tone, as if he'd worsted an adversary.

Dr. Gully had to deal with patients who were drinking too

much, a great deal too much, and needed drastic control, but he had never met with anything quite like this. With every faculty alert, to see if he could detect a clue, he said, feeling his way: "I am afraid no one could persuade you out of this fatal habit, unless they knew what had led you into it in the first place."

The strange being answered: "That would be telling, old boy, that would be telling!" A zany smile overspread his face, turning into a glare at once fierce, mocking and cruel. Dr. Gully had scarcely time to feel alarmed, when it disappeared, and there was no one in front of him but a poor, sick young man, trying to put the best face he could on his wretched condition.

"Never mind me, Doctor," he said brokenly, "I'm in poor shape, but never mind me. You take care of my wife, that's what you've got to do." His anxious affection made him sound pitiable.

"I am doing my best," Dr. Gully said, "and I am happy to tell you that Mrs. Ricardo is greatly improved in the last fortnight. I hope another month or so will see her quite well." Captain Ricardo seemed to have dismissed the matter from his mind. He looked around.

"Where's my fellow?" he said. Field must have been within earshot for he appeared immediately.

"Bring—bring some brandy and soda," Captain Ricardo said. "Some for this gentleman, too. I don't know who you are, sir, but I daresay it's all right. Have a drink by all means."

Dr. Gully rose. "Not now, I thank you," he said. "I'll say good evening, Captain Ricardo. I hope you will sleep, and that you'll be much the better for your stay at Malvern."

He took up his hat and went out into the hall, out of the front door and lingered a moment. If he could speak to Field, well and good, but he could not hang about and besides, he wanted to get home to send the summons to Mrs. Rideout. He stood at the small iron gate that gave in to the pavement; he was about to turn and go when Field came hurriedly out of the front door and asked if he would care to come in. When Dr. Gully entered he led the way to a small anteroom where he set a chair for the doctor, remaining standing himself. Field had been in the army and looked it every inch: spare, dapper, with a promise of wiry strength.

"I'm glad to have a word with you," Dr. Gully said. "Mrs. Ricardo is under my care and I'm very anxious that nothing should throw her back in her recovery. Is your master usually in this condition?"

"This or worse, sir."

"It isn't the sort of case I understand, but there are physicians who—"

"Lord bless you, sir," said Field, "they wouldn't be able to do nothing for him!"

This was so nearly Dr. Gully's own opinion that he did not press the point. He went on: "Your master doesn't lead a normal domestic life at present? He doesn't take his meals with Mrs. Ricardo?"

"No, sir. He doesn't take regular meals, nothing at all regular except first thing in the morning."

"And what does he take then?" Field said that before he got up the captain took a tumbler three parts full of liqueur brandy, filled up with champagne. It put him on his pins, the captain said. Dr. Gully exclaimed that it would have knocked any ordinary man off them, but Field said it stopped the shaking enough to get him dressed. He drank brandy or curaçao at intervals during the morning. For lunch, if he took anything, it was a mouthful of deviled chicken or some curry or smoke-cured fish, and the same at dinner. He fancied a hot taste, it made the claret more refreshing.

"And the vomiting?" said Dr. Gully. "I understand that is sometimes very severe?"

"It has been, sir. It usually comes on when the captain has been fancying gin a good deal."

"Gin!" repeated Dr. Gully fearfully. "Can't you prevent him from getting that?"

Field said simply: "It would lose me my place, sir."

"I suppose so." Dr. Gully gave an involuntary sigh. "And these outbursts of violence, are they the result of gin drinking?"

"Gin or whiskey, sir. As long as he keeps to brandy, he's much quieter."

"Well, Field, I see that it would be very difficult for you to refuse to supply the gin if your master insists on it, or to prevent him from getting it for himself. But at least I must impress on you that Mrs. Ricardo's safety is your responsibility, yours and the other servants'. There is a lock on her door and her maid will be sleeping in the dressing room, but if there are outbreaks of violence, you must let me know immediately and she will have to be removed."

"Yes, sir," said Field. He spoke impassively but Dr. Gully felt that he was to be trusted. He got to his feet, and as Field escorted him to the door, he gave the man the name of The Priory House and told him how to get to it.

He walked home rapidly, in deep thought. The situation for a woman in her state of health was thoroughly unsatisfactory and would require most careful watching; but though outbreaks of violence would be shocking and injurious to witness, what he had been most afraid of was that she might be the victim of drunken lust, and a young man so weak and debile, even if fired by ardent spirits, was not likely to present this danger—at least, drinking on this scale was indeed a wife's protection, since it was almost bound to result in sexual impotence.

Chapter 6

FLORENCE had now established the habit of natural sleep. As he looked at her each day in the fresh morning light Dr. Gully realized how much of her personality as well as her beauty had been obscured by the illness, whose disfiguring traces were vanishing. There was sometimes a gay imperiousness in her manner, a spritely impatience of a very pretty kind that charmed him, and made her sudden lapses into helplessness, her unconscious appeals for protection, moving to a strange degree. There was still an air of delicacy; the coloring of the lips and cheeks was faint, but her skin was the healthy white of a white rose petal. Altogether the improvement in the last month was wonderful; if only it might be allowed to continue!

His society was at present the most exciting thing in Florence's life. She regretted that he came so early; she would have liked to look forward to his visit for the greater part of the day.

Occasionally he would appear unexpectedly in the evening; she would lead him out to the garden to walk for a brief while. One very fine evening the first week in June, she saw him coming from the staircase window and was in the hall as he appeared at the open front door.

"How strange you should arrive just now!" she exclaimed, the color of her cheeks and eyes deepened by delight. "I was just thinking of you and wishing you still came in the evenings as you did at Malvern House." With perfect naturalness she took his arm and they walked into the drawing room, making for the French window. A figure prone in a lounging chair seemed to pay no heed as they passed, unaware; when they were out in the garden a head was raised, sideways, to look after them, the red eyes fixed in a hard, hostile stare.

It was two days later, on June 7, that as he arrived at Orwell Lodge, the maid Rogers put a narrow envelope, addressed to him, into his hand. He came into the hall, put down his hat on the table and adjusting his glasses, took out the note. In a flowery but decisive hand, it said:

MY DEAR DOCTOR,

You will be surprised at my sudden departure, I am so anxious to explain. Early this morning the servants told me my husband sent the kitchen maid for a cab, and got himself to the railway station. He caught the next train to Paddington. He has left no address with me. I have telegraphed to my mother in Lowndes Square. Poor Field is distressed that my husband gave him the slip. He comes up with me to London. I will write to you from Lowndes Square as I am sure you will wish for news of us. I shall return to Malvern and your care as soon as I am able.

Yours sincerely,

FLORENCE RICARDO

"Well," said Dr. Gully, "here's a pretty kettle of fish!" He looked so kindly at the nervous girl that she felt comforted. "Laundon has gone with your mistress, I daresay?"

"Yes, sir."

"So you are by yourself at present, but you'll have the landlady and her servants for company."

"Oh, yes, sir. I don't a bit mind that. As long as they can find the master."

"Yes. Everyone will be anxious until that's done."

"But Mr. Field—the mistress seemed to think he'd be able to find him. There's places, sir, places where the master's been before."

"I see. Well, I daresay someone will write to me from London; if they send you any news, will you be so kind as to bring it to my house? And if you are in want of anything, or if you feel lonely, come around to The Priory House and my butler and cook will look after you."

Rogers was suddenly too grateful to speak. She had been taken up by the mistress's trouble and the general confusion; now it came over her how far away she was from her home in the Pentonville Road and that, though they'd promised to come back or send for her, she had only seven shillings of her own. She curtsied, blushing and smiling, but didn't say anything in case she started to cry.

Dr. Gully retraced the Southfield Road, walking briskly but deep in thought. He had a heavy round to make that morning and no leisure to think about other affairs but as he came home to lunch, Florence and her trials were vividly present to his mind, with anxiety for her health, her comfort, her safety, even. Fortunately she was going to the house of her excellent mother. He told his sisters of the hasty departure when he met them at the lunch table. Ann said what a good thing it was that Mrs. Ricardo was so much recovered; she would be able to bear it better, poor dear.

"*That's* all due to James," Ellen said.

"And to hydropathy, my dear," said Dr. Gully gently.

Two days later the post brought him two letters. One was from Mrs. Campbell, thanking him for his friendly care, but saying that her unfortunate son-in-law had been found, in rooms kept by an old servant, suffering from a shocking bout of delirium tremens. He was now shut up in his own rooms with Field in attendance. He refused to have Florence in the room

with him and Mrs. Campbell could only be glad; his unkind-
ness at least spared her daughter something; she could at present give Dr. Gully no idea of their plans.

He took up the other letter, in a narrow envelope of superfine
quality, hot-pressed with a wreath of flowers embossed on the
flap. It said very much what her mother's had said; but she
added her own warm thanks: "I can never be grateful enough
to you that I am now so nearly well myself," and saying that
though they were giving up Orwell Lodge, she meant to return
to Malvern as soon as she could, to complete her cure under
his guidance. He sighed. When he had briefly, sympathetically
answered Mrs. Campbell's letter, he tore it up, but Florence's
he put away in a little drawer. Before he closed the drawer, he
read the letter again. He was touched by what she said of returning to Malvern but he was afraid there was little chance
of it. Later in the day he heard through Pritchard that a housekeeper had come up from Lowndes Square and seen to all the
packing up and had departed with Rogers and the boxes that
morning on the eleven o'clock train for Paddington, and that
Rogers had left her respects for the doctor.

Chapter 7

Above the hills there was always a zest in the Malvern air, but in the town, a hot summer made hard work harder. The grass was brown, the trees oppressively silent in their heavy leaf. Dr. Gully began to feel that the people whose faces he saw every day demanded an expense of nervous energy from him which he was barely able to meet.

Then, one afternoon as he was turning over the post on his library table, he saw a handwriting he couldn't mistake though he had seen it only twice before. He slit the envelope with his silver paper knife and read a letter that astonished him.

Florence wrote that her husband's attack had been dreadfully severe, but he was now recovering, though much exhausted and reduced, and he agreed with her that a return to Malvern would do them both good. Here followed the part of the letter that surprised Dr. Gully most. Florence on her own initiative had secured, through the Malvern letting office, the lease of another furnished house; all their preparations for return were made and they expected to be at Stokefield in four days' time. She hoped he would call.

This totally unexpected display of energy and competence in one barely emerged from a state of nervous prostration acted upon him with tonic properties. His first sensation was surprise, his next, great satisfaction at the recovery she had achieved; then came a feeling of personal pleasure that he would see her again so soon.

He knew Stokefield; it was one of a few graceful, Regency houses scattered along the Graham Road, which ran at right angles to Church Street; opening out of this busy thoroughfare, the road became secluded very soon. On its left side, the hills towered up into the air. From many sites in Malvern their height appeared diminished; here it was seen impressively. Graham Road lay at the foot of what looked almost like mountain ranges.

Dr. Gully knew of the party's arrival when he met Field outside the Italian Warehouseman's where he had been for capsicums and *Patum peperium*. The latter greeted the doctor with respectful enthusiasm. Dr. Gully could not discuss the captain's symptoms in the street but he learned from Field that his master was, for the time being, a good deal recovered. When he got home, he sent a note to Stokefield, saying he was glad to hear of Captain and Mrs. Ricardo's arrival and would give himself the pleasure of calling that evening at six o'clock.

A little after six o'clock he was ushered into the ground-floor drawing room of Stokefield whose French windows looked across the road to the great height of the Beacon. He was looking out at the upper reaches of the hills, massive in the transparent evening sky, when there was a slight rustle, and turning quickly around he found her in front of him; her hand was in his, her face raised with a look of eagerness that delighted and touched him.

Florence had been looking forward to this meeting; how much, she had not known herself till she saw him standing in the window, handsome and authoritative, with a gracious, indulgent smile. She answered his first inquiries almost at random, then collected herself with an effort and assumed the air of the lady of the house entertaining a visitor in her drawing room.

He saw some change in her; she was not quite so well as when she had left Malvern; but he was gratified to see that there was no return of the nervous collapse in which he'd seen her first. In fact she looked firmer, more in command of herself than when she'd left his care. She rose and went to a silver tray loaded with filled decanters and brilliant glass. He had risen also, but when she said, "Will you have a glass of Madeira?" he replied: "No, thank you. Not even with you to give it to me."

"Then sit down again." As he took his chair once more he said gently: "I hope you don't drink wine at this hour?"

"I do, sometimes. Do you think it wrong?"

"Yes, a very harmful habit. I should not like to see you take wine at your meals except occasionally. Between meals it should be quite forbidden." It was too pointed, now, to ask after Captain Ricardo's health and he was wondering how he had best introduce the topic when she got to her feet again and trailing her skirts across the carpet, went to the open French window.

"There is my husband," she said. They moved out onto the small lawn in front of the house.

The young man, followed by Field at a discreet distance, was coming up the drive. He walked as though he were wading through deep water, feeling carefully for the ground. He stopped as the others approached. His ruined face had a purplish tinge; there was an expression of misery on it that made his attempt at a smile and a friendly greeting almost heartbreaking. Dr. Gully spoke to him with warm kindness; the young man said in exhausted tones he was glad to see Dr. Gully. Then a look of being hopelessly lost filled his eyes; he added something indistinguishable and moved toward the open window.

Florence sighed. Dr. Gully was silent. He had his hat in his hand and as the quarter of an hour permitted for a call must now be up, he decided not to return indoors; in saying good-bye to Florence however he told her that his sisters were hoping very much to see her at The Priory House. Would she come to tea?

"I should like to so much," she said. "And I want to consult you. I would like to go on with some of the treatment now I am here again. Nothing has ever done me so much good."

"My sister will write, asking you to take tea with us. Then if you wish you can consult me afterward." He bowed over her hand with an air more like a friend than a doctor.

Ann Gully's note arrived next day and on the following afternoon, Florence drove up to The Priory House in a carriage hired from the stables in Graham Road. She came by herself. She felt that, what with her return to health and being by now an habituée of Malvern, she could dispense with any attendance.

The tea was very pleasant; the china was beautiful, and the meal was such as one could enjoy only in a country district; the milk in the large silver jug was thick with yellow cream, and this and the Malvern water made the tea most delicious; the bread was homemade and spread with such fresh butter—it was more of a delicacy than any cake.

While she talked to his sisters, he looked at her. Her hair which was dressed out in a frame around the face and a chignon at the back of the neck, and the voluminous draperies at the back of the skirt emphasized the slightness of her neck, her waist. He did not admire the fashion, which seemed to cumber most women, but now he saw it for the first time as it was intended to look. He could hardly take his eyes from her.

His sisters and the guest had most of the conversation to themselves. Ann was her usual self; welcoming, sympathetic and interested. Ellen, always a little gauche with people she didn't know, sat bolt upright, talking with forced animation, but it was all very agreeable and the announcement of Mrs. Ricardo's carriage quite took them by surprise. His sisters parted from her with mutual wishes and plans. He then conducted her across the hall in silence. As they reached the open front door and she stood with her hand in his, even then he seemed unable to say a word; but Florence said: "I meant to ask you when you would give me an appointment. Will you send a word to say when you can see me?"

"I will," he said. The hired carriage had no footman, so it was for Dr. Gully to open the door and, standing close beside it, to hold out his arm for her to lean on as she mounted the step. Her diaphanous masses of muslin were mounted on silk that whispered as she turned around to take her seat. The faint scent of White Rose came from her, made by Piesse et Lubin, with a troubling hint of patchouli under the extract of triple rose. She seemed unconscious of her fashionable dress and the sophisticated scent, fixing him with the direct, demanding gaze of a little girl.

The carriage drove off with her and he stood at the open door in the warm evening, amazed and longing. He hardly understood himself; what he did know was that he had shaken off the satiety and fatigue of the last few months.

Chapter 8

❧❧

HE did not send any word to Stokefield for the next three days. The matter of a consultation was not urgent and he needed the pause to examine his feelings. Florence, who understood hers perfectly, was irritated and wearied by the silence.

On the morning of the fourth day, Alexander was in the garden at the back of the house, lying in a wicker chaise longue, a Panama hat tilted over his eyes, a tumbler of brandy and soda in the holder on the chair's arm. Indoors Florence was walking restlessly up and down the shaded drawing room. She took up a small guide to Malvern and read: "That Malvern was occupied by the Druids is beyond question." The *Druids*, indeed! She tossed the book aside with impatience and contempt. She continued her walk up and down the room; she did not want to go into the garden.

Just then a note was brought to her. In it, Dr. Gully said with his compliments, that he could, if convenient to her, see Mrs. Ricardo at The Priory House at five o'clock that evening. Would she send an answer by the bearer? Florence went to the front door which opened at the side of the house and found Dr. Gully's liveried coachman standing in the glass porch among begonias and geraniums.

Griffith was a good-natured man, rather wild-eyed, very clever

with horses. In his stable or on a carriage box he was much
more intelligent than he was anywhere else, though he could
be trusted with a simple message. Florence asked him to say
that she would keep the appointment and Griffith touched his
cockaded hat and walked briskly away. He was due to drive
the doctor over to Malvern Link.

Florence now went down into the garden. Her husband mum-
bled: "Come here, Flo, and sit by a fellow."

"I'm coming," she said, and Field brought out a spoon-back
basket chair for her.

She sat down and Alexander began saying in rambling tones:
"I'm no good to you, no good to you."

"Don't keep saying that," she said impatiently but not un-
kindly. "We should be very happy if you would give up drinking."

"No, no no," he repeated, "no good to you. You don't know
it but *I* know." Florence had long given up attempts at conversation when he was in this state, but she knew her presence
gave him satisfaction, so she sat on. The heat was drawing out
the velvet scents of phlox and stock and late wallflowers. She
entered a sort of trance. Presently she noticed that the hat which
had been tilted over his nose was pushed sideways and one
reddened, unhappy eye was watching her.

"The old fellow," he muttered. Then he fell into a brief doze.
Florence got up and went into the house.

She thought as she sat opposite Dr. Gully in his consulting
room that evening, "How much has happened to me since I was
here before!" She had not remembered the wallpaper, a green
flock patterned with ferns.

But she was recalled by Dr. Gully's speaking.

"I am concerned to find," he said, "that you drink wine—
spirits, too, perhaps—between meals?"

"I did not think there was anything wrong in the little that
I take."

"But it's a habit that doesn't stand still with you. You have seen enough—too much—of where it may lead."

"Yes. It's because my life is sometimes very—" she stopped.

"Very hard and difficult, that you feel you want the support of wine?"

"Yes. I do not think I can be blamed if I take something to help me."

"First, you must understand that I am not blaming you. I am deeply sympathetic. But I see you in considerable danger and I must do my best to protect you. My very strongly worded advice is that you take no wine or spirits between meals and only one glass of wine at luncheon and dinner; at only one meal would be better, at none, best of all. Women like you, sensitive and brilliant, are at the greatest risk in forming this habit and of being ruined by it."

Florence was looking at his right hand that lay on the desk. On the little finger was a ring, an oval of dark green bloodstone with his initials carved on it. The hand and the ring formed a magnet to her mind, she felt she could gaze at them forever. After a pause, he said: "Will you give me this undertaking?"

"Yes," she said instinctively, not knowing exactly what she was called on to promise.

He began to speak again about the importance of fresh air, fresh water, regular exercise of one kind or another. How did she sleep now? Florence said that on her hurried return to London, her nights had been shocking, with hours of wakefulness and her heart beating as if it would choke her when she lay down, but this had all got better again as she came back to Malvern.

He looked very grave. "The shock and strain of your domestic situation is very harmful to you. All I can say is you must take every opportunity you have at present of building up your health. If the sleeplessness should return you must go back to a regular course of sitz baths. Meanwhile, I will order you three packings a week."

"Please do. I am so anxious to have some treatment again. I missed it so, during those dreadful weeks, and having no one to—of course my mother was as kind as could be, but I had no one who could *really* advise or help."

He got up, saying: "I shall be so glad to be of any help I can, medically of course, and in any other way."

"Then I wish you would call sometimes. It was so nice when you used to, at Orwell Lodge."

"I will. I will take my chance of finding you at home one evening between afternoon tea and dinner."

He called at Stokefield the next evening and Florence welcomed him with a startled but trustful gaze. "You won't see my husband," she said. "He's been drinking all day. He's shut up with Field and he won't let me into the room."

As they sat down in one of the windows beneath the veranda, he said: "Has your husband ever been given any treatment to stop him from drinking?"

"No, I do not think he would have taken it."

"Were you ever given any advice on how to treat him without his knowing it?"

"No. How could that be done?"

"It is sometimes done by putting a strong emetic in the patient's wine. He comes to connect the idea of drink with violent sickness and it's hoped that will create a disgust for it."

"Alexander *is* violently sick sometimes."

"So I heard. I wondered if that treatment had been tried."

"I think not, I am sure not. No one could have done it except Field and he wouldn't without—"

"No. It's a drastic remedy and of course shouldn't be used without medical advice."

"What *is* used?"

"Various substances; ipecacuanha, sometimes tartar emetic, a solution of antimony. It occurred to me that something of the sort might have accounted for that vomiting in the spring."

"Field says that was brought on by gin; as long as he keeps to wine and brandy he is not *very* sick, only just sometimes." He looked at her with inexpressible pity, the beautiful young creature who had been brought to regard this state of her husband's as something to be grateful for. She knew what he was feeling as well as if his emotions had been played to her in music.

"Sometimes he gets better," she said gently, "and we talk as we used to. Then a terrible, sly look comes over his face and he says something that sounds as if he were mad."

"My poor child!" The words burst from him.

"But it makes such a difference, to have you to talk to about it." Her words carried their relationship forward, like a boat pushed out from shore.

He got into the way of calling at Stokefield when he could, before dinner, usually four or five times a week. Often he saw Captain Ricardo. The latter would begin by greeting him civilly; it was pathetic to see how good his manners must once have been. Sometimes the actual personality would emerge, in a charming smile, some consecutive sentences of friendly talk; then he would lapse suddenly into marked hostility, which in turn would give way to a state of blank incomprehension. It was like talking to several men one after the other. There were other days when, though uncertain and confused in speech, he was his own man; deciding on a walk or drive, giving orders to Field. As September went by, these lucid intervals lengthened. Though always seeming wretchedly ill, he began to go up to London for a few days at a time, to see his tailor, to have his hair cut, to show up at his clubs. Field went with him, so the worst of the anxiety was removed, and while he was capable of making his own decisions, no one was in a position to control him. In these absences, Dr. Gully and Florence met with the unspoken understanding that they found each other's company utterly delightful. At the end of a warm September summer clothes were still being worn and one afternoon when he came to tea, Florence appeared before him in yet another muslin dress, piled up like clouds, descending like waterfalls. Beautiful as it was, he could not approve of such elaboration—on any other woman.

She offered to refill his teacup but it was still full.

"It'll be quite cold by now."

"No, just warm, as I like it."

"I like mine to be very hot. But you disapprove of that?"

"I disapprove, but of course I only concern myself in these matters with people who are under my professional care." Florence received a shock of dismay. She wanted to take her tea hot; she didn't want to be told that unless she were his patient, it was all one to Dr. Gully how she took it.

"Am I not under your professional care?" she asked faintly.

"I hope so, but it's for you to decide, of course." She poured half the contents of her cup into the tea bowl and added milk to the rest. She was nearly crying. To prevent the need for speech she began to drink, slowly.

"Well, is it so very disagreeable?" he asked kindly.

"No. Not very."

Chapter 9

FLORENCE liked Laundon; she appreciated her skill and was comfortable in her hands, but she sometimes felt a little uneasy about Field—why, she could hardly have said. He was not only valuable, he was almost irreplaceable, and his manner to her was invariably correct; but there was occasionally the faintest possible tinge of disrespect to be seen fleetingly in his pale eyes, that made Florence wish that he and Laundon were not so much in each other's confidence. There was nothing on which she could actually put her finger; if she had found any cause for complaint she would have made it; she was never afraid of servants.

With Laundon however she felt quite at her ease. The girl seemed to her always thoroughly respectful and sympathetic, and since she could scarcely put into words what she objected to in Field, she decided to ignore it. Indeed, it would have been impossible to live in the same house as Alexander without him.

An attempt had been made to dine at The Priory House but on the afternoon of the day Florence had been obliged to send a note to Miss Gully, saying that Captain Ricardo was too unwell for him and Mrs. Ricardo to keep the engagement. This was answered by an invitation to Florence to tea on the following day and this by others. When Dr. Gully called of an evening

he would invite her for an afternoon which he could keep free
of appointment.

Florence had discovered that if, instead of turning left out of
Stokefield, down Graham Road to Church Street, one turned
right to the far end of the road, one got onto the Victoria Road
which led back, passing the back gardens of Graham Road, and
came out into Church Street almost opposite The Priory House
gates; when she went to tea there, Florence would now tell
Laundon that she was at liberty for the afternoon, and take the
sequestered route by herself. She seldom met anyone at all on
it. Once a clergyman coming out of a gate saw the veiled,
quickly moving figure gliding along under the garden walls—
on some errand of kindness, no doubt. He raised his hat, thinking she was probably one of the Priory Church congregation. She
bent her head and hurried by without looking at him. That was
right, he thought. Malvern was a place where women could
walk about alone without remark, but even here it was just as
well that they should make for their destination without lin-
gering.

Dr. Gully was alone at home this afternoon; his sisters knew
that Mrs. Ricardo was expected but they were obliged to go to a
sale of work to raise funds for the society that provided free
hydrotherapy. Ellen had embroidered a cushion cover, a wreath
of pale-gold, pink-tipped honeysuckle on a green satin ground.
He had given his sisters some money to spend, as his contribu-
tion, and told Ellen to buy the cushion cover for him if somebody else hadn't bespoken it already.

Over tea which Pritchard brought them, Florence asked Dr.
Gully if he had read the novels of George Eliot. She was reading *The Mill on the Floss*.

"No," Dr. Gully said, he really was no novel-reader.

"She is not, I believe, married to the man she lives with?"

"She is a chaste and serious-minded woman, I am sure, and one of us on whom the laws of society are very hard. I think you have heard, long ago, that I have a wife living?"

"Yes, Mama told me." She gazed at him with eyes dark with compassion and love.

"Miss Evans, as her name is, deserves praise, in my view, for the courage she has shown. However happy her lot, and I am sure that it is happy, she must undergo a good deal of suffering—much more than would fall to the share of Mr. Lewes."

"I hope—I expect he makes it up to her."

"I believe they are devoted to each other. They came here—nine years ago it would be, in 1861."

"Oh! Did they? To you, I suppose?"

"Yes. I managed to put Mr. Lewes on his legs again; very bilious, with prostrating sick headaches. The lady conceded that I had 'really helped to mend George,' as she calls him, but I heard she told her friends that 'Dr. Gully was certainly a quack.'"

"Good gracious! The impudent, ungrateful, ignorant thing!"

"Well, well; a distinguished woman, but not altogether consistent in her opinions. If I had been in the habit of noticing such remarks, I would have liked to ask her: 'Is it better to have your husband—or the gentleman who bears the courtesy title of your husband—cured by a doctor whom you call a quack, or left uncured, as had been the case so far with Mr. Lewes, by a number of medical advisers on whom you would have bestowed a more dignified title?'"

"Oh, I *wish* you had. And I hear that she is very plain."

"She is not beautiful, certainly. But some plain women have great powers of fascination."

"Oh. Perhaps you *prefer* plain women?" Her eyes were round, starry with an indignation that, though pretended, had something real about it. He looked at her in silence for a moment.

Then he said: "You're a very naughty little creature, aren't you?"

"Yes."

"Aren't you?"

"I *said* yes. Why must I say it again?"

"Just as well to have the point clear."

"It *was* clear. You were simply being tyrannous and cruel." It was an exchange where the words themselves meant almost nothing; the game, suddenly so exciting, could have been played with other counters.

He got up and said: "Tyrannous and cruel I may be, but I can't allow you to walk back to Stokefield unaccompanied. It's nearly dark. If you would like to come now, I will give myself the pleasure of escorting you. If you will wait till my patient is due, Griffith shall take you in the carriage."

"Let us come now," she said. It was deep twilight. The lamps were lit in Church Street but only a few indistinguishable figures were going up and down. They got themselves into Victoria Road with a delicious sensation in Florence's mind of privacy and safety. As they walked together under the long stretch of wall, arm in arm, she said: "My sister Effie is coming to me next week."

"I am glad she is to be with you."

"Yes, they have been abroad. I haven't seen her this long while. I shall be very glad of her company. I only hope that— that nothing will happen while she's here. She knows already about our trouble but she isn't used to it, as I am." He made a pitying exclamation under his breath.

They were now at the gate of Stokefield. He took her hand in both of his. On the other side of the road the towering hills increased the gloom. Along their summits a long stream of mist was scurrying before the evening wind. The air was damp. He could hardly bring himself to say good-bye. Suddenly, lamp-light rose up in the ground-floor windows of the house.

"You must go in, my dear." He added: "I'm afraid the weather has broken."

"The *weather* doesn't matter," Florence said.

Chapter 10

EFFIE was less remarkable in appearance than Florence but she had the air of being more successful; she was now the confident young wife of a rich, good-natured, devoted husband. Her fairness and her small figure gave her a doll-like air, in piquant contrast to her straightforward, affectionate manner.

She had brought no maid with her for this brief stay; Florence had said that Laundon could attend to them both. The first evening they sat over the fire in Florence's bedroom, in their peignoirs, brushing their hair and talking, not about the present and its miseries, but of those scenes that began with "Do you remember."

"I always thought you were so beautiful, Flo," said Effie earnestly. "You were the first person I thought of as beautiful." Florence sighed; then her eyes brightened; without knowing what had led to it, she began to talk about Dr. Gully.

"He must be quite an old man now," Effie said.

"No!" said Florence with energy. "Not at all; or rather, it doesn't matter what his age is."

"Perhaps not," said Effie politely. "It's wonderful what he's managed to do for you. Mama always says he's such a clever doctor."

"Mama, yes, and hundreds of people from all over the world. He is so famous, it's quite amazing!"

"Fancy! Well, we ought to be very grateful to him, I must say. I'm tired, Flo, with my journey, and I'm sure *you* ought to be going to bed. Alexander doesn't come up here, I suppose."

"No. His rooms are downstairs at the back of the house."

"Not that I want to shun him, poor dear."

"Oh, no. And he'll be glad to see you tomorrow if he's well enough."

Next day, all hope had gone of any return of the beautiful late-autumn weather. The sky was dark with rain. The sisters spent a desultory morning during which Alexander appeared; he spoke civilly to Effie without any idea that she was his sister-in-law. Afterward, Effie settled herself to write letters and Florence, because she knew that Dr. Gully would wish it, walked up and down the roads, breathing the pure, rainy air and buffeted by gusts of wind. She returned with damp hair and glowing skin, and after lunch the sisters went into the drawing room for a long comfortable afternoon of talk and needlework. Florence had a talent for creative embroidery; she was at work on a tiger lily, orange and brown-spotted, on an ivory satin ground. Effie admired it wholeheartedly; she herself was content with crocheting yards of lace in a pattern like snow crystals.

It was toward six o'clock when they were roused by sounds, indistinct but alarming and becoming louder. In another moment there was a fumbling at the door handle, then a rain of blows on the panels and Alexander's voice was heard, shouting in maniacal fury. The young women were on their feet, cowering in each other's arms.

"Surely he isn't trying to get at *you?*" Effie breathed. The din grew louder but retreated from the door. Then there was a prolonged noise of breaking glass.

Florence boldly went to the door and opened it. On the other side of the hall, where jagged holes stared in the walls of the porch and the floor was strewn with glass, Field turned around.

"Keep out of the way, madam," he said in a voice she didn't know. She withdrew, almost shutting the door, keeping hold of the handle.

He came across the hall, uttering yells like a wild animal. Effie shuddered, holding her hands over her ears. Florence leaned against the door, her eyes tight shut, exclaiming: "I can *not,* I can *not!*"

Presently the shouts ceased and Field's voice could be heard, encouraging, consoling. Then came convulsive sobbing and words that couldn't be understood. After an age, there was quietness. Effie raised her head. Florence was still leaning against the door, white as a sheet.

"I can't stay, I can't stay in this house," she said. "We must go to The Priory House. He'll take us in. Tell Laundon—ring—"

Effie pulled the bell beside the fireplace, and as the door opened to admit Laundon, a new outbreak of noise was heard from below. Florence said: "Mrs. Chalmers and I are going to The Priory House. I want you to come with us."

"Shall I order a carriage, ma'am?"

"No, I can't wait. We must walk. Fetch our outdoor things and yours, quickly." Laundon disappeared, nimble and competent, and as they waited for her to come downstairs, a fresh outburst of sounds came to them, muffled by distance. Laundon, dressed, reappeared with their hats and mantles and they picked their way through broken glass to the front door. Outside, the November dusk was deep, with clouds scudding overhead. Florence led the way down Victoria Road, almost running. All three were light on their feet and in less than ten minutes Pritchard was receiving them in the lighted hall. Astonished at their wild, damp appearance, and at there being three of them, he showed them into the dining room while he decided what to do next.

"The doctor is with a patient, madam," he said. "I will inform him as soon as he comes out."

Florence stared in indignation. A patient! Was not *she* the patient? Effie, seeing her sister taken aback, said they would be very glad to see Dr. Gully as soon as he was at liberty. Meanwhile, said Pritchard, making up his mind, if they would come into the drawing room, he would tell the ladies of their arrival. He led them into the drawing room, glowing dimly from a strong fire, lit the lamps and left them.

Florence had now begun to tremble in long, shuddering fits. The others made her sit on the sofa and in a few moments Ann and Ellen were with them, surrounding them with sympathy, tenderness and sense. Effie gave the story as well as she could but she had come to the house as a stranger and hardly knew how to speak for Florence. The latter was crying and her efforts to speak were incoherent; Laundon now ventured to give a concise account of the affair; when she spoke of the yells, blows and broken glass, Ann got up from her seat beside Florence.

"You and your sister must stay here, my dear," she said. Ellen added that a bedroom should be made ready at once. "You would like to be together, I daresay, and your maid shall be next door."

"Yes, thank you so much, you are so kind," said Effie.

"Then, ma'am," said Laundon, "shall I go back for the night things?"

"If you aren't afraid," asked Effie doubtfully.

"Oh, no, ma'am, I shall keep out of the way, and the mistress and you must have something with you."

"An excellent young woman," said Ann, as Laundon disappeared. She was sitting beside Florence again, wishing that James would come, not knowing what ought to be done meanwhile. The crying increased and she was afraid it would become hysterical. At that moment, to her intense relief, she heard the door of the consulting room open and steps sounding on the hall flags. She restrained herself from rushing out, Pritchard would tell the story; and in half a minute, James was in the room. Florence jumped up and went blindly toward him, her hands outstretched. He took them, and stood, holding them, while he listened to Ann's explanation and Effie's alternately.

"You did quite right to come here," he said. He put Florence into a chair, standing beside her, for she clung to his hand, shivering and crying still.

Ellen came in, saying that their room was ready. "Then I think," he said, "that she had better come upstairs right away." They all moved into the hall; Ellen, saying "I think we shall be rather too many," fell behind. In the bedroom a wood fire was already burning, a double bed was made up with sheets turned back, candles were lit on the mantelpiece and dressing table and a maid was putting woolen covers over the brass cans of hot water on the washstand.

Dr. Gully pushed a chintz-covered armchair up to the hearth while Effie took off her sister's hat and cloak; he left the room and came back shortly with sal volatile and water in a glass. Florence was still crying so much that Effie doubted if she would be able to drink it, but he put one hand on her forehead, gently pressing her head back against the chair, and a second or two afterward, held the glass to her lips. She drank some mouthfuls till he took it away. She was calmer and Effie, who had stood gazing anxiously at her, now took off her own hat and mantle. "Mrs. Chalmers," said Dr. Gully kindly, "let my sister take you downstairs; we dine at half past seven. I don't think Mrs. Ricardo should sit up for dinner. When the maid has brought her things, she'd better go straight to bed. I will stay with her for a little while, until she feels more comfortable."

On the stairs Effie said: "I am anxious to hear about poor Alexander."

"You must be," Ann said. "No doubt Laundon will have something to tell us when she comes back. I shouldn't wonder if he's quieter now you are all out of the house."

Dr. Gully had left the room in the wake of the others. He went into his bedroom, washed his hands and changed his coat, his habit when the day's work was finished. Florence had not noticed his going out. She suddenly found that she was alone in the candlelight. She got up. Her chest was still heaving but the tears were drying on her burning cheeks. She walked distractedly about the room; then she began to wonder in some indignation how long she was to be left alone like this. No sound reached the room from the rest of the house; the stillness was absolute. She longed for him to be there. She could not keep still but walked quickly, aimlessly, from the hearth to the curtained window and back to the hearth again.

Someone knocked. She cried impatiently, "Come in!" and when he appeared she went toward him stretching out her arms.

He left the door ajar, with habitual discretion, but at the sight of her, flushed and brilliant-eyed, with face and arms raised toward him, demanding and helpless, sense and experience forsook him. He took her in his arms. It was the first embrace she had ever known that gave her comfort and absolute delight. Her head reached his shoulder; his weight and firmness gave her the support to lean against that she needed. She raised her arms above his elbows and joined her hands at the back of his neck. He gently kissed her head, her eyelids and temples. After a while she murmured: "I had to come to you. Please take care of me."

"I shall," he said. "Don't be frightened anymore." He tightened his hold, but unlike anything she had known before, the increased pressure didn't cause her discomfort or suffocation; it only intensified bliss. Everything that she had ever felt for him had brought her at last to this exquisite moment. And then, a dress basket in each hand, Laundon was standing in the room.

He had too much dignity and presence of mind to show that he was disconcerted. He gently released Florence, saying: "Mrs. Ricardo has been so much frightened and distressed, she had better go to bed at once."

Laundon's eyes were lowered as she said, "Yes, sir," but there was the faint smirk that he had expected to see. He forced himself to maintain his ground.

"You will ring for anything Mrs. Ricardo wants. Mrs. Chalmers is in the drawing room." Then he said to Florence, "They will bring you some dinner when you are in bed, my dear," and left the room.

He did not return to the lighted drawing room; he went into the library and stood over the fire with his hands behind his back.

The embrace, especially in a bedroom, had been preposterously indiscreet; but even so, he found that he didn't regret it. But after this contretemps he must be particularly careful, for both of them. The maid—whom he'd never entirely trusted—was on trial too, even if she didn't know it. If she presumed on what she'd seen—his face took on an expression of iron severity that it wore very seldom. It passed; the idea most in possession of his mind was to protect Florence.

This violent drunkenness wasn't going to end; the man's case was hopeless; and though she might gain a separation, she would still be tied to him, till he destroyed himself. He would, sooner or later, but with partial recoveries, it might be years hence. Expectations of death, however reasonable, when death would bring release to other people, were apt to prove unfounded, as his own wrecked life could show. He and she were both victims of an established order, cruel and immutable.

But there were certain possibilities, calling for determination and courage; he could not explore them now; his only immediate concern was to protect her, because she was in desperate need of his protection and because she was so precious to him.

At dinner he was his usual charming self to their other guest, but his sisters thought he looked distrait. A doctor's family are accustomed to having claims imposed on them, but that trouble should be brought actually into the house was something they hadn't bargained for. However, they went willingly up and downstairs, superintending the invalid's dinner, and the evening was not a long one, for Effie, exhausted, went to bed early. Ann and Ellen came into the bedroom with her; Dr. Gully stood for a moment on the threshold, asking whether they had everything for comfort. Florence from the bed called out in a weak voice, saying thank you and good night. She was still awake, watching the glow fade from the ceiling, while Effie slept beside her. She knew, as certainly as he knew himself, that extreme caution and restraint were now binding on them both, but for the present she was serene and satisfied. The assurance of his love was so overmastering she could not look beyond it.

Chapter 11

THE ladies' breakfast was brought to them in their room and they were still in their dressing gowns when the Misses Gully came to hear their plans.

"I can't go back to that house," Florence said in a heavy, dogged manner unlike her usual spirited utterance.

Effie said: "I think we should write to my mother—if," she added tentatively, "we might stay here till she comes?"

"Of course you must stay," said Ann. "My brother wouldn't hear of anything else."

When they were dressed, she took Florence into the library, empty but with a bland, fragrant atmosphere of a wood fire and sun-warmed leather chairs. Florence was not seated at the doctor's desk but at a little davenport near the fire and supplied with writing materials.

Effie meanwhile, accompanied by Laundon, went off to Stokefield to superintend the packing of clothes, ready to fetch away. While she went up to the bedrooms, Laundon excused herself and slipped downstairs where Field, spruce as ever though in his shirt sleeves, was sponging the front of a jacket with a flannel dipped in water from a simmering kettle. The captain, he said, hadn't rung; he was still in a heavy sleep. Laundon couldn't wait to hear more; she eagerly poured out her experience of yesterday evening.

Field said: "Ah! and you mean to say you didn't know what was going on there?"

"I had my ideas, of course."

"Your ideas, they'll be everybody's ideas before long. You must look out for yourself before that. Don't let them come it over you."

"What ain't I to do, then?"

"Fair's fair. In good service, you give your notice if you see anything off color. It's expected of you. If you oblige by staying on, it's only right there should be something extra in wages and consideration."

Laundon was silent, thinking.

"I like her," she said at last.

"That's your lookout, but don't stay without making yourself felt, or you'll get nothing for it and be at a loss when you go."

"Such an old man, isn't he? If she'd got to have somebody, you'd think a young fellow—"

"Ah!" said Field in an oracular tone. He went on sponging and pressing, and after staying away as long as she dared, Laundon went upstairs again. Effie was busy with her own packing; she told Laundon she didn't want help and asked her to get on with putting up Mrs. Ricardo's things. Presently she herself went downstairs and summoned Field by ringing the drawing-room bell. From him she heard that the captain had been talking of going to London; he believed they would be off as soon as the captain was on his legs again. Effie told him that Mrs. Ricardo would be going to Buscot Park as soon as Mrs. Campbell arrived to fetch her, and all arrangements had better be referred to Mrs. Campbell, there or at Lowndes Square. Field bowed slightly.

"I wish anything could be done for the captain," said Effie

wistfully. Field approved of Mrs. Chalmers, young, nice-natured and a thorough lady.

"It's a sad business, madam," he said kindly. There was nothing else he could say.

It was half past eleven. The November sunlight poured through the tall library window; Florence's letter had been taken to the post office and now Dr. Gully had seated her in a chair by the hearth. He was standing at the corner of the chimneypiece.

"I allowed my feelings to be shown too plainly last night," he was saying. "I must apologize."

"No!" she said, shaking her head.

"I am glad at least that I did not offend you."

"No, no!"

"There is so much I want to say."

"Tell me!" Her round, dark-blue eyes were fixed on his, her lips slightly apart. He smiled, but realized that he must show sense for both.

"You are in a very difficult, a cruel position; you need protection and guidance."

"If I can have yours, I—"

"It is one of my dearest wishes to protect you. I wish I did not love you, then I could perhaps be more useful to you."

"Don't say that. To hear you say you love me—you mustn't want to take away the delight that gives me."

"My dear! But there are other matters I must discuss with you. Your maid saw me last night—"

"Yes."

"Did she make any remark?"

"No, none at all. I do not really mind her being in my confidence. I do not think she would take advantage."

"You may know her best. I confess I am a little doubtful. But if she should, you must get rid of her right away."

"Yes, I would. I shouldn't dream of allowing a servant to be impertinent to me."

"Quite right. Don't think me interfering—"

"I couldn't ever think so. I wish you could tell me what to do about everything."

"My dear, my dearest child! I wish I could—"

"I wish I could stay here. But now I have written to my mother, she will expect me to go home with her."

"Yes, and it is right you should. But we shall be in close touch with each other, I hope." Whether he put his hand out first, or she hers, their hands held fast together. Florence was entirely contented by the contact. It thrilled and satisfied her, she wanted nothing further.

Presently he took out his watch. He was obliged to leave her. She remained sitting over the fire—she could not have said for how long—until Ann came in and told her Effie had returned. Florence got up at once and hurried upstairs after her sister and heard Effie's account of affairs at Stokefield.

After luncheon, Ellen asked if they would like a walk. Effie said she would, she would like to see Saint Anne's Well; Florence said she was tired and would rather lie down, and Dr. Gully, looking at her pale cheeks and shadowed eyes, said, "That would be wise, I think, but come and walk around the garden once while this sunshine lasts." On the paved walk, she took his arm and they strolled down the lawn to the ornamental water. It was only two o'clock but even as they stood there, the brightness of the day was over; there was a silence, a stillness all around; she leaned on his arm in their slow walk, too full of emotion to speak, nor did he attempt it. After a few turns about the lawn, he led her back to the house and she went upstairs.

Laundon, who had watched them from the shelter of the window curtain, removed Florence's dress and helped her on with her dressing gown. Florence pulled the combs out of her hair and walked toward the bed.

"My mother will be here, I expect, tomorrow or the next day, and we shall return with her to Buscot or London." Laundon had the brown moiré dress with its heaped-up, trailing skirt, over her arms.

"The doctor will miss you, ma'am," she said, "but perhaps he will be visiting you at Buscot, or London?" Florence was astounded. If she had expected any signs from Laundon, it was not this.

"What do you mean?" she said coldly.

"I only mean what's plain to anybody, ma'am. I don't want to be disagreeable, but as Mr. Field says—"

"What does he say?"

"That this is a family where the servants have something very particular expected of them."

"Captain Ricardo does unfortunately need very special attention."

"Not only the captain, ma'am, is it? But I'm quite prepared to be helpful so long as—"

"As what?"

"Well, as long as it's realized, as you may say, and taken into consideration."

"Laundon," said Florence calmly, "we shall have to part. I don't think you would have spoken to me like this of your own accord, but since you have, I can't keep you with me. You must take a month's wages instead of notice, and leave when I go away with my mother. I suppose you can go to your home at Camberwell? I will provide for your journey."

The young women had thoroughly astonished each other. After this, it was awkward to be thrown a good deal into each other's intimate society for the next forty-eight hours or so; but Laundon's training in good service and Florence's determination of character and her experience of dealing with servants, very long considering her youth, combined to smooth the way. Each, too, had a motive for keeping things as pleasant as might be; Florence wanted Laundon's discretion to be used in her favor; Laundon for her part wanted a really valuable reference.

In that pleasant evening lull, when the day's work was over, before people separated to prepare for dinner, Florence was coming downstairs to join the others in the drawing room. As she reached the lighted hall, she saw him at the open door of his consulting room. She came toward him, saying, "I have something to tell you," and he made way for her to come in. He did not shut the door but stood just inside it. She told him how she had been obliged to dismiss Laundon, and he remembered how she had brushed aside his warning—so positive, and so mistaken!

But he only said: "You have done the right thing. I would not say anything to anyone in this household as to why you are parting with her. In fact, you need not mention that she is leaving you. I suppose you will explain to your mother that she tried to make capital out of seeing me kiss you."

"I may, but I don't think Mama ever cared for her very much. She will be satisfied to hear that she didn't suit me and that we have agreed to part."

The dressing gong now sounded.

"Dear me," Florence said, "just as I've come down. Now I must go upstairs again." She walked across the hall, the tail of her skirt crisply sweeping the flags. He watched her mount the stairs, her head bent as if by the weight of the great plaited bunch of copper hair at the back of it, as big as the plait on a harvest loaf, the looped-up train dragging behind her, and thought he'd never seen such grace. His sisters and Effie came out of the drawing room and followed her up the staircase. He turned into the room and put away some papers that were lying on the desk. When he came out to go upstairs himself, a tall, slender figure in black with a white apron, carrying two brass hot-water cans, came though the hall to mount the staircase. At the sight of him, standing in the doorway looking at her, she gave a second's involuntary pause, then went on her way again.

The anger she had not felt against Florence, Laundon felt against Dr. Gully. He should now have been in her power. He was an old man, making up to a young woman; that should have put him into an inferior position to start with, and at the mercy of all young women. Then, he'd been seen by her kissing Mrs. Ricardo in her bedroom; a scandal, if you like! He ought to have been, by this time, frightened of her, trying to make peace with her in every way he could think of. Instead of all that, he seemed as powerful as ever and he had a stern look on his face she hadn't seen before that cowed her, though she was annoyed with herself for minding it.

Chapter 12

❦

MRS. CAMPBELL telegraphed next morning to say she was coming to Malvern at once. She arrived at The Priory House about six o'clock, prepared, after seeing her daughters, to go to a hotel, but the Misses Gully welcomed her cordially and told her a room was ready for her. A cup of tea was brought to her in her daughters' bedroom, where she alternately soothed and questioned Florence, while Effie unpacked her mother's traveling bag.

At dinner, Dr. Gully observed his old friend had put on weight in the last twelve years and her face showed the ravages of anxiety and fatigue but she was still a pleasant-looking woman with an honest charm about her. After dinner he said to her: "You will feel too tired now for us to have a conversation?"

"No, indeed," she said, rousing up. "I am not at all too tired, if you are at leisure."

"Then let us have our coffee in the library."

"I can't tell you how grateful I am for your assistance," she said as he settled her in a chair by the fire.

"Flo's letter shocked me—poor child! These endless horrors! Can nothing be done for him? Other doctors have tried, but *you* are so clever."

"No doctor can prevent a man from drinking himself to death if he wants to."

"Aren't there ways of preventing him from wanting to?"

"There may be. I do not know them."

"It has gone on for so long now—what the rest of her life is to be, I dare not think."

"In my opinion, she should be separated from him."

"Separated! That is a very serious suggestion!"

"My dear madam, of course it's very serious. This is a very serious matter."

She said tremulously: "No one can feel that more than I do."

"Of course not. And I am sure you feel that your daughter's health ought to be the first consideration. From the condition she was in when she came to me last May, I believe it is dangerous for her to go on living under this man's roof."

"Of course she mustn't be exposed to violence, but she can always come to her father and me when she's driven to. Shelter is always available. What would she gain by a legal separation?"

"She would gain release from a domestic situation that is threatening to destroy her nervous system. As long as her husband can call her back to him in temporary recoveries, as I understand has happened several times already, she undergoes the intense nervous strain of these repeated efforts. She has youth on her side at present; she has made a satisfactory recovery—"

"We owe that to you."

"Well, I think you do, to me and Malvern. But if she is to undergo these sufferings repeatedly, the time will come when she won't recover."

"It's terrible to hear you say so, and nothing, almost, can be as important to me as her well-being. But physical well-being is not our *only* care. A young woman who leaves her husband, from *whatever* cause—society will say—"

"I'm not arguing about society. I'm speaking to you plainly as a doctor. It's dangerous to her sanity to leave this man with any power of compelling her to live with him. In one of the states of America—I think it is Maine—they have the power to commit a man to an inebriates' asylum if he's declared to be dangerous at large. If this were Maine, Captain Ricardo would be in that asylum now. The authorities have power to detain the patient for a year while his situation is examined and his family given protection from him if he's thought not likely to recover. Over here, we fine the man if he's disorderly in the street; we ignore the sufferings of the wife. The law allows her a separation and society exerts all its influence on her to prevent her from taking it."

Mrs. Campbell was almost crying. "I'm sure I only want what's best for her, my poor darling."

"I know you do."

"So does her father, but he would never consent to such a step as that." He did not say that a married woman, if she were over twenty-one, had no need of her father's consent, legally speaking. He knew that Mrs. Campbell was thinking of prohibitions outside the law. As long as a woman endured evil treatment from her husband, she was a dignified figure, her social position was impregnable. If she chose to release herself —she could be "talked about," as someone subtly degraded, and the taint would spread from her reputation to her family's. Mrs. Campbell would be inclined to make even this sacrifice for her daughter's happiness. Her husband, she knew, would never make it. She wiped her eyes.

"Well, Doctor," she said, "however it may be ordered, I shall never forget what we owe to you."

He made a gracious gesture; then he said: "By the way, there have of course been no live births, but has she had miscarriages?"

"No, I think not, I am sure not. In fact I have sometimes wondered if everything were quite right between them, as there was never any sign of anything." He was silent, looking into the fire. She went on: "My daughter has never complained, or even spoken about the matter and I did not like to trespass on her reserve."

"Well," he said, "however it may have been at first, drinking on this scale must have made Captain Ricardo incapable of marital intercourse this long while."

"I suppose so."

"There is another matter. I have noticed her taking wine as a stimulant. She hasn't done so in my house. As a rule I have wine only for guests and I didn't bring up any for her and Mrs. Chalmers."

"Then I'm afraid that delicious claret was on my account."

"It gratifies my butler to bring it to table. But of course she should drink wine only at mealtimes and very moderately then. She hasn't asked for any since she's been here and I hope that when she feels in safety and at ease, she won't want to resort to it."

"I'm sure she won't. One can hardly blame her, in her trials—"

"No one blames her, but it's a dangerous habit that must be firmly checked. When she is with you at Buscot Park, you must be watchful, and if you notice her drinking between meals, you must speak very seriously. I do not think that she is likely to take too much at table, though one glass should be the limit; the danger is in resorting to it at other times."

"Yes. It would be quite dreadful. I will do everything I can." She sighed. He felt deeply sorry for her.

He suggested her going to bed early and she said that she would be glad to go at once. In discussing her arrangements for the morning she said she did not feel she could leave Malvern without some word with Field. It was not practicable to send for him to The Priory House, for he could scarcely be spared from where he was, and Mrs. Campbell decided that as the doctor had kindly placed his carriage at her disposal, she would drive around to Stokefield soon after breakfast and return to take up her daughters and go on to the station. Dr. Gully said a message should be sent early in the morning to the outporter, telling him to call for the ladies' luggage, and one to Stokefield, telling Field to expect Mrs. Campbell.

The next morning the doctor and his sisters were standing in the hall with Mrs. Campbell, who was dressed for the journey.

"I should recommend you not to go into the house," he was saying. "But are you sure you would not like someone to come with you?"

At that moment Effie joined them, in bonnet, cloak and muff.

"I am going with Mama," she said. "I am sure she had better have someone in the carriage with her." The carriage now wheeled up, Griffith bringing the horses to a halt, delicately, on the exact spot of gravel that he had in mind.

The doctor went out and said: "Griffith, you must take Tom with you. When you get to Stokefield, he is to ring the bell and tell Field to come out to the carriage. The ladies won't get out, mind that."

"Very good, sir," Griffith said. "Please to hold them." He jumped down and ran off, and Dr. Gully stood with one hand on the nearer horse's bridle, his other hand caressing the beautiful neck, while the horses blew softly and jingled the harness. Griffith returned, followed by the stableboy, shuffling into a respectable coat. Dr. Gully handed the ladies in and watched them drive off. Ann Gully went into the kitchen to speak about sandwiches and the filling of Mrs. Campbell's tea flasks, and Ellen went upstairs to offer help.

Florence was already dressed for the journey and so was Laundon, who was to go with the party to Buscot and from there to London the following day. The latter was putting a novel and a bottle of lavender water into Florence's valise. Ellen began to ask her how the tea and sandwiches should be packed: in the valise or in a separate basket? While she and Laundon were speaking, Florence, with perfect self-possession, walked out of the room and down the stairs where the pale November sunlight came through yellowing leaves and filled the hall with ethereal brightness.

He was on the threshold of the consulting room. Without a word she went up to him, they went in and he shut the door. She was now trembling like a thrush. He put his arms around her waist; she did not dare put her head on his shoulder for fear of disarranging her bonnet and her hair, but he felt, pressed against him, the rich textures of velvet and moiré and fur, and breathed a scent as fresh as morning.

"I was afraid I should have to leave without saying good-bye." She whispered because her voice had deserted her.

"I would never have allowed that," he said.

"I will write to you."

"I shall look forward to that, more than you can perhaps imagine."

"And hope very, very much to see you soon."

"We shall meet, indeed, how soon I can't say but whenever it can be. But never forget how dear you are to me, send to me at once if you need help, and let me have the comfort of knowing *you* want us to meet." She put her arms around his neck; he kissed her, but gently; this was five minutes to ten in the morning and she must appear, almost at once, elegant and *soignée*, for a drive to the railway station. He drew down her arms and held her hands tightly. Presently he led her to a chair and stood over her, still holding one of her hands. Each felt there were things this was the opportunity to say but the emotion was too strong for words. The pale sunlight pouring through the tall window made the fire on the hearth pale too; the silence was language.

After an uncounted time he drew out his watch and looked at it. She gave an anguished sigh, but he put it back in his waist-coat pocket without comment and took her hand again in both his own. She knew that the time of parting must be advancing toward them with scythelike edge. She withdrew her hand and peeled off her gloves, taking his hand again. He spread out the small fingers of each of hers. On the left was the wedding ring, on the right the great emerald of the Ricardo family. He would have liked to take off both of them.

At the distant sound of wheels on the gravel he lifted one of her hands and kissed it, then the other. She picked up her gloves and rose; as they walked to the door he held her by the elbow, which he might have done under the eyes of anybody.

The hall was full of movement. Mrs. Campbell remained seated in the carriage and Dr. Gully went out to her. Effie had descended to come in for Florence. The Misses Gully, Pritchard, the dark, discreet figure of Laundon, getting into the carriage and sitting down with her back to the horses, all passed before Florence's eyes without her recognizing them. She knew that he was helping her into the carriage; she did not look at him.

They wheeled about and drove up Church Street to the turning that led to the station.

"Very much the same," her mother was saying. "Quite exhausted still, but he had told Field he wanted to send his love to you, Flo."

Chapter 13

CHILL autumn in Buscot Park, rain, wind and gloom; indoors, richly burning fires on marble hearths under lofty gilded looking glasses, and the attentions of numerous willing servants—there was really no comfort to be found anywhere such as there was in her parents' house.

Florence had her breakfast upstairs and she did not join the family at luncheon or dinner when, as often happened, there were guests. To appear without her husband was to court inquiries about him which no one wanted to answer.

Her mother was all tenderness and anxious care; her father had, of course, greeted her warmly but from the trend of his remarks Florence knew that he looked upon her visit as a short one before rejoining her husband.

Effie had left Buscot to rejoin her husband the day after their arrival, and Laundon too had departed, generously paid. Mrs. Campbell had too much on her mind to notice anything of this except that Flo was making a change; there was no hurry to replace Laundon; there were plenty of maids here to look after her till she should suit herself again. The poor darling was distraite, and no wonder, but her mother was thankful that there were no renewed signs of the dreadful nervous illness.

On the afternoon of her third day at home Florence came in

from a walk in the park and went up to her bedroom. She meant to get out of her corset and lie down before tea, and she had already rung when she saw it on the table: the oblong envelope with the Malvern postmark. The maid who answered the bell paused in the doorway. Mrs. Ricardo was sitting in the window, reading a letter with such intense attention, the girl didn't like to disturb her but went quietly into the dressing room for a few minutes.

Florence had a blue morocco writing box, with pockets in the lid for stationery and a locked compartment for letters, which so far she had never used. Next morning she put the box on the table in her window overlooking the park and settled herself to write.

She had that morning received a letter from Laundon, apologizing for the impertinence that had caused her to be dismissed and hoping Mrs. Ricardo would be so good as to give her a reference. Florence began her answer easily enough. She accepted Laundon's apology and regretted having been obliged to part with her. "I like you personally and you suit me in every way. I will do all I can to procure you a good situation and hope you may soon succeed in getting one." She paused. Would it be wiser to end here? She felt sure that the doctor would say so; but she had an innate confidence in her own judgment which at times could overcome even her confidence in his. She took a quick decision and wrote: "I hope you will never allude *in any way* to *anyone* of what passed at Malvern. Let it all be buried in the past. If *anybody* questions you, please refuse to answer any inquiries. With kind remembrances to yourself, Yours truly, Florence Ricardo. Burn this." With a sense of having committed herself, but all for the best, she fastened the envelope.

The wind swept across the park with a sound that was almost a scream, hurling yellow leaves with demoniac force, then sank suddenly, leaving them for dead on the ground. Unheeding, she began another letter: "Dearest, wisest and best of doctors." It took her a very long time.

In the hall, on a marble table resting on gilded lions' feet, the postbox stood, a tall cylinder with the times of collection lettered on it. She dropped the two envelopes into its mouth and went upstairs again with a private sense of security.

Her father did not unlock the postbag and dole out its contents at the breakfast table as some antediluvian persons still did. Florence arranged with the maid to collect her morning letters from the butler. The afternoon post was spread out on the marble table. Florence knew what time to expect it, and could secure a letter that it brought her, before anyone except the butler had time to notice the recurring Malvern postmark. There was a little pile of letters now in the locked compartment of her writing box, beginning: "My dear Mrs. Ricardo," "My dear Florence," "My dear."

About other letters she was almost childishly open. Scrawls in poor Alexander's broken-backed writing, begging for another chance to begin their life together again, undertaking, promising, she showed to her mother as they came. "May I show this to Papa?" Mrs. Campbell would ask, and Florence, weary but docile, would answer: "Yes, of course."

At the beginning of December Florence said she must go to London for a day's shopping and would take a morning train from Faringdon.

"Tell them you want the carriage," her father said.

"Or the dogcart."

"The dogcart, my love!" exclaimed her mother. "In this weather! You'd be blown to pieces before you entered the train!"

"Of course she can't go in the dogcart," said her father impatiently. "If you don't want the carriage, take the brougham. And tell them which train you'll come back by."

"I shall hardly know that, Papa. I can take a cab at Faringdon."

"Nonsense. Tell them the first of the trains you might take. They'll be there for that, and if you don't appear, they'll put up at the Arms and wait till you do." Mr. Campbell did not like opposition in a daughter even in his kindnesses.

The train from Faringdon brought Florence to Paddington by half past twelve. In the station refreshment room she had a cup of coffee and a Bath bun; she did not want them but she knew it was only sensible to take something. A hansom carried her the long drive through crowded, noisy thoroughfares, teeming with omnibuses, cabs, hansoms, drays and foot passengers, with the speed of a good horse pulling a very light vehicle. They danced through Leicester Square and down Charing Cross Road and drew up at the doors of Morley's Hotel, the long, white, pillared building that lay all along one side of Trafalgar Square and turned the corner so that its bow-windowed coffee room overlooked the Strand.

Before she had her money in her hand, the hotel doorman was opening the hansom. The driver touched his hat with his whip as he drove off and Florence, in the vestibule, had not time to wonder whom she should speak to: Dr. Gully was before her, taking her hand and bowing over it. The shock of delight at seeing him, actually there in front of her, was tempered; he looked so formal, so well dressed, so important as he led her up the shallow stairs to a landing and opened the door of a private sitting room. When they were inside he said with great courtesy: "This is so good of you. I was afraid you might find it too fatiguing, coming up from Gloucestershire and down again in one day."

"Oh, no." It should have been easy, irresistible even, to meet him exactly where she had parted from him three weeks ago, and now there seemed to be rough edges that would not join.

Tears of disappointment filled her eyes. She said coldly: "We often come up from Buscot for the day."

He smiled and said: "Won't you take off your coat?" She unfastened the heavy garment of violet cloth and he took it from her, laying it on a chair. Meanwhile she pulled off her gloves. He took those too, then he took her bare hand and raised it to his lips. In an instant her tears turned to a prismatic radiance. She smiled on him and they sat down opposite each other. He did not take a seat on the sofa beside her, for though this was a private sitting room it was in a London hotel. She was conscious of his restraint, but his keen, florid face, his commanding gaze were so exactly what she had been seeing in her mind ever since they parted, to see him actually there gave her a sense of heightened existence.

"And now you must tell me how it is with you," he was saying. She told him of Alexander's letters.

"I know my father thinks I ought to go back to him. But I—" she stopped.

"And what do you think?"

"I've told you already what I feel."

"Yes, but in a personal matter like this, feelings vary, very naturally. They ebb and flow."

"Mine don't. I've made up my mind. I'm never going through all that again. I thought you didn't want me to."

"I don't want you to. If you told me that you meant to return to him, I should regret it most bitterly, for your sake, and for mine because your health and safety are so precious to me."

Her gaze sank to the hands folded in her lap. He said: "You will let me talk to you as a doctor as well as a friend, will you not?" She lifted her eyes now, surprised and startled.

"Of course I will."

"I think that ever since your husband began to drink on this scale, you and he cannot have had the relations normal between married people?" He looked at her narrowly; she kept her startled gaze on him but said nothing.

"Before your marriage, did your mother, I wonder, tell you in what those relations consist?"

"She said something but I didn't really know what she meant. She said that my husband would know what to do and I must learn it all from him and do whatever he wanted."

"Well, and were you and your husband happy doing what he wanted?"

"No. He always seemed so unhappy himself; that is, we were happy in the daytime, sometimes, but at night, he seemed to be so upset, he made me quite miserable. I used to wish we'd never got married." He thought of one of William Acton's passages: "Here is material for a woman's social misery, the domestic wretchedness of ruined health, the idiocy or brain disease of the semi-virgin."

He got up, standing against the window, and said with all his authority: "I repeat what I said to your mother. I think that so far from contemplating a return to your husband, you ought to be separated from him."

"Do you mean legally?"

"Yes. It could be arranged, I am certain, if you wished it. Your father, I understand, would object—"

"Yes, he would. But it wouldn't be for him to decide, would it?"

"No. The matter would be between you and your husband. Have you a solicitor?"

"My husband has, of course."

"I think you need one of your own. If you like, I will find a well-recommended one, to suggest to you."

"Oh, yes, please do! Could I not use yours?"

"No, my dear. I think you should employ someone who does not act for me or for your family either."

"Very well." She stood beside him. Out of the window they could see the base of Nelson's Column, the four great leaden lions at its feet; in front of the columns of the National Gallery, the fountains played through fugitive gleams of light. It was too chilly now for throngs of idlers. Beggars with trays of matches and bootlaces stood shivering, but all the other figures in the scene were crossing the square purposefully, one way or another. Florence began to think, early as it was, that she would like some tea. She said so, and Dr. Gully rang the bell, opening the door and leaving it wide open, afterward. He ordered tea from the waiter who appeared, then asked her what train she meant to take at Paddington. She said that there were trains to Faringdon at half past three and half past four. Knowing that the journey took two hours and that there was a three-mile drive at the end of it, he decided that the half past three, which would enable her to reach Buscot Park at six o'clock, was the appropriate one to return by, after a day's shopping. "If you will allow me," he said, "when you've had a cup of tea, I'll take you in a hansom to Paddington."

"It will be like our drives at Malvern," she said, "at least, not *like*, but reminding me."

"London streets, particularly in the direction of Praed Street, are not like our Malvern roads, certainly. But there will be charms about this drive that even Malvern does not own."

"Yes. I was so ill then, and now you've made me quite well."

"And we know each other better." This was an approach to the conversation she longed for; but now the waiter came with the tea tray: tea, small iced cakes, cress sandwiches and fingers of hot buttered toast under a plated cover. The man shut the door on them and in this uncompromising but delicious privacy, she poured out Dr. Gully's tea and her own. He would not eat anything but when he had questioned her about her lunch, he encouraged her to eat up most of what was on the plates.

When it was time to go, he told her she would find a ladies' room at the end of the corridor, and went downstairs to have a hansom summoned.

There had been some apprehension and even some sore feeling in Florence's mind at first, but the meeting had grown steadily more incandescent as the time flew on, and their journey in the hansom, side by side with her arm drawn through his and his hand in both of hers, was one of those voyages to Cythera, where the rapt travelers are approaching the source of light.

In Paddington Station, the noise of hissing steam and of the moving crowds was diminished by the extent of the station and the loftiness of its vast roof. The train was already at the platform and Florence had a return ticket, so he escorted her to a first-class carriage at once. There were two ladies in it but they were talking to each other, and when she murmured as he stood on the steps, "Don't wait, I'd rather you wouldn't" (for she felt that to be pulled away from a last glimpse of him would be more painful than to say good-bye now) they noticed nothing except that an elderly gentleman (probably an uncle) was seeing into the train this pretty, grandly dressed young lady, and very proper, too—not the sort of girl who should be about by herself in London. As the journey proceeded, she seemed to their discreet observation to be a little older than they had thought at first; when they consulted her about shutting the window, she replied with great self-possession, almost with hauteur.

Dr. Gully intended to return to Malvern the next afternoon. When he got back to Morley's Hotel he wrote a brief note to Mr. Brookes, a solicitor with offices in Godliman Street, leading out of St. Paul's Churchyard. He knew of Brookes from having met his mother-in-law, Mrs. Lea, at Malvern. Brookes had the reputation of a humane, good-natured man; it was a fact that he was an able solicitor with a large practice. Dr. Gully wrote that he hoped Mr. Brookes would be able to see him when he called at eleven o'clock on Friday morning. He posted the letter himself in the post office in the Strand and returned to the hotel for an early dinner before going to the Royal Opera House to hear Sessi in *La Traviata*.

The experience kept him waking all through the night. As he turned and turned again on his pillows, he felt it strange that though he had been devoted to grand opera all his life, it was now, at the age of sixty-two, that he felt most keenly the emotional impact of a story of passionate, ill-starred love, brought home to the listener with all the force that music could command.

When he did sleep, he slept heavily and got up with not much more than time, before his appointment, for a late breakfast and a stroll around Trafalgar Square in the uncertain sunlight. He was irresistibly drawn to the fountains, their cloudily gleaming arches falling into the great basins where the water quivered all the time as it did in the marble basin at Saint Anne's Well; but here, though the water was glassy, it did not look pure; he would not have liked to put his lips to it.

Mr. Brookes turned out to be a blunt-featured, bearded man with spectacles and a snub nose. His manner was heartily cheerful but sometimes the smile left his face and the eyes behind his spectacles looked very shrewd. Dr. Gully liked the shrewdness quite as much as the good nature. When Mr. Brooks had listened to his account of Mrs. Ricardo's situation, he said: "If she instructs us, we shall be very glad to act for her. By the way, you are quite certain she wants this separation?"

"Wants it! She's determined on it."

"I ask, from experience of this type of case. You sometimes find that after you've done all the work and are ready to act, the wife tells you she's made up her mind that she doesn't want to leave him after all."

"I think you'll find that this is a very positive young woman."

"So much the better. Shall we have to fight the husband?"

"I doubt if he's in a condition to fight anybody."

"She's of full legal age?"

"Twenty-five last month."

"Then, if she perseveres in wanting this separation, I daresay we shall get it for her."

"Her welfare is a matter of much concern to me. She's virtually friendless. The parents, who ought to protect her, are against it; at least, the mother I think is sympathetic but she can't influence the father. I shall be very glad to feel that her affairs are in such competent hands." He got up and Mr. Brookes rose also.

"You may rely on our doing everything possible, once she's instructed us," he said. They shook hands warmly and Dr. Gully, having been shown out by a civil young clerk, made his way to the churchyard again and walked down Ludgate Hill and back to the Strand. He felt confidence in what he'd seen of Mr. Brookes and was pleased with his morning's work.

Chapter 14

❦

As Christmas approached Ann and Ellen were making the usual preparations: mince pies—James thought them unwholesome but did not object to their being distributed, once a year, to those in sound health—and a Christmas tree, to be decorated for Susanna's children. A week before Christmas they heard that measles would prevent Susanna from bringing the family. They gave the news to James as he came in for his afternoon cup of tea. He said: "I am sorry for the cause, but it is just as well, perhaps, for Susie not to be with us this Christmas. I have something to tell you that it would be difficult for you to keep from her and I do not want it generally known as yet." They looked at him, interested but tranquil.

"I have given Fernie twelve months' notice of my leaving the partnership, dating from the end of this month," he said.

His sisters could hardly understand him: Had he and Dr. Fernie fallen out?

"Yes," he went on, "I have been very weary for some long while. I must retire presently, and I would like to go before my powers are noticeably failing and while I still have energy to make something of the rest of my life."

They knew that this decision must have to come in time, but they had never expected to hear it from him at a hale sixty-two.

They were stunned into silence. Then Ann said: "Do you mean to leave Malvern?"

"Yes, my dear. I shall be in no hurry, naturally, but we will find a house in or on the outskirts of London. I have no plans at present, but we shall all remain together, of course." They could not say a word.

"Fernie and I shall choose our own time for making the decision public. I do not want it to get about in any unauthorized way."

"*We* shall say nothing, of course," Ellen said.

"I spoke to Pritchard this afternoon. You and he are the only ones who have heard of it so far." When he had briefly conveyed the news to Pritchard, he had added, "I hope you will never leave me, Pritchard," and Pritchard had said: "I won't, Doctor, you may take your Bible oath of that."

He could tell that the shock to his sisters must be most painful: to be torn away, at fifty-five and fifty-three, from the scene that had so happily absorbed them for twenty-seven years. He had known it must be so, and felt it better not to talk to them about the change until their feelings should have recovered a little. Their sense, their courage, their loyalty to him, made them summon up all their resolution to reconcile themselves to the prospect; all the same, for the next week or two they were noticeably pale and quiet. Dr. Gully, on the other hand, was looking uncommonly well. One of the letters in small envelopes which came for him every few days told him that Florence had seen Mr. Brookes in his office and found him very helpful and reassuring; that she had openly discussed a separation with her father: "But Papa is afraid that people will think less well of the family if I am separated from my husband. He does not seem to understand that *I* am the one who ought to be considered."

A letter from Brookes himself gave him the other side of the picture: "The first time she came into the office I was almost startled. Young, of course, I knew she was, but I was hardly expecting anything so brilliantly handsome and so tastefully dressed; quite a bird of paradise in our dry as dust retreat! She seems however a most touching and interesting young woman, and her situation strangely friendless, except of course for the excellent friend she has in you." There had been two other meetings, and Brookes was as much interested in the client's cause as Dr. Gully himself could wish.

His deep preoccupation with her and her affairs had the effect of making his life sometimes mechanical and half conscious. When a patient was before him, the instincts of a lifetime were aroused, and he thought of nothing but the patient, but at other times, though he saw, moved, spoke, thought, even, as he had always done, it was at a remove; nothing had quite the actuality and importance for him of normal existence. For his sisters, the present was a state of painful reality; the last Christmas at The Priory House, the last New Year, soon it would be their last quarter of office in the town charities, the last meeting with friends, the last tasks about the house, the last look at the hills. They were thankful that James wanted the removal kept secret for the present; they could hardly have borne, yet, the good-natured astonishment, the regrets, of neighbors and friends.

Dr. Fernie, though with some regrets and misgivings, was elated at the prospect of being in sole command of the practice but he was naturally anxious to get every benefit he could from his partner's experience while it was still available, and he now discussed cases which before he would have dealt with on his own initiative.

Pritchard, Dr. Gully could see, was not altogether sorry for the impending change. Pritchard knew that the doctor was a tired man, and also a well-to-do one; wherever the family might settle, Pritchard would be prepared to be interested and to make the best of it. He was, as ever, a clearinghouse for local news. It was he who told the doctor that Captain Ricardo had gone away, abroad, some people said, and that the lease of Stokefield had been surrendered by the captain's man of business.

"Stokefield!" Dr. Gully thought. "Orwell Lodge and Stokefield"—those names would always be dear to his memory.

The pile of letters in his drawer increased and in February came the one he had been waiting for: "I have had a dreadful quarrel with Papa. Mr. Brookes wrote to him and he ordered me to take my affairs out of Mr. Brookes' hands. This I will not do. He now says that until I drop all idea of a legal separation he will not pay me the income due to me on the marriage settlement he made me. The next installment of this is due on March 25." He was about to write to Brookes, asking if it were legally possible to withhold money due on a settlement when another letter from Florence arrived, postmarked "Sydenham."

"You will be surprised at this address. I have come to the Crystal Palace Hotel with Plascott, who is now my maid; she looked after me at Buscot and does not wish to leave me. Papa gave me his ultimatum yesterday, that he will withhold my income, until I consent to his wishes. I came up at once to see Mr. Brookes. I asked if he knew of a small furnished house I could take in his neighborhood and he offered me a part of his house: two bedrooms and a sitting room. While Mrs. Brookes makes ready for me, I am staying here; then my address will be: Brookefield, Streatham Common."

Dr. Gully felt that he must see her at once, if only to make sure that she wanted nothing he could do for her. He planned a visit to London in four days' time, arranging a call at the Crystal Palace Hotel in the afternoon after he had visited Mr. Brookes to whose office he had himself driven as soon as he arrived at Paddington.

"Surely," he demanded, "the man can't legally refuse to pay the money if he's settled it on her?"

"I don't think he can. If he perseveres, she can file a suit demanding that he should submit his trustee accounts; that's the first step toward getting the money. But these actions are expensive and disagreeable. I would advise waiting to see what income the husband allows her, before we take further steps. After all, once the separation is accomplished her father may accept defeat without further trouble."

"Very true. And the matter of the separation is in hand?"

"We are in treaty with them on the other side."

"Excellent. She tells me you and Mrs. Brookes have most kindly offered her accommodation meanwhile?"

"Yes. It seems the best arrangement she can make, pro tem, and my wife and I are very willing. Mrs. Ricardo insists on very generous terms."

A tender, gratified smile appeared on Dr. Gully's face for an instant. He said: "I am sure she values the kindness of yourself and Mrs. Brookes exceedingly." He added that if funds were wanted to tide over, he would be happy to advance them. Mr. Brookes, however, said that he hoped the income under the deed of separation would be decided in a very few weeks.

The railway took him to the Crystal Palace station, and a cab up the long pull of Anerley Hill. The hotel, a small-fronted eighteenth-century building with premises thrown out at the back, was on very high ground from which steep roads ran down, Fox's Hill, indeed, commanding a view all over Kent which in its extent recalled Malvern.

In 1862, a scheme had been on foot to found a hydropathic establishment here. It had never come to anything, naturally; there had been no first-rate intelligence behind it. In the park opposite the hotel (renamed to suit), stood the Crystal Palace itself, removed from Hyde Park and converted to a Winter Garden. The curved roof and the two towers of this structure of a million panes of glass were visible for miles around, appearing in unexpected glimpses, now grayish like thawing ice, now clear and sharp as crystal, now burning like diamonds. The nearer one got to it, the more it was concealed by trees.

From the entry of the hotel, Dr. Gully saw that it was warm, neat, with prompt and cheerful service. He was shown upstairs and she met him at the door of her sitting room. She lifted her head to kiss him but he held her down by the elbows, restraining her (where was Plascott?). She led him across the small room to a sofa. Answering his thoughts she said: "Plascott has gone over to Clapham to see her aunt. It's a long journey by omnibus." Then he kissed her but only once. He sat with his arm around her waist, congratulating her on the turn of events and telling her of his conversation with Brookes that morning.

Her composure and determination surprised and almost shocked him. She showed no tremor, no uncertainty; when he spoke of her going to Brookefield, she nodded. "I am sure that will do extremely well for the time being," she said. "It's so fortunate they have room for Plascott as well. Of course I couldn't have gone to them without her."

He touched her temple. "You couldn't put up all this beautiful chestnut hair by yourself?"

"I don't think anybody could do it for themselves, as I am wearing it."

"What time will Plascott come back?"

"I gave her leave till six o'clock."

"I will stay, then, till half past five, if you will allow me." If Plascott should return before her time, there would be no bones broken. He must, he must accustom himself to being with her merely as an affectionate family friend, or he would not be able to visit her freely at the house of Mr. and Mrs. Brookes.

And was she quite comfortable, he asked, with everything she wanted, for the present?

"Yes," Florence said, "for the present." Neither of them could have framed a plan at that moment, but each was convinced that they were approaching some undefined state of bliss.

"Will you have a cab, sir?" asked the waiter. "The hotel can put one to."

"No, thank you," Dr. Gully said. The spring twilight was magical; in the gardens, forsythia and almond blossom stood out ethereally against brown leafless boughs and deep-blue distance. As he walked rapidly down Anerley Hill, full as his mind was, he spared a moment's amused recollection that this was where they had thought they would establish a rival to himself and Malvern. There was nothing here but groups of houses and the enormous, strange, transparent creation of the Crystal Palace among the trees.

Chapter 15

As he approached Malvern he forgot, for once in his life, to look out after Worcester for the first appearance of the hills. It was not until they almost loomed in at the carriage window that he remembered them.

He was beginning to consider when he and Fernie should make their announcement, when a letter brought him news of such rapid developments, he put his own affairs aside.

> March 28.
>
> Mr. Brookes says my husband has agreed to a separation; I am to have an income of twelve hundred pounds a year. The deed will be sent to Mr. Brookes' office. It must be signed by two trustees on my behalf. Mr. Brookes will be one, will you be the other? You are my dearest friend, there is no one I love and trust so much.

He wrote immediately to Brookes to say that he would sign as co-trustee and to her to say that he had done so. He felt an exquisite tenderness as he thought of himself in this relation to her. That Brookes was in the same relation, he brushed aside. On March 31 he came down to London and signed the large parchment in Brookes' office: writing James Manby Gully MD,

Great Malvern, with satisfaction. As he shut up his gold pen he said: "Where is the poor fellow, do you know?"

"Abroad, we hear, in Cologne, with a female companion who, I daresay, understands him. I am told that his expectation of life is not great."

"So I should suppose. When they drink on that scale they stop eating; so if pneumonia or some other infection supervenes, there's no resistance."

"Doctor," said Mr. Brookes, "did she ever tell you the terms of the will he made on the marriage?"

"No; she may have had only a vague idea of them."

"Possibly. But if he predeceased her, she was to inherit forty thousand pounds. I say was, because the likelihood is that he will alter the will."

"Well, the man is alive. Perhaps we ought not to speculate." But they shared a moment's thoughtful silence.

The fountains of Trafalgar Square were sparkling, as if the water were in sympathy with them. He and Florence stood at a first-floor window in Morley's Hotel while waiters laid a luncheon table behind them. A quiet luncheon at midday after a considerable absence, he felt, would cause no remark. The champagne too seemed to be in sympathy, it rushed with such force into their glasses.

"Fancy you allowing champagne!" said Florence when they were alone. "I thought you disapproved of it."

"I do as a rule, but this is a very special occasion."

It was: Each had gained a degree of freedom, she, the legal separation, he the prospect of the lifting of his great professional burden.

"Plascott went to Buscot and brought away my trunks," she was saying. "It would have been too disagreeable to have gone myself. Poor Mama! She sent her love to me and told Plascott to tell me that she would write. But I don't want her to, just yet."

"No. Presently your mother will view the matter differently, I am sure. And you go to Brookefield at the end of this week. I hope you will like Mrs. Brookes."

"Oh, I daresay I shall," said Florence carelessly. "And the first thing I must do is to find somewhere near, where you can stay. Because you will come to see me, won't you?"

"Yes, if you will allow me." He raised his glass and said: "To your future happiness."

"And to yours," she said, hardly above a whisper.

Brookefield was a comfortable, roomy modern house, fronting on the road called Streatham Common; its large garden backed onto the common itself. Florence and Plascott had adjoining rooms on the first floor; downstairs Florence had been given the breakfast room, from which French windows opened onto the garden.

Mrs. Brookes was a round-faced, round-eyed woman, who was capable of making a scene but would then collapse, not knowing how to go on with it. "My wife is the best woman in the world," Mr. Brookes was accustomed to say. She had three daughters and now suspected that she was pregnant for a fourth time. She was always uncomfortable in the early stages and would not have chosen this time to have other people in the house, but her husband wanted the arrangement and had described this lady as one of his most interesting clients, rich, beautiful and unfortunate.

Rich and beautiful she certainly was. The first sight of her in the dove-colored silk, with her cock-feathered bonnet, had filled Mrs. Brookes with amazement and respect; and the charm of being treated by this dauntingly fashionable young woman with

friendliness and gratitude made the meeting unexpectedly enjoyable.

Florence for her part found herself very comfortable. Brookefield was an improvement on the Crystal Palace Hotel. Mr.
Brookes whom she met at dinner in the evenings was pleasant
and devoted and Mrs. Brookes good-natured. The little girls
were nicely behaved, and the youngest one was in the charge of
a daily governess whom Florence was prepared to like also.

Mrs. Cox was a widow, of about thirty, who, it turned out,
had three sons whom she was anxious to educate. She could
never have been good-looking, Florence decided, even if she
hadn't had to wear spectacles, but she was neat and deft and
light-footed; her manner, as well as her movements, was very
quiet. Her skin was a yellowish ivory, her hair very dark. Florence thought she had a touch of colored blood and it came
out that Mrs. Cox had been born in Jamaica and only left it
on her marriage. This link with the doctor's birthplace gave
Florence an immediate interest in her, and she very soon grew
to like Mrs. Cox for herself. The latter in her quiet way was
very companionable. She was a different sort of governess from
what their own had been, but from what she picked up, Florence
thought that the things Mrs. Cox did know, she taught well.
Lucy was beginning to speak French very nicely; she practiced
the piano diligently under Mrs. Cox's supervision; she could tell
the name of every flower and plant in the garden and to what
order it belonged; and she was in a fair way to knowing a great
many of the answers to *Mangnall's Questions*.

The April weather was lovely; the beds were full of wallflowers, hyacinths, white narcissus; and the warmth brought
out the hot scent of bushes of pink American currant. Outside
on the common there were constellations of daisies, and in a
dell Florence found cowslips. She stooped to pick them and
heard a cuckoo shouting. The balmy, exciting warmth suited

the state of her feelings. She usually had a letter in her pocket that had come by the morning post, and she would sit down to answer it in the evening lamplight. On the morning of April 24 she had news that demanded immediate writing. Her letter arrived at The Priory House by the same post as one from Mr. Brookes. On April 19, Alexander Ricardo had died in Cologne.

Florence had written: "I can't help, poor boy, thinking of him as he was when we were engaged. He really did love me, but he made me so unhappy I nearly died of it. I can never, never, never forget what I owe—" Delightful as the words were, he put the letter down for further reading and hurriedly slit open Brookes'. This confirmed the news and added a momentous paragraph. Not only was Captain Ricardo dead, he had died without altering his will. His widow had now inherited forty thousand pounds.

Mr. Brookes, a solicitor of considerable experience, was not often surprised by any turn in his clients' affairs but when he received this news from the dead man's solicitors, being alone in his room he got up and walked about the floor. He was saying to himself: "If she still wants to pitch into her father about that settlement, by George, she can do it!"

When Dr. Gully had read Brookes' letter twice and hers many times, his triumphant satisfaction was edged with bitterness. The latest report from Brighton had been: "In wonderful health, considering. Eats well and enjoys her drives." Seventy-nine! And no signs of finishing her mortal course. He had long since taught himself not to dwell on the possible nearness of her death; events now would make this self-discipline harder to practice.

Meanwhile Florence had written: "Do come, I long to see you, to talk about everything!" and she had sent him the address of The Coach and Horses, a small commercial hotel just off Upper Streatham High Road, a few minutes' walk from Brookefield.

The parlormaid at Brookefield said, to his perfunctory inquiry, that Mrs. Brookes was not at home, and led him to the breakfast room.

There she stood, against the open French window, in a black dress, supplied at an hour's notice by Jay's, the great mourning emporium of Regent Street. Black, but not the lusterless black of widow's weeds; this was a black silk that might have been worn at any time and the widow's cap on her piled-up hair was a mere cobweb with streamers, almost invisible, of transparent gauze.

His delight at seeing her was heightened by this sensible manner of dressing herself, decorous but with no insincere parade of stifling crape and bombazine. Her eager approach and their embrace, from which however he gently disengaged himself at once, gave him a sensation of purest happiness which seemed diffused into the April afternoon.

"Shall we walk a little in this charming garden?" he presently said. She picked up a shawl, also supplied by Jay's, a soft ivory cashmere with a border of weeping willows and funeral urns delicately printed in black. He wrapped it around her and they walked out onto the gravel path that led to the wicket gate on the common. The warmth and sweetness of the air was intoxicating.

"And now that this news is known at Buscot," he said, "now that the cause of your father's displeasure is removed, does he intend to obey the law and pay you the income on your settlement?"

"No, I don't think he does. He says he won't discuss anything with me till I have taken my affairs out of Mr. Brookes' hands and come back to Buscot."

"And what have you said?"

"That I shan't do either," said Florence coolly. "I must have Mr. Brookes' assistance, considering the way Papa is treating me; and if I went back to live at Buscot, you couldn't come to see me as you can here. Because you will come, often, won't you? Could you not come down once a week?"

It crossed his mind that she had lost sight of the distance from Malvern and of his commitments there, but he did not want to remind her of difficulties. She gave him exquisite pleasure by demanding his presence. In view of his retirement he was now his own master to a degree he had never been before; he *could* come down once a week if he chose; he told her that he would. In a moment of extreme delight Florence had the unselfconscious look of a little girl. The look was on her now. He was touched beyond expression.

Mrs. Brookes had been right in suspecting that she was pregnant, the usual discomforts were making her life difficult to bear; and as a married woman and mistress of a family she began to be made first irritated and then censorious by the repeated visits of Dr. Gully, who, she learned from the cook, did not stay at The Coach and Horses anymore, but had an arrangement with a maiden lady in Leigham Lane, who sometimes took in visitors, to let him have a room once a week. The doctor, she understood, was a highly distinguished not to say important man, but in Mrs. Brookes' view and that of her women friends, men, however distinguished, were, none the less, men. Her attitude was sharpened, perhaps unknown to herself, by the fact that Mrs. Ricardo was a very attractive and fashionable woman and that she was a plain one, with as regards dress, what Mrs. Ricardo would have called "simply no idea."

The cordiality with which the acquaintance had begun was waning, though both of them remained outwardly polite: Mrs. Brookes because she did not want to distress her husband; Florence because the place suited very well for the time being.

One of its minor attractions was that she really enjoyed the society of Mrs. Cox. Florence had very few female friends. She had never been to school, that great place for forming lifelong friendships; her early marriage had cut short her season as a debutante, and on the whole, her beauty and success and her critical spirit had tended against other young women's being much drawn to her. Unreserved conversation with an interested, sympathetic, admiring listener of her own sex was a very agreeable novelty. Not that she had many opportunities for talking to Mrs. Cox; the latter began Lucy's lessons as soon as she arrived in the morning, and lunched with Mrs. Brookes and the girls, while Florence, if at home, had a tray in the breakfast room. Mrs. Cox remained till four o'clock, then she had liked to go back to her lodgings as soon as she could, but since she became friendly with Mrs. Ricardo, she would sometimes accept her invitation to a cup of tea, and remain till perhaps five o'clock. Mrs. Cox had of course by this time heard of Dr. Gully but she had never seen him till, at eleven o'clock on a fine morning in May, Florence came to the French window and approached Mrs. Cox who was turning up an edge for Lucy to hem, while Lucy read one of La Fontaine's fables aloud, as they sat on a garden seat.

"Come in and meet Dr. Gully," Mrs. Ricardo said. Mrs. Brookes had, Mrs. Cox knew, driven out in a hired landau to look at maternity gowns at Pratt's, the chief drapers in the High Road.

"Just for a moment, then," she said.

Dr. Gully, who got up to bow to her, was dressed comfortably for the warm weather, a white rose in his buttonhole, a straw hat in his hand. She was impressed by his ruddy, vital face; his manner was one of great courtesy, great decisiveness. They all sat down, Mrs. Cox where she could keep Lucy in full view, Florence at one side of the window making lace on a pillow.

Dr. Gully said: "I was saying to Mrs. Ricardo that it is just a year since Mr. Dickens died."

"A great loss," observed Mrs. Cox. "We heard he quite shortened his life by giving those lectures when he was so far from well."

"Far from well!" repeated Dr. Gully. "How any self-respecting physician could have allowed it is beyond my power to fathom."

"Perhaps they couldn't help it, you know," said Florence, looking up with an ingenuous air.

"Ah," said Dr. Gully. "Well, perhaps not." She bent over the pillow again and smiled as if his words conveyed some enchanting message.

In a few moments Mrs. Cox excused herself and said she must go back to her pupil. Dr. Gully bowed very pleasantly and Mrs. Cox went over the grass to exclaim at Lucy who was making a daisy chain, and to ask her to go on reading where she had left off.

In the few snatches of leisure during her day, Mrs. Cox thought a good deal about the morning's meeting. So this was the elderly friend, the distinguished Dr. Gully. A widower, no doubt. He was clearly very much interested in Mrs. Ricardo but he was far too old for her, not only so young, but so beautiful as she was. He would probably be there very often, and as she herself might become a part of Mrs. Ricardo's circle, he might possibly become attracted to her as the second best. It was a situation that frequently arose. She was not vain, she had no mistaken views about herself, but unlikelier things had happened.

Mrs. Cox had hardly ever in her life given way to unfounded optimism; if she failed in a scheme, that was the luck of the game; she had not to incur the sickening disappointment of ridiculous hopes. But for once, within ten minutes, she had been led out of her usual course. Before she recognized her feelings she had found this man attractive; a warm current of pleasure had been set flowing in her veins and for a short time she had allowed herself to be carried away into imagination.

She was very soon reined up. Now that her confidante had seen Dr. Gully, Florence found it easier to talk about him. Mrs. Cox learned that she had made two grave mistakes; Dr. Gully was not a widower and neither he nor Mrs. Ricardo regarded his age as any obstacle to their romantic friendship; and almost as soon, Mrs. Cox understood from his straightforward, courteous, unchanging attitude toward herself that he had not and never would have the smallest interest in her. The delusion, so brief, so completely checked, unsuspected by anyone, was buried deep.

Chapter 16

A FEW days later Mrs. Campbell drove out from Lowndes Square to Streatham. At the door of Brookefield she asked for Mrs. Ricardo but Mrs. Brookes met her in the hall and civilly asked her into the drawing room.

Mrs. Brookes saw at once that Mrs. Campbell was genuine and good-hearted; Mrs. Campbell recognized in Mrs. Brookes (a well-meaning, anxious woman in delicate health) a person whose views on many subjects would chime with her own.

"I will not disguise from you, Mrs. Brookes," she said, "that her father is extremely displeased at my daughter's taking legal advice independently of the family solicitors. I mean no reflection on your husband naturally."

"I am sure you cannot, ma'am. My husband, after all—and Dr. Gully made such a point of it."

Dr. Gully! Mrs. Campbell gazed at her in silent dismay, and Mrs. Brookes went on in a sudden burst: "Whatever my husband may think and no doubt he knows best—but *I* say, that these visits from Dr. Gully are far too frequent. Once a week and sometimes more—"

"Indeed!"

"Not that I suggest there is anything wrong—"

"Of course not—"

"But *I* was brought up, Mrs. Campbell, to think that it's wrong to *look* wrong."

"Certainly. And I am sure my daughter—you know I daresay how very sad her married life was, driving her into serious illness. And Dr. Gully has done so much for her health! It's natural he should continue to take an interest."

"*I* don't want to say anything ill-natured," said Mrs. Brookes, "but I must and do say," she added more firmly, "that twice a week is too much, and all the way from Malvern."

Mrs. Campbell rose. "I shall certainly represent to my daughter—" she began. Mrs. Brookes got up too and rang the bell, and the smiling Plascott appeared, to lead the old mistress to the breakfast room.

Mrs. Campbell had taken Florence in her arms and kissed her before she realized what was amiss. Then she exclaimed: "My dear child, your weeds! Surely Jay's could have provided you by this time?"

"Jay's made this frock," said Florence, looking down at it. "I don't intend to wear crape."

"Not wear crape!"

"Dr. Gully says the mourning expected of widows in this country is barbarous; he says it's the English form of suttee."

"Dr. Gully says! What in heaven's name is it to do with Dr. Gully? And any right-thinking man would expect to see you in weeds with your husband dead only a month."

"Dr. Gully is the best friend I ever had," Florence said. It wounded the mother desperately to hear herself and her care and love put aside. She began to say something but her eyes overflowed and she brought out her handkerchief. Florence gave a frown of annoyance and compunction.

"Mama, the one thing I wanted was a separation from Alexander, and you and Papa tried to force me to go back to him."

"There is no need to discuss that now, my dear. We thought we were acting for the best."

"Not the best for *me,* Mama. You were thinking about all kinds of other things. But Dr. Gully thought about *me* all the time. He felt it was his duty, because I was his patient, to put my health and happiness first. That's why I regard him as my best and truest friend."

"Well, my love, I am not finding fault with that. But, my dear, these visits of Dr. Gully's are all too frequent. Mrs. Brookes tells me that he comes down from Malvern twice a week."

"Not exactly that. He comes once a week, but sometimes he has come on a Sunday for a couple of nights and then again on a Friday; so she probably had the impression that he was coming twice in the week."

"Her impression, at least, is that he comes much too often; it has a *most* indiscreet appearance, my dear, you aren't a child, you must see that for yourself. It really won't do, Florence, you must tell him that for both your sakes it must stop."

Stop! Florence repeated the word under her breath. A very strange look came into her eyes. She said: "I shouldn't dream of telling Dr. Gully to discontinue his visits. If Mrs. Brookes objects, I can go somewhere else. I came here at her own husband's suggestion."

"Mr. Brookes has played a most unfortunate part in our family affairs," said Mrs. Campbell heatedly. "I do not say that I blame him altogether—professional men, I suppose, are obliged—but it's *not* suitable that you should be living here, as a lodger. Your proper place at present is with us, in Lowndes Square or at Buscot, and Papa and I wish you to come home at once. When you have shown a proper respect for your father by doing as he asks, he will pay you the income on your marriage settlement. He is withholding it until you consent to behave in a dutiful manner."

Florence said: "I don't blame you for not knowing this, Mama —I didn't know it myself until I took legal advice—but Papa *can't* withhold my money, whatever I choose to do. He must pay it. If he says he won't, the Lord Chancellor will make him. He must know this himself, or if he doesn't, he ought to."

"Do you mean that you will have the law on your father, your own father?"

"I shall file a suit, obliging him to submit his trustee accounts. It will rest with him whether we go to law after that."

Mrs. Campbell turned her head away in despair, at the familiar experience of being defeated by Florence, headstrong, untamable, immovable. She began on a different track.

"I cannot understand why you should refuse to come home. If you want an establishment of your own presently there could be no objection. But why not come home now? You and Papa would have nothing to quarrel about then."

"I can't come home while you take this attitude about Dr. Gully. I can't part with my dearest friend when I feel I need him so much."

"Do you really mean that Dr. Gully is more important to you than your parents?"

"I mean I can't give up his friendship and the right to see him as often as we please."

"Florence, this is absolute infatuation!"

"Call it what you like, Mama."

"There *can't* be anything in it, there *can't,*" Mrs. Campbell told herself in a state of rising panic, as her carriage and pair took her briskly along Streatham High Road on the long journey to Westminster Bridge, which they must cross before returning to the fashionable quarter of Belgravia. At several of the crossings where the horses were obliged to draw up, tired women gained a glimpse of her, sitting back on the cushions of her high-sprung carriage that swung so easily above its wheels and next instant bore her out of sight. They thought it must be a fine thing to lead a life like hers.

Mrs. Campbell's usual instinct was to put the best face she could on Florence's behavior when discussing it with her husband, but she could conceal nothing from him of this afternoon's interview; the stark facts admitted of no shading off.

His anger was savage, as she had expected. She was too much exhausted to try to conciliate him. While he shouted, she took her collapsible fan out of her pocket and fanned herself. Mr. Campbell declared that his daughter's conduct was so infamous, she must have been put up to it; this scoundrel of a lawyer, in whose clutches she now was, saw his market in it. As to her obstinacy on the other matter, what propriety and decorum could you expect from a woman who'd thrown off filial duty? Until she consented to obey her father's wishes, she should never be received by any of her family.

The pleas that Mrs. Campbell would have made were choked in her throat by the dreadful suspicion, the unnamable fear. There *could* not be actual immorality—the characters of both, the difference of their ages, made it, surely, impossible; but the indiscretion was so serious, Mrs. Campbell for once entirely agreed with her husband: To receive Florence at home while she persisted in it would be conniving at a situation no decent family could condone. And Dr. Gully, of all men! Even supposing a marriage with him were suitable, he could not marry. What was he about? She got up out of her chair and went heavily upstairs; grief, agitation and fatigue had brought on a racking headache.

Mr. Campbell when calm enough to hold a pen wrote to Florence, demanding her presence at home and a promise that she would drop all communication with Dr. Gully. Three days later he received his answer; not from Florence herself but in the form of a notice from Mr. Brookes' firm saying that on behalf of their client they had filed a suit against him in the Court of Chancery.

He was now obliged to consult his own solicitors who advised him to pay his daughter her income without further question. That he realized he must act on their advice made his anger the hotter. Though he now relinquished the matter of the settlement, he wrote to Florence repeating that she was to be cut off from all family intercourse till she consented to give up her present way of life. He was buoyed up by his anger; his wife agreed with his verdict, but it cost her hours of weeping.

Without actual discussion, Mrs. Brookes understood that any remonstrance from Mrs. Ricardo's mother had been useless, and that Dr. Gully's visits were to continue as freely as he pleased. She made up her mind that next time he appeared, which she calculated would be next week, she would really say something to Mrs. Ricardo about the awkwardness of this sort of thing getting about in the neighborhood. She was a little apprehensive, but was winding herself up to make the effort in about four days' time. The shock was considerable when, next morning, she passed the open French windows in the morning sunshine and heard a man's voice, a ringing, decisive voice, and looking in, saw Dr. Gully sitting on a chair with one leg over the other, his stick and hat lying beside him on the sofa. Florence, who was arranging the sprays of lilac he had brought in a tall, opaline vase—her own, the Brookeses had nothing so beautiful—looked up and saw at once that Mrs. Brookes had come to make trouble. The latter said as she walked in: "Mrs. Ricardo, I think the time has come for me to say a word. When we let part of our house to you, we did not expect it to be used for an improper purpose." Florence's surprise was so great, she dropped a spray of lilac and let it lie unnoticed on the carpet.

"Improper purpose!" she repeated.

"Yes," said Mrs. Brookes, hot and trembling. "I do not want my home to be used for visits which every respectable person must disapprove of."

Dr. Gully had stood up when she came in. He now said in quiet but formidable tones: "What do you mean, Mrs. Brookes?" Now that she had the chance of saying what she meant, Mrs. Brookes found it unexpectedly hard to seize, but she made a valiant effort.

"You must know what I mean, sir. Everyone else does. Mrs. Ricardo's mother is most upset by your coming here so often, and all our friends wonder that my house should be made use of for something scandalous." She was now trembling violently and she made for a low, stuffed chair. Dr. Gully pushed toward her a harder, higher-seated one.

"I think you will find this sort of chair more comfortable at present," he said with cold kindness. Mrs. Brookes sat down on it thankfully. "Florence," he went on, "will you ring and ask Plascott for a glass of water?"

"I am quite all right, thank you," said Mrs. Brookes, struggling to regain her commanding position as the lady of the house.

"I hope you are, but as you have spoken in this injurious way to Mrs. Ricardo, I must, if you please, say something to you, and of course I am anxious not to cause you discomfort or distress." It was clear beyond hope, that he and not she was the one in authority. A glass of water, misted with the coldness of the rising main, was handed in at the door. Dr. Gully took it from Florence and gave it to Mrs. Brookes, telling her to drink it slowly. She obeyed and the action helped her to listen with calmness to what he was saying.

"You want to accuse me and Mrs. Ricardo of using your house to carry on an intrigue—is that it?"

She nodded.

"This is not true, and when you go about among your friends, telling them that it is, you give grounds for an action against you for slander."

"I never told my friends—" she stopped.

"You told me just now that all your friends were surprised at your house being used for a scandalous purpose. How could they think it was, if you had not told them?" She said nothing.

He went on: "My visits to Mrs. Ricardo are made by day, and in this room, to which you have access whenever you choose. When she comes out with me, we go to a picture gallery or a concert or for a drive. If you or your friends had had us followed by private inquiry agents, you could have proved that to your satisfaction."

"I never—wanted or thought of such a thing."

"That is a pity, because it would have disposed of the matter." The tears began to fill her eyes; he took the glass from her and put it down.

"I think you know what a hard time Mrs. Ricardo has had," he went on more gently. "She needs a friend, and I am the closest friend she has at present. I agree that my visits are frequent, but I never thought that this would give offense to you or your husband."

"My husband has never said anything," said Mrs. Brookes somewhat hastily.

"Well, I should feel surprised if he had; but of course Mrs. Ricardo must leave this house if the lady of the house wishes it." Mrs. Brookes was now twisting her handkerchief and looking nowhere.

"I did not mean—" she said, and stopped again.

"I do not think we had better continue this discussion at present. You will no doubt talk the matter over with your husband and if you want Mrs. Ricardo to leave you will tell her so. But if she stays it will be on the understanding that she can see her friends here when she wants to."

Mrs. Brookes lived on terms of complete confidence with her husband. That evening she followed him into his dressing room and gave him a very full account of the morning's conversation.

"Dear, dear, dear!" he said, but not in annoyance.

"I felt I had to speak."

"It would have been better if you had consulted me first."

"But you would have told me not to." He laughed. "You don't think there is anything—really wrong, do you?"

"I think he likes a pretty young woman—"

"But not—"

"Certainly not, or I would not have asked you to put up with it."

That evening the small party at dinner was pleasant. Mrs. Brookes wore almost a pleading air; Florence was obliging and companionable; Mr. Brookes himself was a great asset, good-natured and cheerful and making it possible for the others to behave as if nothing awkward had occurred.

Chapter 17

DR. GULLY was not comfortable in leaving Florence at Brookefield. He turned over a scheme, and when he had discussed it
with his sisters, he suggested that Florence should come to The
Priory House for a long visit; after all, it was the last time he
would be able to entertain her there. Miss Ann Gully followed
his letter with an invitation in form.

Neither of the Brookeses wanted to sever their connection with
Florence. She was a valuable client and beautiful heroines were
not rife on Streatham Common, but the visit to Malvern would
make a welcome break in an intercourse that had become
strained.

To Florence the invitation was a prospect of heaven; not only
to be in the same house but openly to throw in her lot with him,
under such respectable auspices. The rupture with her home
carried with it a suggestion of being *déclassée* and to be a guest
in the distinguished Malvern household would be very gratifying,
as well as promising glimpses of utter bliss.

Plascott packed and on the afternoon before their departure,
took the trunks in a cab to Paddington. Florence meanwhile
was having a last cup of afternoon tea with Mrs. Cox.

"I shall miss you sadly," the latter said, quietly but with much
feeling. Florence was moved to think of Mrs. Cox in her life of

lonely drudgery after her own interesting self had departed. She determined that they should meet again. Mrs. Cox's company was very pleasant to her. On every occasion when something was needed, Mrs. Cox knew what to do. She was generous with her scant free time, and Florence was quite shocked to find that she had been to Miss Butcher's Berlin Repository in the Streatham High Road for embroidery twist and silver beads for her. Mrs. Cox would talk about Jamaica if Florence asked her to, about the dense blue-green of the trees on the mountain sides and the brilliant white beaches of powdered coral; but she never ran away with a subject; she had the delightful trait, that she would rather listen to her friend's affairs than talk about her own. Florence promised very seriously to write to her from Malvern.

It was the fifth of June. They arrived at Great Malvern Station in the middle of the afternoon. Outside were the hills and in the foreground the doctor's brougham with Griffith and Tom on the box. At the sight of the brougham, the porters behaved with special devotion.

It was heavenly to wake up in the morning to the calm joy of being under his roof, knowing that she would see him at intervals during the day—at lunch, in the garden, for a few moments' conversation when they were left alone by chance.

Ann and Ellen were unfailingly kind, offering to make expeditions, to take her with them to their social engagements, but Florence said with ingenuous sincerity that she was perfectly happy to be left alone, in the house or garden.

The lovely June weather made it possible to be out of doors all day. Sitting in a basket chair or on a garden seat, walking at the edge of the ornamental water, the hills in the sky, his house across the lawn, she felt that all strains and miseries were soothed away. The liquid notes of a few birds among the trees, the peace and silence thrilled through with the expectation of seeing him at some moment, alighting from the brougham on the gravel drive, or coming out onto the terrace, gave her, for the time being, endless content; offers of entertainment were as irrelevant to her as to someone who had just entered paradise.

Ann and Ellen hardly knew what to make of their beautiful guest. It was strange that she was so content to be idle and solitary, for no one could suppose that she was suffering grief; but though they were anxious to make her stay as happy as possible they were relieved that she hardly ever wanted to go out with them. The most unassuming of women themselves, at the same time they knew what was what. It was their considered private opinion, now, that Mrs. Ricardo wanted tone. With her striking appearance, it would have needed great modesty and retiringness to appear thoroughly ladylike. A self-willed carriage, with her youth, her vivid beauty and grand clothes, made her presence a little surprising.

On a Sunday morning in July, the house was absolutely quiet, the windows open all around it. Ann and Ellen were at church; he was sitting in the library, considering a letter that had come yesterday from his wife's solicitors.

He put the letter in the drawer where he kept documents of his wife's affairs. He looked out. Florence was slowly crossing the lawn between the cedar tree and the cotoneaster. She had a book in one hand, in the other a furled black parasol ruffled with black gauze; on its long, slender black handle it looked like some exotic black bird, long-legged and sharp-billed.

He leaned from the window; she saw him at once and came toward him as if she had been drawn into some field of magnetic attraction.

He said: "It is kind of you to come and talk to me; I have had one of the letters that always make me sad."

"From Brighton? How is she?"

"It seems that there is a little mental deterioration but that often tends to prolong life."

"I wish I could comfort you."

"You do comfort me. You are all my comfort." Such a look of life and joy came into her face that he said: "If I were free, in spite of the difference in our ages, I should ask you to marry me." She smiled with downcast eyes as if she were actually listening to his proposal.

"If I had been able to, I wonder what answer I should have had?" With the suddenness of lightning and thunder, she frowned, her eyes filling with angry tears.

"It is cruel to ask that!"

"Cruel? My love!" She was in his arms, in the first entirely free and unrestrained embrace of their joint lives, the only one she had ever known that gave her complete, ecstatic bliss. She put her whole soul into it, she could not have kissed him with more fervor; but he still held something back. As he saw, taking place before his eyes, the wonderful intensification of color in her face, the cheeks becoming deeper rose, the mouth geranium, the eyes shining through moisture, the hair itself seeming a stronger tone because the forehead and temples were so white, he felt a deep, protective tenderness toward a creature over whom his power was so great.

Presently she said: "You must know what the answer would be."

"It makes me feel so unworthy. I can't offer you marriage for an indefinite time, and if we became lovers—I should not, in our circumstances, think it a crime, but society would be merciless, especially toward you. You would be absolutely cut off from the life you ought to have."

"I don't want any life without you. And besides, we *are* lovers."

"Yes, dearest. But our situation isn't that of lovers. There is so much happiness for you to give and receive that you haven't experienced yet; you should give it to some man who could marry you."

"I could never marry again, anyone except you. And if you won't be my lover, I won't have one."

"I must try—try not to take advantage. We must decide nothing in a hurry; you must consider thoroughly what you would be sacrificing, the extent of the injury I should be doing you." He looked down at her with somber gaze, but she was smiling in secure content. She was not afraid of considerations, however numerous, however serious. The decision, the only one that mattered, had already been taken.

That evening Ann and Ellen had a conversation in which they startled each other by admitting everything they had noticed and feared during the past weeks. They agreed that if James were to continue this romantic friendship while he had no near prospect of being able to marry, it would not be possible to go on living under his roof. Ellen spoke vehemently of danger; Ann said nothing, her face stamped with anxiety and grief. That James—James of all people—could contemplate anything undignified and rash! Suffering as they were already at the idea of leaving Malvern, this dread turned their misery into something infinitely worse.

One evening he followed them upstairs after dinner and said with his comfortable directness: "We must have a talk about our plans for the New Year. We have to find a house for the three of us. I shall go abroad for January and part of February; Mrs. Ricardo will come with me; we shall take Pritchard and Plascott with us. By the middle of February I shall be ready to settle into our new abode. If we start to look for the house now, you will have plenty of time to get it arranged to your liking."

"And Mrs. Ricardo?" said Ellen breathlessly.

"She will look for a house somewhere in our neighborhood."

"James," said Ann, "Ellen and I have been talking about this. We have no wishes for ourselves; we are only anxious about your happiness." She would have liked to add: "And safety."

"I know you are, my dear."

"And we feel that this friendship, in your circumstances, is very, very dangerous."

"I must be the judge of that."

"Yes. But we are obliged to tell you what we feel."

"I know. I appreciate it."

Ellen longed to say, in desperation: "*Can't* you give it up?" But the useless words died on her lips.

Ann went on: "We feel, dear James, that we should not be comfortable, and you would not be comfortable, if we went on living in your house."

"Well," he said, "there is perhaps something in that. But it is not *my* wish that we should part. However, if a small house to yourselves would suit you best, I will willingly arrange it. As to my affairs, it is not only that I am very much in love with her, and she with me. I am taking a step which requires much thought and courage. I think that in cases like ours, society is wrong, and the enlightened men and women who disregard it are right; and that I am right to do what society calls wrong." His sisters were silent. "Even if you can't agree with me, don't tell me that this means a breaking up of our family relationship."

"Oh, no, no, never, never!" cried Ellen. He drew her hand through his arm and patted it—but a little absently.

Chapter 18

THE news of his retirement at Christmas was now out and the ordeal Ann and Ellen had feared was upon them: every fresh person stopping them to exclaim, to lament, to be astonished; but the sharp edge was blunted because they were enduring worse things.

Also, there was a great deal of hard, tiring work to be got through: Possessions, household and personal, accumulated through thirty-seven years, had to be selected, divided, disposed of, or their storage decided. After studying London street maps, and reading the notices supplied by various agents, a short lease was taken of a small, trim house in a terrace just off Marylebone Road from the coming December quarter. They went to see it and confirm the choice, spending two nights with William and his family at Queensborough Terrace. William made no comment of any kind on his father's retirement except to say what a loss he would be to Malvern and to the medical world, but as he had always been very fond of his aunts and grateful for what they had done in his childhood, he was really glad at the prospect of their coming to live in London. The sincere kindness with which he told them so cheered Ann and Ellen greatly. When they got back to The Priory House, they said how pleasant it would be to see a good deal of William and his wife and children.

"And of me too, I hope," said Dr. Gully.

"Dearest James!" said Ellen, between laughing and crying, for they had had two exhausting days. She and Ann now saw that the best possible arrangement had been made. In the little house in Marylebone, he would be to them what he had always been.

Florence had kept her promise of writing to Mrs. Cox. She had told her that she would be abroad in the New Year, without however saying that she was traveling with Dr. Gully; she also said that she wanted a small furnished house, in, she thought, the Streatham neighborhood, to take possession of in February. To look for this, she was arranging with Mrs. Brookes to return to Brookefield at the end of September, and quit it finally at the beginning of January.

Mrs. Cox was delighted at the idea of seeing her kind and charming friend again, and of her being afterward in the neighborhood. The Brookeses were pleased, for her to come and for her to go. When the baby was born they would want the rooms themselves, but they, too, liked the idea of Mrs. Ricardo as a neighbor and Mr. Brookes began to make a few inquiries as to available houses that might suit her.

Meanwhile Florence felt an increase of confidence in walking about The Priory House and garden. She knew that great discretion must be observed, but she no longer felt the slight diffidence of a guest. She often walked freely into the stables. She was fond of horses and liked to watch Griffith as he combed one of the bays, making the hissing sound between his teeth that grooms always made during this operation. On the morning of the Misses Gully's departure to London, she found her way into the yard where Griffith was combing and hissing while the bay shuddered his flanks luxuriously and gave soft, muted whinnies.

Besides the attractions of a stable yard, Florence felt an interest in Griffith. She knew he and Plascott liked each other. The doctor was going to lay down his carriage when he retired; he thought that hansoms would serve the turn in London; but Florence intended to keep one, and she thought she might take Griffith into her service. Then, if he and Plascott married, it would be very comfortable. This morning she picked her way over the cobblestones of the yard among bits of straw and rivulets of sharp-smelling urine, to the harness room, where she examined brushes and polishing cloths and jars of saddle soap. In the open cupboard, among combs and basins and flasks of oil, was a bottle full of white crystalline powder. She picked it up.

"Don't go for to touch that, ma'am," said Griffith, behind her. "That's poison, that is."

"What is it?"

"Antimony, that is. Some calls it tartar emetic, it's all the same."

Florence paused. Tartar emetic was used to make people sick when they were drunkards! "What do horses want it for?" she asked curiously.

"Quarter of an ounce in a pint and a half of water is a lotion for sores, or put as much as would stand on a threepenny piece in a bran mash and it'll clear the worms."

"There seems to be a lot here."

"Ah," said Griffith. "It's those chemists. Mr. Clarke wouldn't let me have it without I gave the doctor's name. Which I done. But doctor don't want the horses treated with anything except water."

"You mean, you said the doctor had ordered it, but he hadn't?"

"That's it, ma'am. Don't do to do it too often, so I bought plenty, just the once."

Really, Florence thought, servants were all the same; no notion of *exact* obedience. If they were good ones, the most you could hope for was that they'd do the best they could for you in their own way. Griffith clearly was a very good one; the horses were in excellent condition and perhaps after all he was right to use his own judgment.

That evening she and her host behaved in the empty rooms as discreetly as if numbers of people were observing them. At the little dinner at which Pritchard waited as usual, the latter asked, over the bottles of Malvern water, whether he should bring up any wine. Dr. Gully looked searchingly at Florence and said: "I do not know that Mrs. Ricardo cares for any?" and she shook her beautiful head. The quietness and sobriety of the meal was matched by the exquisitely clear, fresh-tasting water, drunk from his heavy crystal goblets.

Afterward there was a long, heavenly evening of conversation in the library, by evening light, by starlight, at last by candlelight. They parted with an embrace that lasted a long time, but then he lit the candle in the silver bedroom candlestick for her and stood in the hall while she went upstairs with it. Plascott had already been run for and was waiting in her room; Pritchard crossed the hall on his way to lock the front door.

But the next evening, the last of their solitude *à deux,* they sat in the library with their chairs drawn close together so that her hands could be clasped around his arm and her head rest on his shoulder while he read aloud to her from one of the books kept in his locked bookcase. It was Dr. George Drysdale's; the words, read in his strong, softened voice, gave her a deep sense of reassurance.

"It is not unmarried love but mercenary love and the communication of disease, which disgrace an individual." Outside the windows there was no darkness, only a twilight full of stars.

Chapter 19

IT cost him a pang when she left his house, but it was best that she should not be there for the final leave-takings.

The preparations for leaving The Priory House went on all the time; faced with this formidable amount of work, Ann and Ellen tried never to go to bed without having done something toward it. They were quite calm now but the suppressed misery was roused at every turn. The china and glass not in daily use was laid out in the washhouse ready for packing. Ellen let the flower vases go with it; she would not pick the late roses. The idea that she would be doing it for the last time was too painful.

At Brookefield, Florence too was busy, but on a surge of joyous energy. She had found a house in the Leigham Court Road and taken it on a two-year lease. The road ran at right angles to Streatham High Road, just opposite the little Streatham Hill railway station. Broad and graveled it went gently uphill, made a wide sweep and came down again on Streatham Common. The house was one of two semidetached, on the right side of the hill, a couple of minutes' walk from the railway station. They were solid, gracious buildings of about 1840, a front door under a fanlight, round-headed windows on each side of it. There was a good garden at the back, with stable, coachhouse, and coachman's cottage, and Florence was very well pleased with her find. She sent him enthusiastic descriptions of it, and then, a letter saying she had also found, on Tooting Bec Common, a house of which the lease could be bought for seven hundred pounds. It was so near the Leigham Court Road, she was wild for him to come and see it; the neighborhood was expanding and houses weren't easy to find. Her eagerness was irresistible. He came and saw it and did not like it. It was new but already shabby, with ugly tiles, mean ornaments, poor kitchen quarters; still, it was near hers, it was available, and time was drawing on. He paid the seven hundred pounds; and then she was contrite but ecstatic; the most amazing thing had happened just at that moment: In the Leigham Court Road, a furnished house was up for letting, almost immediately opposite her own. Think of that! Think of it! He could dispose of the lease of the odious one, and if he lost anything on it, she would reimburse him. She felt she could hardly wait till he had secured it.

He came. Hillside was also one of a pair but very recently built, of grayish brick with three gables sheltering dormer windows, and large rooms on each side of the front door. It was commonplace but so infinitely better than the other, and the situation, as she said, positively ideal, that he agreed to take it on a two-year lease. It was not, he decided, foolish to take this one, the mistake had been in taking the other. Let that now be put right as far as might be. His solicitors did their best; they got the previous owner to buy the lease back for two hundred pounds. When Florence heard this she declared she would pay him five hundred pounds. Quietly, in a tone as near to severity as he could use to her, he told her to say no more about it. "I shall always *feel* that I owe it to you," she persisted.

He arranged another visit to make a final inspection of the rooms, to assess their capacity and decide which of his things must be sent down from Malvern. Florence was already measuring and considering in the house across the way, and he agreed

to call for her there so that they could make the decisions together.

They walked into Hillside early on a fine October afternoon.
The room on the left of the front door he had chosen for his
study, the one on the right was the dining room; the drawing
room was a long-shaped one at the back, overlooking the garden.
They went upstairs to the first floor and entered one of the rooms
overlooking the road. Florence approached the window. "Just
look how plainly you can see my house!" she said. "I shall put
a lamp in that window every evening. When you see it you can
think of me."

"Yes, but I shan't wait to see a lamp before I do that." She
turned and threw herself into his arms.

"My dearest!" he said, but he drew her away from the window.
Out of sight of the road, he held her in a long, close embrace.
They exchanged uncounted kisses. At last she said: "I have never
been so happy."

"There is much more happiness to come."

"I suppose so," but she thought, the happiness she would always find the keenest was this passionate excitement which
needed nothing more.

They went downstairs for a last look at the basement. As she
darted about, her head held at inquiring angles, her silk skirt
brushing the flags with a sharp hiss, he followed her, his heart
sore because this house was not to be her own. The shadow
hadn't fallen on her; she was alight with excitement because
their houses were to be so near together.

In the back kitchen where someone had left a cracked piece
of yellow soap and a withered blue bag on the clothes copper,
she came toward him for a last embrace, and lifting her brilliant face, said: "Do you love me?"

"Florence!" he exclaimed in despair, gathering her into his
arms. When, several minutes later, they came up to the front

door, he made her stand back while he opened it and went out
onto the steps. He glanced up and down the road; there was no
one in sight but a milk boy on his afternoon round, coming
down the hill, pushing a great brass-necked milk can between
two wheels, with a pint and a half-pint dipper hanging from
the handles. He came on whistling, and noted that Hillside
looked as if it would be a customer again, with the board down,
and that elderly gent a-airing of himself on the steps.

His obsession, for such it now was, anesthetized the pain of
the final partings at Malvern except the one from the male and
female bath attendants. They had subscribed to an ormolu clock
for him, inscribed on the base, presented to him as a parting
gift "from your old servants." For this ceremony he invited them
to a supper at The Priory House. The tables were laid in the
dining room and the library and he passed from room to room,
helping to charge glasses and fill plates. The presentation was
made in the drawing room, and it moved him to the heart.
He told them that he couldn't have done his work without them,
that he held every one of them in particular gratitude and regard, and that their beautiful timepiece would remind him, for
the rest of his life, of all he owed to them. He felt, then, standing
in his own house, surrounded by those faces, what it was to
leave so much; and when his eye fell on Mrs. Rideout he remembered only the skill, kindness and reliability with which she
had aided all his patients, without a thought of one unique
patient.

Christmas passed and New Year's Day with innumerable concerns and engagements, details requiring decisions and the arrangement of private plans.

In January came the last of the presentations, from the resident tradesmen of Malvern, who had always recognized him
as the founder of their prosperity. They brought a most handsome piece of silver, an *assiette montée* for the center of a dinner

table. Their spokesman was the characterful Mr. James Nott, by occupation a grocer, but a self-taught local historian, who spoke in a wild, impressive way of his own. He remembered Dr. Gully's coming to Malvern, and had seen the development of his brilliant career. "Some of us," he said, "have had your firm hand laid on us when life has been trembling in the balance; had it not been for the skill and care you then showed, we might have been now among the clods of the valley." He spoke with glowing warmth of the affection Dr. Gully had inspired not only as a doctor but as a man who had given much of his spare time to working for the town. This was what they would never forget. He exclaimed: "You have made thousands of earnest friends who would ever be ready to fight for you, and if need be, to meet danger on your behalf." Dr. Gully could not think of any danger in which the staunch defense of the people of Malvern could be needed by him, but he was deeply moved. He told them so as he thanked them heartily for their silver ornament and, for what was to him even more valuable, their affectionate friendship. He reviewed the course of his life to them, the struggles and successes, the enthusiasm he had felt for everything that concerned the prosperity and growth of Malvern.

Though he looked forward to some years of leisure now, he would never forget them and their friendship.

It used to be said of him that he was so regular in his morning walk that people could set their watches by him, but the last one he took was so early, no one was abroad to see. He let himself out of his house at half past seven on a January morning when the moon was still in the sky. Houses and shop fronts were scored by slits of light behind curtains and shutters as inmates prepared for the day. The air was sharp, the earth crackling with frost. The sky was transparent indigo, its color thin-

ning above the hilltop. An eerie light came from the moon
high overhead, a radiance that cast his ghostly shadow on the
ground. He walked rapidly up Church Street, up the Worcester
Road, to the path beside the little Unicorn Inn that led up
onto the hill. When he looked back he could see the white
buildings glimmering below him and the great plain, half familiar, half altered, like a landscape in a dream.

Chapter 20

THEY were to spend some days in Paris before going on to Leghorn. The journey was an escape to paradise; it was also thoroughly comfortable. They could not have found two better servants for traveling than Pritchard and Plascott: the one, dependable, clear-headed, always in a good humor; the other, inexperienced but with her wits about her, gentle-mannered and obliging.

He was of course perfectly discreet in his conduct to Florence in public, but it amused him to see that the French took it for granted that they were lovers. Monsieur Taine said in his comparison of France and England: "Novels, criticism, art, philosophy, the instinct of curiosity, do not here submit to the fetters which religion, morality and convention impose on them on the other side of the channel." He might have included social *moeurs*. After the constricting months in England, always cautious, always apprehensive, to be in Paris was to move in a summerlike ether of encouragement and sympathy. Hotelkeepers, restaurateurs, shop assistants, cabdrivers, showed by their faces that they admired her beauty and congratulated him upon it. The French saw at once how the land lay; it would have been impossible to get them to change their opinion; his homage, her acceptance of it, their mutual passion were as plain as day to the French, and their respectful, gallant behavior was a continuous tribute to it.

The pace in Paris was indeed far more rapid than in London. At the fall of darkness, a glowing festivity set in. Diners out could be viewed through the windows of restaurants against red damask walls and rich golden lights; doorways poured out light and glitter and chattering throngs; people spoke louder, quicker and gesticulated as if they were mad. At the theaters to which he took her, the Comédie Française, Les Bouffes Parisiens, to a foreigner the audience seemed part of the theatrical entertainment: a loquacious, exclamatory, scintillating sea. Sitting beside him in a loge, in a black velvet dress with six strings of seed pearl around her neck, her beauty attracted so much attention, it filled him with delighted pride. Offenbach's music was no longer the first object of his evening—it was a flavoring, exquisitely delicious.

In one of the letters he had written during their separation, he had said: "My darling, I look forward with inexpressible longing to the creation of a very deep relationship between us. I want a complete union of our souls and bodies. I long, I long to make you mine and awaken you to all the delights of love." She also looked forward, with impatience and delight, shot through with something like fear.

The stay in Paris was too disturbing in its novelty and excitement to be the setting for a romantic climax, but when they arrived at Leghorn, as she came into the hotel, she knew that one stage in her life had ended and another was beginning.

The bedrooms were all on one corridor, but the two prepared for them had doors opening into a sitting room as well as the doors giving on the landing. The bedroom beyond the sitting room was her own. The walls were pale, sweeping festoons of muslin curtains crossed the windows, worn, dark velvet ones hung at the head of a high-piled double bed. The room was very quiet because it opened onto a little plant-filled courtyard, where a broken, graceful statue of a girl stood holding a lapful of flowers.

When they were about to go to bed, instead of saying good night, he asked if he might come to her presently; though the tone was gentle, it was a demand rather than an entreaty. She said the one word, "yes," and disappeared into her bedroom where Plascott had lit all the candles and had found the jugs and ewers full of water, but all cold. "Never mind," Florence said.

Nearly two hours afterward, when she had alternately feared his approach and been angry because he hadn't come, the door to the sitting room was quietly opened. He carried a lighted candle but extinguished it as he came in, for one was burning on a marble-topped table; its dim beautiful light barely reached the bed.

His face buried in her hair, he whispered, "I have waited so long for this!"

"I have been waiting for you," she said, but her voice was not her own.

In spite of the fearful dangers that would attend discovery, the few hours before them were a time of absolute safety. His gentleness and patience, as well as his ardor, made it the most enjoyable of lovemaking. The gasps which she gave under his caresses were none of them disregarded; he was all the time awake to the sensations of the living creature who was at his mercy. He brought her to the pitch where, though she was not entirely willing, she would have suffered if he had drawn back. She was grateful that at the point where, though she had committed herself, she would still have evaded him if he had allowed her to, he was then so firm that no retreat was possible.

He was very careful; the fright was momentary, the pain less than she had expected; but of the ecstatic enjoyment for which he was pouring out his thanks and devotion, she felt none whatever. He had warned her that the first time would hardly bring it to her, that it would come from experience, but still she felt a blankness, a sullen dissatisfaction. His adoration presently soothed this displeasure. From his whispered words she understood that she had achieved some wonderful success and bestowed something on him that all his devotion could never repay; also that she was to be praised and worshiped for being the most beautiful little creature in creation.

She woke up at five o'clock, her watch told her, and found that he had gone. She spread out her arms and legs, missing him but finding it comfortable to have all the space to herself. She was pleased and thankful that a very important feat had now been accomplished, but the excitement that his mere appearing caused her, so that she sometimes felt almost faint when he came into a room, a sensation which ought to have increased a hundred times by being in bed with him, had deserted her.

Meeting him after breakfast in the sun-filled sitting room, with her stately clothes and the great pile of hair behind her head, she appeared with a somewhat haughty remoteness; but it was her privilege to behave as she chose on such a morning. He was devoted, deferential but extremely satisfied; she was cool and detached. They made a drive around the harbor. Sitting very upright, she was almost unnaturally alert in noticing the sparkling green sea. "To think that it's still winter at home!" she said, as if she had nothing in her mind but a tourist's impressions. But as evening came on, she began to long for nightfall; the second night advanced them much farther toward mutual bliss. She began to feel, in fits and starts, that this man in whose arms she was lying naked, was, actually, the man who had been the target of her thoughts, hopes and wishes for so long, who had caused her rapture by coming to her, and whose leaving her had taken the light out of the day. On the same night that she felt the identification was complete, she unexpectedly, surprisingly found herself carried away in a swooning sensation of physical enjoyment, so intense that she cried out, as she had not done for the pain. From having merely accepted his gratitude she now began to understand and return it. From that night on, from the morning of the next day, she was changed. She was infinitely happier, self-confident without assertion, reigning calmly over everybody.

That afternoon she was resting on the sofa in the sitting room; he had been out on an errand and she was just beginning to suffer from his absence when he came into the room. He sat down beside her and took out of his pocket a small ivory box; inside it, pushed into a cleft in a white velvet cushion, was a plain gold ring.

Not a very interesting thing, she was beginning to think, but he took her left hand and drew off the wedding ring. Then he replaced it with his.

Though the memories of Paris remained sharp and vivid, she afterward retained very little distinct recollection of Leghorn. It was to her only the seat of heaven. The beautiful scenes and their colors were an expression of her emotion rather than a spectacle in their own right. She did not leave them with regret, for what they meant to her, she carried with her. When it was time for them to leave, her thoughts and ardent wishes turned toward the Leigham Court Road.

Chapter 21

❧❧

FLORENCE's house had been called Alverstoke; by a natural association of ideas, she altered this to Stokefield; and the name, painted on the gate, gave him pleasure whenever he saw it. She had now assembled a household of a cook, three housemaids, Plascott as her lady's maid, a gardener and Griffith for her coachman. The latter had been on board wages since Dr. Gully laid down his carriage at Christmas, and was pleased to be taking up his new duties. He liked being in the same household as Fanny Plascott, and since he couldn't continue in the doctor's employment, he was glad to be in Mrs. Ricardo's as the next best thing. She had bought a landau from Offard's, the carriage builders in Oxford Street, and she jobbed a pair of horses.

Florence had lived so much of her married life in other people's houses, now that she had set up for herself even in a furnished house, she had a great deal of household shopping to do. This interested her, whether it was for prosaic matters such as servants' sheets or flower vases for the drawing room.

Hillside was more completely ready because Dr. Gully had had his sisters' services. His study desk and chair, his bookcases and books, his bachelor chest, his pictures and precious mementos, his chosen plate and china as well as everything that Pritchard needed for the domestic staff were all arranged for him before he came back. In return, he paid a special visit to the little house in Marylebone to see if anything were wanting for their comfort. They declared that nothing was; but he bought a small table for tea at the fireside and a stand to hold a collection of flowering plants.

They asked him friendly, impersonal questions about his tour, and if Mrs. Ricardo were now comfortably settled. He told them of her frequent shopping expeditions, and added that Griffith was very glad of his new place.

"I always liked Griffith," Ellen said.

"He is a likable man," agreed Ann; but they both said he was lost when he was out of his stable or off his carriage box. He never seemed even to know what day of the week it was.

Well, Dr. Gully said, perhaps it did not matter so much, Griffith's not knowing it, so long as somebody knew it. He was an extremely skillful coachman, he himself had never had a better.

Florence took almost more pleasure in her new carriage than in any of her possessions. She never got into it without a critical look at the horses and to see that the brasswork was gleaming, the varnished sides immaculate, the spokes and rims of the wheels free from mud and dust. To ride in her own landau with James beside her was an exquisite happiness.

The Leigham Court Road was faced on both sides with houses, separated though they were by ample grounds, almost to the summit of the hill. He did not choose to be seen entering her front gate more often than need be, and they would arrange for the carriage to pick him up at some distance. On the lovely mornings of April and May, these expeditions were inspired with a heavenly gaiety. His walking pace was so brisk he had usually passed their rendezvous before the clop of hooves behind him made him pause. He would then turn around, to see the carriage coming up the wide, quiet road, the whole equipage lustrous in the sunlight, Griffith touching his cockaded hat with a smile as he drew up, and inside, Florence in a bonnet so small and perched so far to the back of her head, that there was some excuse for the muslin parasol held between her and the bright-blue sky. Leaning out, she would say: "Oh, how do you do, Dr. Gully. May I set you down anywhere?"

As he climbed in beside her, he would say debonairly: "Thank you, I should like to go wherever you are going!"

Griffith would drive them all over Streatham Common, across Mitcham Lane and onto the commons of Tooting Bec and Tooting Graveney. Road after road, the houses were going up fast, but between them the common land still stretched unspoiled for acres. The grass was richer than in the uplands of Malvern. After rain, pools of water stood under trees; in little coppices the soil was ankle-deep in damp leafmold. A feature of the Tooting commons was their ponds, small and large. Great, old trees tilted over their margins; in their depths were little islands, loaded with bushes and saplings and their murky foliage. The shores were of clean brown sand, scattered with pebbles. It was delightful to walk beside them.

Florence would stop the carriage saying she would like to walk for half an hour, and Griffith would then drive away to give the horses a round, bringing them back to the spot at the appointed time solely by instinct; his sense of time was so exact, he often left his watch unwound.

On these occasions, they had the common to themselves as far as the eye could see. Walking slowly, she leaning on his arm, they enjoyed a kind of rapturous tranquillity. To be alone with him had always made her happy, but once it had been an excited, scared happiness; now, with no one able to part her from him, she realized a deep, absolute content.

His own physical happiness, his ecstasy and satisfaction, were more strongly felt than hers but his happiness altogether was less complete. She asked nothing more than this charming, tame, south of England scene; he could not help sometimes regretting the wild grand beauty he had left. She was delighted with the Streatham Spa Well in the Valley Fields beside the Leigham Court Road. Its pretty little well house she had thought would please him too. He drank a little of the water, enough to find how flat it was compared with the ethereal freshness of a Malvern spring. The greatest happiness of all was edged by discontent. They never spent the night in each other's houses but every few days when they agreed to meet to go to bed, she would come over to Hillside after lunch and he, watching for her from his study window, would open the front door so that she need not ring. The servants were in the basement kitchen, from which occasional clattering rose; when the maids wanted to go to their rooms on the top story, they would use the back staircase; there could be no accidental meeting; in his bedroom, behind a locked door, he and she were as free and safe as they could be in this world; but there were times when, accustomed as he had so long been to a position of undisputed authority, the idea of being at a disadvantage was hateful to him. He did not feel that he was a wrongdoer; he believed that he had already done her inestimable good, and he meant to spend the rest of his life protecting and cherishing her, to be truly a husband to her in everything but name; and he was galled because he was driven to be furtive in deference to conventions he despised. When she was sitting propped up against the pillows of his bed, bare-armed and bare-legged in her chemise, her cheeks a burning pink, her eyes brilliant but sleepy, it was painful to have to hurry her to dress. One afternoon they were later in getting up than he had meant to be; he urged her to get dressed and went himself into his dressing room. Florence was thinking dreamily how much she admired him in his gray dressing gown with the dark-blue quilted satin collar and dark-blue frogs. She was always excited by anything formal in his appearance; this was how he had looked when he had first aroused her passion. When he came back, dressed, she was still in the same position, her clothes, like the plumage of swans, lying on the chair, the floor, where she had dropped them. The rapidity and competence with which he began to put them on her made her laugh, but he was thinking that at five o'clock Pritchard would be bringing tea into the study.

But the drawbacks were only spots on the sun. Before he left off practice he had occasionally wondered if he would find the days difficult to fill. He was surprised now to find how happily he passed the time doing very little. The greater part of the day he spent with her. When they did not drive out, he spent hours sitting at her side in her drawing room which, opening into the garden, was charmingly private. He usually took tea in his own house, spending the hours afterward in reading and writing, then he would dine at Stokefield, or less often, she would come to dinner at Hillside.

He entered into all her plans for new furniture, for planting out the garden and for filling the little glass conservatory which clung to the back wall of the house and was entered from the staircase at first-floor level. Her clothes too were a matter of personal interest to him. He thought she spent too much on them, but he was so charmed by every new dress she put on, he had not much resolution for scolding. She had now given up black—at least a year before it was correct to leave it off; but mauve was half-mourning, and it suited her exquisitely. She had a dress of moiré, the softest shade of amethyst; and as the summer advanced, muslin ones of lilac and heliotrope.

He had been down into London to buy a few books and some learned journals, and on the counter of the bookshop he had seen a reprint of Mrs. Lynn Linton's famous diatribe: *The Girl of the Period*. He brought it over to Stokefield next morning, where Florence sat in the drawing room embroidering, in a muslin dress whose train, mounted on rustling silk of a deeper tone, was frilled and tied up with bows to match. He leaned over her and kissed her with the long, firm pressure of his mouth that she loved, her head afterward falling away from his and drooping on its white throat.

"Mrs. Lynn Linton is very much shocked at you, my dear," he said.

"Oh, that!" said Florence, looking over his arm. "I never read it. But I am not a girl," she added.

"You are, in my view," he said, "and it will be wholesome for you to hear what Mrs. Lynn Linton says."

He read aloud the now celebrated description: "'She dyes her hair and paints her face as the first articles of her personal religion. . . .'"

"In other words, she makes the best of herself."

"'In time of crinoline she sacrificed decency. In time of trains, she sacrifices cleanliness.'"

"No, I do not," Florence interrupted. "You can hold up a train with a loop if you want to; otherwise brushing and sponging are all that's needed." He pressed his hand on hers, to enjoin silence.

"'Her bonnet,'" he continued severely, "'is cut to four straws and a rosebud, or a tag of lace and a bunch of glass beads. . . .'"

"That's rather attractive," she said critically.

"What she principally objects to in you, is imitation of the demimonde: slang, bold talk, fastness, love of pleasure and indifference to duty. There!"

"Silly old besom," said Florence impatiently. "Of course, if cosmetics, and fashionable things, and talking like a modern person instead of somebody out of the Old Testament, really meant that you were wicked and—and criminal and that sort of thing, I should object to it myself, and I don't approve of vulgarity any more than she does. But she doesn't know what she's talking about. Those frumpish women never do. It doesn't mean that you've given up all your duties to everybody if you make your hair a rather different color. And if people like us are driven to live for a time in a way that society says is wrong, she ought to understand that that's the fault of society, for being so narrowminded and cruel."

He had meant to amuse her by Mrs. Lynn Linton's strictures; he hadn't expected this outburst. He took her hand and kissed it. He was impressed by the fact that the ideas he'd given her had been so thoroughly adopted, she now brought them out as if they'd always been her own.

"Look at your George Eliot and that Mr. Lewes, if it comes to that," she added.

"I would much rather look at you, my beautiful one."

Chapter 22

THE infatuation was made more intense by possession of each other. It was engrossing, but even so, he was capable of an active, enjoyable life outside it. He often visited William's family in Queensborough Terrace, lunching there, taking "the chicks" into Kensington Gardens just across the Bayswater Road. He looked up old friends and made new ones; he lunched at the Reform Club and the Athenaeum; he spoke to medical societies, and listened in the strangers' gallery at the House of Commons.

Florence had no social amusements independent of him, but she did not miss them. Completely, or almost completely happy for the first time in her life, she wanted nothing, at first, except his presence, and regretted their not being married because they had to part so many times a day. As she had never known the bliss of mutual passion before, she supposed that it would last forever, and that the rest of life would never interest her again. That no one called at Stokefield, that ladies emerging from the gates of other houses passed her on the pavement with unseeing eyes, gave her no concern. If they had made advances, she would have thought it a nuisance. They had both suffered so much from the restrictions imposed by society, isolation was the lovers' paradise. Though he did not imagine, as she did, that it would last, as it was, forever and ever he did believe that the love was everlasting. He would not accept the view that this was an amour, a scandalous connection; they both lived in the firm intention of marrying, and the hope that they might be able to do so at any time.

On this other side of the Streatham High Road was a large building, the Magdalene Hospital, for the reception, maintenance and employment of penitent prostitutes—patron, Her Majesty the Queen. The consulting physician, he found, was an old acquaintance, Dr. Frodsham, who had come from Worcester. He was glad to see Frodsham now, to welcome him at Hillside, to take him across to call at Stokefield. Frodsham was urbane and a man of the world, there was no *gêne* in introducing him to Florence, but it galled Dr. Gully to think how many minds would connect Florence with the girls in the Magdalene Hospital in an association that nothing on earth would break.

The servants in both houses behaved as if nothing were in question but affectionate friendship. Plascott's manner was invariably gentle and respectful; Pritchard's loyalty, discretion and decorum were so perfect that though Dr. Gully had known them for fifteen years, it seemed to him as though he had never fully recognized them till now. He was going into town one morning and as he could not lunch at Stokefield he walked over for a few minutes of her society before he left. She had asked him to have himself photographed and this he had done, at Mayall's of Regent Street. She had the print now, in a broad frame of claret-colored velvet with delicate brass filigree at the corners, but she had said she would like a small picture of him to wear in a locket.

"Have you a locket?" he asked.

"No, but if I could have the picture I would get one." This was the errand he was going on now, before a luncheon appointment with an American doctor visiting England, who was interested in spiritualism.

In the hall of Hillside, above the umbrella stand, was a set of branches with brass hooks, from which hung clothes brushes of different sizes, large, oblong ones for serious mud and little ones with handles for brushing up the nap of a silk hat or removing specks from a lapel. He returned to his house to exchange his Panama hat for a low-crowned bowler, and was about to walk out of the front door, when Pritchard advanced on him with one of the little brushes, and saying, "Excuse me, Doctor," deftly removed three long, curling, copper hairs from his shoulder.

In New Bond Street he went to Hunt and Roskell and chose an oval gold locket, the face ornamented with a pearl set in a star of small diamonds. This he took to Mayall's, who had prepared a miniature copy of the photograph; while he waited, it was trimmed to fit the locket, pressed in with a mount, and the glass fitted over it. He took it away, feeling how charming it was to be making this present to her. He had never yet given her anything so expensive but this, like the gold ring, was a symbol, a sacrament.

He returned to Leigham Court Road in the late afternoon and presented himself at Stokefield for dinner a little earlier than usual. Florence was still upstairs, dressing. He walked out of the French window to pace up and down the garden till she should appear. It irked him that he could not go upstairs and watch her, but Plascott would be there. As he turned at the far end of the lawn and came toward the house again, he saw her, glimmering within the room. She saw him coming and as he crossed the threshold she held out her arms.

Presently he brought the little box out of his waistcoat pocket. When she had exclaimed over the locket and the photograph, he fastened the sleek, heavy gold chain at the nape of her neck.

The shops in Streatham High Road were really surprisingly good; the fishmonger, poulterer, butcher, greengrocer and provision dealer made one quite independent of London. After a printanier soup they had some trout and a dish of strawberries, with a bottle of dry white wine. She drank two glasses and prepared to take a third.

"My love," he said, "two glasses of wine are enough."

"But I am thirsty."

"Then take some Malvern water—you have some, surely?"

"I don't know that we have."

"I will send some over, but you must keep plenty on hand. I ordered a hundred quarts last week from Burrows' in Cannon Street."

"Good gracious!"

"But for now, take some strawberries, without sugar. They will be thirst-quenching." She did as he told her. She did not really want wine when he was beside her.

She had a piece of domestic news for him after dinner. Griffith and Plascott wanted to be married in July. Plascott, no farther away than the coachman's cottage at the bottom of the garden, would be available to some extent, until she had her family; but a new lady's maid would have to be found, and trained in Florence's ways. It was tiresome. He agreed and sympathized. Then he examined the new Broadwood piano in a case of black and gold. She had never heard him play; on the few occasions on which they had had music, he had made her play to him. Now he sat down and played one of Chopin's nocturnes, the perfect music for an evening in early summer.

The prospect of having to give up Plascott next month turned Florence's thoughts in a novel direction. Since she had been established at Stokefield, she had resumed her friendship with Mrs. Cox. The latter now came to tea with her quite often. When she had finished her duties at Brookefield, she would walk to the upper end of Leigham Court Road and all the way down it to Stokefield, more than a mile, but she was so nimble and light-footed, she did not mind the distance. With every visit, Florence liked her better. She did not want acquaintance with neighbors, whom she probably would not like even if she knew them, but with no family intercourse, no society, and James obliged to leave her so often, a chosen female friend filled a want that had begun to make itself a little felt, in spite of the great happiness. It *was* very pleasant to have someone to take an admiring interest in all one's things, to listen and give such sound advice about household matters. She did not explain to Mrs. Cox the terms on which she was with Dr. Gully but her face when she spoke about him, the numbers of times she said "we," made the emotional situation clear, at least. Mrs. Cox had seen Dr. Gully once or twice since the return to Streatham, when she had stayed a little later over tea, or he had come in to dinner a little earlier than usual. She had thought how well he looked, admiring his keenly intelligent face with its bright-blue eyes and bladelike nose. The baldness of his forehead was, she knew, said to be a sign of virility. His presence was always stimulating.

Florence's plan took shape one afternoon when Mrs. Cox told her sadly but with resignation that their engagement for her to come to Stokefield the next Saturday afternoon must be given up. Mrs. Brookes was expecting a large family party to see her new baby; the house parlormaid was away nursing her mother; and Mrs. Cox's deft services were very much in demand. Florence was annoyed, for James was spending the afternoon with his sisters, but she saw that the point must be conceded. Then it occurred to her how pleasant it would be to have Mrs. Cox in her own employment, endlessly sympathetic, endlessly useful, and always there when she was wanted. Of course, her presence couldn't be allowed to interfere with anything—anything important—but Florence did not think that it would. All her life she had been accustomed to a great deal of service;

in her experience, employees gave inconvenience by not being there, not by their presence.

Before she offered Mrs. Cox the post of companion-housekeeper, she told Dr. Gully of her intention, one evening after dinner when the Stokefield drawing room was looking particularly charming in the sinking light, its air faintly delicious from great bunches of white roses in urns of milk glass. At first he found the news thoroughly displeasing, but even at first he did not say so. He had deprived Florence of so much, it was not for him to object to this arrangement if she wanted it; and as he thought the matter over, he began to see that it might have advantages for them both. When he and Florence went anywhere in public, the difference in their ages, between sixty-four and twenty-seven, was no protection to them against occasional furtive but knowing glances. He was conscious of these, in a theater, a restaurant, even on a station platform. With her beauty, youth and fashion, she drew the eye in any case, and then it was seen how much they were enjoying each other's society. Their faces as they talked to each other, the radiance of hers, the tenderness of his, made the thing plain to people who knew the world and had eyes in their heads. How woefully different from Paris! Here the matter was one for avid, hostile curiosity. He could not alter the situation; his happiness and *bien-être* made him content to ignore it; but if the interval before marriage were to be very long, and they were to travel about to English resorts, as he would certainly wish to, their reception at hotels might be awkward at any moment; with this confounded woman as the *tertium quid,* that danger at least would be avoided. Two ladies would be traveling together, with an elderly gentleman in attendance. The question was whether their precious freedom wouldn't be curtailed to nothing.

Florence of course said no—never! Mrs. Cox would be sure to know when she was in the way.

"I suppose, my dearest," he said, "you will provide her with a housekeeper's room, a sitting room, where she can have her family photographs and so on, so that it won't be any penance to her to be expected to sit in it?"

"I thought of giving her the large front room on the second floor. The servants don't use it."

"As a bedroom? That wouldn't be quite enough, I think."

"Well, she can have the room over the front door. I can finish furnishing it."

"Excellent. But, oh, my darling"—he gathered her in his arms —"how I long for us to be married, to be all in all to each other, with no need of other people who keep us apart!"

"We are all in all now," she said, "and no one is going to keep us apart." The beautiful glow of her eyes and cheeks as she spoke comforted him with its assurance.

The dusk was getting deep. To prevent the parlormaid's being rung for, he found the stand of sulfur matches on the chimney-piece and lighted two pairs of candles in candlesticks hung with glass lusters, that as the flames rose, glittered like fairy fingers. Then he took her in his arms again and though they were by themselves he said in lowest tones: "Will you come to me tomorrow afternoon?"

"Yes," she said. When he left the house a few minutes later at the decorous hour of half past nine, crossing the quiet road in the twilight he was divided between ecstasy that his lot was so blissful and despair that it should be so hard.

When he went to bed it was a long time before he could sleep. He thought over the question of Mrs. Cox with the force and clarity of mind he was accustomed to bring to bear on problems.

Florence had said she should not tell Mrs. Cox that they went to bed with each other. That a woman of Mrs. Cox's experience and sense didn't know this, or wouldn't soon find it out, he did not believe; nor, apart from observing ordinary discretion, would he take any pains to hide it from her; to do that would be to live in fear of discoveries, something which he would never endure. He would go on as he had begun, not denying, but by his strength of will, forbidding any comment. Mrs. Cox herself was no doubt willing and well meaning enough, but he had a stronger ally than her good nature: It was her self-interest. She had not only herself to support but three sons of school age, and she belonged to the group of women he had seen described in a review devoted to social questions: the impoverished gentlewomen who, forced into an overcrowded labor market, formed "one of the greatest social problems of the day," "one of the burning questions of modern political economy." If she accepted the post, as she was quite certain to do, it would be of overriding importance to her both to keep it and to behave as though it didn't compromise her respectability. These calls on Mrs. Cox's tact and discretion would be no doubt somewhat heavy but as, in his heart, he resented the idea of her presence, he did not feel much compunction.

Chapter 23

THE first time he came across to Stokefield after Mrs. Cox's being installed, he feared what he might find; but Florence was alone in the drawing room, she kissed him, plainly without fear of their being interrupted, and in fact Mrs. Cox did not appear until the gong sounded for lunch. At table, he admitted to himself that her manner was good. She was quiet, volunteering very little, and answering pleasantly and concisely. He studied her discreetly. She was difficult to place; she had at least a touch of colored blood, West Indian probably as she came from Jamaica, and the slightness of her frame, her jet-black hair and colorless olive face bore out the idea. She was a plain woman, not improved by wearing tin spectacles. Her upbringing had not been among well-born people; her accent, her turns of speech, were thoroughly provincial; her laugh was disagreeable, high-pitched with a sound like creaking wood; but in spite of all this, she was not uncongenial, her dress was scrupulously clean and neat, she wasn't in any way stupid, she was tactful and *serviable*.

After lunch coffee was brought into the drawing room; and in ten minutes time Mrs. Cox got up and said, "Will you excuse me, Mrs. Ricardo?" He rose and opened the door for her and she went out noiselessly as a cat.

He had to get used to her being there. It was impossible for him to take a moment's pleasure in her society, a moment's interest in anything she said, but as she was always polite and inoffensive and showed, too, considerable readiness in making herself scarce, a very tolerable state of things was soon established. There were hours when he could sit beside Florence undisturbed, they took their morning drives together as before, and whenever Mrs. Cox went into London to see about her affairs—she had invested all her capital in a house in Lancaster Road, No. 150, and let it off in apartments, which required some supervision—or when she went to visit her boys at their school, or to pay a call of duty on some patrons of hers, the Bravos—the family of a wealthy, retired Jamaican merchant living on Palace Green—then Florence would spend the afternoon at Hillside, so long as nature hadn't thwarted them by making her indisposed. All the same, these visits were not quite so regular, so frequent as they had been.

There was one advantage, however; now that he could say Mrs. Ricardo had a companion-housekeeper with her, he felt able to suggest that he should bring Florence to lunch in Queensborough Terrace. His son and daughter-in-law gave a cordial invitation; he himself was always welcome, and they had a lively curiosity to see Mrs. Ricardo in whom Papa took such an interest, and of whom they'd heard something in guarded terms from Ann and Ellen.

On a Saturday at the end of August, a day of deep-blue sky and rounded masses of white cloud, Griffith brought the carriage to the steps of Stokefield at 11 A.M. for the long drive to Bayswater.

She looked lovely as usual and Dr. Gully told her so; no, he said, lovelier than ever. Her dress was a dark-gray poplin, with a very small, flat bonnet of white net, tied under the chin with a white bow, and a white parasol festooned with bunches of white muslin like the cumulus clouds overhead. The colors seemed to him appropriate and discreet, and this pleased him; the effect of the whole ravished him.

For the first couple of miles as he sat beside her he was making love to her, talking of her beauty, his happiness, the exquisite pleasure of being alone with her. She sat a good deal of the time in silence under her parasol, listening and smiling. When the road was not crowded and they were going too fast to be overlooked, he held her left hand. Griffith drove at a rapid pace till they came to Westminster Bridge where the heavy traffic began. The carriage drew up outside 65 Queensborough Terrace at quarter to one and Dr. Gully helped her down to the pavement, her bonnet strings and gloves still immaculately white.

The luncheon was successful. His son and daughter-in-law were a charming host and hostess and Florence, a little tense and positive in utterance, was painstakingly agreeable and correct, while her lovely appearance at his son's right hand kept him in a state of perpetual enchantment. The chicks, James, Edward and Gertrude, seven, five and four, came into the drawing room after lunch to see Grandpapa, and were told to say how do you do to the beautiful lady in the little white bonnet. She was very pleasant and asked the boys if they had ponies to ride.

"No," they said, "we haven't."

"Grandpapa should see to that," the lady said, looking at Grandpapa and laughing, her eyes very blue and large. Gi-gi was leaning against his knee. She said decisively: "*I* don't want a pony."

They got up to go at half past two and Mrs. Ricardo was most kindly pressed to come again. Griffith, who had been told to bring the carriage back at quarter past two, was sitting on the box alert and upright, the horses' heads toward the Bayswater Road. Young Mr. Gully came out, said a civil word to him and opened the carriage door; then the doctor came out with Mrs. Ricardo and the two gentlemen helped her in. Having watched the carriage drive off, William went upstairs again to the drawing room. He and his wife exchanged a few noncommittal remarks, and then she said with her sweet, candid air: "After all, it isn't her fault that she's so beautiful—nor Papa's either."

"No," he said, "but it would be rather more convenient for everyone if she weren't."

As the carriage was driving down Park Lane, Dr. Gully said: "My son's a handsome fellow, isn't he? He has the good looks I missed, and the height I ought to have had."

"Well—yes."

"You sound doubtful," he said, in a displeased tone. "I must say I never met anyone else who didn't admire Willie's appearance."

"I do admire it. He's more regularly handsome than you and he is taller. But—he isn't—he hasn't—when *you* are in the room, one doesn't want to look at anybody else."

"Well, well—I don't know that you should say that."

"*I* know I should."

The expedition, reminding him of the idyllic freedom they had enjoyed only a few weeks ago, made it the harder to endure Mrs. Cox's presence with resignation. However it had to be done, first, because Florence wanted her in the house, secondly, because the arrangement was obviously a good one; but a feeling of dissatisfaction perhaps played its part in leading him to take up an old friendship.

Charlotte Dyson, forty years old, unmarried, still lived in what had been her late father's house. It stood on Streatham High Road a short distance from the mouth of the Leigham Court Road and was called Vernemore, a solid, restful house in a tree-shaded garden. Miss Dyson had left the interior much as it had been in her parents' time, in the taste of the 1850's. Whatever she herself had added was in the *art nouveau* manner: chairs and cupboards of spare, medieval lines, a Morris wallpaper, a few pieces of pewter. She was tall and slight with faded fair hair, a short, beautiful nose and grayish-blue eyes like opaque glass. He could not have told anybody how she dressed, except that she sometimes wore a necklace of small amber beads with an amber heart hung on it. She was very quiet and, he thought, very intelligent. He saw a row of Mr. Ruskin's works in her drawing-room bookcase and asking her what she thought of *The Stones of Venice,* he was delighted by her remarks on Italian pictures. She had been teaching herself Italian—he wondered how far she had got with *that!* When she read aloud a passage of *Il Paradiso* so that he might help her with the pronunciation, he saw that she had got very far indeed. Now that he had discovered her again, he called every fortnight or so, and found that in talking to her, time went increasingly fast. Social questions interested her deeply: education, nursing, the aftercare of discharged prisoners. What did she think of women's rights? he asked. She said she was afraid she was selfish; she had all the rights she herself wanted to exercise, but no doubt conditions pressed hardly on some women, and one should take an interest. He did not think she was very strong; there was a slight defect of physical energy, though the mind was active and clear.

After some time he spoke of her to Florence; Miss Dyson, he said, would like to meet her, he was sure. Florence was not jealous—it was hardly possible that she could be—but the mere mention of another woman slightly startled her. She said: "Oh, very well, if you like." He arranged one morning in October, that they should call at Vernemore in the course of their morning's drive.

Charlotte Dyson had been so calm and gentle with him, he

got a new sight of her as she exerted herself for a guest who was a stranger. She made conversation with Florence, who responded correctly. They spoke about greenhouse plants, art needlework, the novels of Mr. Trollope, of which *Phineas Finn* was lying on the sofa table. Florence had tried one of them, but it seemed to be all about an old man and she hadn't cared for it. Miss Dyson said in a deprecating way that she thought the political parts of this one were interesting but she didn't pursue the matter. Did she ride? Florence asked. Oh, no, Miss Dyson said, she had always been too gawky and clumsy, she would certainly have fallen off.

They remained a quarter of an hour only and then departed for their morning's drive.

Charlotte Dyson was glad to have seen her, very glad. It was clear, it must be clear to anyone who saw them together, that Dr. Gully's affections were entirely engaged, and it was just as well, indeed it was essential to know these facts about friends or acquaintances, so that everything might be comfortable, perfectly comfortable, that no misunderstandings of any kind should arise, and things go on in a sensible manner. In that first call of his, in which he had taken up the threads, he had told her that his wife was still living, and she was afraid that this friendship might turn out a cause of suffering. She could only hope and pray that matters might go well for him—for them both. She did not suggest calling on Florence, she knew it would give no pleasure. The next time she saw Dr. Gully she said she hoped he would bring Mrs. Ricardo again. She did not expect that he would.

Florence, now that she had Mrs. Cox's company in the house, in the hours when she was not with Dr. Gully, wanted for no one else, at present. She would have been glad, really glad to see her mother after an interval of nearly eighteen months, but since this could not be, without the concessions she refused to make, she thought no more of it. James made the color and richness of her life; to see him from an upper window, coming across the road, to be summoned from the garden by the words, "Dr. Gully in the drawing room, ma'am," affected her like the opening bars of an overture. Whatever he said was interesting; it was delicious to sit in the window sewing while he read aloud to her, though his presence and his voice meant more to her than those words of somebody else's that he was reading.

They loved giving each other presents. She had given him a gold pencil case to hang on his watch chain and a square morocco box for handkerchiefs. She had lived so long in other people's houses that she had not a set of appointments for her own writing table. He bought her some of a kind that was all the rage: a brass inkstand, coffer and blotting book, all studded with round knobs of black, white-streaked onyx. He had found in the Burlington Arcade a sentimental keepsake for her: Framed in sapphire-blue velvet, it was an Italian photograph, deeply, brilliantly colored, of the harbor at Leghorn. These were non-committal gifts; it was sweet to him to be able to buy for her also things that were meant for lovers' presents. One of them was a pair of little scent bottles closed in a large shell of mother of pearl. If he had been asked, before he knew her, whether he liked women to use scent, he would have said no; her use of it charmed him. Lavender was the one most poignantly associated with her, but she used White Rose too, and in her bath, Eau Verveine, a refreshing attar of orange and lemon. He did not, even now, approve of cosmetics, but he could not refuse when she asked him to bring her from town a preparation she'd read of: Piesse et Lubin's Milk of Roses. He bought it at Savory and Moore's in New Bond Street, a firm of dignified repute; they told him it was not injurious, "though between ourselves, Doctor, perhaps it does not do quite everything that is claimed for it."

He gave it to her when they were alone in the study at Hillside. She eagerly peeled away the wrapper and read aloud from the label: "It is harmless as an April shower on the verdure of spring."

He merely replied, "Well, we must hope so," and collected the wrappings, dropping them in the wastepaper basket.

Their intimacy was still showing them new aspects of each other. He found she was hardy and active to a degree that delighted and astonished him. She had taken up her hobby of driving again, and they drove out several mornings a week, while autumn faded and changed into winter. Once they were on one of the commons, Griffith would be made to relinquish the reins, to one and then the other. The doctor was a competent driver but Mrs. Ricardo was what Griffith called a winner. He'd always known she must be good with horses, he hadn't known how good till he saw her at it. She had what coachmen called "hand," and he watched her as one artist watches another, driving the pair from the high box seat, doing everything as he would have done it himself, but with the extra bit of dash that wouldn't have been becoming in a coachman. The doctor was good enough to bring the horses along, and you could trust him not to be run away with, but anything like the polish of Mrs. Ricardo's performance, you'd go far to see.

One December day they were driving over Streatham Common, the wheels crackling on ground swollen with frost. Florence, in a gray ulster and a black postilion's hat with a peacock's feather in it, was highly excited by the exercise and the sharp air. She was driving with Griffith on the box beside her and Dr. Gully had taken his seat in the carriage. Griffith was saying to him: "You can get a glimpse of the Crystal Palace over there today, sir; just how the light strikes it; can't see it in the ordinary way."

"I think I got it just now," Dr. Gully said. Florence declared she must see it, and told Griffith to take the reins. When they had changed places on the box, she remained standing up.

"Sit down!" Dr. Gully exclaimed, getting to his feet.

"I don't see it," she cried. "Yes, I do—I did then." She had caught a gleam on the skyline, no sooner come than gone, like a great diamond.

"Sit down!" he cried angrily. She sat down, somewhat piqued by his dictatorial tone.

"Don't you realize that's very dangerous?" he went on. "If they'd made a sudden move, you'd have been thrown out—very badly hurt." They drove on in silence; she felt that James ought not to speak to her like that, in an angry tone that had actual dislike in it; and he had a sudden, uncomfortable perception that she would, if she wished to, disobey him even in a matter of danger.

Chapter 24

ANY dissatisfaction with each other was momentary, lost sight of in a constant, glowing physical happiness. As a doctor, he did away with all the discomforts of wounded modesty. To him, and so to her, under his influence, all bodily functions were important and interesting; none of them gave rise to shyness or disgust. This freedom from shame and oppressive concealment, combined with his discretion and good manners, made a state of comfort she had never before imagined.

He was very careful always to calculate the date of her next monthly period and often knew it had arrived before she did. He soon found that it was apt to be very late, but irregularly so. Had it always been like this? he asked. "Oh, I think so," she said; she had never had much interest in the calculation. When a period was unusually late he was always anxious, though he believed he had been unfailingly careful. An undercurrent of anxiety he now accepted as perpetual.

Florence now had the best of both worlds; her highest delight was to be alone with him, but apart from that, she thoroughly enjoyed possessing, at last, a congenial woman friend, and he admitted to himself that Mrs. Cox was an asset. Without a sympathetic female inmate to share her domestic interests, the difference between Florence's existence and his own would have been too marked.

Sir Percy Shelley put him up for the Garrick Club which elected him in January. There was no club he would have preferred in the whole of London. Fond of the theater as he was, he loved the rows of portraits of actors and actresses, hung on paneled walls, their frames gleaming in the light of branched silver candelabra, and the sight of actors who entertained their friends in the dining room or came as guests—the tall, gaunt figure of Irving occasionally appearing—but this, though delightful, was in the nature of background. An intense interest of a scientific kind had now developed; now that he was at leisure he had taken up the scientific investigation of spiritualism.

Daniel Home, his career trailing like a meteor across clear skies of winter, was in Russia, married to the Princess Aksakoff, wearing on his hands brilliant sapphires and diamonds given to him by the czar. In 1871, however, he had lent himself to scientific experiments by William Crookes. This gifted physicist, a fellow of the Royal Society, was already noted for his researches in the fields of analytical chemistry, electricity, optics, astronomy, photography. The material collected from the experiments with Home he published as *Researches into the Phenomena of Spiritualism*.

Dr. Gully was familiar with some of Crookes' writings; he had read "The Spectral Phenomena of Opals" in 1869; their mutual friendship with Home introduced them to each other and Dr. Gully became a very frequent visitor to Crookes' house, in a street behind Mornington Crescent in Camden Town. The comfortable rather shabby house was roomy; it housed Mrs. Crookes and nine children, and had also a large laboratory. In the course of these meetings all Dr. Gully's old interest in spiritualism revived; he felt himself magnetized into the investigation with a drawing power only less strong than his passion's.

In April of this year, a society was formed, the National Association of Spiritualism, with premises in Great Russell Street, and he joined it as a founding member. He addressed it several times and when he attended lectures given there by other people, his contributions to the discussions afterward were so distinguished, they were often reported in the account of the lecture. His attitude, though as engrossed as anyone's, showed a scientific temper that was by no means universal. "We had better be in ignorance," he said, "than in error from too rapid conclusions." Always sensitive to public opinion even when he scorned it, he was not only aware that the subject aroused almost maniacal prejudice, he accepted the fact that it was lamentably at risk from weak-mindedness, sensationalism and sheer fraud. He wanted strongly to see it purged of all disreputable elements and raised to one of pure scientific inquiry. Good repute was very dear to him; he wanted it for whatever he loved; he yearned to give Florence the position before the world that was her due.

Florence of course knew of his interest in spiritualism and the meetings he attended, but as she was not intellectually interested in the subject he did not discuss it with her. With Charlotte Dyson, he felt, he could have talked about it by the hour, because, whether she were personally drawn to it or not, she would have listened earnestly, holding her clear, tranquil mind like a looking glass to his. He forbore to tell Florence any stories of dramatic experience, afraid that with her vivid nature and her lack of scientific approach, she might become one of the sensation-hungry public. The subject occasionally came up in general conversation. Mrs. Cox said that in Jamaica, families in houses on the edge of old sugar or coffee plantations took it for granted that in the early evening, the ghosts be walking.

"Were they alarmed?" he asked.

"No, I don't think so, but the nurses used to bring the children indoors at that time. It was only superstition, you know."

He said nothing. By degrees he was becoming almost reconciled to Mrs. Cox's society. A person who is there for a great deal of the time and never makes a mistake can accomplish wonders. He had heard by now as much of her family circumstances as Florence knew. He had once seen her three sons at Stokefield, aged thirteen, eleven and nine: sallow, small beings with dark eyes and bullet heads. He was always ready to like children and their faces, cautious and hoping for kindness, he thought rather engaging. Two of them were already at an excellent school for the sons of distressed gentlefolk, and their mother was anxious that the third should be taken. Admission was a matter of votes, bought for money. He gave Mrs. Cox five pounds to secure a vote, and was glad to hear presently that Leslie Cox had been admitted. She had really valuable patrons in those Bravos at Palace Green. Mr. Bravo, proud of having married a wife of pure white extraction, was immensely fond of her. She was a beautiful, haggard, hunted-looking woman in her early forties. In her extreme youth she had made a disastrous marriage with an Englishman named Turner. There had been something extremely sinister about this man; of their three children, one daughter was imbecile and one deaf-mute; only the son was normal. His stepfather as well as his mother appeared to dote on this young man; Mr. Bravo had sent him to Oxford and was now supporting him at the bar; and his position at home was that of the beloved son of the house. Mr. Bravo had helped Mrs. Cox in many small ways and the boys were invited to spend the day at Palace Green two or three times a year, when Mr. Bravo would tip them a gold half sovereign each.

She clearly felt herself very fortunately placed at Stokefield, although the servants didn't like her, he could see, and resented

having to take orders from her; she was clearly very fond of
Florence, as well she might be. She performed innumerable
services for her instinctively; she almost never had to be asked
to do anything. He began to feel that he could take her into his
confidence and one day when Florence was not in the room
he said: "I am anxious about a habit Mrs. Ricardo has of taking
too much wine. Don't ever propose her taking any, especially
between meals. Check it if you can, and speak to me if you see
it growing worse. With her highly strung nervous organization
she would be in great danger if the habit of intemperance got
a real hold on her."

Mrs. Cox promised. He hadn't much faith that her influence
would succeed, but at least she might be depended on for a
warning. Florence did not drink much at his table or at her own
when he was there, but he sometimes smelled sherry on her
breath when he came over to dinner; she had been drinking it
in her bedroom while she was dressing, and once he had detected it in the middle of the morning. When he taxed her with
it, she denied it. Her fibs were both unconvincing and delivered with great earnestness; she lied like a vehement child
who doesn't grasp that its falsehood is blatant. This made her
untruthfulness seem innocent, not the odious thing that lying
was as a rule; but it did not do anything to relieve his anxiety.

Chapter 25

THE passing of time had made them less romantic to each other but it had not loosened the tie of affection and passion. He yearned for another idyllic spell such as they had had, briefly, at Leghorn, and she agreed that it would be delicious. The mere idea of traveling abroad was alluring; though their servants would be behind them, everyone else would be strange; the freedom of a foreign country was more absolute than any privacy at home.

For various reasons he decided on Bad Kissingen, a little spa east of Frankfurt. It was in Bavaria that Wilson had found Priessnitz; the Kissingen waters were very interesting medically and the salt-mud baths of the spa were held to be useful in cases of intestinal obstruction, liver complaints and abnormalities of menstruation. They might do Florence good. The place itself was said to be charming, with beautiful scenery and a town of simple, kindly inhabitants. They made their plans to set out early in August. Pritchard was to go with them and the maid Humphries who had replaced Plascott; a cheerful, energetic young woman, glad enough of a bit of travel to liven things up.

Kissingen was indeed enchanting. It was in a valley through which the little river Saale ran fast, transparent as glass and bordered by willow trees. The meadows on each side rose into sloping orchards and vines, and the summits of the hills were crowned with old oak trees growing among broken rocks. The town's houses and buildings, all bright and white, were connected by bridges thrown across the stream. The chief buildings of the spa were in a large grove of trees, all laid out with promenades. In a glass-roofed hall, a spring hollowed into a deep well and protected by a glass hood rushed up to the well's rim. For two hours it stayed there, surging and foaming, then sank into the ground with a groaning sound. An hour later, a hollow noise underground warned that it was rising again.

Dr. Gully arranged for Florence to take a course of the salt-mud baths. His name procured her a great deal of attention and interest among the resident physicians but this couldn't prevent her from finding the baths very disagreeable. She was obliged to lie in a warm, gruel-like mixture of peat and mineral water, which needed to be washed off afterward in a hot bath—a world away from the water cure at Malvern, just as the glasses of mineral water she had to drink morning and evening, salty and nauseous, made her long for the fresh-tasting Malvern water —but she was no longer the young woman who had taken the Malvern treatment; she had come out of a dewy dawn into the broad light of a hot, bright day.

When the horrid treatment was over, the rest of the day was given to pleasure. They walked arm in arm by the Saale, beside the willow trees; they drove into the uplands where the air smelled of apples and grapes; they visited the little town of Bochlet to see Bohemian glass, and Florence, enraptured with it, bought a tazza of violet glass striped with clear and a pair of ruby goblets with lilies of the valley enameled on their sides.

They were both in perfect humor; the feeling of health in the clear, limitless air made them conscious of their bodies only to take pleasure in them; they loved the sight of each other.

Pritchard and Humphries, by enjoying the stay themselves, enlarged the climate of cheerfulness and contentment. Not only did they perform all their personal services in a faithful, considerate way; their attitude was reassuring. The doctor had brought Mrs. Ricardo abroad for her health, and there was nothing peculiar in that; the baths she took, poor thing, they wouldn't have undergone if you'd paid them. Dr. Gully and Florence, too, deeply appreciated this tranquil acceptance by devoted servants. In the nights, which were sometimes only twilight because the moonlight came through the thin curtains as if they were deep water, in each other's arms for hours they felt a security they had never known before; the friendliness of the outside world was there, surrounding the passionate delight of solitude.

In the day, however, Florence was altogether in command of herself and he saw for the first time how managing and dictatorial she could be now that she was completely recovered from the illness which had brought her to him two years ago. She sat one morning in the sitting room of the entresol, writing letters on her blue morocco writing box, while he sat by the window sometimes reading a four-day-old *Times,* but mostly looking over it at her determined little face.

A letter from Stokefield showed that in their mistress's absence, Mrs. Cox was having trouble with the servants. The footman who had been boarded out while his mistress was away had come back to sleep at the house. Florence reminded Mrs. Cox that she had told the man he was to sleep out and added: *"My order is to be obeyed."* Then one of the housemaids had been having her sisters to see her a good deal, and when Mrs. Cox remonstrated, had said something about Mrs. Ricardo's having said she might. Florence wrote, "I never gave her permission to have her sisters at the house," and she enclosed a peremptory note to be given to Anna. She asked Mrs. Cox to compare the prices of two local coal dealers, and to get the cellar filled. The last housekeeping check had not been acknowledged. If it had arrived, would Mrs. Cox please say so immediately? If it had not, she must stop it at the bank. She had run over the contents of Mrs. Cox's letter to James and he watched her, admiring and amused, as she dealt with them. She paused, considering whether there were anything more to say before she signed herself, "Yours affectionately, Florence Ricardo." He smiled and said: "You are quite a woman of affairs, my love!" She said with her imperious, impatient air: "Everyone must look after their house, I suppose?"

"Everyone *should* look after it, undoubtedly." She bent her head again. The sun struck her hair, the gold tassel of her earring and the gold chain of his locket.

They were back in the Leigham Court Road the last week in September. Florence was agog to take up all the concerns of Stokefield again, and though Hillside meant less to him, poor place as it was after The Priory House, still it was his own house and as such he was glad to get back to it, and to resume his London life. The Kissingen holiday had the hallmark of success, that it had been intensely enjoyable while it lasted and had sent them back with a renewed zest for home.

The restricted intercourse of Leigham Court Road, after weeks of uninterrupted bliss, was galling, but this was not the only trouble that now bore on them, or the worst. September ended, October went by, November came and Florence strained and white, said to him: "It's no use; I can't wait any longer. It's got to be done."

He said gently, impressively: "It shall be done, my dearest. I will do everything that has to be done." His words gave comfort and relief although she was so angry with him. He could not remember ever being so thoroughly angry with himself. It had been the carelessness of his supreme content, and she had to suffer for it.

A liaison could be hidden from the world at large but not an advanced pregnancy. Society's censure, bigoted and cruel, he could think of as a rule with philosophic disdain; now that he had put her within reach of its brutal power, disdain was changed to sheer fright; but he was never a coward; a challenge called up all the capacity he possessed. He said: "I can't forgive myself; but you can trust me now."

"Yes. Very well."

"But you must think once more. If you decide you want this child, I'll take you away to live abroad, wherever you like."

"No," she said fiercely. "I would like a baby but I don't want a bastard. And I don't want to live abroad for the rest of my life. I won't."

"Very well," he said tenderly.

"And you—would you want—" He held her in his arms, bending his head over hers.

"You are all, all I want."

He went down into London that afternoon and bought several things, including a sheet covered with vulcanized rubber, the invention of Charles Mackintosh. He said to her when they were alone in the Stokefield drawing room that evening: "It will not be formidable, my dear, but there will, I am afraid, be some pain afterward."

"That won't matter once it's over."

"It will be over; but you'll need a little nursing. I shall be there, all the time, but you'll want Mrs. Cox to take care of you as well?"

"Yes, but I don't want her to know."

"She won't know. I shall tell her I am removing a small tumor."

"Don't let her be there."

"Of course not. No one will be there except me."

When he came into her bedroom the following afternoon she was sitting in her nightgown and dressing gown, looking pale and alarmed but resolute. He stood in front of her, willing her to calmness and passed his hands rapidly before her eyes, several times. After some minutes he raised her to her feet and led her to the bed. She knew all the time where she was but consciousness had retreated a short distance. She lay on the pillows, her blue eyes wide open and unmoving. She felt no fear and no distress. She saw him in his shirt sleeves, and had the strange feeling that what was happening was happening to someone else, quite near her. He passed away from her sight, carrying something, to a part of the room she couldn't see because it didn't occur to her to move her head. Then she was sick, and he was holding a towel under her chin.

When her mind had come back into focus again her face had been sponged and wiped and there was a pungent smell of carbolic in the air. He was standing by the bed; she smiled at him and he picked up her hand and kissed it.

It was four hours later that the pain came on. He had gone over to Hillside telling Mrs. Cox he would return in half an hour, but after ten minutes, Mrs. Cox sent one of the housemaids across to ask the doctor to come to Mrs. Ricardo at once. He came immediately, Pritchard following him shortly with a bag containing what he would want for the night.

The hours between evening and early morning were harrowing. He had never tried her with an opiate, having always got sleep for her by natural means, but he remembered that chloral had made her ill and had brought a mild preparation containing opium, but he now found hers was one of the organisms on which this acted in the opposite manner, increasing wakefulness and distress, and though Mrs. Cox produced a bottle of another sort, he did not dare try it. The pain took her quite beyond her own control. He found that sometimes she was aware of his presence and quieted by it as she held his hand; then the influence would wane and the moaning would begin once more. It was six in the morning before she was asleep.

He was exhausted and bathed with sweat. Mrs. Cox had all the time been his most efficient aide and seconder. She had proved herself a thoroughly skillful sick nurse; quick-witted, deft, tireless. At six o'clock, just as the servants were coming downstairs, she went down to the kitchen and shortly returned with a pot of coffee which she took into the dressing room, suggesting that he should go there and lie on the sofa, saying that she would fetch him as soon as Mrs. Ricardo woke.

Two hours later Florence opened her eyes and said: "Where is he?" Mrs. Cox said in a low, soothing tone, "Let me just make you comfortable and then I'll fetch him." She removed a soaked bandage and was putting on a clean one when Florence said: "I want him *now*." Before Mrs. Cox could go to rouse him, he was there, feeling her forehead with the backs of his fingers. The guttered candles and the tumbled bed, the close air and the fire covered with ash, created a scene of deplorable squalor, but Mrs. Cox very soon made an improvement. Florence was propped up to drink a cup of tea, the hearth silently swept and when the fire was burning strongly again, one of the windows was opened at the top. Dr. Gully satisfied himself that there was no fever, that the hemorrhage was not violent and though still in distress she was not in danger. Leaving her in Mrs. Cox's hands he went across the road for bath and breakfast and returning in an hour, told Mrs. Cox to go and lie down, that he would take charge for the rest of the morning.

Florence slept for some time which gratified him but when she woke she was suffering acutely from backache. No position gave her any ease; the pain was relieved when he rubbed the lower region of her back on each side of the spine but it returned when he left off. When Mrs. Cox reappeared, before he expected her, fresh and composed, he asked for pails of cold water and towels and between them they applied a cold-water compress to the lower back. This, constantly renewed, had a good effect at last. There was not a sitz bath in either Stokefield or Hillside but he got one up from the invalid-requisites department of Savory and Moore, and when it was ready, he helped Mrs. Cox to lower her into it, for three minutes at a time, morning and evening. This treatment, which Florence had always enjoyed, brought its usual sense of freshness and soothing.

He found he need not give any directions about the patient's food; Mrs. Cox brought up cups of chicken broth and beef tea, with beautifully hot toast, milk puddings and jellies made from fresh oranges.

After nearly a week she was able to come downstairs and lie on the sofa in front of the drawing-room fire, the room full of flowers which he had got from Covent Garden, roses and freesias in the milk-glass urns, and on the sofa table a bunch of heliotrope in a cornucopia held by a glass hand. He played to her Beethoven, Weber, Chopin; she liked everything he did for her, but she was querulous and exacting. His forbearance and kindness were inexhaustible, but then, she thought, so they ought to be. The memory of those hours of suffering in the candlelit bedroom remained with her, an unforgettable injury.

Filled with regret and remorse as he was, humbly accepting peevish replies to his tenderness, he was sometimes so worn down by her crossness that he was almost glad to get away.

His chief interest at present, outside Stokefield, was in a series of experiments Crookes was conducting in his house in Mornington Road with a young woman called Florence Cook, who seemed to have the powers of a materializing medium; when she went into a trance inside a cabinet or curtained recess, after an interval there appeared outside the niche the form of a young woman, barefoot, clothed only in a white shift with a white veil around her head. She called herself Katie King, and could be spoken to and touched by the watchers.

Crookes took photographs of the materialization; he invented a mixture of magnesium powder and sand which, when ignited, gave a steady, brilliant silver light, by which the exposure was taken. One of these showed Dr. Gully himself, holding the hand of Katie King as she emerged from the cabinet, rapt and blind-looking. His own face was in profile; his eyes were shut against the glare of the magnesium light.

Accounts of the phenomena, attested by witnesses, were published and caused much comment. The *Sporting Times* said: "If I had my way, they should be sent to the treadmill for a few weeks. It would do them good." But the *Spectator* said: "The number of individuals of honourable and upright character who have witnessed the phenomena, justify further, cautious, investigation of the subject." And the *Standard* said: "If there is anything in it beyond imposture and imbecility, there is the whole of another world in it."

He brought up as many topics likely to interest Florence as he could collect, but though he told her of the investigations in Mornington Road, he did not enlarge on them, nor did she ask to know more than he told her. She was however rather interested in a book Mrs. Cox had produced for her amusement, an ephemeris, which contained a section on character based on the rising sign, and an outline of what was likely to befall those born under the twelve signs of the zodiac.

James, it seemed, when she asked him, had not given any attention to astrology. He assumed there must be something in it but he disliked any vulgarization of the occult, and reading destiny by the stars seemed to him to rank with servants' telling fortunes in teacups. He picked up the book as it lay on the sofa table, and put it down again. Florence however read it with considerable, though passing interest. Her own birth sign was Scorpio, and she found that it promised her magnetic good looks, and great good fortune of a material kind. It went on to say: "Some love affair will injure or advance the position, affecting

the honor one way or the other very much." She looked up, gazing about the empty room; that was strange! And it prophesied
a loss of some loved friend in or about her thirtieth year. That
would be about 1875? Not the loss of Janie, she devoutly hoped.
Since Mrs. Cox's goodness to her in the past fortnight, they had
become, at her invitation, on Christian-name terms with each
other. Please heaven she was not to lose the only female friend
she'd ever had. She turned the leaves to see what was said about
James. As his birthday was March 14, he was a Pisces subject,
and the book had in fact more to say that suited him than it
had for her. Pisces was a water sign and its subjects succeeded
best in undertakings connected with water. This was really interesting. They were attracted to the remote, to poetry, mysti-
cism, spiritualism. Another score! Their wealth would be due
to their own work and efforts. Yes. Two marriages were foretold; in one of them the partner was an invalid or afflicted in
some way. Really, this was almost uncanny. Servants would
cause confusion and trouble; well, anybody's might do that, at
almost any time. There would be a treacherous friend who became a secret enemy; that sounded mere melodrama. The nature was slow to anger but very hard to appease. Perhaps. She
was not likely to have an opportunity of proving that. At last,
it referred to Pisces as "the sign of self-undoing." That, at least,
didn't suit James' case; James had an uncommonly good idea
of looking after himself.

Chapter 26

THE leases of Stokefield and Hillside would expire at the March quarter. Should they be renewed?

On a still, cold afternoon in December, Griffith was driving them across Tooting Bec Common when Florence noticed a board saying THIS DESIRABLE RESIDENCE TO LET, on the palings of a house that rose, pale, above leafless garden trees. She had long since known that such a house was there, but now, for the first time, it really caught her attention. It was in the toy-castle mode, with one narrow wing, three stories high, rising behind a square block of only two stories. The first-floor windows projected under little battlements, and under them were the French windows of the ground floor. At each corner of the various roofs, was a turret with a battlemented top; they gave the whole building an effect of soaring into the wintry air. As the carriage came over the common, the house, to the right of the road, presented its garden front; the drive and entrance were around to the left, opening on Bedford Hill. This long, sloping road ran down between commons, sprinkled with trees and thickets till it reached level ground. Here, at its foot, was the Balham Railway Station and a large, imposing public house, the Bedford Hotel, which comprised bars, a billiard saloon and a livery stable.

A road had been laid across the common at right angles to

Bedford Hill on the right side going down, and several houses had been built on it already; lower down there were three large houses giving onto the hill, and lower still, above the Bedford, was a newly built row of six solid, comfortable villas, their front gates on the pavement, but with large gardens enclosed from the common at the back; otherwise, the hill was green and silent. The turreted house that stood at the top of it, in ten acres of its own, was in a leafy retirement.

When Dr. Gully dined at Stokefield that evening, he found that the vision of the afternoon had quite taken possession of Florence's mind. She talked about it with driving enthusiasm. He sat back in his chair after dinner; she was always interesting to watch when she was determined on anything; her face became bolder, the beautiful coloring more intense; one was conscious of the muscles of her neck and shoulders, arms and hands. He watched, and listened fondly, agreeing that the place would be well worth an inspection. Mrs. Cox sat at a little distance with her needlework; she was also listening, intent but silent.

The next day Florence got an order to view; the house, she found, had been built in 1822 and was originally called Bedford Grove; the rage for medievalism had quickly changed its name to The Priory. The sight of it, arresting her at the moment when she wanted a house, had so worked on her imagination that she was now absorbed in the project of having, for the first time in her life, a house entirely her own to be furnished and arranged exactly as she pleased.

Two days afterward, she stood arm in arm with James on The Priory drive. The front door was like the door of a church; to the left of it, a small greenhouse projected over the French window of a sitting room; to the right was the large window with pointed upper panes of what was clearly the dining room. This room and the large drawing room behind it, and the master bedroom on the first floor, were really spacious; the other rooms, though convenient, were smaller; the house contained fifteen altogether. It was perhaps a little large for her—but might not a house be needed, at any time, large enough for both of them? He murmured something about this and she responded by a pressure of her arm to the pressure of his. The idea of living with him was a prospect of solid happiness that she looked forward to, it was the hoped-for thing in life. It was not the idea of magical excitement it had once been.

The house had not stood empty for long and was in excellent condition. It required, she decided, considerable redecoration, but what remained of the work of 1822 she meant to retain, it was too good to demolish. The hall, with a groined roof, had woodwork painted to look like marble, dark green with red and yellow veins; the banisters were olive green picked out with gilt; and in two of the downstairs rooms there were the original wall coverings: In the room on the left of the hall that opened into the greenhouse, there was a red-patterned paper with a frieze of Prince of Wales feathers delicately traced in black, and the walls of the drawing room were buff, with a dado four feet above the floor, of flowers and arabesques, in purples, blues and muted rose colors.

The stable and coach house, to which she led him after their tour of the house, were at the left of the front door, standing on two sides of a yard that had a drain in the middle of it. They had stalls for four horses and room for two carriages, and she began to think that as well as the carriage and pair she would have a little phaeton and a pair of ponies to draw it; she could then drive herself all about the common without having the carriage put to; the carriage would of course be needed for journeys into London.

There was a small ornamental lodge at the far end of the garden where a gate opened onto the common, and this would have to do for Mr. and Mrs. Griffith for the time being but it was not commodious, and walking down the drive with Dr. Gully, she had decided, before they reached the gate on Bedford Hill where Griffith was waiting for them with the carriage, that another lodge, *en suite* with the house, must be built at that entrance.

"This is where your lodge will be!" she called up to the box, waving toward the grass plot beside the entrance gates. Griffith touched his hat in cordial assent. She climbed into the carriage and Dr. Gully got in after her. In her enthusiasm, she seemed a creature of fire and air. To draw her earthward, as they drove down the hill, he covered her hand with his and said:

"And where am *I* to live, meanwhile?"

"As near as you can, of course," she said at once. "I thought you had been looking at one of those six houses?" He had. He had wanted her to ask about it, but with her head so full of the furnishing of fifteen rooms, as well as of the contents of stables, flower beds and a greenhouse, she had not had leisure to think of anything else. She was now, however, as ready to hear as he could wish. The house was called Sutton House, at the end of the row nearest the Bedford. It was five minutes' walk away from The Priory. "Five minutes of *your* walking," she said, with a memory of Malvern.

The six houses, all alike, were solid, comfortable, dignified, even. Each floor contained two large rooms and two smaller ones, but on the ground floor, one of the latter was taken up by an entrance hall. This had a fireplace where a bright fire would be welcoming on a cold day, and the panels on each side of the front door were of engraved glass: urns full of plants of a moonstone opacity on a clear ground.

The large front room had a black marble chimneypiece, the large back one, one of fretted white marble; these were the dining and drawing rooms respectively. Their modern windows,

wide sheets of plate glass without glazing bars, let in an un-
stemmed flood of light.

The room which attracted him immediately was the one next
the drawing room. Its smaller area made it seem lofty. On the
left-hand wall was an arched fireplace; a tall French window
flanked by shutters opened onto a little wrought-iron balcony,
from which a flight of ironwork steps led down to a garden.
Unfurnished as it was, its proportions, its air, made him feel
that this was his study and that nowhere, not even at Malvern,
had he had one more completely to his mind.

In a surprisingly short time after he had seen its outside, he
was, in imagination, as firmly settled in the house as Florence
was settled in The Priory. Having decided to move into it, he
meant never to move again, unless, until, he set up house with
her as man and wife.

It was the beginning of January, with less than three months
before the March quarter. Florence, ably seconded by Mrs. Cox,
entered on a campaign of choosing furniture, curtains, upholstery, wallpapers and carpets. Mrs. Cox was invaluable. She
made lists of what was needed for servants' bedrooms and the
servants' hall, for stocking kitchen and scullery, butler's pantry
and laundry. She found the drapers, crockery shops and hard-
ware merchants which sold the durable at a reasonable price,
setting Florence at liberty for the stimulating work of furnishing and decorating the principal rooms. Mrs. Cox shopped up
and down Streatham High Road while Florence drove into London to consult Heals, Maples, Shoolbreds and Nosotti of Oxford Street, the shop for looking glasses.

She chose the room on the left of the hall for her morning
room, taking up the tone of the walls in crimson moreen curtains and a crimson carpet covered with flowers and ferns. Over
the hearth she set a mirror surrounded by small shelves and
brackets, on each of which she stood one of her pieces of glass.

In three corners she placed tiers of ornamental shelves to take further pieces, so that all around the room the eye caught a fugitive sparkle, called out by the aqueous light coming through the greenhouse. A sofa, padded and buttoned, covered with crimson satin, stood between the fire and the view of plants and exotic greenery.

A dining room did not allow much scope for personal views—a suite of Spanish mahogany, a brown-and-yellow flocked wallpaper, heavily framed paintings of fruit and dead game—and Florence passed on to the drawing room. Here there was a large French window opening on the lawn at the other side of which stood a giant oak tree, whose arms, viewed from a distance, seemed to stretch halfway across that side of the house. At the left-hand end of the drawing room was another French window, and Florence had already determined to build a little conservatory over it. Meantime, she chose blue as the prevailing tone. Satin curtains of lapis lazuli blue hung from pelmets cut to look like battlements; the chairs were upholstered in azure brocade; on the carpet, wreaths of flowers twined on a deep-blue ground. The black-and-gold piano stood at an angle against one wall. She bought a cabinet of ebony and gilt, decorated with porcelain medallions of shepherds and shepherdesses, and a set of small chairs and a settee, with frames and canework all of gilt.

The intensive choosing and shopping and arranging kept her faculties on the stretch and she could never have accomplished her designs so rapidly without Mrs. Cox's help. Mrs. Cox knew when the shops would deliver and when the painters, carpenters and upholsterers would come, and she was always at The Priory before they arrived, to supervise and direct. Many a morning she set out on her half hour's walk to be at the house before nine o'clock, while Florence came later in the carriage, sometimes going on to the bottom of the hill to see how the doctor's workmen were getting on.

The doctor's ideas of house decorating were on a simpler scale than hers, but his solid, elegant furniture, which had been in store since he left Malvern, and the curtains and carpets Ann and Ellen helped him choose (his sisters' taste, he felt, was more in keeping with his own than Florence's, even if she had been able to spare him any time at present) created a comfortable, harmonious interior, into which his cherished objects fitted beautifully. The study fulfilled the vision he had had of it as he stood on its echoing boards. On the right-hand wall his bookshelves went to the ceiling, the top ones reached by his library steps. Facing them, his desk stood, a little out into the room, so that the light as he wrote came over his left shoulder. On each side of the hearth were cupboards full of shelves; over them he hung his two favorite paintings, copies of a Carlo Dolci and of two angels' heads by Fra Angelico on a gold ground. The colors of the room, soft greens and browns, showed off his polished brass and silver: the heavy silver and crystal inkstand inscribed by a grateful patient, the silver candlesticks, the ormolu clock on the chimneypiece that the bath attendants had given him.

Though his schemes were carried out with the concentrated energy that produces speed, they did not take much toll of him, but Florence, he saw, was becoming feverish with activity. Pleasurable creative occupation was a great aid to spirits and therefore, up to a point, to health, but even this could be overdone.

Since the illness in November they had meant to go somewhere to give her change of air, but it was useless to travel in England for health in December; then these preoccupations had seized them; but now that the greater part of the work was done, he suggested to Florence that they should have a fortnight at the sea. She agreed willingly—she was feeling quite knocked up. She said that Mrs. Cox must come with them, but affairs at The Priory were so forward, she could leave them in the hands of her reliable cook and an excellent housemaid, Mary Ann Keeber, if Pritchard would walk up every day and take a look.

Dr. Gully was resigned to Mrs. Cox's presence in their party, but he was, secretly, affronted by Florence's saying that she and Mrs. Cox would share a bedroom. He was not a man to invade any woman's bedroom and since the calamity of November he and Florence had tacitly agreed that their union as lovers must not continue for the time being, but he felt he did not deserve this treatment. However he said nothing, from a feeling that he owed her a great forbearance, as well as from a sense of personal dignity.

They set about deciding where to go. When he spoke of the south coast, Mrs. Cox asked if he meant Brighton. But he said Brighton was now becoming disagreeable from the numerous flash persons who crowded it, cheek by jowl with the trippers, brought by excursion trains. The idea that he might see a bulky form propped up in a carriage, a face glancing at him with hideous, jeering recognition, poisoned the whole neighborhood for him.

They settled on Bognor, on the borders of Sussex and Hampshire. To the west, along the coast, was Bournemouth. He wished he could have made a tour, taking Florence to see the Shelleys. When she should be his wife—he sighed and began turning the pages of *Black's Guide* to find a hotel.

Bognor was charming, with an out-of-season population of well-bred visitors who had come for peace and the February sunshine. In the first half of the morning the shore was almost unpeopled. He and Florence walked on hard sand washed clean by the retreating tide. The waves left narrow reaches of shingle and stones that were full of curiosities: fringed clusters bearing brown pods covered with raised orange spots, pieces of sea-green bottle glass worn opaque and smooth, a beautifully veined pebble, a fernlike seaweed, glistening pink, pressed flat against a white stone. Florence had brought with her a book, *Sea-Weeds: Instructions How to Find, Preserve and Classify Them*, and had provided herself with frames, blotting paper and an album. Everything she found on the shore that she liked, he put into the tin vasculum slung over his ulster and carried home for her.

In spite of a nervous organization that was liable to prey on her health, Florence, as he had already observed, was essentially a hardy little creature. With her light feet almost printless on the sand, her face turned to the sea wind, her hair, worn loose under a small hat, blowing out in a fan behind her head, her shepherd's plaid wrap billowing in sculptural folds, she was the very spirit of what he thought most attractive in women. They would walk on the shore for two hours before luncheon. In the afternoon she drove out with Mrs. Cox; sometimes he went with them. In the evenings they all sat in a private sitting room, Florence busy with her apparatus for preserving seaweed, Mrs. Cox in the intervals of needlework, looking on, admiring and giving help with a deft finger when it was needed. Their conversation was almost all about the work going on at The Priory. As Florence's firm white fingers spread out and attached the seaweed, her mind ran on paperhangers and carpet layers.

He sat at the other side of the table, sometimes reading Gosse's work on marine biology, oftener watching her fingers and her bent head. He knew that Mrs. Cox was sometimes watching him, but he did not care.

This seaweed album was not the only one in Florence's possession. Two years ago, while she was at Brookefield, she had bought a very handsome one, covered in violet velvet with thickly gilded leaves. This was to preserve all his published writing of an ephemeral kind, every article he contributed to a learned journal, every letter he wrote to a newspaper, every report of a speech. At first she had been very busy with it, for he had a collection of items awaiting arrangement of some sort. She had devised a method of hinging the papers on the album leaves, so that each side could be read. For some time she had snatched up everything he brought her and mounted it immediately. Now there were several cuttings tucked into the book, awaiting a convenient moment for mounting them all together.

Working on her collection of seaweeds reminded her of the other album and of the arrears. As he sat watching her work from the other side of the lamp, she knew that it was in his mind also and she felt some compunction, a little irritation at the same time.

Next morning when they were on the shore, he said: "I have been thinking of altering the name of Sutton House."

"You have?" she said, her eyes bright with the reflection of light from the sea.

"You changed Alverstoke to Stokefield, and Bedford Grove was changed for you to The Priory." Her little hands were clasped on his arm.

"Yes."

"So I think I shall call my house Orwell Lodge—our third name. Do you like the idea?"

The shore was empty for leagues around, the glassy, bitter, relentless waves were racing toward their feet.

"Yes, I do," she said. Their lips met in a kiss such as they had not given for a long time.

Chapter 27

IN spite of being so much occupied by their new houses, they would have liked to stay longer at Bognor. The holiday had charms for all of them. To Dr. Gully, being under the same roof with Florence meant that he had hours and half hours of being with her, of strolls with her, in the hotel garden or on the esplanade, all impromptu, unintended, which at home would have required arrangements to bring about. Mrs. Cox, whose life had been one of self-denial, anxiety and hard work, enjoyed every moment of her stay in a luxurious hotel, with a companionship that meant a great deal to her. To Florence the visit gave another pleasure. She naturally attracted the discreet admiration of the male visitors as she came in off the beach, brilliant from wind and sun, or descended to dinner in a black silk dress with a train shaped like a wave sweeping after her. This she accepted as a matter of course, without appearing to notice it; but in this hotel, the women visitors, ladies with husbands and children, highly born, shy sisters accompanied by brothers, pairs of ladies taking a holiday together, all accepted, as perfectly *comme il faut,* the young married lady with her companion and the elderly gentleman who was with her. They made polite remarks to her about the weather and the state of the tide; there was nothing that could be called conversation, but their friendly "Good morning," the smile and thanks of a mother as she retrieved a large colored ball from a flower bed and rolled it back to a very small, solemn boy, soothed and gratified Florence in a way that took her by surprise. She and Dr. Gully decided that though they were called home now, they would return for another little holiday in a month's time. "Shall we come back here?" she asked, on his arm, walking under the shelter he provided against a rather boisterous sea wind; but the pleasure of taking her about, even in Mrs. Cox's company, made him eager to find a new scene; he suggested Southsea, a place that had the character of the Sussex seaboard, before the coast gave way to the rich warmth of the west. From there they could visit Lord Nelson's flagship laid up at Portsmouth, and take a pleasure steamer across to the Isle of Wight. In the airs of April, these expeditions would be enchanting. She agreed. Even in her state of absorption over The Priory, the prospect allured her.

At home once more, she entered on all her affairs with renewed enthusiasm. The Priory required a large staff of servants: a butler, a footman, a cook and three housemaids, the lady's maid, a gardener and two assistants, Griffith the coachman, a groom and a stableboy. These had now been assembled, and Florence found that a part of almost every morning had to be spent in dealing with one or other of them and listening to their representations. She did not delegate anything of this kind to Mrs. Cox; she liked to feel that she was in control of her own establishment. Though not indulgent she was anxious to be fair and as the quarters were comfortable and a good table was kept in the servants' hall, a general contentment reigned.

The furnishing of the house was now, in all essentials, complete. Her bedroom was the large room on the first floor above the dining room, with one of the projecting windows that looked over the common. In the right-hand wall, the fireplace, of steel and brass, was arched and fretted like a medieval tomb, and over it a great pointed arch rose to the ceiling. These antique features could not be disguised, but the furnishing was modern and expensive, in tones of green and pink. There was a deep-piled flowered carpet and facing the big window, a large glittering brass bed, of the kind furniture dealers called Arabian, with a canopy and vestigial curtains at the head. These curtains were of green brocade with pink and cream-colored flowers; those at the window were similar with an inner pair of white lace ones, mounted on pink tarlatan; the blinds were white Venetians. There was a tall cupboard in the corner to the left of the window; a chaise longue stood at an angle across the floor.

Leading out of the bedroom, through a door at the bed's head, were two dressing rooms, one beyond the other. There was no bathroom in The Priory and in the smaller room Florence had a washstand, the sitz bath brought from Stokefield, and a hip bath with its cans and pails. In the further room were the cupboards for her clothes, chests of drawers for underlinen, a cheval glass and a dressing table. The windows of the dressing rooms, and the small windows of the bedroom were in a row above the front door, all wreathed with wistaria.

The other bedrooms on the first floor were considerably smaller than the master bedroom, so Florence had given Mrs. Cox the large room at the end of the upper story. The rest of the rooms on this floor were servants' bedrooms but this one was a magnificent room with a window in each of three walls, the middle one looking out into the boughs of the giant oak. Mrs. Cox had never occupied, seldom even seen a room of such size and airiness. She had no furniture of her own to bring to it, but Florence furnished it with lavish attention to comfort and convenience. The fire was lit morning and evening by the housemaid who toiled up the extra flight of stairs with the hot water for Mrs. Cox's morning bath and for her washstand at night.

The servants were not obliging in their manner to her. They resented having to wait on her when they regarded her as beneath themselves because of her touch of colored blood; but Mrs. Cox had been accustomed to this sort of thing all her life; it had no power now to injure her content and happiness.

The flat roof of the lower block made a wide, lead-covered floor outside the windows of the top story, reached by a small door in the wall outside Mrs. Cox's room. As the lovely April weather came on she would steal out, walking on the leads; the turrets and the chimneys rose above her; a pierced stone parapet ran around the three sides of the roof; and she would pause, leaning on it, above the stable yard, or above the front drive, or overlooking the lawn and the great oak with the common spreading beyond it and the spire of Streatham church rising above distant trees.

The previous occupiers had left the garden in good order and Florence, since January, had been instructing the gardener with might and main. The beds all around the house were filled with bedding plants, now breaking into spring flowers. Quantities of standard roses had been set and their buds were already forming: damask roses, moss roses, tea-scented roses, Noisette, Bourbon and Maréchal Niel. To the right of the lawn, close behind the paling dividing it from the common, was a natural dip in the ground; this had been turned into a small sunk garden, led down to by three circular steps, with pebbled paths between its beds. The plants had been chiefly roses and Florence increased them, setting Provence roses among the rest for the sake of their heavenly scent. She had an iron garden seat put here, molded in the form of overlapping fern leaves. When the roses should be in full flower and scent she meant to sit here with James.

The Priory entrance on Bedford Hill consisted of three wooden gates, the large central carriage gate and a small one on each side. The middle one and the right-hand ones were bolted at night and sometimes during the day; the left-hand one was fastened by a lock and anyone could get in who had a key. Florence had had three cut; she and Mrs. Cox kept one each; the third she gave to Dr. Gully.

It pleased him that he should not always have to ring for entrance. When the housemaids came down first thing in the morning, one of them unbolted the front door, the French windows of the dining room and drawing room, the French window of the morning room and the greenhouse door that opened onto the path. He usually came to lunch and then he would ring the front doorbell but sometimes he walked up soon after breakfast, let himself in at the gate, took the short walk down the drive to the greenhouse, opened its door and passed through delicate, fragrant greenery to the French window of the morning room. If she were not there he would seat himself in one of the crimson satin chairs, knowing that she would come soon. Mrs. Cox was frequently—usually, in fact—to be found in the drawing room; she did not appear to use her own room as a sitting room—but the morning room was free from her.

He had now accepted Mrs. Cox's presence with almost total resignation. He was not a man to consent to an arrangement and then grumble and repine at it. His cheerful, humane temperament, his intelligent capacity for enjoyment, enabled him to make the very best of the matter while it was necessary. He had, at odd moments, kindly questioned her; she had not dwelt on the details of the grim poverty of her widowhood, the anxiety for her sons, the wearisome career of a daily governess by which she had eked out the meager income from letting the apartments in her house in Lancaster Road; but a man of his experience could fill them in. Smooth and neat as she was, he thought her face bore the marks of this hardship, though the spectacles she wore made it difficult to read her eyes. He was even glad that fate should have, for the time being, dropped this astonishing bonus into her lap: luxurious living conditions, a generous salary, frequent presents for her wardrobe, a fostering attitude toward her children, and all at the hands of an employer with whom she was on terms of an equal friendship.

Florence had, he knew, established a completely confidential relationship with her, except over the one matter as to which, he assumed, Mrs. Cox needed no confidences. It was not to be wondered at. Not only was Mrs. Cox sympathetic, trustworthy, devoted, she had, he had come to think, some of that strange quality possessed by Negresses who had been body servants in the families of slaveowners, and Indian ayahs who nursed white children now, a genius for taking care of people, which gave the ones they waited on a sense of comfort and security that in the case of neurotic women became like a drug. Florence had said to him: "I could never do without her now." To this he had said nothing. If—when—he became her husband, he would speak from a vantage ground. Till then, it was better to be silent.

Mrs. Cox, he could see, was not only deeply thankful for her lot; she loved Florence. She never obtruded her feelings but they inspired everything she did. He knew, too, that Mrs. Cox admired him, that she liked his company and conversation, and yet that she was—jealous was too strong a word—was sorry that Florence had a stronger feeling for him than she had for her companion. All this was irrational, totally absurd, but it was suppressed, and he was sure it always would be; and that being so, he really did not care about it. He had lived too long in a position of authority to be inconvenienced by merely knowing of such feelings; he was kind and liberal to people who behaved themselves sensibly; what they felt was their own affair.

Though the distance was greater between Orwell Lodge and

The Priory than between Hillside and Stokefield he dropped in even more frequently than he had in the Leigham Court Road. The spaciousness of the house and grounds made it possible to be there without ostensibly seeking her. He took, besides, a great interest in the place. He would stop to see how the building of the lodge was going on, and walk around the house to see how far the workmen had got with the conservatory over the drawing-room window. Florence's burst of creative energy in her furnishing and decoration had surprised and delighted him; her garden, her morning room, had inexpressible charms for him because they were hers. The belief that their marriage, however delayed, was coming nearer all the time, that in all probability this was the house where they would live together, led him gradually to assume that he had a right to be in it.

His right was thoroughly recognized by Florence; she expected, demanded to see him daily, though often she treated him more as a husband, to be argued with or taken to task, than a lover whose every word was a revelation. She spoke to him now, if she felt inclined, with an utter lack of restraint, was irritable or contradictory or even abusive. Their fallings-out were almost always over her drinking. He had several times seen her take sherry or Marsala between meals. Once he had laid his hand on hers as she was filling a glass, and said: "Won't you leave it, to please me?" and she had let him put his arm around her waist and take her into the garden; but this was once only. One morning when she was not in the morning room he walked across the hall and saw her by the dining-room sideboard. A full glass of brown sherry was in her hand. She saw him approach and put it hurriedly to her mouth. She set it down empty. The speed with which she had drunk it horrified him. He said, "That is not good for you."

She burst out angrily: "Can't I take a glass of sherry in my own house without *your* permission?"

"You can't take it *with* my permission, certainly, at this time of day." When raised, her voice was surprisingly strong.

"I'm sick of this!" she shouted. "There's no harm in just the amount *I* take. I don't take more than ordinary people do!" But he feared she did.

During a seaside holiday he would be able to control her more easily than when they were at home. One of her reasons for flying to the sherry bottle was the sudden exhaustion that overcame her when she had tired herself out. That he could prevent when they were at the seaside with everything planned for rest and recreation.

When they were alone, discussing a plan for enjoyment, she would sometimes revert to the old manner, returning his kisses with passion. To be held in his arms was, at present, all her idea of sexual pleasure; the memory of pain was still too keen to let her think of anything else. In her bedroom they would sometimes lie in each other's arms on the chaise longue, exchanging kisses. He did not ask for a renewal of intercourse—he knew that the idea of it frightened her—but he spoke sometimes of their future marriage, when there would be no fear and their love would have the final, exquisite bliss of completion once again. Lying in his arms and listening to his murmured words, she was almost willing to let him take her; then the knife-edged recollection made her shudder and she clung to him as a protector, against himself.

But to be under the same roof with him at Southsea, so that she could have his society at all hours, and, in the frequent absences and withdrawals of Janie, his kisses and embraces, was a prospect very agreeable to her; and so was the idea of moving among ladies who would accept her as their equal, their superior, even, whom they would like to speak to, but would fear to intrude upon.

Chapter 28

In his intermittent correspondence with Dr. Fernie Dr. Gully had mentioned his plan of visiting Southsea and Dr. Fernie had told him of an excellent establishment, a very superior boarding house on the South Parade, where they made you thoroughly comfortable and the sea was so near, it looked as if it were going to pour through your windows. Dr. Gully engaged two bedrooms and a sitting room, Florence having again told him that she and Mrs. Cox would share a bedroom, and that this time she would be taking no maid with her. Humphries was about to leave and her successor would not be available till their return. Florence's turnover in the matter of servants, he told himself, was somewhat rapid. He was afraid that her peculiar situation had an unsettling effect on her household; he was very glad that the head housemaid, Mary Ann Keeber, was such an excellent girl and hoped devoutly that she would turn out to be a permanency. Meanwhile Mrs. Cox had assured Florence that she could do everything for her at Southsea that Humphries would have done.

"That is very obliging of Mrs. Cox," Dr. Gully said when he heard of the arrangement.

"Oh, she will like it," said Florence. "It pleases her to do things for me. . . ."

Before they set off, he had a work to make ready for the publishers. He had accepted an invitation to act as the next president of the National Association of Spiritualists, beginning his term of office in August, and he felt he would like to mark his presidential year by a publication he had long had in mind. He had at last persuaded Sir Percy and Lady Shelley to consent to the publication of some of the spirit drawings made by their niece nine years ago. Of two hundred and forty-eight drawings made over to him, he had chosen twelve, the first in chronological order, illustrating the spirit's parting from the body, its welcome by angels and its hovering over the ones it loved who were still on earth. The radiant quality of the figures, the poignant emotion they conveyed, made him long to see them published. The frauds of disreputable mediums and the brutal contempt shown to people who had investigated the matter by those who had not, inspired him with a yearning to give the public—some of the public—a chance to see these speaking drawings for themselves. The firm of E. W. Allen, in Ave Maria Lane off Ludgate Hill, was bringing them out in the form of a book; the child, now a young lady of twenty-one, was not to be mentioned by name nor were her relations; but he himself wrote a signed preface, describing the origin of the drawings and vouching for their genuineness. He added that if the public showed interest in this first series, he would publish others of a kind more arresting still. With this task completed, he left with the ladies for Southsea.

The weather was delicious; opposite their windows the Isle of Wight lay low down in the heaving, glittering sea, which, as Dr. Fernie had promised, seemed as if it would pour into the rooms. Florence had originally thought that she would prefer the comings and goings of a hotel, but actually the smaller size of this establishment meant that contact with the other guests was more frequent, in the dining room or the glassed-in veranda where they sat in wicker chairs, reading newspapers in the morning sun. The old gentleman with his wife and sister-in-law, the anxious mother with the little girl who had been ordered sea air, at whom Dr. Gully looked without appearing to look, a couple of elderly ladies, dowdy and vigorous, two parents with their child and its nurse, all of them quiet, ordinary and well bred, were glad of a word now and again with the interesting young woman, of high fashion, accompanied by the companion, clearly a most valuable person, and the distinguished elderly gentleman—someone said he was a well-known doctor, probably a relation, or at least a very old friend of the family.

The weather being so warm they made an expedition every day, one of the first to Portsmouth, to look at the *Victory*. To Mrs. Cox it was a treat to go anywhere, and Florence, naturally, was alive with interest at the spectacle of the great ship, so fresh, clean and stately, with the sea dancing beyond it. The brightness on deck made the cockpit seem at first as dark as night, till they made out the midshipmen's berth where Nelson had died. Florence, holding his arm, said softly: "Could you have done anything for him?"

"No, he was shot through the spine. I suppose we could have made it a little easier for him, during the three hours it took him to die."

"With chloroform, or laudanum?"

"I don't think he would have taken them; he wanted to be kept aware of the progress of the battle." As they came on deck again, he was thinking of Tennyson's line:

Mighty seaman, tender and true.

Leaving his wife for Emma Hamilton had earned Nelson the second half of this tribute, from no less a one than the poet laureate. How far would this generous feeling be extended to lesser men who did the same sort of thing?

They took a pleasure steamer to Ryde the following day, a voyage that would have enraptured him if he could have had Florence to himself; but though Mrs. Cox, to her credit, retired below stairs to the saloon, leaving them on deck to enjoy the sea and air, they presently found, leaning on the rail, the two strong-featured, sensible, tedious ladies from their lodgings who, when Florence bowed and smiled to them, came up, tentatively, to exchange remarks, and were welcomed by her so cordially that they remained a party of four until Mrs. Cox rejoined them, to make five, a few moments before the steamer reached the end of the long wooden arm of Ryde pier. They parted company from the ladies on landing, and he set about finding a carriage to take them to Carisbrooke Castle; but beneath the charming interest of the drive itself, and the pleasure of being at least in the same carriage as Florence though not alone with her, was the uneasy perception of how much pleasure she now took in chance friendly encounters with such women as Miss Selver and Miss Puddifoot; once she would have voted their society a dead bore and have brusquely avoided it. It was painfully clear that the social isolation she had once vowed she did not mind was becoming irksome to her, and it was something he could do nothing to mend.

Twelve miles across the island in a westerly direction was Freshwater Gate, outside it, Tennyson's house, Farringford. Once, finding himself in the neighborhood, he would have written to ask his former patient if he might call; he believed he would have received a cordial answer. Now, since he could scarcely go by himself, he could not go at all.

It was natural to have a pocket edition of Tennyson's poetry with him on this holiday, and he was reading it next morning, sitting by himself in the glassed-in veranda while he waited for the others. The idea of Farringford and The Solent made him turn to "Maud"; he read the passage that had stirred his imagination years before: the ominous rising of the wind after the troth plight of the lovers, first rattling the laurel leaves, then swaying the cedar boughs, while its sound came off the sea. The noise of the wind rising on The Solent, the presage of storm, could be heard, it was said, a mile inland:

> Is that enchanted moan only the swell
> Of the long waves that roll in yonder bay?

This holiday though so similar in kind to the recent one at Bognor had already assumed a different emotional coloring.

At home once more, he wrote to Queensborough Terrace for news. His daughter-in-law was expecting her fourth child; and Ann and Ellen were there, helping to take care of the others. The baby, a girl, was born safely on May 26; he received a letter saying so on May 27, and walked up to The Priory after breakfast to give the news to Florence. She delighted him by her sympathy and her ready congratulations. Then she exclaimed: "I should like to be a godmother!" He paused for a fraction of a second, then said warmly, "I'll tell them so when I go." The situation was perhaps slightly awkward, but in all the circumstances, he felt that he could not refuse to try to get her this gratification.

He paid his first visit to the baby a few days later; she was a lovely, healthful little thing, but when the nurse brought her into her mother's bedroom, she had taken a crying fit and was refusing all attempts at consolation. Her penetrating wail distressed her mother, her father, her two great-aunts, everyone present except her grandfather. Dr. Gully took her in his arms and she became quiet at once. He looked at her little face with close attention.

"I think she will be a beauty," he said.

"*We* think so, of course," said Willie, "but can you really say, as soon as this?"

"That is how she strikes me," his father answered.

Downstairs, he mentioned to Willie that Mrs. Ricardo would be pleased to be asked to stand godmother. Willie said that unless Bessie had already committed them to two godmothers, an invitation should certainly be sent. He would have found it very hard indeed to refuse his father's known wish, and neither he nor his wife wished to slight the lady who at any time might become the wife of their child's grandfather.

Florence was deeply gratified by the invitation to stand which she received in the course of the week. She did not, with what Dr. Gully felt to be praiseworthy tact, accept the invitation to the ceremony, leaving the child's other godmother to carry her to the font; but as the baby, christened Florence Julia, was to be called Florence, she sent her the beautiful little gold repeater watch with "Florence" enameled on the back, and her six-stranded seed pearl necklace. These presents were the finest the baby received. Dr. Gully was glad of that.

Like water finding its own level, life between the two houses settled to a pitch of contentment varied by the same recurring dissatisfactions. Florence and Mrs. Cox came perhaps once a week to dine at Orwell Lodge. The walking distance though short was not practicable for a lady of Mrs. Ricardo's position, and Griffith would bring them in the carriage and call for them at half past nine. These occasions gave Dr. Gully the sort of pleasure a man expects from a domestic engagement—pleasant with some irritations; but sometimes the unhappy element overcame the agreeable. One evening when he came into the hall to greet them, Florence reeked of sherry. She and Mrs. Cox went upstairs to the smaller of the spare rooms on the first floor, which was always prepared for them with hot water and towels. Mrs. Cox usually made a point of descending a minute or two after Florence so that she and the doctor should have time for a few kisses. On this evening he was shocked at Florence's breath being so loaded with spirit; her face too showed what a stiff dose she had taken. He took her in his arms but did not kiss her. "My dear, you've had a great deal to drink," he said gently.

"I've had *something* to drink," she said, in loud, angry tones. "Why shouldn't I, with the life *I* lead! Anybody would think we *were* married, the way you talk to me!"

In the open doorway of the drawing room, Pritchard's face showed, for an instant, shocked dismay. Then he said: "Dinner is served, sir." As he retired, Mrs. Cox came into the room. Dr. Gully felt that there was nothing for it but to ignore Florence's words, and could only hope that his doing so wouldn't provoke another outburst of drunken captiousness.

They sat down to dinner. Florence at first said she wanted nothing, but his influence, which, after all, was very great, persuaded her to take some spoonfuls of soup. She looked about the table and said suddenly: "I took some sherry while I was dressing because one never gets anything to drink here."

This was untrue; wine was always on the sideboard and brought to table if asked for. It was there now.

"Pritchard," Dr. Gully said, "I daresay the ladies will take a glass of wine." Pritchard retired to the sideboard, muttering soundlessly.

One glass, Dr. Gully felt, might be risked in the interests of peace. If she demanded more, he would force the issue and speak with angry severity. With time, however, and the taking of some food, the effect of the sherry began to wear off. For once he was glad of Mrs. Cox's efforts at uninteresting conversation.

The immediate result of this evening was an improvement but the memory caused him considerable anxiety. He thought that if he were with her all the time, he could probably keep her from drinking the sherry and Marsala that she took between meals; her drinking of table wine remained, as far as he saw, moderate; but while he was separated from her by the length of Bedford Hill, he couldn't exert the hourly influence that was needed, and the habit was getting slightly but perceptibly worse. If only he could marry her by special license in the next twenty-four hours!

She seemed now, for the time being, rather more affectionate. He loved spending hours in her house and garden but it gave him peculiar pleasure to have her at Orwell Lodge by herself; she sometimes would come in the carriage without Mrs. Cox, in the afternoon, stay to dinner and be called for by Griffith at half past nine; on these occasions there were still halcyon spells when they charmed each other with the old passion. One afternoon at the end of May she came down in the carriage with four pots of carnations that she had budded for him in the greenhouse. Pritchard and the doctor carried them into the house and stood them on a table in the drawing-room window, where their scent began to rise and hang in the air. The large, three-sided window let in an afternoon light which made the colors of the room glowing and tender. The walls were rose red, and many of his pictures in softly gleaming gold frames hung above the white marble chimneypiece. A creeper edged the window with leaves of translucent green. All around were the easy chairs, fringed, padded, buttoned, that she had known at Malvern. On the sofa was the green satin cushion Ellen had embroidered with a wreath of honeysuckle, beside it a volume of Shelley's poetry, open at "Prometheus Unbound." Florence picked it up and put it down again.

"Ah," he said, "it was a very long time ago that I first read those lines—so wild and gloomy and mysterious—"

"And so dull," she added. He smiled indulgently. She took a copy of *Punch* from a small table by the hearth and sat down, her feet stretched out on a crystal-beaded footstool. He was frequently in two minds as to whether to give up taking *Punch*. The excellent drawings gave him so much pleasure—the beautiful ones of Du Maurier, with their observation, if a one-sided one, of social life, the rough, humorous ones of Charles Keene, creating life itself; but he objected to the tone of some of the letterpress, particularly to the persistent, crude and vulgar attacks on spiritualism. Florence, however, did not bother with the reading matter; she enjoyed looking at the pictures, and had sometimes thought she would take in *Punch* herself, only as she could always see it at Orwell Lodge, there would really be no point in this. Her black silk stockings were open-worked on the instep, so much *à jour* that the white skin seemed to be covered by black lace; her black kid slippers had winged bows on them. In these shoes and stockings her feet had an exotic look, like orchids or tropical shells, but were not so beautiful as when they were bare: slender, arched feet, as undistorted as other women's hands. He came and stood over her; the subtle, gracious light in the room, the scent of the carnations, the solitude, helped create one of their heavenly moments. She dropped the magazine and leaned back against him, and he caressed her temples with his fingertips; she had forgotten how delightful the sensation was. Presently, in the infinite quiet of the room, she said: "Of course it doesn't matter now, but I haven't been unwell for quite a long time." His fingers stopped their movement.

"Indeed! For how long?"

"Oh, nearly nine weeks, I think."

"Why did you not tell me before?"

"I didn't think it mattered, now."

"Well, in that sense, of course it doesn't, but it's very important to keep this function working. If it doesn't, the irritation it's meant to throw off may become a burden on some other function. It may affect the brain or the lungs or the kidneys."

"Oh, dear!"

"There's no need to be alarmed. I am only explaining why we must put the matter right."

"How can that be done?"

"There is a method, in hydrotherapy; it involves a daily treatment, rather rigorous and complicated. Otherwise there is a prescription that is usually successful."

"I would rather have the medicine."

"Well, I think it might be best, in the circumstances. But once, you would have been willing to have the water treatment, wouldn't you?"

"Yes, and in a way, I would be now; but I have so much to do, at present; and the treatment does make rather an invalid of one, every day!" The inconveniences it would entail were obvious; he did not even sigh.

Next morning he wrote a prescription for oil of savin, bromide of potassium and tincture of chloride of iron and took it to Smith's, the chemist he used in Balham, directing the bottle to be sent to Mrs. Ricardo at The Priory. He had once written: "I would warn all women against the employment of ferruginous medicines given for the purpose of forcing on the monthly illness." Now he was prescribing tincture of chloride of iron, though in a minute quantity. He had become more eclectic as he grew older. The medicine brought on the period, and he said it must be repeated next month if necessary. She seemed otherwise well and only the drinking gave him any anxiety. The more enjoyment she could have, of a healthy kind, the less this weakness was likely to encroach, and he approved heartily of her scheme of getting a pair of cobs to draw her in a little phaeton. He had told her once of a pair of piebald ponies and a small basket carriage he had had at Malvern; they had been quite a feature of the neighborhood. Lamb's Library had supplied a series of the double photographs used for viewing through a stereoscope, including as many as possible of local interest. There had been one of himself standing, hat in hand, at his front door, and another of the ponies, harnessed in their carriage. Susanna had been their chief user; after her marriage he had sold them because he wanted another carriage horse. He was discussing Florence's project one evening after dinner in The Priory drawing room.

"A little carriage like that will be such a nice thing for a lady to drive," said Mrs. Cox. "I own I am always rather frightened at seeing her on the box of the landau, it is so high up."

"If it's a question of being frightened," Dr. Gully said, "I'm afraid there's more to alarm you in a pony phaeton. The higher up you are, the more control you have over the animals. A gig is more dangerous than a carriage, and a phaeton is the most dangerous of all, where you're right under their heels."

"There's no danger in any of them, if you know how to drive," said Florence impatiently.

"No. I was only teasing Mrs. Cox with a little unwelcome information."

"I'm afraid the doctor is a sad tease," said Mrs. Cox with her creaking laugh. "But fancy there being more danger in driving little ponies than great carriage horses!"

"Some little creatures are very *méchant*," Dr. Gully said. Florence did not notice the insinuation as she would have done once; her head was full of bargaining at Tattersall's, the instructions she must give Griffith since she couldn't go into the auction ring herself, and where the ponies must be brought for her inspection before she made a purchase. As usual when her mind was set on something, she retreated into a world of her own, where no one could reach her.

Chapter 29

❧❧

THE cobs were a very handsome-actioned pair, bright bay-colored; their names were Victor and Cremorne and they had cost two hundred guineas. Dr. Gully thought this too high a figure; she could have suited herself for a little over half that amount, he said, but Florence disagreed with some vehemence. The horses were exactly what she wanted, beautiful, in perfect condition and trained as a pair. She was completely delighted with them.

She had always taken an interest in her stables, far more than she ever took in her kitchen or butler's pantry. Now that Victor and Cremorne were in the two remaining stalls, she visited them every day; the cobs knew her footfall and would whinny, expecting pieces of apple or lumps of sugar. She often came into the harness room and she always found that Griffith kept things in good order. The implements he had used at Malvern—the combs and brushes and basins, the cloths and oils and soaps—had been sold off with the contents of the doctor's stables and everything replaced at Leigham Court Road, but he had brought with him from Malvern the bottle containing now, rather less than two ounces of antimony crystals; he had kept it in his portmanteau between leaving Malvern and coming to Streatham; it stood now in the harness room cupboard. It was labeled "poison" so, as Griffith said, if anybody took and gave it to himself, that was his lookout.

Griffith had a professional pride in the turnout of the cobs and phaeton—an approval which included the mistress. Mrs. Ricardo wore when driving a jacket with turnback cuffs like a livery coat, a large bow under her chin and a hat with an ostrich feather around it. This was what driving ladies wore now, but none of them that Griffith had seen looked a patch on Mrs. Ricardo.

She still went out in the carriage alone with the doctor, two or three times a week, and sometimes the drives recalled their idyllic ones *à deux*. In quiet moments, James' presence close beside her gave her, still, a deep, sensuous content. His smell was most agreeable to her. There was no rank, masculine odor in it, only one made up of skin washed with Brown's Windsor Soap or Wright's Sapo Carbonis, the natural smell of clean hair and freshly laundered linen. All together these made up an indefinable, soothing, delicious feature of his presence and she recognized it still; but the physical pleasure of each other's society did not prevent disputes or even quarrels. However devoted and magnanimous, he would not accept without protest some ignorant assertion or some inaccurate remembrance (and her memory was sometimes surprisingly inaccurate—he wondered if this were a result of her drinking) but Florence had grown very intolerant of being put right. She would perversely uphold her original statement, pushing out her chin. Sometimes he would lean back in the carriage, admiring her beauty and saying, "Well, well, if you wish to say so," but at others he would retort very sharply: "That is nonsense, my dear, you are being very foolish." At these moments there was a state of defiance between them almost like hatred.

Her house and garden, her stables, the paddock with its chickens and geese, the apple and plum trees, the strawberry

and asparagus beds, the melon pit and cucumber frames, were
now all in absolute order, and though she was surrounded by
servants, with Janie for her companion, and James, who still
magnetized her more than any living creature, for her lover, she
sometimes realized a blankness, a loss. He did sometimes bring
friends to call; his sisters came occasionally; but these were all
people, as she knew very well, who would be trusted to take a
large-minded view; she would have liked, now, to see a gay
party walking about the lawn, women, even if she didn't care
for them, taking tea in the blue drawing room, a dinner party
in her own house or someone else's where she could once again
wear full evening dress. All her evening clothes now, though
beautiful, were demitoilets, for dining quietly in hotels, at Orwell Lodge or at home with James as the only guest.

His own interests continued, varied and deep. When he had
spent hours with William Crookes, or chaired a meeting of the
National Spiritualist Association, or dined in stimulating company at the Garrick, his journey back to Balham made him
feel that he lived on two levels, in two worlds which had no
connection with each other. The train from Victoria took him
to Balham and from the station half a minute's walk brought
him to the Bedford Hotel that rose like a cliff on the corner of
Balham High Road and Bedford Hill. Almost immediately outside the hotel, Bedford Hill was spanned by a triple arch carrying the railway on which the trains ran close beside the
windows of the hotel's first floor. The wide central arch covered
the road, the narrow ones covered the pavements going up each
side of the hill. Dr. Gully always took the pavement running
under the left-hand arch, leading him up to his front gate. He
thus walked past the Bedford Hotel every time he came home
on foot from Balham Station. It was a lofty, handsome building,
three stories high, with large, globular gas lamps hanging over

its three entrances. He understood that it was very well kept; he did not expect ever to see the inside of it.

Once through the tunnellike arch, and emerging on the green-sided hill with its thickets and trees, he entered the other world, private and enclosed, of anxiety and happiness, annoyance and love.

In the transparent, golden September weather, their gardens were glowing with flowers and fruit. At Orwell Lodge raspberry canes, currant bushes and the strawberry beds were in a heavy second fruiting. There were Michaelmas daisies in the beds and tea roses climbing to the iron balcony outside his study. He stood on the lawn one evening looking at the gold light resting on a little path grown over with green velvet moss and hearing subdued sounds from the basement windows as his dinner was being prepared. His mind was filled with peace. He had already a love for this house which surprised him, as he had been here barely six months.

Florence had established her fernery in the little conservatory built over the drawing-room window. Here were some tree ferns, exotically beautiful, which had cost her twenty guineas each, and a crowd of smaller ones—some like green blades, some with fronds curled like green feathers, some spread in lateral green fringes, some that looked like showers of delicate green drops held motionless. She had an expert knowledge of what each one required, how much moisture to give, how often and by what method: The rare *Trichomanes brevisetum* grew by water-falls, so in captivity it needed watering by spraying from above; she knew in which fern pot to enrich the soil with leaf mold, in which to aerate it with gravel. Dr. Gully was much impressed by her competence in treating her patients.

The rose garden was now heavenly; every day fresh roses opened while yesterday's were still perfect; the scent they breathed out was held in the unstirred air. One morning he let himself in at the gate and went to wait for her in the rose garden instead of in the morning room. He was beginning to wonder if he should not go back to the house to look for her when he saw her come out of one of the French windows, and the gardener stop his scythe to direct her to the rose garden. She was wearing a dress of ordinary Holland, but made up by an expensive dressmaker, with silver filigree buttons and string-colored lace. She trailed across the lawn, the sun on her hair, and the sight of her filled him with tenderness and joy. She sat down beside him, and as the dip of the ground, though shallow, was enough to conceal them from the men working in the garden, they kissed. He could not have said why, a few seconds afterward, his eyes were directed to the parapet of the flat roof. Behind it, Mrs. Cox stood, watching them.

She was not merely loitering, sunning herself for a few moments, ready to return a wave if they noticed her. She was stock-still, her head craning forward. Florence was sitting half turned away from her; his own face he thought was protected by the roses. They were helplessly exposed to her, but she, unknowingly, was exposed to him. There was nothing in her seeing them kiss; she had seen it scores of times; when he met Florence for the first time in the day, he would give her a husbandly kiss, whether Mrs. Cox were there or not. No, there was something in her pose that spoke of a keen, insatiable vigilance—something that surprised him.

Not that he cared; but he did not choose to stay there as an object of it. He said to Florence, "Let us take a turn about the grounds, my love, and see how your plums have come on. If you would like some of our raspberries, Pritchard shall bring up a basketful."

"Yes, I should," Florence said.

Chapter 30

THE impression he had formed of Mrs. Cox, long since, that some of her feelings were carefully concealed, had remained at the back of his mind, disregarded; the sight of her watching from the roof had brought it into conscious force, but even so he was not disturbed by it. Whatever her feelings, she showed a warm appreciation of his presence and conversation, and he listened good-naturedly while she related her affairs to him and asked his advice. This summer she told him that she had an aunt in Jamaica who owned a small business which she intended to leave her niece, and she wanted Mrs. Cox to come out, so that she could be put in the way of understanding it before she took it over; but, Mrs. Cox told him, she didn't want to inconvenience Mrs. Ricardo by such a long absence. He saw at once that she wasn't going. He did not give her any advice; she wouldn't take any that didn't fall in with her private schemes. He heard also, from time to time, a good deal about her friends the Bravos and their house on Palace Green: one of two handsome red-brick mansions lately built, in the avenue of plane trees that led off Kensington High Street. Its situation was most *recherché;* only a strip of turf on the opposite side of the avenue divided it from Kensington Palace itself. Mrs. Cox was actually talkative on this theme; apart from her position at The Priory, her connection with the Bravos was her sole claim to consideration. Mrs. Bravo, she told them, was not an invalid, exactly, but a lady in very poor health; her nerves plagued her cruelly and her beauty was almost destroyed. Her husband, elderly, wealthy, affectionate, devoted his life to taking care of her and he thought the world of his stepson, Mr. Charles Bravo, who was, in Mrs. Cox's opinion, a most gentlemanly, interesting young man, no doubt he would go far in his profession, though of course it took a long time, as well as industry, to make headway at the bar. Dr. Gully thought of Willie; he didn't say that besides time and industry, what it also took was outstanding ability. His poor mother, Mrs. Cox said, with the dreadful visitation of her two daughters, the deaf-mute who lived with them at Palace Green, the one who was not quite like other people kept in seclusion elsewhere, with every attention and kindness—naturally Mrs. Bravo was wrapped up in her son, and thought nobody good enough for him. Nor had Mr. Charles thought so, said Mrs. Cox, with her chuckle like a woodpecker's; up till now, he was living at home as a bachelor, but when he could find a suitable match, everyone would be glad to see him marry. He was nearly thirty.

"Just my age," Florence observed carelessly, snipping off a thread. She was sewing dark-green velvet ivy leaves on a white satin cushion cover. It was an evening early in October, and they were sitting in the drawing room after dinner. The curtains were draped across the French window; at the far end of the room the fernery was closed up by shutters. Florence and Mrs. Cox sat at a round table covered with a blue velvet cloth; he sat in an armchair by the fire, listening benignly as Mrs. Cox discoursed on the splendors of Palace Green. The scene was one of solid domestic comfort. Though Florence had made for him the great sacrifice of respectability, a considerable appearance of respectability was maintained. To a man less sure of himself, his establishment at The Priory without loss of dignity would have been difficult. He had noticed, before it was quickly masked, a look of surprise on the maid Keeber's face the first time she had seen him, quite early after breakfast, sitting by the morning-room fire reading the newspaper, though she hadn't let him into the house. From then onward she encountered him at all hours, in that room, the drawing room, the dining room, on the stairs, but she had never opened the front door to him. Now, the first time she saw him in the day, she curtsied and said: "Good morning, sir." The servants liked him, he was authoritative in such a calm and genial manner. Griffith was of course attached to him, the gardener was always glad of a word. The Priory servants were also on very friendly terms with Pritchard. There was always a welcome for him in the servants' hall, and a glass of ale and a plateful for The Priory menservants in the kitchen of Orwell Lodge. This being so, almost everything that went on at The Priory was known down the hill. Pritchard would give the doctor the news, slightly edited, as it came in; the most recent items were that what had caused an underhousemaid to leave had been that she didn't take to Mrs. C. managing everything, and that it had come out that Mrs. Ricardo kept a bottle of brandy in the corner press in her bedroom. To the first item, Dr. Gully had replied, "That is very foolish of the girl, but if she'd rather give up a good place than take her orders from Mrs. Cox, that's her affair, I suppose." To the second he merely said, "Do not mention this to anyone else, Pritchard," and Pritchard had said: "Not a word, Doctor." His face showed that the caution had been unnecessary.

This October there burst on London the extraordinary success of Mr. Irving's *Hamlet* at the Lyceum. As the weeks went on, it seemed to Dr. Gully that everyone he met, especially everyone he encountered at the Garrick, was talking to him about the performance and telling him he ought to see it. He was not anxious to do so; *Hamlet* was not a favorite with him. An inability to bring the mind to take decisive action made interesting matter for medical investigation; he didn't feel it endeared a tragic hero; but no doubt the presentation was extremely fine, and if this phenomenal run continued, he dared say he would fill a stall at the Lyceum some night or other. It was not a play Florence would be likely to enjoy, and he did not in any case think it wise to appear with her in a box at a London theater, even with Mrs. Cox as chaperone. He had once or twice offered to get tickets for her and Mrs. Cox for some show he thought would amuse Florence, but she had always refused. An outing of this kind without him in attendance, even with her own carriage to set them down and take them up and her own footman to escort them through the crowd, had no attraction for her.

She was, however, very much interested in an outing she made with Mrs. Cox toward Christmas. She had gone up to London in the carriage for a day's shopping and had set down Mrs. Cox at 2 Palace Green so that the latter could spend some hours with the Bravos before Florence called for her on the way home. That Mrs. Ricardo's footman should ring the front doorbell and then, under the eyes of the Bravos' butler, return to help Mrs. Cox descend from the carriage and pair, gave Mrs. Cox acute satisfaction; and when, during the afternoon, Mrs. Ricardo returned to take up Mrs. Cox, and Mrs. Bravo sent a message downstairs asking Mrs. Ricardo to come up to the drawing room, the satisfaction was complete. She had demonstrated the grandeur of her patrons to her employer and the wealth and elegance of her employer to her patrons. That evening she talked freely, relating everything she had heard from Mrs. Bravo and putting her hearers *au courant* with the latest developments of the family's history and troubles.

"And what did *you* think of the house?" Dr. Gully asked Florence when he had an opportunity, made by Mrs. Cox's going off to the morning room to fetch some skeins of silk which Florence believed she must have left there.

"A very fine house, very handsomely appointed; in a beautiful situation, the Palace is in view over the green."

"And Mrs. Bravo, was she pleasant?"

"Yes, I think so, I think she meant to be, but as Janie says, so much ill health; she looks cross and anxious; there is a look of suffering on her face all the time. I should have thought she didn't like me—only I believe it is all ill health."

"And the famous young man—did you see him?"

"Yes, for a few minutes. He was in the drawing room and he handed me downstairs."

"And what did you think of *him?*"

"Good-looking, I thought, pale, rather heavy, with dark hair —rather strange eyes."

"Well they may be," thought Dr. Gully, "with that family background."

"Strange, did you think, dear?" said Mrs. Cox, returning with the silks. "I've always heard people speak of him as such a handsome young man—"

"Well, I do not say he is not. But that was what happened to strike me." In spite of Mrs. Cox's having brought the silks, Florence got up and said somewhat abruptly that she was tired and would go to bed. He went out with her into the dimly lighted hall and walked with her the few paces to the foot of the stairs. The servants were all in their quarters; there was no one in the morning room or the dining room; in the drawing room there was only Mrs. Cox. Yet she did not stop to kiss him, she barely said good night, and went straight upstairs with steady, swift ascent. He felt a miserable certainty that she was making for the brandy bottle in her bedroom.

During the next few days, though she did not take anything in front of him except wine at table, he could see that she was drinking heavily; she was flushed, excitable, restless, and on the third evening, she did not come down to dinner at the usual time. Mrs. Cox said nervously that she believed Mrs. Ricardo was dressed—she would go and see.

"No, stay here," he said. "I will go to her." He found Florence in her bedroom, in her evening dress, but dazed and breathing heavily, the brandy bottle and a glass on the floor beside her. She could not speak to be understood; she tried to get to her feet but was unable. He found her negligee in the dressing room and coming back with it, he began undoing the rows of hooks and eyes of the closely fitting bodice, and got the dress off her, with some difficulty as she could not stand up. He undid the corset and took off her shoes and stockings, then put her arms into the sleeves of the negligee. Keeber had not yet been up to turn down the bed, so he stripped off the counterpane and replaced the down quilt that was protected by a muslin cover with great bows at the corners. Then, half carrying her, he got her to the bed and heaved her onto it, arranging the clothes over her. She was overcome with sleep already. He pulled the pins and combs out of her elaborately dressed head so that they shouldn't stick into her scalp. The hair was clean and silky but he could not smell its characteristic scent of herbs because the brandy's odor was so strong.

Mrs. Cox's face now appeared around the bedroom door; she came cautiously up to the bed; Florence was sound asleep and breathing stertorously; there seemed every sign that she would stay there till she had slept it off. He picked up the bottle and glass from the carpet and went across to the corner cupboard. In it was a half-empty bottle of sherry and a wineglass, unwashed, lying on its side with the stem broken; a strong smell of spirit came from the saturated wood. His face became for a moment like iron. He said to Mrs. Cox: "I'll take these bottles downstairs. Of course that won't prevent her from bringing up more; but I'll have a very serious talk with her tomorrow. I think the time has come to persuade her to have some drastic treatment."

The spectacle, facing them, of the inside of the cupboard was so significant, Mrs. Cox felt obliged to say: "I hope you don't feel, Doctor, that I have been to blame in any way." It was no use now, saying that she should have warned him. He would not discuss the matter. He courteously declined her suggestion of dinner and went back to Orwell Lodge. Pritchard was sorry to hear that Mrs. Ricardo wasn't so well, but his immediate concern was to see that the doctor took something to eat. The cook being out, he brought up a basin of soup to a little table by the study fire and went downstairs again to make an omelet.

Next morning, sitting with Florence in the morning room, he spoke with all his impressiveness. She was pale and heavy-eyed, and though the headache with which she'd woken up was better, there was still enough of it to make her miserable.

"I know it's very naughty," she said.

"My love, what I want you to believe is that there's no quicker way to lose your youth and beauty. You've had a horrible experience of a drunken man—women who drink are even more shocking. You, you with your beauty and your charm, the loveliest woman I've ever seen—Florence, I can't endure the idea of what you'll make of yourself if you can't give this habit up." She was silent. He took her hand and said: "Won't you let me save you?" She sighed.

"Yes, I will," she said. He told her there was a prescription in powder form that would have no effect on her if she didn't take any wine or spirit. If she did, the alcohol on top of the powder would make her very sick. This was a way of creating a distaste for it. She agreed to take the treatment, a little sullenly; her head was aching.

The prescription was a well-known one for dipsomania and instead of having it made up at Smith's, his chemist in Balham, he thought it more discreet to take it to Epps' in Piccadilly, whom he used for homeopathic preparations. For the next few days he made a point of taking tea at The Priory, so that he could give Florence one of the powders in half a wineglass full of water about five o'clock, for he believed that the time when she was most prone to drinking was between tea and dinner. There were no ill effects, and he began giving her another powder in the middle of the morning. Then, one evening just before dinner, she was violently sick. The distress and the business of washing and sponging and clearing up, and not being able to eat, made an invalid of her for the rest of the evening. For several days this seemed to act as a cure; then there was another attack of sickness before lunch on Christmas Eve.

That Florence felt unwell and dispirited on Christmas Day did not much interfere with arrangements at The Priory; there was no festivity, no presents and visits among large numbers of relations and old friends. For the last three Christmases she had not felt the lack of a family gathering; at Brookefield, at Stokefield, James' presents and his love had made all the Christmas joy she wanted. Now, looking about the large rooms of The Priory, she had to stifle a wish to see her father and mother there, and Effie; Effie would have come to her before now, having by this time developed enough dignity and assurance as a successfully married woman to ignore, tactfully, their father's edict; but she was still abroad with her husband and the meeting both the sisters wanted had to be postponed.

Florence gave Dr. Gully a malacca walking cane with an amber top and he gave her a gold bracelet mounted with an oval cameo showing Venus in a chariot drawn by doves. He gave Mrs. Cox at the same time a handsome pair of scissors in a tooled leather sheath. After the exchange of presents they went in to Christmas dinner but Florence felt too languid and sick to eat much. She did not sit up for the evening meal either but went upstairs about six o'clock. He went up to her room to say good night; she was in the dressing room with Mrs. Cox, and he opened the door of the corner cupboard. It still smelled strongly of spirit but it was empty.

The new year opened without alarm, but there was another attack in the middle of January. Florence was recovering from this and one afternoon after lunch she went into the fernery to see how one of her new exotics was bearing its change of home. Dr. Gully went into the morning room expecting to find her there, as she usually lay down on the sofa in that room after lunch, and he would sit by her, helping her to fall asleep. Not finding her there, he began going up the stairs to her bedroom, but hearing her step in the hall he came down. Seeing him at the foot of the stairs, she burst into sudden, passionate exclamations and ran into the morning room. When he hastily followed her, she turned around, shouting: "It's a nightmare! Nightmare! Always here—attempting me—"

"*Attempting* you!"

"Yes. Attempting me or else making me sick. Wherever I go—all over the house. I can't be free anywhere, always there, in every room, on the stairs, wanting to—"

She wasn't drunk, he was satisfied of that; there was nothing he ought to do for her, so he could obey his own wish and leave her at once. The hateful accusation, so utterly unjust, so affronting and so cruel, filled his mind as he walked down to Orwell Lodge. He could not dismiss it when he settled to read over the study fire. It was a little after three when Pritchard knocked at the door, asking if he would see Mrs. Cox.

He went into the drawing room. The fire was not lit; in the

chill twilight Mrs. Cox's dark bonnet and mantle absorbed the gloom.

"You had better come—" he began.

She interrupted. "I am only here for a minute, Doctor, to beg you to return to Mrs. Ricardo. She's so much put about, she's afraid she may have been a little bit thoughtless in what she said to you."

"Well?" he said.

"Well, Doctor, if you could see her, you wouldn't hold it against her, I'm sure. Won't you come back with me and let her tell you it was all a mistake?"

"Has Mrs. Ricardo sent you to ask me to come to her?"

"Yes, of course, Doctor. She wants you to come back with me now."

He paused, then said: "Please tell Mrs. Ricardo that as she says she wants to see me at her house, I will be there at six o'clock."

"But that's such a long time away, Doctor. She wants me to bring you with me now."

"That is the only message I have to send, Mrs. Cox. If you will be so kind as to take it, I shall be obliged to you." He opened the front door for her himself, though Pritchard was hovering at the back of the hall.

He was wondering all the while till six o'clock how he should meet her, what to say, but when he came into the morning room, he had no need to think; she threw herself into his arms, her eyes reddened and heavy, filling with a gush of tears. She could not imagine what had made her say those things to him, she had not meant one word of it; his anger nearly killed her, his love was the only thing in the world that really mattered to her! They sat on the sofa, her head on his shoulder, and she begged and implored him to say he forgave her. He would not do that quite at once, but he held her fast, saying how sorry he was that the remedy was so painful and disagreeable, but could she do without it? He was afraid that if he stopped giving her the powder—he fell silent. She looked up at his face, so grave, so awe-inspiring, so gentle. He must do as he thought best, she said.

Chapter 31

HE thought that as traveling for pleasure kept her contented and free from the desire for alcohol, and as there was no reason why they should not travel as much as they chose, they might as well plan a foreign holiday for the spring. They agreed on an Italian tour: to go via Calais, Paris and Mâcon, to Turin, Rome and Naples, and return via Venice, which he had never seen. For every reason he looked forward to the tour, and felt that to see Venice would be the crown of it.

When they embarked at the end of March, the great wave of new impressions at first washed away all personal irritations and disharmonies; but gradually the discontents wore through the charm and novelty, the interest and grandeur. He tried not to remember the time in Leghorn in 1872. Its contrast with the present was too painful. Then, he had been in the paradise of her bed; now he was prevented from even saying good night to her in her bedroom, because it was Mrs. Cox's bedroom also.

Mrs. Cox, he had felt for some time, was increasing almost daily in her quiet assurance; at first he had not exactly minded this, he had merely made a note of it. But as their Italian journey progressed, she was getting to treat him, he felt, almost as if he were a courier. "Mrs. Ricardo wants to do this," she would say, "Mrs. Ricardo has decided to do that." Venice itself was almost marred for him by the presence in the foreground of Mrs. Cox in her spectacles, her black straw bonnet and dark-green traveling cloak. On the first morning after their arrival he wanted to explore with Florence (and Mrs. Cox, of course). He was waiting for them on the steps of their hotel when Mrs. Cox approached and told him quietly that Mrs. Ricardo was a little tired and would stay in bed till lunch time.

He looked about him at the splendid scene. On the roof of the cathedral of San Marco, the central arch framed the four gilded bronze horses, removed by Napoleon and very properly restored by the victorious allied powers. The basilica's Byzantine decoration of variegated marbles had a striped effect, infinitely strange and arresting to an unused eye; in the foreground the gilded group of the winged lions of Saint Mark flashed in the sun under a sky of brilliant blue. Good God in heaven, had he come so many hundred miles by sea and land, to find himself in the Piazza di San Marco—with Mrs. Cox?

Whether Florence were gracious to him or not, he was of course invaluable to her, in promoting her enjoyment and comfort: reading Baedeker for her, speaking Italian with more strength and fluency than she could muster, guiding, amusing and protecting her. Their most successful expedition was not to see pictures or frescoed palaces or the interior of San Marco itself, with its gloom and richness, its treasury of mosaics and jewels, but the island of Murano which Florence had long wanted to visit as the factory of Venetian glass. There it all was, pierced through with the bright light, as lovely as she had imagined. She bought a bowl of sea-green glass powdered with gold dust, a vase with a swirling pattern of opaque white lines and a tazza of crimson glass, its lid and stem decorated with gold. These purchases put her in very good humor and it was almost like old times when she thanked him radiantly because, when she hesitated over buying a final piece, of green and white *ritorto,* he bought it for her.

Next morning they were standing at the bottom of a flight of steps, with Mrs. Cox in attendance, waiting for a gondola to take them up the Grand Canal, and he had one of those instants, rare in a long, close intimacy, of seeing her as a stranger would see her. She had lately put on some weight, not unbecomingly; her figure was elegant, with a rounded bosom above a still-small waist. The lovely coloring of her face was unaltered, but there was now a little heaviness of chin. What was immediately noticeable was an air of determination; all traces of girlishness, of invalidism, had disappeared within the last two months. He could not believe that this young woman, self-possessed, youthful but mature, would ever cry and cling to him again.

It was not only she who was standing in the revealing light. When he formed this impression of her present state, Florence was looking at the green canal in a musing way; but before her eyes fixed themselves on the water, they had taken a sidelong look at his profile and his neck. Lines, hollows, configurations she had never noticed stood out plainly. He was an *old* man.

Chapter 32

THE summer 1875 was a very fine one; the common in June was pleasant with flowering elder thickets and a march of yellow flags across the great pond.

Once he had noticed the change in her he began to notice it all the time. She was tinting her hair. He begged her not to, to return to the chestnut color he loved, but she persisted in making the shade deeper and redder; it was handsome, of course, with her white skin and dark-blue eyes, also it was very well done, but he regretted it. She used pearl powder on her face; when he noticed it, he told her she didn't need it. She ignored these comments, looking away from him with a fixed stare.

He had loved the scent of lavender on her but she had given it up altogether for a heavier scent, Eau de Chypre, formed on musk, ambergris, vanilla and triple extract of rose. He confessed to himself that he enjoyed it. Taught by her, his tastes had become broader, more catholic; he was pleased now by luxury, brightness, voluptuousness. It was the fashion at present for bodices to be cut low; in some of her new frocks they were cut very low; when she kissed him and leaned against him, he admitted that he wouldn't, now, have her any different.

They had settled down to a level of accommodating each other. She was drinking, he knew, but not to excess. He had discontinued the powders but he was prepared to administer them again if she should need them. He would, occasionally, revert to the accusation she had made, for which she had so frantically begged his pardon, asking with mock ceremony if he were expected to wait on her the following day. She would say how unkind he was.

Meanwhile, she was getting to treat Orwell Lodge more and more as her own house. She took away *Punch* and Bell's *Sporting Life,* asked that Pritchard should come up to wait in The Priory dining room when her butler was on his holiday and left her possessions strewn about the drawing room: a piece of needlework on the sofa, a necklace on a side table because its clasp had broken and it had fallen off her neck. One afternoon she left a bottle of Eau de Chypre on the white marble chimney-piece, a little round bottle with a stopper like a crown. He was expecting his friend Dr. Moore and two other doctors to dine with him and he only saw the bottle as he came into the drawing room before dinner. He caught it up and carried it into the study where he put it into one of the cupboards that flanked the hearth.

This slackening of restraint which might have been so comfortable had the disagreeable effect that she didn't mind quarreling with him in front of Pritchard. It was correct, of course, up to a point, to behave before servants as if they weren't there, but he felt rather than saw how Pritchard took it when, as he waited on them at dinner, and his master said, "I think it would be prudent," Mrs. Ricardo answered in a high-pitched tone: "I really don't care what you think; it's my affair and I don't need your advice about it." Pritchard's very back expressed the view that the doctor was patient to a fault; but the latter tried always to make allowance for her equivocal position and its effect on her nervous irritability.

He did the little that it was open to him to do; Florence had been invited to Queensborough Terrace to see the baby, and Willie and his wife had come out to lunch at The Priory on a Sunday in June when everything about the place was in high perfection. The luncheon, of salmon and guinea fowl, a great pile of strawberries in a silver dessert basket and a correctly chilled white wine, had been praised by Willie to his father afterward as tip-top. Dr. Gully on this occasion had been particularly careful to behave as if his position in the house were merely that of a neighbor, addressing the hostess as Mrs. Ricardo and showing no familiarity with her domestic affairs. Mrs. Cox, in a black silk from Florence's dressmaker, almost looked the part of friend on an equal footing.

His son and daughter-in-law rose to take leave at quarter past two; the occasion had been a great success but everyone understood that it couldn't be repeated too often.

Among the few other callers at The Priory were friends of Mrs. Cox, Mrs. Harford and her daughter, Mrs. Ffoulkes. Florence did not make one at their tea drinkings. In spite of her circumstances, these really were people whom she could not wish to see, and it was better that she should be absent; her brilliant presence would arouse a keener curiosity than Mrs. Cox's discreet references.

The mere absence of calls from neighbors however was not the only sign of her reputation. Florence assumed, with impatient annoyance, that at least some of her servants gossiped with the servants of other houses round about, there was no way of preventing that; the certainty of it confronted her abruptly one July morning in the waiting room at Balham Station.

She had never used the station before, but on this day when she intended to go to the Chiswick Flower Show to examine new roses, a lame horse made the journey by carriage impossible. Florence ordered a cab to take herself and Mrs. Cox down the hill, and descended from it at the station, very beautifully dressed in gray muslin with lilac bows, white gloves and a shady black straw hat on her russet hair. The occupants of the waiting room were a lady with her child's governess and the child herself, a self-possessed, supercilious little miss, who led a Maltese dog on a rose-colored ribbon.

A moment after the entrance of Florence and Mrs. Cox, the lady stood up and quietly made for the door, followed by the governess. The child moved after them but at the door she turned and stared at Florence.

"You have a very pretty little dog," Florence said. The child took no notice of the words; she maintained a hard, inquisitive stare, a faint, contemptuous smile on her face. From the platform her mother looked around and called her sharply; she turned her back on Florence and walked out.

A day at the flower show was bound to be fatiguing; it was natural that in the evening Florence should be tired and cross. In the drawing room after dinner Mrs. Cox was sitting at the round table, working with gold and silver sequins; a few of each were scattered on the blue velvet cloth, winking in the lamplight. Dr. Gully pressed his finger on a gold spark; it stuck to the skin and he transferred it to his palm.

"Zecchini, little coins," he said. Mrs. Cox had stitched two handbreadth scraps of black net with a sprinkling of sequins, one gold, one silver, to try the effect of them on a bonnet veil.

"Which do *you* think, Doctor?" she asked. He glanced at the great loops of hair near him in the lamplight. "The gold, surely," he said, "if either."

Florence shrugged; it was clear that in the final clause he had committed another of his offenses. In her present mood, no happiness was possible for either of them; he could only hope that tomorrow she would be feeling better. Her look was so discouraging that for once he said good night and left without kissing her.

The night was lovely; instead of going out onto Bedford Hill he turned left at the front door and went to the common. The moon was full, an enormous, radiant circle with the four patches of shade that looked like features; at the right-hand corner of the triangular mouth, the dark spot of the Mare Nectaris could be seen with the naked eye. All around the moon the light was so strong, no star could show; she appeared to be alone in heaven. The peace and silence were exquisite. He remembered Maria Vilda's singing *Norma* at the Royal Opera House a year ago. The notes of *Casta Diva* were sounding in his head; they expanded and went ringing around the sky:

> *Casta Diva, che inargenti*
> *Queste sacre antiche piante*
> *A noi volgi il bel sembiante*
> *Senza nube e Senza vel!*

Peace! Chaste goddess! Peace! He half-turned and found The Priory unexpectedly near. In Florence's bedroom the curtains were drawn but moonlight gleamed on the glass. The shadows of the giant oak freckled the pale walls. He turned away again, lifting his head to the solemn bliss of the light-pouring sky.

Unclouded, unveiled, chaste goddess! She had filled the sky with her influence—but alas. He turned, leaning on his stick, and slowly retraced his steps across the grass, his shadow thrown before him by the vast light behind his head.

He did not feel equal to suggesting and arranging another trip for the three of them this year, and when he was invited to attend a medical conference in Paris in the second half of August, he decided that he would spend a few weeks in France by himself, looking up old friends and taking up introductions he had never had the opportunity to use. Florence heard his intentions calmly; she said it would be a good occasion for her to take the sea air at Brighton as he didn't like the place and they did. He took an affectionate interest in her plans, discussing hotels and lodgings with her; they both seemed to look forward to an absence from each other and to meeting again after it.

He was to spend a few days in Queensborough Terrace at the beginning of August, and he went up there in charge of cordial remembrances to Mr. and Mrs. William Gully and Florence Julia.

The heat was more felt in Bayswater than at the height of Tooting Common, but it was dry and not disagreeable. As he turned one afternoon into Queensborough Terrace, he thought the scene very pleasant; the quiet, sunbaked street had been sprinkled by the water cart, of the porticoes that lined both sides of it, one-half were in the shade; housefronts were gay with geraniums and striped window blinds. He paused before entering the portico of No. 65, and glanced to his left, where Kensington Gardens showed green behind the railings of the Bayswater Road. He reflected that a walk straight across the Gardens would lead to Palace Green, the abode of those Bravos whose ambiance was so rich and sinister. He thought sadly that it was the isolation their love affair had brought on her that made his lovely dear glad to be introduced to people such as those; but in spite of his remorse for a position he had always foreseen, of which he had indeed warned her, he did not feel that he had essentially injured her; what he had given, was giving and would give, was more important than the deprivation he had caused. He had a sense of power and assurance, the garnered results of his long professional career, a quiet feeling of mastery that went well with the hot, tranquil afternoon.

Before he mounted the step under the portico, a paper boy ran past him up the terrace; noticing a potential customer as he flew by, he turned and came back with a thudding of bare feet, yelling: "'Orrible revulsions! 'Ere you are, sir!" Dr. Gully gave him a shilling. The boy let out a hoarse crow, bit the coin and tore away again; instinct had told him that this old buffer wouldn't demand his change.

Dr. Gully entered the house, hot, drowsy and shaded with blinds. He went into the ground-floor study and began to read the paper which had cost him a shilling. The horrible revelations on which the boy was selling it were those in the case of Colonel Valentine Baker, convicted at Croydon assizes of assaulting a young woman in a railway carriage. Poor fellow! Of course, if he were guilty, the offense was a shocking one and merited the severe punishment of public disgrace, but any man of experience, particularly if he were a doctor, was apt to feel uneasy about these sexual cases where the evidence rested entirely on the word of a woman; women were apt, in these matters, to make up a story to satisfy some need or craving of their own. This wretched man would have had a careful trial and it must be hoped he had suffered no injustice. The paper gave a graphic account of the public, endeavoring to force themselves into a court already crowded to capacity. Two ladies, so called, were hoisted up to a windowsill, seven feet above ground level, "pulled in by friends from above, amidst the jeers and shouts of the mob." Great heavens, what a scene!

Chapter 33

HE missed her in Paris; the image of her as she had been in 1872 was a sweet, aching memory: but he missed her as she was now, with her mature, vivid beauty which had such a hold on him that he would rather she were there in a bad temper than not there at all. Yet, it was comfortable to be completely at his own disposal, free to call on people who received him with the French mixture of excited enthusiasm and elaborate courtesy. It made him realize how cramped and unrewarding some of that journeying *à trois* had been; but all the time at the back of his mind was the wish to see her; it became stronger as the time approached, especially when her letters reached him, affectionate but brief. She and Mrs. Cox were enjoying themselves at Brighton, and Effie had been down to see her; that had made her very happy. She was glad to hear what an interesting time he was having. He had at home a complete collection of every letter she had ever sent him; he reread the ones that came now, and put them away carefully, to be added to the rest.

The lodgings in King's Road seemed to suit her, for before he returned to Balham in the second week in October she and Mrs. Cox had gone down there again. The letter he found awaiting him at Orwell Lodge told him this; he was disappointed not to see her that very evening but the letter asked him to

come down to Brighton as soon as he got back. This was Saturday night. He telegraphed saying that he would be with her on
Monday.

When they met, Mrs. Cox had the grace not to be in the sitting
room and he held Florence in his arms till she gently disengaged herself. He then saw that in spite of the famous sea air,
she wasn't looking very well. Her face was rather pale with a
stamp of anxiety. She told him that Effie had said their mother
was ill; this, it seemed, had roused all the family affection in
Florence which had been dormant for so long. She did not
sound as though she wished to be questioned about Mrs. Campbell's state; "internal inflammation," Effie had said; and with
nothing more than that to go on, there was really nothing he
could say, except that he was concerned and sorry. "I wish I
could see her!" Florence exclaimed. He was a little surprised, but,
though unexpected, the impulse was natural. He said: "How
ardently I long for our marriage. Every happiness of mind and
body is bound up in that."

"Yes," she said faintly. He took her hand and though she
did not return his pressure she left it in his hold.

He asked when she meant to come home. She did not quite
know, she said. It was pleasant to have sunshine here still though
in London it had faded away. There was no immediate hurry.

"Only on my part," he said gallantly. At all events, he said,
if she did not return at the end of the week he would run down
again. The blight that affected the whole scene, the pale streets
and terraces and squares and the sparkling sea, was still there,
but the delight of seeing Florence again had made him almost
forget it.

During the next few days, Tuesday, Wednesday, Thursday
and Friday, he wrote to her twice but he was busy enough. He
had to take possession of Orwell Lodge again, confer with
Pritchard, speak to the gardener, read and write. His presidential

year at the National Spiritualist Association was finished but there was a good deal to discuss at their headquarters. A Mrs. Kimball was introduced to him, a quiet lady in black; she had mediumistic powers that were said to be very remarkable. She and Dr. Gully met in the committee room at Gower Street; there were several people there, the new president, the secretary and some members who were anxious about policy. Mrs. Kimball was taking no part in the discussion; she sat apart by a window. He found himself looking at her with an intense, impersonal stare and receiving one of the same kind from her. He could not have told anyone afterward what she looked like.

He took the opportunity of calling on Charlotte Dyson who was alive to everything he had to say about Paris. The sensitive and tranquil atmosphere of Vernemore had become very dear to him. One of the charms of her society, he had long since discovered, was that she was eminently teachable. She knew nothing about medicine—how should she? But when he explained something to her she listened, with all her considerable intelligence because what he said was interesting, and with an emotional eagerness because it was he who was saying it. He would have liked so much to talk to her about his dearest interests, those that he was forbidden to mention to her.

On Saturday morning he was breakfasting as usual at half past eight; and presently through the large plate-glass windows he saw the postman turn into the drive with a handful of letters. A moment later Pritchard brought them to the breakfast table, with one from Florence on top of the pile. As Dr. Gully had nearly finished he left a piece of half-eaten toast and took them into the study where the fire was already lighted.

"It has been in my mind a very long time. I would not write while you were away, I did not want to spoil your holiday and when you came here I had not the courage to tell you. We must part. I am determined never to see you again. No one will ever be dearer to me than you are, but I cannot bear to go on in this way, hurting and offending my mother and always aware of her distress. I could never forgive myself if she died without my being reconciled to her. There is no more I can say. You must accept my decision. Florence Ricardo."

How long he remained in a shocked condition he couldn't afterward have said. People spoke to him and he answered, he went out on the common and came in, went out again without remembering where he had been. On Sunday morning he was himself again and by then several points were clear to him. If her happiness now depended on a reconciliation with her family, he must not even attempt to stand in her way; he would tell her so. Secondly, he did not really believe—accept—that the reconciliation must mean a total separation; such an annihilating prospect there was no need to face. She was not a girl; she could accept some of her parents' terms and impose some of her own. Thirdly, the edict that they must *never* meet again was sheer nonsense. He would run down to Brighton and talk it out with her.

Leaving it till Monday morning so as to be altogether in command of himself, he wrote, beginning as he always did: "My dearest." He said that it would be a very good thing to be reconciled to her parents; whatever she thought best for her own happiness, that was what he wished her to do; but, he added, he could not accept her decision that they must part immediately. He would come down tomorrow, Tuesday, and be with her a little before lunch time. A telegram arrived from her next morning while he was at breakfast. It said that Mrs. Cox would be on the Brighton train that stopped at Croydon at eleven twenty, adding, "Please join her."

This mandate annoyed him and yet there was something to be said for the arrangement. So much had gone on, unknown to him except by its cataclysmic result, the opportunity to get some information out of Mrs. Cox was not unwelcome.

When the Brighton train ran alongside the Croydon platform, Mrs. Cox's face was at the window of a first-class carriage. They had the carriage to themselves and Mrs. Cox began by saying that Mrs. Ricardo would be glad to see him. He did not tell her to keep her breath to cool her porridge; he said nothing at all; and as the train hummed over the lines, swaying a little as it gathered speed, she began to talk about Florence's desire to see her family again and how very, very unhappy over the past four years the separation had made her. This drew no reply from him either, and though once or twice she stopped expectantly, when she saw he was not going to give her any encouragement she went on without it. She said how sad it was for Florence to be deprived of any social life in the neighborhood—so much talk going on in Balham, it was quite distressing. As this was something for which he acknowledged that he was responsible, the consciousness was bitter enough to him as it was; he positively was not going to discuss it with Mrs. Cox. His face assumed a sternness and coldness that would have been formidable to someone who was not immunized already.

It was quite a treat, Mrs. Cox said, for Mrs. Ricardo to meet people who would accept her on the footing she ought to occupy. Mr. Charles Bravo and his father had been in Brighton. Mr. Charles was there still; he had called and dined and driven out with them and it was refreshing to Mrs. Ricardo to have a little ordinary society.

"No doubt," Dr. Gully said. The train swung and rocked between the chalk cuttings that proclaimed the nearness of the south coast. He did now exert himself to take a part in the conversation. How long, he asked abruptly, had Mrs. Joseph Bravo's health been so poor? Mrs. Cox, surprised, said, well, for some years, certainly. And the daughter who was put away, did Mrs. Cox know anything about her condition? Oh, no, nothing at all, Mrs. Cox said, except that *every* care and attention—

And the daughter at home, Dr. Gully pursued, was she, apart from her disabilities, of normal intelligence?

Oh, dear, yes, said Mrs. Cox eagerly; quite one of the family circle. It was *only* that she was deaf and dumb; otherwise there was nothing at all. And she was most ably taken care of by their cousin Anne Bell. Miss Bell's brother was a surgeon in Harley Street, Mr. Royes Bell. Did the doctor know him?

Dr. Gully said he believed he had heard the name. He leaned back in his seat and took out his watch.

"We shall be in, in another twenty minutes," he said. He fixed his eyes on the flying landscape, making it clear that he determined to have no more talking.

Brighton Station was not crowded and as they approached the barrier he saw her standing outside with the determined air so much at variance with her small frame. She advanced on them and said to Mrs. Cox: "Janie, will you wait for me in the ladies' waiting room?" To him she said: "Will you come to the Prince Regent? It's only a step—we can talk there."

Astonished, he allowed himself to be guided to the small hotel and to an unoccupied corner between two windows with a distant, bright view of the sea over tamarisk hedges. They sat down and he gazed at her. Her hat was black velvet; nothing could have suited her hair better. Of all their meetings in hotels, was this to be the last? She sat upright with hands clasped, but it seemed that words had deserted her.

"Well," he said tenderly, "as I told you in my letter, it is a very good thing for you to be reconciled to your parents; and if you wish it, our close association must cease. But I can't accept that we are *never* even to see each other again."

She said, pressing her hands together: "But they won't see me unless I promise that I will never see you anymore."

After a silence, he said: "And have you agreed to that?"

"James," she said. "I wish you would try to understand my point of view."

"I am trying to understand it. That's why I'm asking you."

"It would have been better if you'd just accepted my letter."

"Better for whom?" She shrugged, but her color rose.

"Haven't I the right, after all this, to hear from your own lips that you mean to dismiss me?"

"Yes, I suppose so; but you are making it very difficult for me. And you always did say that if I ever—" she stopped.

"If you ever what?"

"Could form another attachment, you wouldn't stand in my way."

"And have you formed one?"

"No—no, certainly not."

"Are you," he said bluntly, "talking about Charles Bravo?"

"I have become friendly with him."

"Are you engaged to him?"

"No."

"Has he asked you to be?"

She hesitated. "He cannot do that until his mother allows it."

"His mother! Why should a man of thirty need his mother's consent? His mother doesn't provide his income, does she?"

"No; but her influence is everything with his stepfather. Mr. Joseph Bravo provides the money."

"I see. But if he does find himself able to propose to you—"

"He has not done so; it's no use talking about it."

"Well, I can understand that; but am I allowed to give one piece of advice?"

"Naturally."

"If this proposal is made, I think you should take three or

four months to answer it, so that you can get to know his family before you commit yourself."

"If he does propose, I will."

"There is nothing more I can say, except to ask you, looking back on these four years, if you really want us to part forever?" She would not look at him; tears of vexation rose to her eyes and gushed out. She fumbled for her handkerchief; the scent of Eau de Chypre came from it.

"I don't want to make you unhappy, my darling. As I see your mind is made up, I'll say no more to distress you. Are you going to give me some lunch at your lodgings?"

"Yes, if you like." She got up, and while she went to summon Mrs. Cox, he engaged a cab on the station rank.

At the lunch table an extra cover had to be laid, which showed him that she had not meant him to be there. His powers were always called out by a challenge and he made the meal pass off with enough general conversation to prevent awkwardness. The ladies retired for a few minutes afterward and Mrs. Cox came back alone; he could see from the way she came up to him that she had been briefed.

"Forgive me, Doctor, if I sound interfering," she said, "but now that things are over between you and Mrs. Ricardo, don't you think it would save you pain if you were to move away from Balham?"

He was at first too surprised to speak.

"Leave Balham—leave my house!" he said. "No, Mrs. Cox, I don't think I'll do that. But perhaps I may pay a long visit to Jamaica; it is my birthplace, after all."

"I am sure you would find it well worth a visit."

"And do you mean to go there yourself, as your aunt seemed to wish?"

"I think Mrs. Ricardo would not like to spare me at present," she said evasively. The ease with which Florence was sparing *him* made him realize the deathly approach that he had been fighting off; a sickness of heart came over him and a terrible fatigue. The brightness of the air made him want to close his eyes to it. He was almost glad to make his farewell. When she was to return he did not even ask.

Four days later however a note from Mrs. Cox was handed in at Orwell Lodge. It said that Mrs. Ricardo felt, in sincerity to the promise she had given not to see Dr. Gully again, it was right that she should return to him all the presents he had made her. Mrs. Cox would bring them down in the carriage that afternoon. Would the doctor oblige by having ready, at the same time, all the presents Mrs. Ricardo had given him, so that they might be taken back to The Priory?

At half past two he was standing in the study beside an assembly of objects: pictures, vases, pen wipers, the malacca walking stick, the gold pencil, books, boxes, the china bowls in which she had grown hyacinths for him, a set of dominoes, a cashmere traveling rug in shepherd's plaid. There were also three photographs of her: two large ones, in a velvet and a silver frame, and a small oval one in a frame studded with brilliants; this had stood in his bedroom among his private treasures.

Mrs. Cox arrived with her arms full, followed up the steps by Pritchard, equally loaded, for he had seen the carriage draw up as he looked through the window of the front kitchen. Griffith could not leave the box and Pritchard and Mrs. Cox each made a second journey. Their burdens were laid on the study floor and Pritchard without a word began collecting the objects to be taken out to the carriage; with a tray and a large basket he effected the removals with wonderful quickness. When he had finished he retired and closed the door.

Dr. Gully stood by the French window; his attitude made it clear that he saw no reason for detaining Mrs. Cox, but Mrs. Cox had something to say. When the door was shut she allowed a second to elapse, then she said, "Mrs. Ricardo says, Doctor, that you have a great number of her letters to you. She would like you, please, to give them to me." She stood looking at the floor, meek and triumphant.

The letters! With a memory like a drowning man's, he saw all that they contained—the passion, the intimacy, the promises of everlasting love. His gorge rose at the idea of putting them into the hands of Mrs. Cox. He said in even tones:

"I won't do that, Mrs. Cox, but you shall see me burn them." He chose a key from his ring and unlocked one of the drawers in his desk. The bundle he took out, tied up with a strand of lawyers' pink tape, was compact but it contained nearly a hundred letters. She had once written to him every day.

The fire under the round-arched fireplace was glowing; he flattened the pile of red coals and laid the packet there, holding it in place with the poker till it was scorched, blackened, consumed; the white corners that had escaped he drew together and pressed down into the red-hot bed; in a minute nothing was left, nothing. Mrs. Cox's eyes as usual were screened by her spectacles, but her lips moved as if she were eating.

He said: "You will tell Mrs. Ricardo. My own letters to her—"

"Oh, she has destroyed those already." He bowed.

She had gone, and unable to bear the sight of the presents or to think about what to do with them, he opened the left-hand cupboard and bundled into it pictures, ornaments, jewelry, glass, porcelain, marble, silver. He had shut the door when on the floor by the sofa he saw something bright. It was the jeweled locket with his photograph in it.

He thought of cramming it into the coals, for the heat to do what it could on it; but the gold, the diamonds and the pearl wouldn't be destroyed by a domestic fire, they would be damaged but they would remain; it would be foolish. He prized out his photograph and tossed that into the fire, then threw the locket into one of the desk's little drawers. This done, he rang.

"Pritchard," he said, when the latter appeared. "Mrs. Ricardo has behaved very badly to me. From now onward neither she nor Mrs. Cox is ever to be admitted to this house."

A look of absolute satisfaction spread over Pritchard's face. "Very good, Doctor," he said. "You won't have to repeat *them* orders."

Dr. Gully had forgotten what a supporter he had in his affectionate, faithful servant. The comfort of his home began to make itself a little felt. He thought with indignation of the suggestion that he should leave it. He couldn't but remember the episode of 1872 when at Florence's vehement urging, he had first taken and then relinquished the house on Tooting Bec Common, losing five hundred pounds on the transaction. Then, he had willingly forgone the money; now he did not feel inclined to give up the house that was his home because, having thrown him over, she would find it more agreeable if he left the neighborhood.

He determined to read, but he sat down without a book and was still sitting unoccupied when Pritchard brought his tea two hours later.

Chapter 34

DAY followed day of the strange, maimed existence. On the morning after the return of the presents he remembered something he ought to do. He summoned Pritchard and gave him the key of the outer gate.

"I want this taken back to The Priory at once," he said. "Give it yourself to Mrs. Cox, or to—give it to Mrs. Cox and come back and tell me when you've done it."

He knew that The Priory servants continued to frequent his kitchen. Through this source he heard a few days later that Mrs. Campbell had come to visit the mistress, and it had been Mama here, and Mama there, no end of a setout, and Mrs. C. brought forward, looking as though butter wouldn't melt in her mouth.

Well, she had gained the thing she wanted, the thing that had cost him so dear. Once she had thrown over her family for him; now he was sacrificed for her family. He could not condemn her in spite of her ruthlessness and his suffering.

A fortnight went by and in the complete blankness and silence to which he was left, he began to doubt very much if this engagement to Charles Bravo would take place. There seemed so much against it on both sides. What was known of his family was surely enough to deter Florence, and if the man knew the truth about her past, would he marry her?

One of the thoughts that tormented him was that though he could maintain that their love affair was respectable while it was still in being, while it was a private engagement, a pre-marital union, once it was broken off, all the arguments supporting it were made void, it became a criminal intercourse, merely. This must tell against her in the eyes of the man and his family if it were known. Not that he accepted the blame for this; his intention had been marriage. It was not his responsibility that if she broke her engagement with him, another man would be unlikely to make one with her.

On Tuesday, November 9, he had attended a meeting in Gower Street and returned to Orwell Lodge about nine o'clock, on a dark night with the moon not yet risen. He let himself in; the fire in the hall was cheerful, and as he took off his coat he saw a small envelope on the salver; the sight made his heart beat—but the handwriting was Mrs. Cox's. He carried it into the study.

The shutters had been closed, the fire was throwing a light up one wall. He lit the two candles on his desk and the two on the chimneypiece and slit open the envelope.

"Dear Dr. Gully," he read, "Mrs. Ricardo wants you to know that her engagement to Mr. Charles Bravo is announced, and that the wedding will take place from her father's house in Lowndes Square on December 14." He saw it all now; the desire for a reunion with her mother had been used to lever him out of Charles Bravo's path.

He sat for a long time in a chair on the hearth. At last he got up and took from the right-hand cupboard a green morocco solander with his initials stamped in gold above the lock. Turning back the lid he found a sheet of writing paper; the mild glow of candlelight bathed the page, covered in Tennyson's sensitive hand.

Child, if it were thine error or thy crime,
I care no longer, being all unblest,
Wed whom thou wilt, for I am sick of time
And I desire to rest.

In this room he had shown her the verses, shown her too the poem printed with alterations in *The Keepsake*, saying he would always prefer the version given him by the poet. He put the precious paper back into the box and returned the latter to the cupboard shelf, pushing it a little against some slight obstacle, leaving the door ajar.

He stood looking at the closed shutters as if he could see through them. Outside, the thickets and trees on the common would be black, barely distinguishable against gloom. His mind carried him up to The Priory, its brilliant interior glowing against the surrounding darkness. He stopped; he would not wonder in which room she was or who was with her. As he stood, returning in consciousness to the dark waste, he was pierced by a pang of incredulous amazement. Her scent was in the room.

He turned. There was nothing behind him but the room itself, empty in the candlelight, but the scent was becoming stronger, Eau de Chypre, sweet, sensuous, troubling. He gazed about him, aghast in the dim light, at the gleam of silver and brass on his desk, the gold background of Fra Angelico's angels. Silence, emptiness, silence, and the scent rising in power like a materializing spirit.

His eye fell on the cupboard door and he remembered how he had hidden away the bottle she had left in the drawing room. He stooped, pulling out the solander again, and there at the back of the shelf was the little flask on its side with the crown-like stopper half out.

Pritchard came with hot water and a flannel. He said they must have the door and window wide open tomorrow morning; meanwhile as the fire was burning in the doctor's dressing room, he suggested that room should be used, as the drawing room took so long to warm. As the doctor wanted to write letters, Pritchard carried the silver inkstand upstairs and Dr. Gully followed with writing paper.

"Have I not behaved to you with every consideration and gentleness? Did I deserve that you should allow Mrs. Cox to give me the news of your engagement, instead of writing to me yourself? I have never denied that you were at liberty to form another attachment; I only wish you had formed this one before I ever saw you. You might not have been constant to this man either but that would have been his affair. Then I should not have left Malvern where I was at the height of my success and given up everything for a woman on whom my devotion was wasted."

To Mrs. Cox he wrote briefly: "I am obliged to you for the information in your letter and must congratulate you on the success of your endeavors. I hope that the marriage of Mrs. Ricardo to your friend will fulfill your hopes in every respect."

The notes were taken up to The Priory next morning and for some hours he was gratified by the memory of what he had written, but in a day or two the balance of his humane, sympathetic nature reasserted itself. He began to regret the terms he had used and he wrote again to each of them, regretting his harshness, and saying to both of them that he sincerely hoped the marriage would prove very happy.

The struggle that he made for calmness was not always successful but he knew he owed it to himself to make it. He took his walks on the common, avoiding the stretch of it commanded by The Priory windows, striking out to the right at the top of Bedford Hill and making for the largest of the ponds. He would pause sometimes on its shore. The ground was a rich, pale brown mixed with gravel, the water, ridged with spreading rings, like green tourmaline. After every rain a rivulet scarcely a handbreadth ran down from the saturated grass into the pond. It had worn for itself a little channel scattered with tiny pebbles. By stooping over it he could just hear its faintly murmuring flow. The sound was apt to be blotted out by another. To the left, across the farther common at a distance of some eighth of a mile, the view was bounded by a railway embankment, where the Victoria-Brighton line train sped by under a rolling banner of steam, the sound, according to the weather, loud and insistent or a subdued, rumbling hum.

The November weather, damp and dim, suited a pensive mood, and he had much to think about. Ann and Ellen, Willie and Bessie, Susanna and Charlotte Dyson were all in his mind. When he could do so calmly, he meant to tell them all that Mrs. Ricardo was going to be married and it had been decided that they should not meet again.

Pritchard saw that the doctor was looking older but that he had also become more impressive. He moved more slowly but with the air of added intellectual strength, of quietness and dignity. Pritchard had not, so far, told him the latest piece of news from up there, that Mrs. Ricardo's wedding, which had first been spoken of for April, then fixed for December 14, was now brought forward again to December 7 (something funny there, if you asked *him*).

It was at half past eleven on the morning of November 27 that Mrs. Griffith came to the side door of Orwell Lodge and had a word with Pritchard, who brought her up into the hall, and asked the doctor if he would speak to her.

Dr. Gully said kindly, "Good morning, Mrs. Griffith"—and almost before the words were out of his mouth, Fanny Griffith nervously explained that Mrs. Ricardo would be obliged if he would step up and speak to her at the Lower Lodge. She said afterward: "He looked surprised, but he said he would come."

Fanny Griffith ran back up the hill; ten minutes later Dr. Gully set out. He made the short walk in severe mental conflict, holding down curiosity, fighting off hope. He passed the new lodge, where workmen in hats made of folded newspaper were still occupied in pointing the back walls, and walked along the drive to the Lower Lodge, where he was admitted by Fanny Griffith who, still a little breathless, showed him into her neat parlor. He remained standing with his hat in his hand until, without warning, Florence was in the doorway, in brown velvet with a sable cap on her head. She looked beautiful but strangely charmless. She walked straight into the room and said: "I want to ask your advice."

Whatever his surprise, he merely bowed and said: "Well, do so." She sank into a chair and motioned him to one.

"It is about my marriage settlement."

"And what about it?"

"It is being drawn up by Mr. Brookes."

"Yes."

"The forty thousand pounds left me by Alexander's will is settled on me, so is the twenty thousand pounds on which Papa pays me the income."

"Quite rightly."

"So Mr. Bravo will not gain possession of that money but he will of course benefit from the income as he will live in the establishment which is kept up by it, as well as from any of the income I might make over to him from time to time."

"Quite so. That is a very proper arrangement."

"Yes; but I instructed Mr. Brookes to put all my personal property into the settlement as well. There—there is a great deal here, really; the lease of the house, and all the furniture that was bought only eighteen months ago, and my Venetian glass, and the silver, my jewelry and furs, the two carriages and the carriage horses and the cobs." She stopped, white and breath-less.

"You have had all these things put into your settlement as well as the money?" He was careful not to allow the least surprise to show itself; he asked the question as if he were gaining information about a patient; but great heavens! What sort of terms was she on with this man she had chosen to marry?

"Yes," she said, "at least I told Mr. Brookes to put them in."

"Well?"

"Well—" her voice was almost gone. "Mr. Bravo says that unless all the personal property is taken out of the settlement and becomes his at the marriage, the marriage won't take place." She was staring at him as if she longed to tell him something further; her white lips opened but they didn't move. He sat looking very grave, very attentive and very kind.

"But," he said, "I don't think there is any cause for this distress. I think you should give way over the personal property." Was it relief or disappointment? Some feeling caused her to relax her rigid pose.

"He says, rather than sit on a chair or at a table that isn't his, he won't be married at all."

"That is putting it strongly, certainly, but I don't think his objection is much to be wondered at. You shouldn't want your husband to feel that he isn't master in his own house."

She looked uncertain. He said in encouraging tones: "You have a large fortune, after all, and that is still in your own hands."

"Yes, but this action of Mr. Bravo's has made me feel that he's marrying me for what I've got instead of for what I am."

The benignity of his face changed to a momentary sternness.

"I do not know Mr. Bravo; you do; but I can't suppose that he or any other man could marry you without wanting you for yourself. I think you should give way over the settlement. It's not worthwhile to quarrel about furniture. After all, what he's asking is a small price to pay for happiness."

She drew a long breath. "Very well. I did not like it when it was put to me with such violence, but as you think I should do right to consent, I will. . . ."

Had she half-expected that he would denounce this man as a greedy fortune hunter and beg her to return to *his* protection? There was a shade of bewilderment in her large, expressive eyes. She now added: "I have told my future husband everything about our relationship."

He said: "I hope that will turn out well." Her gloves were brown suede, like brown velvet; he took one of her hands and raised it to his lips; with the glove on, it was a gesture only. "Every good wish for your happiness," he said, and she could see at last, that he was moved.

She said nothing, but still very pale, she walked with a somnambulist's gait to the door of the lodge and turned to the right up the drive.

Dr. Gully came out of the parlor and Mrs. Griffith came out of her kitchen.

"I hope you and the family are well, Mrs. Griffith," he said.

"Very well, at present, thank you, Doctor." Then she said: "We shall see some big changes up here."

He said: "I hope Mrs. Ricardo will be very happy."

Chapter 35

HE decided that he would leave Balham for the time covering the wedding and the honeymoon; he would seek society and change. While he made these plans, he was, without any inquiry on his own part, continually aware of what went on at The Priory. The butler Rowe had told Pritchard all the servants had supposed that on the wedding Mrs. Cox would receive marching orders, but it turned out, no such thing. Well, Dr. Gully thought, he would have arranged matters differently, but perhaps Mr. Bravo was merely biding his time.

Then, the scene came into sharper focus. In the first week in December, Griffith called, and standing in the study, asked the doctor for a reference. A few days before, on Lord Mayor's Day, he had been driving Mrs. Ricardo and Mrs. Cox in Bond Street, and had had a collision with a wine merchant's dray, which had damaged the carriage badly. Mr. Bravo, hearing of this, had declared that Griffith wasn't safe to drive in London and had persuaded the mistress to dismiss him. Griffith was now on a month's notice. He knew that Lady Prescott of Stroud Park, Herne Bay, wanted a coachman; he had applied for the post and Mrs. Cox had written a reference for him, but Lady Prescott, taking a firmer line about letters from Mrs. Cox than anyone else had done up till now, declared that this was insufficient; she said she must have a personal recommendation. Griffith had come to ask if the doctor would be so good.

Dr. Gully had never had a complaint to make of Griffith during eight years' service. Bravo's severity was natural in an anxious bridegroom, but so far as he could, without having been present at the accident himself, Dr. Gully was willing to believe Griffith when the latter declared that it hadn't been his fault. He undertook to call on Lady Prescott at her town house in Grafton Street and say what he believed was due.

He looked very impressive as he came into Lady Prescott's morning room, by appointment. She had of course heard of Dr. Gully and his mere reference went for a great deal, besides his well-grounded recommendation. Her ladyship was much obliged to him for his trouble and they took leave, pleased with themselves and each other. Griffith was engaged to go to Stroud Park on January 3 when his notice at The Priory expired. He was very grateful to the doctor, but he was bitter about being turned out of his lodge. Pritchard had gathered from the servants in general that the master would be affable enough if you were on the right side of him, and that you'd get the rough side of his tongue if he fell out with you.

Dr. Gully now looked forward with anticipation to a round of visits, including one to the Shelleys at Boscombe, and the delightful idea had been started that he should go up to Liverpool where Willie was due at the spring assizes. This proved to be exactly the tonic he needed. He now heard Willie in court for the first time, and his heart was filled with exhilarating pride at the handsome presence, the clear, decisive diction, the commanding ability, the emanation of a humane, modest, trustworthy personality. He was invited to dine at the Judge's Lodging, and he gained the impression that his own view of his son was very generally shared.

All this gave affairs at The Priory a remoteness, as of something interesting but not of painful immediacy.

The bridal pair had returned on January 6; the lodge, vacated by Griffith and his family three days before, was still empty for the new coachman, Parton, had not yet arrived. The stables were in charge of Younger the groom and the stableboy Bob, anxious but not very clever; and Mrs. Bravo on the afternoon of the homecoming lost no time in going out to inspect them. Her well-known step aroused the horses to their usual conversation with her; their hooves clinked and stamped, their soft whinnies answered each other's. She caressed them, looked sharply around the stalls and then went into the deserted harness room.

It had been left tolerably tidy but in a bucket were the large fragments of two broken bottles and one that was not broken; it was uncorked, and had a half-inch stripe of white crystals along the bottom. With an impatient exclamation she stooped over the bucket and lifted the bottle out; it must come indoors and be put in a safe place.

The master had come downstairs and was in the morning room, talking loudly and cheerfully to Rowe. She went upstairs to her bedroom that was now their bedroom. In her dressing room her maid was unpacking her clothes. Florence had relinquished the dressing room leading out of the bedroom to her husband; it was the more convenient of the two as to situation, but the farther one that she had kept for herself was larger.

The master and mistress were not yet settled at home; they went for a visit to her people at Buscot Park and to his people at Palace Green, but they were back at the end of January and Mrs. Cox with them; they all seemed to be very comfortable together.

The menservants told Pritchard that the maids had said that Mrs. Cox was, as ever, always anxious to save Mrs. Bravo any

sort of trouble; she was always with her. The household went
to bed early, Mrs. Bravo sometimes going upstairs at half past
nine, and Mrs. Cox always went with her into her dressing room.
And it was just as well, because before the end of January, the
lady's maid Rolands was got rid of—no fault to be found on
either side, but Rolands understood it was to save expense, and
by putting two and two together, it was made out that this very
strange idea had come from Mrs. Joseph Bravo of Palace Green,
who thought the mistress too free with her money, now that it
was, in a manner of speaking, Mr. Bravo's money, and wanted
to see some economies made. Mary Ann Keeber agreed to take
on some of Rolands' duties; she was willing enough, but she did
wonder what business it was of Mrs. Bravo, Senior, and where
the next interference was to be.

However, all agreed, for once, that it was a good thing Mrs.
Cox was there, because during the last few days of January the
mistress was ill and had to keep her bed. The maids who emptied
the slop pails and the pan in the commode and took away the
bed linen knew all about it, and Mrs. Cox, give her her due, was
a wonder in the sickroom and scarcely ever out of it.

All this was discreetly related to Pritchard, who stored it up
against the doctor's return. He was devoutly thankful that the
doctor was separated from the ladies at The Priory. While his
master was away, Pritchard instituted a grand spring-cleaning
and when Miss Ann and Miss Ellen came, by the doctor's arrangement, to take some lavender cuttings, he asked them to look
over the house; they did so, and declared it to be in apple-pie
order. It was like old times when he brought them tea in the
drawing room (though Miss Ann looked sadly worn; she had
had a slight stroke, and Miss Ellen now acted as the elder lady
and took care of her sister); Pritchard did not retire, they had
so much to say to each other. He talked about Mrs. Ricardo's

marriage, and the ladies said very earnestly how glad they'd been to hear of it and how much they hoped she'd be happy.

"Have you seen the gentleman?" Miss Ellen asked.

"No, ma'am, none of us has laid eyes on him, not even the doctor."

Dr. Gully, before coming home, was spending a few nights at Queensborough Terrace, where his presence was always a source of pleasure to the parents and of excitement among the children. It was convenient to be down in London for he had several engagements.

Mrs. Kimball, whom he had seen only once, without recalling herself to his memory, had written inviting him to her house on the evening of February 18, to sit with Mr. Coleman and Mr. Eglinton and a few interested people. As he studied her strange handwriting, like prints of birds' feet mixed with twigs and stems, he felt, though he could have given no reason for the impression, that there would be something of special interest to him at the séance, and he accepted willingly. Coleman and Eglinton were well known to him by name as materializing mediums. He afterward ascribed some of the extraordinary quality of the evening to the fact that Mrs. Kimball herself sat with them.

In the modest sitting room, arranged, as usual, with a draped cabinet at the far end, the fire a mere glow without lambent flame, and in the light of one candle only, six people including himself sat in a demilune before the curtains. It was announced by one of the mediums that spirits were present who were related to him, and the little hand stroked his face. Then a surprising shower of materializations occurred, so rapid and profuse, he had never seen anything like it, hands, a naked foot, flowers, a woman in clothes like Mary Queen of Scots, all pale and half-transparent like mist in moonlight. He was absorbed in watching this display of disassociated phenomena; then, after some time, he could not tell how long, the curtains parted and a very small girl stood between them with a veil over her face.

He leaned forward in a passion of entreaty, exclaiming: "Can't I see her face?" One of the men answered, "Be patient; when the power is a little stronger," and a few moments later, the child, unveiled, walked into the room.

She was dressed in white muslin, the curls hung all around her head. She stood smiling up at him, so radiant and joyous it nearly broke his heart. "Are you my child?" he whispered hoarsely. The beautiful little head nodded and smiled. So many of his thoughts had been of her as he had seen her last, this laughing look that was she, entirely, came back on him now with a keen thrust of agony and joy. She turned and ran away, out of this world again.

He had never known such sensations; a little more and he would have been over the edge into unconsciousness. After he had left the séance and his mind was working normally again, he remembered the accusations against Florence Cooke, that she herself impersonated the materialized spirit. Of these three mediums, two were men, the third was a grown woman. None of them could conceivably have impersonated a child of two.

Overpowering as the emotional impact had been, he never ceased to regard the subject as, primarily, one for scientific research. Crookes had published the results of some experiments to which Dr. Gully drew the attention of spiritualists, despite the fact that many would not be able to follow them. He wrote: "Mr. Crookes' experiments on the motor forces of light should not pass unnoticed by spiritualists. The discovery opens another point for observation in our complex and mysterious subject."

He came back to Orwell Lodge at the beginning of March. The house, to which he returned as a beloved master, spacious, solid and quiet with all his own possessions in it, was a refuge, a home. He tried to shut out from his mind the unseen domain that was so near.

Pritchard, however, at suitable intervals, gave him all the news of it, and he listened, partly from instinctive wish to hear, partly from kindness which forbade him to tell the man to hold his tongue. Pritchard said that Mrs. Bravo had been very poorly at the end of January and had had to go away for sea air.

"I'm sorry to hear that," Dr. Gully said.

"Lost her hopes, sir, they told us."

"Dear me, I am very sorry. Dr. Harrison attended her, I suppose?"

"So it came through, sir."

Left to himself, Dr. Gully thought that this was strange hearing. Married on December 7 and made really ill by a miscarriage only seven weeks later? He remembered her paleness, her air of desperation at their last interview. Had there, then, been a consummation already? If so, no wonder the man felt able to threaten her. Well, at all events, he himself had given her the correct advice. Better for her, perhaps, to be treated roughly by a man of her own age, than with unfailing tenderness and chivalry by a man of his. He now believed that if the marriage he had so yearned for had taken place, it would not have brought him the happiness he had expected from it once. Since he knew the inside of The Priory so thoroughly, he could not help it that occasionally a vision of this unknown man should invade him, in her morning room, her dressing room, her bed, and cause him pangs; but these were momentary. All in all he did not now ardently wish to change places with Charles Bravo.

Chapter 36

He wanted her to be happy; he did not expect or, except for fugitive longings, even wish to see her again.

Still less did he expect or wish to see Mrs. Cox; but early in March he did see her, on the pavement outside the Army & Navy Stores as he was coming away from Victoria; and when he realized that she had seen him and was hoping for a recognition, his natural kindness made him stop and take off his hat.

He inquired formally after Mrs. Bravo and then he spoke of something that had been on his mind. The album with the collection of his printed ephemera—could he have it? "It can be of no interest to Mrs. Bravo now," he said, "and my children will value it." Mrs. Cox willingly undertook to have the book returned; it was in the cabinet in the morning room; she would bring it down to Victoria and send it by train, directed to him care of the Balham Station Parcels Office. Two days later the package arrived; delivered by hand it would have reached his house within ten minutes but no doubt this course was the best. He was glad to have the album in his hands; as he had expected, there were many loose items tucked into the pages.

Mrs. Cox, it seemed, had lost one set of tenants at the end of February and was having some trouble in replacing them, and this was why she was traveling so often from Balham to

Victoria and from Victoria by the Metropolitan Railway to Notting Hill. On March 23 she overtook him as he was entering Balham Station. This time it was she who had something to ask. The visit to her aunt in Jamaica had at last been decided upon and she wanted from Dr. Gully the homeopathic treatment for Jamaica fever. He promised to write it out and post it to her; then he inquired for Mrs. Bravo. Mrs. Cox pursed her lips and slightly shook her head. Mrs. Bravo, she had to admit, had been indignant at his sending her husband that anonymous letter.

Amazed, he exclaimed: "What anonymous letter? I never sent an anonymous letter in my life!"

Oh, Mrs. Cox said, well, they all supposed it must be from him, though *she* had never thought it likely. It had come to Palace Green, speaking of Mrs. Bravo in very vile terms and accusing Mr. Bravo of marrying Dr. Gully's mistress for money.

He was speechless; that anyone who knew him at all, let alone knew him well, could suppose that *he*—great heavens! What people these were! He raised his hat and left her abruptly; however, as a doctor he felt obliged to keep his promise of writing out the treatment and sending it to The Priory. He would have been very glad for this to be the end of it, but one morning at the end of March, as he was studying the timetable outside Balham Station, there, at his elbow, was Mrs. Cox again. It appeared that in the treatment he had so kindly sent, he had omitted the one for ague, which so often preceded Jamaica fever; would he be so kind as to send her that?

"Very well," he said; then she asked him to address it to her house, at 150 Lancaster Road. So he must not address even a prescription for Mrs. Cox to The Priory? So be it.

The spring, with all its beauty and excitement, was, he had always said, a trying time for the constitution. He was not very well; he had aches and pains and walking was sometimes a little difficult; still, he had not much to complain of; now that the bright season was coming on, he took a walk on the common before breakfast, and the breakfast hour was put forward to eight o'clock.

It was known that a great deal of entertaining was going on at The Priory; Mrs. Bravo's immediate family came, as well as uncles and aunts, cousins and their children, and numbers of Mr. Bravo's friends. There were luncheon parties and dinner parties and a tennis net had been put up; they were really going it, the servants said. It was only to be expected when the mistress had been so quiet before. When their comments on these doings reached him, Dr. Gully said to Pritchard it was a funny thing that with all the times he'd had to pass the gates to get onto the common, he'd never seen Mr. Bravo once. When he said this, Pritchard told him that he himself had at last seen Mr. Bravo. Pritchard had been seeing some of his own friends out of the house; he had stayed, leaning on the gate a few minutes in the spring evening, and Mr. Bravo had come walking up the hill on his way home. He had not looked to right or left, walking purposefully along. Pritchard had had a good look at *him:* a pale, solid, rather handsome gentleman with dark whiskers. Not a good one to cross, but nor was Mrs. Bravo, come to that, Pritchard had thought as he went back into the house.

On Saturday, April 8, Dr. Gully was going to Thornton Heath to lunch with acquaintances whom Dr. Moore had introduced to him. He was feeling his age a little but his appearance was as fresh and spruce as ever. Everyone he met on and about the station knew him by sight and most of them passed the time of day with him. This morning as he bought his ticket for Thornton Heath he realized he had not much time to spare and he was turning toward his platform when he heard himself called and Mrs. Cox was hurrying after him.

"Oh, Doctor," she said urgently, "Mrs. Bravo is dreadfully poorly. She's had no sleep for two nights, such severe pain down the spine. You know she can't take ordinary sleeping draughts. Can you suggest anything for her?"

His train was coming up the line. He said brusquely: "Spinal washings three times a day and a cold sitz bath for five minutes morning and evening might help her."

"Thank you very much; we will try them, and can you prescribe anything to put her to sleep?"

The train was drawing up; he mustn't miss it, his host's carriage would be meeting it at Thornton Heath.

"I will think it over and let you know," he said, and got in at the nearest door.

He should not have been asked for this advice, but since he had been, he couldn't refuse to give it. This sounded like another miscarriage, but whatever it was, that was the correct treatment for backache and insomnia. He was distressed to think of her in this miserable state. He thought, while he was still in the train, of a mild sedative he had never tried her with, a Jamaican specific, *aqua cerasee;* it was a preparation of laurel leaves, poisonous in themselves but in the prescribed dose so mild it was given to children in their teething troubles. When he returned to Balham that afternoon he went into Smith's the chemist; he used allopathic remedies so seldom, he'd forgotten the dose and he asked to see Smith's *Pharmocopeia.* He then ordered a half-ounce bottle to be made up, and presently the little phial was handed to him, its glass stopper neatly bound with white kid. He didn't feel it a matter of urgency to get this into Mrs. Cox's hands; the cold-water treatment was the important thing. On Monday he was calling on a medium who lived in Westbourne Park Road, and Lancaster Road was such a short distance from there, he decided to leave the bottle with his name for Mrs. Cox at No. 150. She could use it or not as she liked.

He told Pritchard casually of the encounter with her. Whether

Pritchard spoke out of a general anxiety that the doctor shouldn't be drawn in once more, or whether he spoke on some impulse that he didn't understand himself, at all events he said with an earnestness that surprised his master: "Oh, Doctor! I think it's *very* unwise of you to have anything to say to them, I do, indeed, sir."

"I don't mean to have any more to say to them," Dr. Gully answered, but when on the following Wednesday morning, April 12, Mrs. Cox again came up to him on the station platform, he could not cut her. He asked after Mrs. Bravo, and Mrs. Cox told him gratefully that the spinal washes which she had given herself, and the cold sitz baths had relieved Mrs. Bravo's back of the pain very much, and she had had some natural sleep for the last four nights. Mrs. Cox could say this, as she was sharing Mrs. Bravo's room to take care of her. She now spoke of the illness as a miscarriage though she had not done so before; he did not ask her any questions, however; after all, Dr. Harrison was presumably in charge of the case. But as they were both going to Victoria on the train that now came in, it would have been difficult to part company with her. They got into the same carriage, and he had some conversation with her, feeling pleasantly magnanimous. He was going to lunch at Queensborough Terrace, he told her, and added that his son was now doing very well at the bar. Mrs. Cox listened with earnest sympathy. At Victoria they both made for the Metropolitan Railway; she left the train at Notting Hill while he went on to Queen's Road. As he walked the short distance to his son's house, he thought with pity and concern about this second miscarriage, which had followed the previous one almost as soon as nature would allow. The misery of her pain and sleeplessness was vividly present in his mind. He hoped fervently that Bravo would be considerate and allow her ample time for recovery, would study her comfort, her nerves, her general well-being. Most women needed gentle handling at such times and a long convalescence before returning to their marital duties; she, especially, was likely to suffer in mind as well as in body. When he remembered the state to which nervous suffering had brought her in 1870, he felt a melancholy anxiety for her.

The affectionate, gay welcome he received at No. 65 made him gladly put such thoughts out of his head. The baby, in pink shoes, walked across the nursery floor to him, holding up her arms. The boys, released from lessons because it was Easter, were full of ideas as to what they wanted to do. He did not think, privately, that either of them was going to be as clever as Willie, but he loved to listen to their eager, laughing talk though some of it was intelligible only to themselves. As for Gi-gi, she had been practicing a new piece on the pianoforte and she played it to him before luncheon, with only a few pauses and hardly any mistakes.

The Easter weekend was fine and warm; at night the Easter moon flooded heaven and earth with a glorious strength of light: mirrored in ponds, reflecting from windowpanes and greenhouses, an insistent presence beyond curtains that had been close-drawn. For Saturday, Sunday, Monday and Tuesday nights the great luminous orb was at its fullest power.

On Wednesday at lunchtime Pritchard said: "Do you hear, Doctor, that Mr. Bravo is taken very ill." Dr. Gully paused in unfolding his napkin.

"*Mr.* Bravo?" he said.

"Yes, sir, the gardener told me that Mr. Bravo was taken very ill yesterday evening."

"What is the trouble, did he say?"

"Sickness and pains. Dr. Moore was sent for and Dr. Harrison last night, and then Mr. Bravo's cousin in Harley Street and another doctor with him."

"Four!"

"And the carriage goes to the station this afternoon to bring his family, his father and mother and his sister, the deaf and dumb lady, and the lady who takes care of her, and old Mrs. Bravo's maid—they're all coming up from their holiday in Hastings."

"I'm afraid that sounds as if it were very serious."

"They say up at The Priory that he's not likely to live, sir."

"How very distressing. I am very sorry for Mrs. Bravo." Acute pains with vomiting might mean one of several things; possibly an inflamed appendix. Well, they had called in plenty of medical advice. He would have liked to send to inquire, but it was out of the question. No doubt news would reach him presently.

It did so in unexpected fashion. Next morning he was reading the paper in his study a little after nine when Pritchard appeared.

"Mrs. Cox asking to see you, Doctor."

"What does she want? You shouldn't have let her in, Pritchard!"

"Mr. Bravo is dying, sir. I thought she'd come to ask you to go and see him."

Still displeased, Dr. Gully said: "I suppose I must see her as you've let her in," and Mrs. Cox was brought from the drawing room into the study. The moment was too urgent for sitting down.

She said in a controlled desperation: "Doctor, Mrs. Bravo begs for your help. Mr. Bravo is dying. He told me he'd poisoned himself, but he denies that he did to everybody else."

"Did he tell you what he took?"

"No. I thought it was chloroform."

"What are the symptoms?"

"First he was unconscious; when he came around he vomited blood and passed blood. Very low pulse. His pupils are dilated. The stomach pains are very terrible."

"That doesn't sound like chloroform. Who is with him?"

"Dr. Moore and Dr. Harrison came first, then Mr. Royes Bell and Dr. Johnson from King's College Hospital; then Mr. Henry Smith, old Mr. Bravo's brother-in-law. Nobody can suggest anything. His sufferings are shocking."

"The case sounds as if it might be amenable to homeopathic treatment: mustard plaster on the spine, cold compress on the belly, *arsenicum album* in water every quarter of an hour."

In less than five minutes, Pritchard, from the window of the front kitchen, saw Mrs. Cox hurrying down the drive.

Next day, Friday, taking his early walk, Dr. Gully saw from far off that on the garden front of The Priory, the blind over every window had been drawn. Some time after breakfast, Pritchard told him that Mr. Bravo had died at half past five that morning.

Chapter 37

THE shocked concern, the curiosity to know what had really been amiss, was in his mind continually. Sir William Gull, eminent, distinguished, famous for his powers as a diagnostician, had been the last doctor called in, bringing the total to six, but none of them, it was clear, had been willing to give a death certificate, for an inquest was to be held within The Priory walls. This opened on April 25 and lasted four days, as two days had to be allowed for the findings of the postmortem to be ascertained.

These, and the jury's verdict, were extremely startling. The deceased, it was said, had taken upward of thirty grains of antimony, and the jury found that he had died of the effects of the poison but there was not sufficient evidence to show under what circumstances it came into his body.

The funeral took place on April 29. Mrs. Bravo, it was understood, attended by Mrs. Cox, had at once gone to recuperate at Brighton.

What on earth was the explanation? Knowing nothing of the man, it was useless to speculate. He was anxious, naturally, to hear any news that came Pritchard's way, and almost at once two items were brought in: One was that everybody knew that Griffith had kept antimony in The Priory stables; the other was a remark that Griffith himself had made on the morning of the wedding, four and a half months ago. It was being repeated "all over the shop," that Griffith, standing in the tap room of the Bedford, had said to the publican Mr. Stringer: "Missis will be sure to have plenty of brandy before she goes to the wedding. Poor fellow, I shouldn't like to be in his shoes. He won't be alive in four months!"

What Griffith could have meant baffled conjecture. Fortunately for him, he'd been at Stroud Park in Kent, long before illness seized Mr. Bravo; but the man's folly had been execrable.

A gradual but persistent oncoming of anxiety was now invading his mind. He had not seen Willie for several days since the verdict of the coroner's jury. He wanted a word with him very much; and then a series of events took place which made consultation between them absolutely necessary.

On May 11, the *Daily Telegraph* came out with an account of the case which it called "Mystery at Balham," and a leading article severely castigating the way the inquest had been conducted. Mr. Carter, the coroner for East Surrey, had occupied this position for forty years and had, it seemed, got to the point of acting according to his own wishes rather than to professional dictates. Convinced before the proceedings opened that this was a case of suicide, and anxious to spare the family's feelings, he had acceded to the widow's request that the inquest should be held in her own house; he had excused her from giving evidence. To further her desire for privacy he had not informed the press, and worst of all he had refused Dr. Johnson's offer to give evidence, saying, "We don't require any further evidence; it is quite unnecessary to examine you." Mrs. Cox, on whose bare assertion that the deceased had told her he'd taken poison the whole case rested, was subjected to the barest minimum of cross-examination. Mr. Carter's conduct had thoroughly upset the jury and they had defeated his efforts by returning an open verdict;

while two of the dead man's friends who had managed to get themselves into the coroner's court had been profoundly dissatisfied, and one of them, who shared Charles Bravo's chambers, had been to Scotland Yard to say so.

A week later the Home Secretary was asked in the House if his attention had been called to the unsatisfactory nature of the coroner's inquest on the late Mr. Charles Bravo. Mr. Cross replied that it had, and he could assure the House that all the papers were now in the hands of the law officers of the Crown. Ten days later, the *Daily Telegraph* amplified this statement; it announced that the solicitor to the Treasury had conducted a private examination of thirty witnesses, which was now closed. It added: "For various reasons neither Mrs. Bravo nor Mrs. Cox, though questioned by the police, has been asked to give evidence."

This last statement appeared ominous, and must have been recognized as such by the ladies' advisers, for it was announced that on June 2, Mrs. Bravo and Mrs. Cox had attended at the Treasury and made voluntary depositions.

The progress of the matter which he followed both in the *Daily Telegraph* and the *Times* was causing him, and Willie, also, uneasiness and disquiet. On June 20, this was suddenly changed to a prospect of acute and imminent menace.

On this day the press announced that the Attorney General Sir John Holker had asked the Lord Chief Justice sitting with two other judges for an order to quash the inquest of April 25 and to grant permission for a new inquiry. The chief grounds for this appeal was a passage in the statement Mrs. Cox had made to the Treasury. The Attorney General read aloud: "'From a mistaken idea of shielding the character of Mrs. Bravo I did not tell the full particulars which I am now anxious to state. There was no cause whatever or the slightest reason for his committing suicide for ——' and here," said the Attorney

General, "comes a name I must not mention; 'and therefore
there was no reason why I should not have stated this before:
"Mrs. Cox, I have taken poison for ——. Don't tell Florence."'"
Dr. Gully read the words with such a sensation of horror, he
laid down the paper, wondering for the fraction of a second if
he were about to have a stroke. He picked it up again. Mrs.
Cox had declared that after a quarrel with his wife, the deceased had said: "Let her go back to ——." She had continued:
"He often said how he hated ——, how he wished he were dead.
He was jealous of —— though he knew all before marriage."
When Sir John Holker had read the statement to the end, he
said: "You see, my Lords, from her own statement, she de-
liberately kept information from the jury."

The Lord Chief Justice said: "There is no use shutting our
eyes to the fact that in your view it is not a case of suicide?"

The Attorney General replied: "If it turned out to be a murder, as I suspect it was, I hope we will be able to elicit facts
which would justify a charge against someone or other."

The Lord Chief Justice said: "I think you have shown sufficient grounds, Mr. Attorney General, to warrant us granting
your application."

The pauses which the Attorney General had made to point
the omitted name were reproduced by dashes—dashes as dramatic to the eye as the pauses had been to the ear. A short
spell of stupefaction gave way to burning anger; the statement
put him almost beside himself; he did not believe one word of it;
it was an impudent falsehood uttered with some intention that
was very dark.

The hardheaded fortune hunter, who'd threatened to break
off the match unless the personal property were made over to
him, who knew that his wife's liaison had been over before he
himself became engaged to her—that this man had been so jealous of her past amour with a man he'd never seen, that he had

been driven by his sufferings to take his life—no sane person would believe it. The lie was preposterous, but why had it been told? If the man hadn't committed suicide, how had the poison got into his body? He sat aghast. Now, it appeared, she herself was offering a reward of five hundred pounds to anyone who would prove the sale of antimony to any member of her household.

Willie was a tower of strength. Saying, "Shall I act for you, Father?" he got in touch with an eminent solicitor, Mr. Henry Kimber, of Lombard Street and explained his father's interest in the forthcoming inquest. Mr. Kimber agreed with him that as soon as the proceedings opened, they must be watched on Dr. Gully's behalf. Willie was so sensible, cheerful and calm, perhaps, apart from his wife, only his father would have been able to see that he was also deeply anxious.

As midsummer approached, the unrelenting heat and brightness began to grow oppressive; it added a feverish horror to a plague that now beset him.

The first letter arrived unstamped so he paid double postage on it; the envelope was dirty, covered with staggering handwriting, a heavy-handed adult's with a child's facility. Inside, the writer's pressure of spiteful feeling and his difficulty in writing it down produced crooked strokes and tumbling letters that looked as if they were bursting from a volcano. Some of the more easily decipherable words were: "Doctors is the wors, they got more chanst you ol villan." He would know better than to open another such envelope as that; but the next one slipped under his guard. It was on good paper, addressed in an unusually regular and beautiful female hand, which he thought he must have known but had forgotten. He opened it and thought it strange that there was no address at the top, only the date. "Dear Dr. Gully," it began, "with regard to your interesting friendship with Mrs. Bravo, I am sure you must—" the plunge into obscenity was sudden and frightful. A page was filled with it, all in exquisite writing. It was signed, "Yours sincerely, Medusa." After a few more of these searing and disgusting experiences he was able to glance very rapidly over the contents of such a letter so that he hardly paused between opening and tearing it up; but apart from the odious impact of the letters themselves was the sensation, like being overtaken in a nightmare, that his privacy, how, he did not know, had been broken into by a hostile, invisible mob.

The knowledge that he was the man whose name the Attorney General had not spoken must have arisen locally; and how devious and wide-spreading the poisonous growth had become already!

The opening of the second inquest was announced for July 11, to take place at the Bedford Hotel. Every time now that he passed the Bedford, he saw that idlers on the pavement nudged each other; and there seemed to be more of these persons than usual, of both sexes, in staring, loud-laughing groups.

About midday on Thursday, July 7, he was sitting in his study; the French windows were wide open and a little freshness came in from the garden. He was obliging himself to read but though his mind took in the words, there were images in his brain that had no connection with them. Suddenly he nearly started out of his chair. The door had opened and a small female shape stood there, in dark muslin; for a brief instant a spasm of incredulity, of outrage, possessed him; then Pritchard's voice said, "Mrs. William Gully, sir," and his daugher-in-law had hold of both his hands.

"Papa," she said, "Willie and I have been thinking that while this business is going on, you would be more comfortable with us. As I drove up the hill I saw a lot of strange-looking people collected on the pavement quite near your gate. I'm afraid they will be very impertinent and annoy you. I've come hoping to take you back with me. Pritchard thinks it would be a wise plan."

Pritchard now came in with a tray containing wine and a carafe of water, one of the best crystal glasses and a plate of Alexandra biscuits.

"Will you partake here, madam," he asked, "or in the drawing room?"

"Here," she said, "if I shan't be in your way, Papa?"

He roused himself and said emphatically: "No, no. Stay here, I beg."

Chapter 38

❧❧

THE second inquest opened at the Bedford Hotel at 10:30 A.M. on Monday, July 11, and on Tuesday the papers were full of it; the *Times* and the *Telegraph* carried verbatim reports. The heat of the day was already felt when, at 7:30 A.M., William Gully took one paper into his study and sent the other up to his father's dressing room.

This time, the widest publicity was to prevail. The Attorney General would ultimately appear; meanwhile the Crown was represented by Mr. Gorst, QC, and Mr. Harry Poland; eminent counsel had been briefed for the two women: Sir Henry James, QC, and a junior for Mrs. Bravo, Mr. Murphy, QC, and a junior for Mrs. Cox. These were sufficiently formidable legal talents, but Mr. Joseph Bravo had secured the services of Mr. George Lewis, who was *sui generis;* with his long hair and long nose, his monocle, his high-carried head, he had the elegance and savagery of some dangerous wild beast. Mr. Henry Kimber had said that he would attend every sitting of the court in person that they might know at the earliest moment when counsel for Dr. Gully should be briefed.

Descriptions, drawings gave a vivid picture of the large billiard room on the Bedford's first floor. An enormous table had been put together; at one end of it sat the coroner, who, after

his lamentable performance at the first inquest, had been provided with a legal assessor. To their right were ranged a jury of
seventeen; on their other side was a row of ten counsel; behind
their chairs, in serried ranks were the reporters and as many
of the public as could cram in. At the door, kept wide open,
two constables were on duty. Over their shoulders could be
seen the onlookers who filled the landing and were standing far
down the stairs. On the pavement was a perpetual throng who
picked up and retailed scraps of news from the tapsters kept
busy in the bars.

The first event was the transporting of the seventeen jurors
to the cemetery in Upper Norwood. Sheltered by a canvas
screen, the exhumed coffin lay on trestles; a piece of the lid
had been removed and the space covered with glass to expose
the dreadful face; a heavy odor of carbolic was nauseating in
its suggestion. One of the jurors was made too ill to go any
farther and only sixteen returned to the Bedford.

In the afternoon, old Joseph Bravo, whose appearance, the
reporters said, showed his West Indian origins, spoke of the passionate family affection in which his stepson had been reared.
His mother idolized him, while, speaking for himself, he said:
"He was my friend and companion." His marriage had been, to
all appearances, extremely happy.

Mr. Lewis asked: "Did your son ever mention the name of a
doctor, a Dr. Gully?"

"Never." Mrs. Cox had told him his son had taken poison.
From his knowledge of the young man he had disputed this with
her "all the way." Nothing would make him believe it.

The days in Queensborough Terrace began at crisis point with
the early delivery of the papers. William left the house soon
after breakfast, having anxiously read one paper which he sent
upstairs to his father who had meantime read the other over his

coffee, which was taken up to his dressing room; a family breakfast, it was felt, would be too great a strain on him.

The second day's evidence included that of Dr. Moore and Dr. Harrison. The latter said that Mrs. Bravo threw herself on the bed beside her unconscious husband, urging him with endearing terms to wake up and speak to her. She then fell asleep and Dr. Harrison had to rouse her and get her off the bed in case she interfered with the patient's breathing.

When roused, she sent the carriage to Harley Street for her husband's cousin Royes Bell who arrived at 2:30 A.M., bringing with him Dr. Johnson, the senior physician at King's College Hospital. Mr. Royes Bell said that Mrs. Cox beckoned him out of the room and told him that Charlie had told her he'd taken poison. Royes Bell at once repeated this to Dr. Johnson and Dr. Harrison; the latter said to Mrs. Cox: "Why didn't you tell me this before?" Mrs. Cox said that she had. "You did not," said Dr. Harrison. "You said you were sure he'd taken chloroform." The tale of the night's doings was re-created by witness after witness. With the uncanny flair of journalists for discovering information, the *Daily Telegraph* printed at the end of this day's proceedings: "It is believed that Mr. Sergeant Parry will appear, representing an important interest in this inquiry."

Sir William Gull, called on the fourth day, said that the decase of suicide though the patient had strenuously denied taking of poison; Sir William had therefore assumed that this was a case of suicide though the patient had strenuously denied taking anything except laudanum for his toothache. Sir William Gull had directed that the vomit, ejected out of the window and still lying on the small lead roof over the conservatory, should be collected and sent for analysis.

Professor Redwood stated that the matter showed that the deceased had absorbed upward of thirty grains of antimony. He further said that, dissolved in water, antimony was virtually tasteless. He gave each of the jury who wished it a sip from a glass in which forty grains of antimony were dissolved in four ounces of water.

On the fifth day the butler Rowe gave evidence. He said that at the dinner on the evening of April 18, Mr. Bravo drank three glasses of Burgundy. Mrs. Bravo and Mrs. Cox between them drank nearly two bottles of sherry. He gave a vivid picture of Mrs. Bravo after the alarm. At Mrs. Cox's order he had already sent the coachman for Dr. Harrison who lived one and a half miles off at the Paragon in Streatham. Mrs. Bravo declared that he must go himself for Dr. Moore who was only a quarter of a mile distant. She rushed into the pantry in her dressing gown. He said: "She kept screaming out between her sobs, 'Fetch someone, Rowe, do something!' She cried out to me, she screamed the words at me."

Mary Ann Keeber was called on the sixth day. He had always liked and trusted the girl, but it naturally gave him a twinge of discomfort to read of her cross-examination by George Lewis.

"Before Mrs. Ricardo was married to Mr. Bravo she was visited by a Dr. Gully. I never opened the door to him but I have found him in the house. I don't know if he opened the door himself when he came. I don't know how old he is"; she added naïvely: "Sixty or seventy, I should think." She said when Mr. Bravo was at home he used the water bottle on his washstand two or three times a day, for cleaning his teeth. She always filled it up at night after he had gone down to dinner; she did so on the night of April 18.

Knowing the rooms as he did, to read of what took place in them gave him a feeling of clairvoyance. That evening, the first since her illness that she had stayed up to dinner, Mrs. Bravo went up to bed a little after half past eight. Keeber was still at supper, and Mrs. Cox went upstairs to help Mrs. Bravo undress. At nine o'clock Keeber had gone up to the dressing room. Mrs.

Bravo, undressed, was sitting at her dressing table; Mrs. Cox was standing by the side of the fireplace, leaning her elbow on the chimney shelf. Mrs. Bravo said: "Mary Ann, fetch me a glass of Marsala." The witness fetched half a tumblerful from the dining room. She stood aside to let Mr. Bravo go upstairs before her. He went into his wife's dressing room and Keeber therefore took the wine into the bedroom and shut the door. She said: "I stood in the dark. The gas was not lit but the fire was burning." When she heard Mr. Bravo go into his bedroom next door she went out onto the landing and met Mrs. Bravo coming from the dressing room; the latter asked where the wine was and Keeber told her it was in the bedroom. Keeber spent ten minutes in the dressing room putting away Mrs. Bravo's clothes. When she went into the bedroom, Mrs. Bravo was in bed apparently asleep, Mrs. Cox sat on a stool beside the bed, almost behind the door. Keeber asked if anything more were wanted and Mrs. Cox told her no; she went out onto the landing, when Mr. Bravo's door flew open and he appeared in his nightshirt, shouting, "Florence! Hot water! Hot water!"

Keeber at once turned back to the bedroom. Mrs. Bravo was lying with her eyes shut but Mrs. Cox got up and came with her. Mr. Bravo stood at a side window, vomiting. Mrs. Cox told her to run for hot water and mustard; when Keeber returned with them, Mr. Bravo had slipped down and was lying unconscious propped against the chest of drawers. Mrs. Cox energetically mixed mustard and water for an emetic and told Keeber to fetch spirits of camphor. Going into Mrs. Bravo's room for this, Keeber roused her: "I touched her; she opened her eyes and looked at me." Keeber helped her on with her dressing gown and she ran into her husband's room. At the sight of him she showed every sign of distress. He vomited into a basin and Mrs. Cox told Keeber to take the basin away, empty and wash it. When she returned, Mrs. Cox was rubbing his chest with camphor and told

Keeber to rub his feet as hard as she could. When the doctors arrived, they were all sent out of the room.

The coachman Parton said that on the morning of April 18, he drove Mr. and Mrs. Bravo into London. Mr. Bravo got out at the Turkish Baths in Jermyn Street; Mrs. Bravo did some shopping, arriving home to luncheon about two o'clock. On the way into town they had turned back because it began to snow, but the weather clearing, they turned about again and continued the journey. They had passed Dr. Gully's house on the way down Bedford Hill. After passing the house, Parton declared: "Nothing was said and nothing was done. I heard no quarreling or high words between Mr. and Mrs. Bravo."

Mr. Lewis asked: "Did you start with the carriage closed?"

"No."

"Whereabouts was it closed?"

"Just at the beginning of Clapham Common when the snow came on."

On the eighth day, Mrs. Joseph Bravo's maid, Amelia Bushell, was called. She had known Mr. Charles Bravo for fifteen years; she had helped her mistress nurse him in his dying agonies. Her mistress was in a state of total collapse and could not be questioned by anybody. She could only say Mr. Charles was the last person likely to commit suicide. She added: "I had no knowledge of Mrs. Ricardo before the marriage. His mother did not approve of the marriage and did not go to the ceremony."

Miss Ann Bell who had arrived with the Joseph Bravos' family party was an admirably lucid witness who impressed the reporters. Mrs. Charles Bravo had walked with her in the garden saying: "We have been very happy and have never had a word together!" On the morning of Friday, April 21, Mrs. Bravo had said to her that the cause of death was a mystery—and would always remain so. But the principal witness on this day, whose every word was scanned with painful anxiety in Queensborough

Terrace, was George Griffith—Griffith whom the family had been accustomed to hear, outside his actual duties, speaking almost at random. What was he going to say now, in answer to expert, relentless cross-examination?

Griffith declared that when Dr. Gully broke up his establishment at Great Malvern, the doctor recommended him to Mrs. Ricardo. Questioned, he said: "I was in the habit of giving the doctor's horses tartar emetic. I kept it in the stables.

"I never got tartar emetic by Dr. Gully's orders."

Mr. Gorst said: "Take that book in your hand. Is that in your handwriting?"

"Yes." Mr. Gorst told the court that this book was the register kept by Mr. Clarke, chemist at Great Malvern, under the Sale of Poisons Act. The entry was as follows:

> June 11, 1869.
>   Name of purchaser. Dr. Gully.
>   Name and quantity of poison sold: 2 ounces tartar emetic.
>   Purpose for which required: Horse medicine.
>   Signature of purchaser: G. Griffith.

Griffith was very shortly reduced to incoherence.

"I am not sure that Dr. Gully knew of it.

"I will not undertake to say that I did not take a note from Dr. Gully to get that poison.

"I cannot swear that I did not buy that for Dr. Gully.

"I will swear that he did not tell me to buy it; if he did I have forgotten.

"I can't swear that I didn't tell the chemist Dr. Gully had sent me for it.

"I may have been sent for it by him; I may have delivered it over to him."

At the dressing-room window opening on the garden below, Dr. Gully laid down the paper and sat motionless. "Dr. Gully, tartar emetic, Dr. Gully, poison." The children had been told not to make a noise on the stairs; the stillness was absolute. He passed the day in a kind of waking trance, replying vaguely to the few, tactful, affectionate approaches of his daughter-in-law. Early that evening a note from Mr. Henry Kimber was delivered at the house. When the court assembled next morning, Mr. Archibald Smith told the coroner that with his learned friend Mr. Sergeant Parry he had been instructed to watch the case on behalf of Dr. Gully and the learned Sergeant would attend in the course of the day.

This morning Griffith said in cross-examination: "I kept the tartar emetic in a cupboard at The Priory stables. I never gave any of it to anyone in the house. Mrs. Ricardo did not know of it. I threw it away before I left—I poured it down the drain in the yard; and as to what I did with the bottle, I broke one or two of them and I may have left one there, but there was nothing in it, I know."

(What would anyone now believe that Griffith could be relied on to know?)

Griffith next denied that he had foretold on the wedding morning that Mr. Bravo would not be alive in four months. Mr. Lewis had Stringer called and asked Griffith if he would repeat the denial to Mr. Stringer's face. Griffith said: "I don't know if I said *four* months, I may have said five or six."

"Now tell me what you meant by it."

Griffith could tell nothing except that he'd said it in aggravation. "It was all one to me," he said, "whether he lived or died."

The evidence of Mr. Payne who had conducted the postmortem was of very great importance. He said that if the poison had been taken in the Burgundy drunk at dinner the deceased would have been sick in less than two hours. If he drank it in water on going to bed, he would probably be sick in about a quarter of an hour. His vomiting and becoming unconscious was consistent with his having taken thirty grains of antimony about fifteen minutes previously.

The coroner meanwhile had sent for Dr. Gully's butler from Orwell Lodge. Pritchard had been to Queensborough Terrace with clean clothes for the doctor and had brought a basket of the Orwell Lodge strawberries for Mrs. William Gully. To read his evidence brought a refreshing sense of consolation to his master.

Pritchard described Mrs. Cox's arrival on the morning of April 20. He was sorry that he'd told her the doctor was at home, because the doctor had told him never again to let Mrs. Bravo or Mrs. Cox into the house. An uproar of comment and laughter broke out all over the room. Mr. Sergeant Parry objected to Mr. Gorst's smiling; Mr. Gorst's smiling was defended by Mr. Lewis.

Pritchard continued: "Dr. Gully gave me orders about not admitting them when they became—I'll say, not so friendly.

"I was aware that there was a great attachment between Dr. Gully and Mrs. Ricardo."

He said: "I have seen Mr. Bravo pass Dr. Gully's house. He took no notice of the house and did not look up." Dr. Gully had told him that he had met Mrs. Cox twice, it may have been three times.

"By appointment?" asked Mr. Lewis keenly.

"How do *I* know whether it was by appointment?" said Pritchard. "*I* don't make his appointments for him!" He added, "I told him I thought it very unwise for him to speak to her. I didn't want my master to be bothered any more with them. Mrs. Ricardo and Dr. Gully quarreled frequently. All Dr. Gully had said about Mr. Bravo's death was that it was a bad business and the last inquest hadn't been satisfactory."

Every word so honest, so simple, so effective! This was the first report that had been read in Queensborough Terrace without strangulating anxiety, but the painful sensations returned with the next day's account of Mrs. Campbell's evidence.

"This intimacy with Dr. Gully met with our entire disapproval. In consequence we saw nothing of her. By her promise to have no more to say to Dr. Gully and by her marriage, she was entirely restored to the affection of her family."

Two letters of Florence to her mother were put in here which struck him, professionally speaking, as of very great significance. One, of April 10, four days after the miscarriage, said: "My back is very painful. I am washing it. It will be some time before I can get about as usual." The next, of April 16, said: "It seems ages before one feels really well, but by sitz baths and spinal washes I have wooed sleep back, one of the most important steps to recovery."

Mrs. Campbell recounted: "When the deceased was at Buscot at Christmas, he spoke to me about my daughter taking too much wine. He said, 'I will cure her of it.'

"Much as I disapproved the acquaintance with Dr. Gully, I believed that no impropriety had occurred between them. I think so still. I said it was a pity Dr. Gully did not leave the neighborhood. She said she had offered to pay his rent if he would go.

"I never heard the deceased say anything myself but Mrs. Cox and my daughter have told me about his talking of Dr. Gully. They said he was unhappy when he passed the house."

He read in this how honest, how unsuspecting his onetime old friend still was. She had no means of knowing that the story of the offer to pay his rent if he would leave Orwell Lodge was quite untrue: part of a fabric of falsehood.

On the thirteenth day something was produced, quite unexpectedly and of great evidential value. Mr. Jepson Atkinson of the Middle Temple, who shared Charles Bravo's chamber and had been at Oxford with him, said that during their intimate friendship of thirteen years, he had noticed the deceased's unvarying habit: on going to bed he always took a deep draught of cold water. "He used to drink it from the water bottle in his or my room, or wherever he was, without using a tumbler." The witness added: "He was a very clearheaded man, with a great deal of common sense and very little sentiment. No feeling for any woman would make him take a painful and uncertain poison with the effects of which he was thoroughly acquainted."

The thirteenth day, Thursday, July 27, was to be the first of the days of crisis. All secondary matters had been dealt with now. He felt like the canoeist whose fragile craft is approaching the rapids, thundering, perilous, inescapable: Mrs. Cox was to be called.

Chapter 39

THE accounts published on the twenty-eighth of July of the previous day's proceedings made it clear that in the unremitting glare and heat, the atmosphere of the crowded court had nearly reached suffocation point. The sash windows, widely open, were screened by Venetian blinds but these did not keep out the large smuts which poured in from the funnels of trains continually passing. Most of the people in the room were ones who washed daily and wore clean shirts; even so the smell of sweat from so many bodies was sickening; and though after a few minutes of it the nose grew accustomed and ceased to suffer, every so often it would realize some wave of overpowering sickly stench. Mr. Willis, the proprietor of the Bedford, had done his best for comfort; numerous rooms had been made ready for counsel and for waiting witnesses, male and female, with jugs and basins and towels and close stools behind screens. All the same, physical discomfort was seriously felt—until mental preoccupation took its place.

The Attorney General had appeared once or twice during the past fortnight, but this morning when the court opened he was already present; it was known that he would conduct the cross-examination of Mrs. Cox.

Reading the reports of these proceedings the following morning, Dr. Gully, in a quiet, shaded room at the back of the second floor at Queensborough Terrace, felt himself transported bodily to the heat and strain of the large, densely crowded saloon.

Mrs. Cox said: "Before the marriage Mr. Charles Bravo used to dine at The Priory and sometimes stop the night. His mother objected to his going home late as he might take cold."

Sergeant Parry said: "That's what he told you, I suppose?"

"Yes."

He paused, looking up from the *Daily Telegraph*. Was this the explanation of the miscarriage only seven weeks after the wedding? He read on, with feverish concentration. "The deceased had a conversation with me about my leaving after they were married. He said: 'I don't wish you to leave.' They were walking in the garden and they told me they'd both made up their minds for me to remain."

(So Mrs. Cox had no cause to wish the man out of the way?)

The pair had gone to Brighton for their honeymoon but three days afterward Mrs. Bravo found herself unwell and had sent for her to come down.

(What a beginning to the married life!) He went on to read of his own meetings with Mrs. Cox: the prescriptions for Jamaica fever, the bottle of *aqua cerasee*, left by him at her house in Lancaster Road within a week of the man's death. The contents of the bottle couldn't have harmed anyone but according to chemist's regulations it had borne a label marked "Poison." Poison and his stables, poison in a bottle from his hands, the connections were forming with a horrible rapidity.

One tribute there was to him, at least: "Mrs. Bravo began the sitz baths on Saturday; when I brought the *cerasee* on Monday she did not need medicine. The baths had relieved her back and she had obtained sleep."

Now she was saying of the dead man: "I heard him refer to Dr. Gully many times; I heard him say he wished Dr. Gully was dead, that he would like to shoot him, that he would like to see his funeral crossing Tooting Common."

Then she described a scene which she claimed to have witnessed on Good Friday, four days before the fatal evening. It had been Mrs. Bravo's first day downstairs and after lunch she had gone to lie down on the sofa of the morning room. The young husband, selfish no doubt, but enamored of her, would not leave her alone to rest. Her nerves, it would seem, were at snapping point, and she had ordered him out of the room in a tone he'd never heard before. An ugly quarrel had flared up which it required all Mrs. Cox's skill to compose. He himself felt no inclination to believe anything merely on her word; but he felt that this scene had a sort of probability in its sound, between an eager husband and a wife whom physical and nervous distress had made almost frantic. That evening, Mrs. Cox declared, he had said: "I despise myself for marrying her. Let her go back to Dr. Gully."

On the morning of April 18 Mrs. Cox had gone down to Worthing to see about a furnished house for Mrs. Bravo's convalescence. She came back just in time for dinner. At table Mr. Bravo was in muscular pain from the cob's having bolted with him over Mitcham Common, and he was angry because his stepfather, having forwarded to him a letter from his stockbroker, opened in error, which told him he'd lost twenty pounds, had enclosed with it a note saying he disapproved of these transactions.

Mrs. Bravo, whose first dinner downstairs this was, went up to bed at half past eight. On the stairs she asked Mrs. Cox to bring her up a glass of wine and water. Mrs. Cox returned for this to the dining room and carried it upstairs to the dressing room, where, the maid being at her supper, Mrs. Cox helped Mrs. Bravo undress, taking down her hair and replaiting it.

When Mary Ann Keeber came upstairs a little after nine, Mrs. Bravo sent her down for a glass of Marsala and then Mr. Bravo came into the dressing room, saying in French, for he thought the maid was behind him: "You've sent for more wine; you've already drunk nearly a bottleful." She had not replied; she was standing with her back to him, folding a cold-water compress.

It was a little after half past nine when Mrs. Cox, summoned by Keeber to his bedroom, found him at his window vomiting, and that he had said to her: "I've taken poison for Dr. Gully, don't tell Florence."

She gave her own version of the facts already given by Dr. Moore and Dr. Harrison, but she added that on Wednesday, April 19, when she was alone with the patient as Royes Bell had gone downstairs to lunch, he had said to her, "Why did you tell them? Does Florence know?" and that she had answered: "I had to tell them. I couldn't let you die." The only being who could have proved or disproved this was now a blackened corpse.

The Attorney General now directed his cross-examination to the relationship with Dr. Gully and Mrs. Cox gave a fluent account of the intimacy between the two households in Leigham Court Road. When she was asked directly if she hadn't realized that Dr. Gully was Mrs. Ricardo's lover, she hesitated, then said: "I knew he was very interested in her and she in him."

"But did you not know he was her lover?"

"I concluded so, from his coming so often."

She disclosed the journey to Kissingen in 1873, unaccompanied except by servants; but she had thought no harm of it: "He was an *old* gentleman."

"Did you know that she had agreed to marry him when his wife died?"

"Yes, I believe she had so arranged."

The witness detailed their holidays at Bognor; at Southsea; "Dr. Gully stayed with us in hotels and lodgings"; and the Italian tour of the previous year.

At The Priory Dr. Gully was a daily visitor; he had a latchkey to the outer gate. Even immediately before the marriage they appeared very fond of each other; they kissed each other frequently.

"Mrs. Bravo never told me she was afraid her husband would find out about her previous conduct with Dr. Gully; she had told him everything."

Trying to assess what the general effect of this evidence as to their relationship was likely to be, he thought that though it must to many people appear highly suspicious, and to some conclusive, on the whole the relationship would be accepted as a romantic attachment merely, indiscreet, improperly so, but not as the irremediably, hopelessly damaging affair which society would describe it, if they knew what it had really been. He would still have defended it on principle but he was pierced with compunction at the idea of exposing her to the murderous contempt and anger of the world. However, it was so much in Mrs. Cox's own interest to maintain a discreet silence; she had, it was known, already left Florence's employment—no solicitor advising the family would have sanctioned their remaining under one roof— and her chances of future employment would be seriously injured if it appeared that she had connived at anything disreputable in her last situation. He must rely on her sense of what was to her own advantage.

On the sixteenth day, Mr. Lewis took up the question of how much of Mrs. Ricardo's past Mr. Bravo had known before he offered to marry her. He asked what part in the matter Mrs. Cox had taken, as a friend of the Bravo family to whom her loyalty was due.

Mrs. Cox replied: "Before the marriage he knew everytl
He told me that Mrs. Ricardo had told him all about Dr. Gu
I left her to tell him what she liked. I did not keep anything ba
before the marriage—well, I did." She trailed her coat and M
Lewis sprang after it.

"What was it?"

"I kept back from him what Mrs. Ricardo told me after giving
up her acquaintance with Dr. Gully."

"What was it she told you?"

"Of her intimacy with Dr. Gully."

"What do you mean by intimacy?"

"You may draw your own conclusions."

"No, madam, I decline to do that. Was it a criminal intimacy
with Dr. Gully that she told you of?"

Witness, after a pause: "Yes, a criminal intimacy."

The paper here printed "Sensation." He could translate it as
sounds throughout that intensely crowded room, sounds in which
no words could be distinguished.

"But," she added, in an attempt to preserve her own respectability, "I did not know about this intercourse when we were
living in the Leigham Court Road. I did not know about it till
last autumn when she told me."

He got up and moved about. The cool room was a refuge but
for a minute he walked up and down it desperately as if it were
a prison. At the open window he looked down into plane trees
standing in the garden below.

It was unmistakably clear that she had courted this exposure;
her enticement of Lewis had been blatant. The determination to
prove jealousy of himself as a motive for suicide had led her to
reveal that the romantic relationship had been also a sexual
union.

Well, if Florence had remained faithful to him, the frightful

consequences of public exposure would never have come upon her; but what motive lay behind this fearful step? If the man had not committed suicide, and to him, at least, it was increasingly plain that he had not, what had they to conceal?

For the first time he regretted that he was staying in Willie's house. He did not know whether Willie and Bessie had known the nature of his liaison. Devoted as he was to his son he had always held the position of a father toward him; he had never treated or wished to treat him as a confidant. Where he had maintained a silence, he expected other people to observe it too. But now—for these revelations to be made while he was under his daughter-in-law's roof—

But when he joined them at dinner that evening he realized that even he had underrated them. They made it clear that they had read the papers, and that their attitude toward him had not changed in the slightest. Willie was cheerful, kind, respectful as ever; Bessie was not only her sweet self; her kindness had a touch of solicitude as if he were an invalid. He was more soothed than he had thought possible. The little that Willie had to say about the Attorney General, about Gorst and Poland and the dangerous Lewis, his father listened to with interest but by tacit agreement they did not discuss the proceedings. As they were parting for the night Willie for the first time gave a hint of underlying anxiety. He said: "I hope you will manage to sleep, Father." Dr. Gully said he should take something from his homeopathic chest. When he was in his room he prepared a dose of aconite. One of his written sayings had been: "Torment is cheated of time spent in sleep."

The following day, the seventeenth, it was clear that Sir Henry James had made up his mind that any further revelations Mrs. Cox might have to make should be elicited by him as Mrs. Bravo's counsel, rather than left for the fell George Lewis. He

drew the information from her with a quiet matter-of-factness intended to discourage sensation.

"I learned on the day before we left Brighton in October that this improper intimacy had been at Kissingen in 1873."

"In November, early in the month, Mrs. Ricardo had an illness. Dr. Gully said it arose from a kind of tumor which, he said, had been removed. No other doctor was in attendance besides Dr. Gully. Mrs. Ricardo appeared to suffer a great deal."

Had she not at least suspected, Sir Henry James asked, what this illness really was? The witness replied: "I gave credence to the facts as they were told to me."

She insisted that Mr. Bravo spoke of Dr. Gully with anger and hatred. These feelings increased because Dr. Gully continued to reside in the immediate neighborhood of The Priory.

After making their depositions at the Treasury she and Mrs. Bravo had gone back to Brighton and stayed there for ten days. Mrs. Bravo was extremely ill with brain fever and a doctor had to sleep in the house; at the end of that time her mother took her away to Buscot and apart from one meeting in London Mrs. Cox had not seen her since. She admitted with some dignity: "Since I have given up my position with her, I have no resources."

This ended Mrs. Cox's ordeal by cross-examination, but before she turned to make her exit through the doorway, which two policemen had some difficulty in keeping clear, one of the jurymen called out to her: "It has been given in evidence that the deceased first called out for his wife: 'Florence! Florence! Hot water, hot water.' Was it not strange that when you came instead of his wife he should tell you he had taken poison and say, 'Don't tell Florence'?"

The witness's aplomb distinguished her to the last. She said: "I did not hear him call 'Florence.' He only called, 'Hot water, hot water, hot water,' when *I* was there."

He was grateful for sleep but the sounder it was, the more painful the waking. As he read this morning's paper over his coffee, he knew that in twenty-four hours he had lost the reputation of a lifetime. The mental sickness was not there because the initial shock was over, but he was now facing an unchanging, illimitable desert of suffering. In the public view, the liaison was damaging enough, but followed by an abortion, performed by himself, a criminal offense, committed by a highly distinguished doctor—family, friends, society, hundreds upon hundreds who respected, admired, were grateful to him—he imagined the thousands of homes where the papers were being read and would be discussed all day; and with a hideous stab he remembered the boast of Cross's Select Circulating Library, that the London papers arrived at Malvern by the first train!

He was so stunned by calamity, he did not remember to think that some people, at least, would be taking his part; that his onetime patients up and down the land were exclaiming as they read that other people might say what they chose, *they* would never forget what Dr. Gully had done for them.

"I *never* liked her!" burst from Ellen's lips as she finished the columns in the *Times*. Ann was sitting on the sofa of their little living room. She looked dazed and her head shook very slightly. They had had one of Willie's excellent, brief letters, and the kindest visit from Bessie, saying that their brother would no doubt be so glad to see them when this dreadful affair was not quite so much on his mind.

In Streatham Church the summer morning light struck the marble wall monuments. The household from The Priory came regularly to matins on Sundays; sometimes the lady herself came, accompanied by her companion; but at a midweek early celebration none of them would be there. It was a small congregation to whom Mr. Nichol, the rector, was reciting the Litany: "That it may please Thee to have mercy on all men." Charlotte Dyson's face was buried in her hands.

"Thy servant, James."

Chapter 40

THE eighteenth day, Thursday, August 3, as hot and oppressive as the days before; "Mrs. Florence Bravo was escorted into court. She attracted the deepest attention of everyone present."

The reporters knew that their readers wanted a mind's eye view of the rich, young, beautiful woman, convicted of immorality and suspected of murder; they described her appearance in painstaking detail.

On this second widowhood she had forgone none of the dignity and impressiveness of widow's weeds, interpreted by a fashionable dressmaker though they were. Her monumental-looking black was covered with black crape; a white tulle scarf was around her neck. When she came in, a transparent crape veil was over her face, but when she sat down, she threw this up over her small, white-rimmed bonnet, and it cascaded down her back, covering the mass of her bound-up hair. When she took off her black gloves, the reporters saw a great emerald ring. She was very pale with a fixed look in her large blue eyes. Her voice was gently modulated, her enunciation distinct. Her poise was remarkable; she seemed unaware of the crowd pressing up to the table within a few feet of her. She was not discomposed by the trains rushing past that almost drowned voices by their clangor.

The revelation of herself, part deliberate, part unconscious, would once have riveted his attention as a lover; now he saw it with a clarity that excluded tolerance or compassion.

Of her first husband's dipsomania she said: "As he was always very miserable when away from me, it was thought that if he were told that he could not be allowed to be with me unless he behaved better, the effect would be to reform him."

Well, the effect of her attractions was very potent; she was only giving an accurate account of it; but this accuracy soon deserted her.

"Dr. Gully attended Captain Ricardo at the same time that he attended me." God forbid that he should approach Fernie, but this was not only untrue, it was demonstrably untrue.

The decision to part from him, she said, was made so that she might be reconciled to her mother. The letter was put in that she had written to Bravo, last October, at the time of his own anguish: "Need I tell you that I have written to the doctor, to say that I must *never* see his face again? It is the right thing to do, whether we marry or not." He read the words now with indignation rather than pain.

Sir Henry James, in view of Mrs. Cox's disclosures, had clearly determined that the evidence of the liaison should be brought out by himself at her examination in chief, not left to be extracted by a vindictive cross-examination. He drew from her the statement: "At one time there was an improper intimacy between Dr. Gully and me." Here she began to cry and was led out of the room. Her emotion roused pity in many who saw it, in thousands who read of it; it left him unmoved. She came back, composed, and drank a little from a glass of sal volatile and water. Then she agreed with her counsel in his questioning: "In November, 1873, I suffered from an illness and I was then attended by Dr. Gully."

"That illness was a miscarriage?"

"It was. I owe my life to Mrs. Cox's attendance on me." (He remembered his own expert, ceaseless care.) "I had acute physical suffering. That terminated my intimacy with Dr. Gully."

She had only told Mrs. Cox the real cause of the illness after her separating from Dr. Gully last October.

"I said then to Mrs. Cox it was very cruel of Dr. Gully to write me an angry letter after the misery I had gone through in 1873."

The all-absorbing egotism of which he had once been only vaguely aware had now risen to sight like a reef of wrecking rocks.

Though she had seen a great deal of Dr. Gully till September last, there had been no improper intercourse between them since 1873. He had never slept at her home except on the one occasion in the Leigham Court Road when she had been so dangerously ill. She described accurately the interview at the Lodge, when he had advised her to meet Charles Bravo's wishes about the settlement.

"Since that time I have only seen Dr. Gully at a distance. I have twice seem him on the Common when I looked out of the Venetians."

He saw the Venetian blinds in her bedroom, through whose slats someone could look out and never be seen at the window. How painfully he had been mourning her total loss during some of those walks over the grass! To think that twice, at least, she had been watching him!

On the evening of the next day but one, Willie, who had not had an opportunity of speaking to him since the papers had been delivered that morning, pointed out to him that when the court had risen on August 18, someone must have spoken to Mrs. Bravo, have reminded her, warned her, that Mr. Lewis's cross-examination was yet to come. She had stated that the only occasion of improper intimacy with Dr. Gully had been at Kissingen in August, 1873. If she wanted to retract that, they must have said, if there were anything that could be brought to light, let her for heaven's sake confess it to her own counsel, not expose herself to the risk of being publicly eviscerated by George Lewis; for at the opening of the next day's proceedings, the reports of which had appeared this morning, Mrs. Bravo had said that she now wished to make some comments she had not made before.

"I was, when I gave evidence, most anxious that I should not appear to have been the mistress of Dr. Gully through all the years of my acquaintance with him."

Sir Henry James said: "In begging you to tell the whole truth I will only ask you to answer yes or no. Were you not improperly acquainted with him before the visit to Kissingen?"

Witness: "Yes." (Weeping.)

"Have you any correction to make about the period after the Kissingen visit?"

Witness (with much emotion): "I have no correction to make in that. Upon my oath, there was no improper intercourse after that time."

Sir Henry James now resumed his examination where he had left off the day before. Mrs. Bravo described in emphatic terms her husband's hatred for Dr. Gully.

"He said angrily that Dr. Gully ought to have removed. He was always abusing Dr. Gully. It annoyed him to pass Dr. Gully's house."

She related a scene which she declared had occurred on the morning of Tuesday, April 18, when she and her husband were driving in the carriage to London. As they passed Dr. Gully's house, "I turned my head away as I always did. He said scornfully: 'Did you see anybody?'

" 'No,' " I answered, " 'I did not look.' He then began his usual abuse of Dr. Gully and said at last: 'We shall never get over it, we had better separate.' "

The money question, he said, could be settled by their keeping half each. She told him he was very unkind to keep bringing up this name. When she had made her confession before marriage, he had promised never to speak of the matter again. He agreed that he had been unkind and asked her to kiss him. She was too angry and too much hurt to comply, and he said with a dreadful change on his face: "Then you shall see what I'll do when we get home." At that she was frightened and did kiss him.

But the coachman had said: "As we passed the house nothing was said and nothing was done." He could say this confidently because the landau had been open; it was not shut till the snow came on, at the edge of Clapham Common.

He was not much mollified to read that she had sent to ask his advice for her husband because she thought he was the cleverest medical man in the whole world; and that though the other doctors would not use the plaster and compress he advised, the *arsenicum* he had prescribed had stopped the vomiting.

As to the advice for herself, she said: "My illness was accompanied by a great want of sleep. The baths and washes gave me relief. I got sleep at once." As she did not need the laurel water, she told Mrs. Cox to put it away.

She made what was, in view of Joseph Atkinson's evidence, a surprising statement. Keeber had said that except during Mrs. Bravo's illness, the couple usually slept together; but Mrs. Bravo said: "I was not aware that my husband was in the habit of drinking water before he went to bed."

A collection of letters had been put in; some written to her by her husband, which she had willingly surrendered, one written by herself to her mother-in-law. Her husband had written on April 6: "If you are as glad to see me as I shall be to see you, two of the happiest people in the world will meet tomorrow."

Writing to her mother-in-law she herself had said: "Charlie and I are as happy as can be and never have an unkind word."

"Now," said Mr. Lewis, "do you mean to tell the jury that your husband was always speaking in disparaging terms of Dr. Gully?"

"I do."

Mr. Lewis left this point but there was another that he was anxious to make. He had been balked of half his prey by the tactics of Sir Henry James, but some of it was still within his reach.

The witness said that after her husband's death she had discussed with her family his jealousy of Dr. Gully as a motive for suicide, though she had not then told them that she had had a criminal intimacy with Dr. Gully. In reply to questioning she said: "I have pledged my oath that no criminal intimacy with Dr. Gully occurred in the lifetime of my first husband."

"Had you," asked Mr. Lewis, "a maid named Laundon?"

"I had." He brought out an old letter.

"And is this your writing?"

"It is."

Mr. Lewis then read aloud a letter dated from Buscot on November 16, of which he said, internal evidence proved that the year was 1870, and read this passage: " 'I hope you will never allude in any way to *anyone* of what passed at Malvern. Let it be buried in the past, and if anybody questions you, please refuse to answer *any* inquiries.' "

How on earth had they found this? Had the woman seen the accounts of the inquiry in the press and offered this letter to the Bravo family for sale? Florence had been uneasy at her understanding with Field. Had the woman married him? Was this his doing?

Mr. Lewis said: "What was it, Mrs. Bravo, that was to be buried and no inquiries answered?"

The witness broke out excitedly: "It was my attachment to Dr. Gully but not a criminal attachment then. That attachment has nothing to do with this case. I have suffered sufficient pain and humiliation already and I appeal to the coroner and the jury as men and Britons to protect me. It is a great shame that I should be questioned like this."

The rows of onlookers crushed back against the walls applauded and stamped their feet. Mr. Lewis waited until she and they were silent; then he said: "You express a hope that she will not allude to what passed at Malvern. Now, Mrs. Bravo, *what* passed at Malvern?"

"She knew of my attachment to Dr. Gully. You, and such as you, it seems to me, think that a woman cannot love a man without what is wrong occurring."

"You use the term 'not to say anything of what passed at Malvern.' *What* passed?"

"I have explained it."

Mr. Lewis relied considerably for browbeating the witness on leading her on to make some assertion and then producing documentary proof that she was lying. In answer to his questions, she declared, "In 1874 and 1875 Dr. Gully did not attend me professionally and prescribe for me," and Mr. Lewis called for Smith's order book in which Dr. Gully's prescriptions for Mrs. Ricardo were written, beginning with: "May 25, 1874, oil of savin, thirty drops."

The witness said: "I had forgotten. I don't remember if I took the medicine which he prescribed."

(*He* remembered that she had taken it, and that it had cured the condition for which he was treating her.)

Mr. Lewis then made her recount the details of the interview in which she had sought Dr. Gully's advice on the marriage settlement. He extracted from her that, as well as having her fortune settled on her, she had tried to put all her personal property into the settlement as well. Then he produced a letter which she had written to her father-in-law barely a fortnight after her husband's death. She was angry because she thought Mr. Joseph Bravo had been attempting to take away Charles' property left in his chambers at the Temple.

"He having left all he possessed to me, nobody but myself has the power to touch one single thing belonging to him. He told me he had two hundred pounds a year coming in from investments, and of course his books, pictures and private property at Palace Green are now mine. P.S. Poor Charles also told me that you promised to allow him eight hundred pounds a year."

Grasping, and wildly inaccurate, the image of her built up by what she wrote and said looked like sheer self-destruction.

"There was a legal separation between myself and Captain Ricardo before his death at my instigation; he wrote repeatedly to me to live with him again." She repudiated the suggestion that the separation had been in any sense the work of Dr. Gully.

"Dr. Gully was not one of the trustees in the separation deed on my behalf. Dr. Gully did not even know of the separation."

Mr. Gorst held up a parchment. "Why, here is the deed with your signature, and Dr. Gully's and Mr. Brookes' as your trustees."

The witness with her beauty and her pallor and her spreading crape, and her air of being in another world, replied with stately indifference: "I had no recollection of it, Mr. Gorst."

To Mr. Gorst's questions she said that her engagement to Mr. Bravo had had no bearing on her separation from Dr. Gully. *That* she had decided on long before. Though Dr. Gully had written to her kindly at first, saying that he wanted her to do what she felt was best for her own happiness, when he heard of her engagement he did write to her angrily. "It was natural that the man who loved me should be angry at losing me. I don't remember what he said and I'm glad I don't. The man had lost me and naturally he would say angry things when he heard I was to be married."

Mr. Gorst: "But he had lost you before?"

Witness: "But perhaps he then looked forward to the hope of regaining me, which he would not do if I married."

When he had so much to contend with, to suffer, it was odd to have consciousness to spare for a distinct annoyance at this picture of himself as rejected yet doting. She had betrayed him under every aspect, small and great. That she herself was an object of the greatest emotional importance to those who surrounded her she was entitled to claim and she had had no hesitation in saying so—himself, her two husbands, her reunited family, not least her faithful servant.

"I treated Mrs. Cox with the greatest kindness and she was deeply grateful to me. I remember the arrangement for her to go to Jamaica. I don't think she cared to leave me. Otherwise, perhaps she was content to go."

Murphy tried to put in a word for the advantage of his client.

"And now, Mrs. Bravo, do you not feel toward Mrs. Cox the same kindly regard you have always felt?"

The witness did not answer for a long time; then she said: "I think she might have spared me many of these painful inquiries to which I have been subjected."

So their collaboration had gone on only so far, the final revelations of Mrs. Cox had been made without her sanction, but in the vital interests of Florence as well as herself? To implement the claim that the man had committed suicide, they had brought up the matter of his own love affair; Florence had thought that could be effective when it was only half-told. Mrs. Cox, with a mind of much greater force, had realized that if the tale were to

DR. GULLY'S STORY   307

be believed at all, it must be told in its entirety; knowing that
Florence would have shrunk, and hung back from this public
revelation, she had made it without warning her, for the sake
of both of them. But what was it meant to cover?

Chapter 41

MR. HENRY KIMBER came to Queensborough Terrace late in the afternoon of August 8. He told Dr. Gully that he would be called next morning, and took him off with him to a consultation in the chambers of Mr. Sergeant Parry. When Dr. Gully came back after dinner, saying he wanted nothing but a cup of weak tea, Willie said in his kind, easygoing tone: "You'll be glad there's no more waiting, Father."

He had felt ill, more or less, for many weeks, and on Wednesday morning the sensations were more pronounced, but the feeling of being braced for an occasion kept them back. He made his usual careful toilet: a cambric shirt, a linen waistcoat, a coat that was formal but of thin material. Unlike many men, he had always known how to dress comfortably in hot weather. Willie, who had gained some insight into what the scene was likely to be, had insisted on his father's engaging a carriage to take him all the way so as to avoid the walk even from Balham Station to the Bedford. The carriage would put up at the hotel and bring him back to Bayswater.

Crowds were already besieging the doors when he arrived. Rude faces were pushed into the carriage and he was recognized but only as he passed inside. Two good-natured, serious constables made a way for him up a staircase already thronged, and showed him into a little room lit by a skylight. The room itself was quiet but immediately outside was a growing noise of shoving and creaking, and cries of: "Make way, if you please" and "Less noise there!"

He was sitting in a Windsor chair, willing himself to calmness, when Sergeant Parry looked in and said a few words in his hearty, engaging manner. He was, privately, much relieved to see his client in such good trim. He repeated his warning of the night before that Lewis would make himself objectionable; this coroner couldn't hold him. Some of his questions to Mrs. Bravo had been outrageous; no judge would have allowed them.

"I shan't mind. My blood is up."

"Excellent. There are only two witnesses to take first: a housemaid and the coachman's wife."

His friend Mrs. Griffith! And soon the coroner's summoner was at the door, saying, "Dr. Gully, if you please," and the two policemen were making a passage for him between people whom he felt rather than saw; then he was in the room. A train rushed past the windows at that moment, clanking and shrieking.

The enormous table of a width like the sea was strewn with portfolios, papers and tall hats. A rack made of netting ran around the walls, into which other hats had been thrown. The towering mirror, the brass of the gasoliers, made an unwelcome garishness in the growing heat. The walls were lined with rows three deep of people staring at him with avid, devouring curiosity, reviling him and picturing him in bed with the beautiful, *louche* young woman whom they had seen standing there in her widow's weeds. The counsel were the only ones present who appeared to take no interest in his arrival. He recognized Lewis at once from the drawings in the press: arrogant with head held up and looking down his nose. In the ring of faces all around the table he identified the coroner's when Sergeant Parry asked if his client might sit down because he had been ill. Some of the jury called out, "No! Let him stand!" and people around the walls applauded. The coroner, for once exerting his authority, ordered a chair to be given to Dr. Gully.

Seated, he got his bearings, and found himself self-controlled, fearless, angry. Sergeant Parry briefly established his professional position and that he was being examined entirely at his own request. Then Sergeant Parry said gently: "We have heard of your unfortunate intimacy with Mrs. Ricardo, now Mrs. Bravo."

He made the only reply admissable to that audience: "Too true, sir, too true. I have read Mrs. Bravo's statement and I am sorry to say it is true and correct. I feel my position most bitterly having to come here and say this."

Parry with effective skill then asked the questions, the replies to which gave the picture of his share of the events.

He stated in firm, impressive tones that he had had nothing whatever to do with Mr. Charles Bravo's death.

Since the marriage he had had no communication of any kind with Mrs. Bravo.

The chemists he had dealt with at Malvern were Hallett for homeopathic prescriptions and Burrow for everything else.

"I never dealt with Mr. Clarke. I most certainly never wrote an order to supply two ounces of tartar emetic to Griffith."

"Did you know of that purchase?"

"Not in the least."

The statement Mrs. Bravo had made about their interview at the Lodge was true and correct. "There was no secrecy about the interview; I was seen by workmen to go to and leave the Lodge." The same was true of his meetings at Balham Station with Mrs. Cox. "Everybody about here knows me and knows Mrs. Cox; the meetings were perfectly open."

At their meeting on April 10 he had prescribed cold sitz baths for Mrs. Bravo; he was hurrying for his train and could not immediately think of a sedative, knowing Mrs. Bravo was driven frantic by ordinary opiates. "In the train, I bethought me of laurel water." Any suggestion that he had caused tartar emetic to be placed in the bottle—he spoke with fierce but controlled anger—*"from whatever quarter it may have come,* is a wicked and infamous falsehood."

Sergeant Parry produced the prescriptions made up at Smith's for Mrs. Bravo in 1874. Dr. Gully said with professional calmness: "I am the author of those prescriptions. I was treating Mrs. Ricardo for a want of action in the uterine organs and a suspension of the natural function. This specific is well known to doctors and of great usefulness. It had the desired effect."

Mr. Lewis got up. Returning to the question of the laurel water, he asked, if it were meant for Mrs. Bravo at The Priory, why should it have been left at Mrs. Cox's house in Lancaster Road? The witness answered simply: "I did not send it to The Priory because I regarded all communication with that place as forbidden to me. I left it openly, with my name. Mrs. Cox could use it or not, as she liked."

Mr. Lewis now directed his attack toward attempting to prove that the liaison had begun during the lifetime of Captain Ricardo, in peculiarly disgraceful circumstances.

Dr. Gully said firmly: "I was not the medical attendant of Captain Ricardo, nor was my partner. Mrs. Ricardo left Malvern in 1870."

"Was it while she was a patient of yours that the attachment commenced?"

"If you like to call it so, yes."

Mr. Lewis, who had treated Mrs. Bravo herself with a relentless savagery that had caused very general indignation, now seemed determined to expose *him* as a ruthless exploiter of feminine innocence and helplessness. It roused his strong indignation.

"You knew she had given you her entire affection, that she had surrendered her name, her family, everything?"

"I knew that in 1871 she had been given the choice of giving me up and had refused."

"You knew she had given up her good name for you?"

"No, I knew nothing of the sort."

"She had been living with you in this state, had she not?"

"She had not."

"Not! Is it all an invention, then? She was not living with you in criminal intimacy?"

"I thought you were speaking of 1871. The criminal intimacy occurred long after Captain Ricardo's death."

"Was it not true," demanded Mr. Lewis accusingly, "that she asked you, for the sake of her happiness, to leave your house, and offered to pay your rent if you would go, and that you refused the proposal?"

"She did not offer to pay my rent for me. I did not refuse the proposal; no such proposal was made to me; nor did it occur to me that Mr. Bravo was jealous of me; I had not the slightest idea of it, and many of his friends had not either, as you observe."

To Sir Henry James, who was trying to rehabilitate his client's reputation for truthfulness, he conceded that Mrs. Bravo might have confused the offer she had made to pay him five hundred pounds, to recoup him for what he had lost over the lease he had taken, at her suggestion, of the house on Tooting Common in 1871, with the offer she had not made, to take over the rent of his house on Bedford Hill in 1875. She had told him at Brighton that if she married Mr. Bravo, she would give him a check for five hundred pounds, and this proposal he had refused.

It was signified that counsel had no more questions to put to him, but the jury detained him, asking if he had ever prescribed tartar emetic.

He said: "I have never used it except in homeopathic doses."

Another juryman asked: Supposing the pills containing oil of savin had all been swallowed at one go, would the effect have been to procure abortion?

Dr. Gully explained patiently that if all the pills had been swallowed at once, probably the stomach would have ejected them almost immediately, but if they had remained in the stomach, then, supposing the patient to be pregnant, probably would have caused abortion. This concluded the evidence before the court. The coroner announced that there would be a day's adjournment and that he would sum up on Friday, August 11.

The carriage took a few minutes to get clear of the hotel yard, and the crowd pushed around it, shouting hoarsely. He could not make out the words but he heard the raucous jeering and could see the horrible relish in their degraded faces. Once the carriage had got into Balham High Road and was going at speed, he blessed Willie for having him transported so quickly from this scene of torture.

He returned to Queensborough Terrace some time after five o'clock. In the hot but shaded hall his daughter-in-law appeared, telling him his tea would be ready in a moment. Willie, home early, came out of the study and faces were looking through the banisters of the second flight of stairs.

"Presently, my dears," Papa called up, "you shall come down and talk to Grandpapa this evening." The boys scampered upward, out of sight, but Gi-gi came down, moved by she knew not what. With her hair behind her ears like a waterfall, she rose on tiptoe and put her arms around her grandfather's neck, feeling as she did so, how hot and tired he was. He held her in an embrace that lasted a second longer than usual. As he released her she darted upstairs again, before anyone could say anything.

Chapter 42

A CAPITAL charge against one, or two, or all three of them, was within the verge of possibility. Willie did not think his father in serious danger; but except when he was actually speaking, anxiety was making his face grave and almost harsh.

The suspense of the intervening day, between the court's rising on Wednesday afternoon and the coroner's summing up on Friday, was so painful, Dr. Gully preferred to be out of the house. He spent hours walking about and sitting under trees in Kensington Gardens.

Lewis' cross-examination of Florence and himself had been clearly aimed at proving an emotional bond between them so strong that its rupture by her marriage might give grounds for a suspicion of murder, perpetrated by either or both. He put the preposterous chimera out of his mind and concentrated on the theory which had gradually formed itself, which had at least the merit of covering the facts.

He remembered, five years ago at Malvern, telling her that tartar emetic was one of the preparations used to make dipsomaniacs sick; he had given her emetic powders himself; she was familiar with the disabling effects of nausea and vomiting.

He went over very carefully the evidence of the pain, distress and sleeplessness she had undergone from two miscarriages in less than three months, with the inevitable effect on the balance of her mind. If Mrs. Cox had told the truth, on her first coming downstairs, the Friday before the Tuesday, Bravo had driven her beside herself by hanging about her, refusing to leave her alone to rest after lunch. Had this warned her that he would soon return to her bed?

If he had said as much, she might determine on a step that would disable him at least for the time being. It was not unknown for women who feared another pregnancy to adopt such measures. If she put a dose of emetic in the water bottle on his washstand—though she had declared she did not know of his drinking water before he went to bed—he was, in fact, almost certain to take it.

On the Tuesday night it would seem that she wanted to nerve herself to something; she drank copiously at dinner; she sent twice for wine before getting to bed. He sat, gazing unseeingly at beds of geraniums, while there rose in his mind the appalling significance of that scene, described though it was by Mrs. Cox, but she would not have related it had she realized what it could convey: that when Bravo, immediately before going into his own bedroom, where the water bottle waited for him, came to his wife's dressing room and reproached her with the amount of wine she'd taken, she did not answer.

She would not look at him. She had her back to him as she folded a cold-water compress.

Griffith had had antimony in the stables; he said he'd got rid of it before leaving on January 3, but the value of his evidence on the face of it was derisory. "I broke two of the bottles, I may have left another but there was nothing in it, I know." The new coachman had not come till the third of February. The groom and the stableboy were in charge till then, but there was not the perpetual presence of a coachman in his harness room.

Between the two inquests, Scotland Yard with Mrs. Bravo's permission had searched The Priory for traces of poison; they had found nothing but bottles of hair dye and a great collection of domestic medicines; how should they, after able hands had made a clearance? The police, Pritchard told him, had dug up the drains; how would that help them, five weeks after the event?

There would be no difficulty in abstracting the poison if it were there; but she would scarcely know the correct dose, and how could she measure it if she did? And on the fatal night, she had had too much to drink. She might have been feigning sleep when Keeber came to call her, but when she threw herself down beside her husband she had fallen into a drunken doze and Harrison had had to rouse her and get her off the bed. To induce vomiting one to two grains of antimony would be the proper quantity; ten grains was a lethal dose; whoever had treated the water bottle had poured in upward of thirty.

She and Mrs. Cox were expecting to hear the commotion of an ordinary attack of sickness. Only when Mrs. Cox was brought to the scene and saw him slip down unconscious to the floor did she realize that dire calamity had overtaken them. From the moment Florence saw her husband's condition, her grief and desperation were unmistakable. The butler bore witness to the frantic state in which she'd screamed at him to fetch Dr. Moore. She sent for medical aid in every direction, including, at last, his own. She summoned the man's family and her family; nothing could exceed the energy, the sincerity, of her efforts. The one thing she could not do, since the consequences had been so frightful, was to admit the act.

Had Mrs. Cox known that she was about to do it? Hardly, perhaps—the recklessness of the dose did not speak of caution and competence; but she knew that it had been done, for when she found Bravo in a state of collapse, she'd at once applied the correct treatment for someone who'd been poisoned. Her statement that Bravo had told her he'd taken poison, he never believed for a moment. Her story had been developed impromptu as she went along and the whole monstrous fabrication of himself as the cause of the man's suicide had been an afterthought between them, most skillfully woven from deceptive fragments of truth.

That Florence, even when fighting for her life, should have sacrificed him, with a series of such heartless lies, left him stunned; when sensation returned, it was with burning anger. In fits and starts, bewilderment still attacked him; he contended with it. Hadn't women betrayed men all through recorded time? But that *she* could have done it to *him*—well, no doubt that was what all the other fools had said.

The lacerating penance made him smart at every turn. Not only were the daily papers full of the case, the illustrated weeklies carried drawings of the court in session, of The Priory, of his own house and pictures of the various protagonists. These were bold, effective drawings, crude but honest; but *Vanity Fair* of the previous Saturday had taken him as the subject of their weekly cartoon by "Spy." Colored, smoothly finished, done with a high degree of skill—conveying the idea of impressive personality and impeccable dress—it was a vicious, an odious caricature in "Spy's" typical manner of enlarging the head and diaphragm and dwarfing the legs. The nose was shaped like a tap. The face wore an air of oily and sinister calm. The letterpress, after commenting on his attainments and his personal distinction, concluded: "The connection of his name with the sudden death of the husband of one of his friends has doubtless caused him as much pain as it has brought surprise to the large circle of acquaintances who had learned to honor and respect him." In drawing rooms, on station bookstalls, on the library tables of clubs—the Garrick! The bitterness was something he could almost taste on his lips.

On Thursday afternoon when he came in, his daughter-in-law persuaded him to come upstairs and have some tea with her. She told him that Pritchard had called with his letters and a parcel of clean clothes, and that she had asked him to come down again tomorrow afternoon, to be with them when the verdict should be known. "I knew he would wish it," she said, with a sweet, deprecating gaze, as though Pritchard's anxiety were a mere personal eccentricity of his own. Dr. Gully said: "Thank you, my dear."

She did not mention it to him, but she told her husband later that Pritchard had said Mrs. Bravo's parents and her sister and brother-in-law were with her at The Priory. He had no information as to where Mrs. Cox might be—not up there, at any rate.

The twilight on these hot, light days seemed as if it would never come, but after nine o'clock, it was dimmer and a little cooler.

Florence was lying on her bed while Effie bathed her temples with eau de cologne. Her father and brother-in-law were smoking in the garden, in a stillness broken only by a train that rushed past, drawing a spangled string of lights along the embankment.

Mrs. Campbell was glad of the presence of her family but she was also thankful for a little time to herself. She sat in Florence's morning room by the open door of the greenhouse. In her mind were thoughts she had told herself she would not admit, because they were there already.

Not in public, not now. Mrs. Manning had been the last, nearly thirty years ago. She had said: "Will it hurt, Mr. Calcraft?" And the hangman had answered: "Not if you keep still, ma'am."

Her eyes were tight shut already, but she pressed her hands

over them. Inside her head, bright on dark, was a vision of Florence, a very small child in a little white dress. The sweat broke and poured through her fingers.

For the first time in three weeks the courtroom was almost empty when at half past ten on Friday morning the coroner began his summing up. This occupied half an hour; the jury then retired and three and a half hours later returned with its verdict. The journalists made a wild rush to the station to reach their offices; before five o'clock the newsboys, bawling, tore up and down the streets.

In Queensborough Terrace, Mr. Kimber was in William's study. The jury had said: "We find that Mr. Charles Delaunay Bravo did not commit suicide, that he did not meet his death by misadventure, that he was willfully murdered by the administration of tartar emetic but there is not sufficient evidence to fix the guilt upon any person or persons."

Mr. Kimber was saying: "I regret the ambiguous tenor of the words, but in essentials we must feel that the result is satisfactory. Not, I think, that there was ever any *serious*—but the case undoubtedly wanted watching." He and Willie were talking; Dr. Gully sat in an armchair and Pritchard stood behind him. The former was composed and self-possessed but his face was deeply flushed and his eyes looked overbright. He got to his feet as his son escorted Mr. Kimber into the hall and they were all in the doorway as the front door was opened.

The moment that the door swung inward, disclosing the figures in the hall, people on the pavement, in the gutter, on the other side of the road, converged on the portico, the foremost ones mounting the steps, craning into the house. As the door was hurriedly shut in their faces, whistles and catcalls sounded in the street, then raps were heard on the door itself. Mrs. William Gully said with calm cordiality: "As it won't be comfortable for you to leave the house just at this moment, Mr. Kimber, do let us give you some tea, or some sherry?"

She took him across the hall into the dining room. Pritchard said: "I will go up to the bedroom, sir, to collect the doctor's linen."

He and Willie were left alone in the study and several loud bangs shook the door, followed by a long, ululating peal at the bell.

"It'll die down," said Willie.

With an effort Dr. Gully said: "Willie, I can't tell you—you and Bessie—my grief for what I've brought on this house."

"No, Father, no; it's you we think of."

Chapter 43

HE meant to return to Orwell Lodge in the course of the week. Meantime Willie had written to Susanna at her home in Sheffield. His father had made the barest mention of her, but Willie knew he longed for some sort of message.

Susanna had known that her father was to appear in connection with the inquiry. She had not had the faintest idea, until she read of it in the newspapers, that he had had a sexual union with Mrs. Ricardo and had performed an abortion on her. The shock, to someone of her reserve and dignity, had been almost annihilating. To her brother's suggestion that she should write to her father, she replied with a passionate outburst of disgust and horror.

Never, never! she declared, never! Papa, of all people in creation! She should never recover from it; the dreadful knowledge was with her all day and kept her awake at night. Papa, whom everyone had respected and thought the world of—and a woman younger than herself! The facts themselves and the disgrace of their being known—she could never bear to see him again.

Though Willie had maintained his usual calmness during the last few weeks, he had borne a very great deal. He had hoped for at least some help and encouragement from his sister in

the task of comforting their father. He did not show him Susanna's letter but he could not conceal its nature. They were
in the study and Dr. Gully was standing at the writing table,
leaning on the back of his hand. He said nothing. To himself
he exclaimed: "Fanny! My darling! Thank God I lost you before
I could harm you."

Reading the comments of the newspapers was a suffering he
felt obliged to court. The *Times* had said: "In violation of the
heavy responsibilities of his profession, and with no excuse from
the passions of youth or even of middle life, he abandoned himself to a selfish intrigue and he cannot complain of having
brought himself to his present condition."

Written, no doubt, by a right-minded man, the utter severance
between the true facts and this picture of them, was something
that the world would never understand. The *Daily News* spoke
of evidence "which, even to have read, raises a flush of shame
and pity. Women should be free from danger with their medical
attendants." Yes, but she was my pledged wife.

The *Standard* sounded the knell whose tones he had heard in
his mind long since: "More than one reputation has been irrepa-
rably damaged and suspicions of the gravest kind have been directed toward persons *previously of some social position—*"

These were the respectable journals, whose views he thought
it necessary to read. The spate of other publications, in blurred
type with grotesque illustrations, he ignored, except that he
found one left behind on the seat of a hansom, a pamphlet
entitled "The Gay Young Widow of Balham." He turned the pages
as the vehicle bowled down Victoria Street. The passage his eye
lighted on declared with a mixture of sanctimoniousness and
spite: "Reverence for a father, love for a mother, could not induce her to give up her lean and senile seducer." He tore the
pages across and put them in his pocket to take home and
destroy. Whenever he had settled into a state of calmness there

would suddenly come into his mind without warning yet another person in whose eyes he had been disgraced. Lady Prescott, to whom he'd taken it on himself to recommend Griffith and who had now dismissed the latter from her service; his old friends the bath attendants at Malvern; James Nott who had sturdily proclaimed that if Dr. Gully were ever in danger, the people of Malvern would fight for him! The names and faces were legion. Friends, patients, acquaintances, colleagues, the recollection of every one causing a separate pang; like the Chinese death by a thousand cuts.

But he collected himself by degrees. After some thought, he had determined that he would not leave Orwell Lodge. Not only was he very fond of the house; when he went back to it there would be embarrassment, suffering, but when these were over as far as they ever could be over, there would be nothing more to fear. If he decamped, fled and settled somewhere else, he would be under ceaseless apprehension of his new neighbors getting to know who he was and bringing all the story up again. No! Better stand his ground. He had refused to leave the house before; he would not be driven from it now.

He made his plans for departure with his daughter-in-law, and tried to tell her, saying he never could tell her, what he owed to her and Willie during these last weeks. When he was alone with Willie the latter said tentatively: "Father, may I give a word of advice?"

"Of course, my boy."

"The great strength of our case all along has been that you parted with Mrs. Ricardo before her marriage and never saw her after it. If, now—I realize that it is most unlikely, but if you were, ever, to renew the acquaintance, on any terms, the danger—"

"Renew the acquaintance!" His father absolutely laughed, a harsh, barking laugh. "My dear fellow, you must have a very low opinion of my sense—justly, perhaps, by this time—but I assure you—"

With his face relaxed into a smile of relief, Willie said: "Not of your sense, Father, but I have been a little afraid of your kindness."

"You need not be afraid of that anymore," his father said grimly.

To be back again, so near, would have disturbed some men, but once the drive past the Bedford and under the railway arch was accomplished and he was inside his front gate, he felt a sense of refuge, of relief. His servants, with Pritchard foremost, welcomed him with smiles, and Pritchard, bringing him his tea, ventured to say he hoped they'd see Miss Ann and Miss Ellen on a little visit presently. He raised his head from his cup, as if arrested by some new idea, and then said he hoped so too.

August turned into September without any break in the weather, only a gradual lessening of the heat. The skies were of glorious clearness, stained at evening with a burning rose color. The parched grass was colorless, the trees were shedding leaves already shriveled, but rich piles of fruit were coming into the market: pears, plums, apricots, melons, grapes.

He soon hardened himself, going about the neighborhood, to the sight of stares and whispers, and of people occasionally drawing aside with their heads in the air as he approached. The constant endurance gave him a formidable air of abstraction and dignity. Among the painful results and consequences was one he had expected. It was conveyed to him that the General Medical Council had decided to remove his name from the Medical Register; but this had been done in as merciful a manner as possible. A technical regulation ordered that a doctor's name should not remain on the Register if his address could not be ascertained. His name was noted as having been removed, "address no longer known." He felt the kindness of this, when his address was known by now to every newspaper reader in the United Kingdom.

After some suspense until the next volumes of their proceedings were out, he found he had not been deprived of his fellowship of either the Royal Medical and Chirurgical Society of London, or the Royal Physical Society, Edinburgh. Most of all, he appreciated the fact that he had not been asked to resign from the Garrick. He did not know whether he would ever enter the club again, but he valued his membership now even more than when he had made so much use of it.

At the end of September he was sitting one afternoon by the open French window of his study in something more like tranquillity than he had enjoyed for a very long time. On a china dessert server at his elbow was a beautiful bunch of grapes, a vine leaf still attached to the woody stem, which Dr. Moore had called with, from the hothouses of his friends at Thornton Heath. He had meant to eat some but in the end, looking at them did as well. There was a discreet tap at the door and Pritchard brought in a note on a salver; he had retired before Dr. Gully roused himself to pick up the envelope—an envelope with a black edge. He stared at the writing, almost paralyzed; then he prized up the flap, shocked to find the gum still damp. The note, headed "The Priory" in Gothic letters, began without any opening words: "If you knew how much I am suffering, you would pity me. I know you have much to forgive, but I beg you to give me the chance to say one word. Let me have the comfort of speaking to you. Let me have an opportunity to tell you the truth. I know that you are at home. Please let us meet, just for me to explain to you. It is all I ask."

He put the note on the table beside him; he did not want to touch it. Tennyson's lines came back upon him now with a more fearful significance even than they had had on that October night:

> Child, if it were thine error or thy crime,
> I care no longer, being all unblest.

He picked up the note and read it through once more. There was of course no fire in the grate and as he was not a smoker there were no matches at hand. He rang and asked Pritchard to bring a box. When the latter returned with it, Dr. Gully said: "If any inquiry is made, there is no answer to the letter you brought just now." Left alone, he stood at the hearth, remembering the afternoon last November when Mrs. Cox was in that room, demanding the letters, courteous, mincing, implacable. Deprived, dispossessed, and brought low in the eyes of Mrs. Cox, he had burned the letters in front of her, rather than put them into her hands.

The whirligig of time! He tore paper and envelope into scraps, dropped them behind the polished bars and put a lighted match to them. They flamed up, then writhed as if in pain.

His mind had not enough energy to pursue the matter, nor did he wish to, but he couldn't but wonder, fitfully, what she was doing or meant to do. Pritchard did not now volunteer information as readily as he used to do, but he was always able to produce it. Dr. Gully had given up *Punch* whose heartless comments on spiritualism, vivisection and the case itself had finally disgusted him; he now took in the *Illustrated London News,* but several copies of this were lying unread in the drawing room. In the third week in October, Pritchard produced the current number and asked the doctor if he'd noticed a paragraph. This said: "Mrs. Cox, who gave evidence at the recent inquiry into the death of Mr. Bravo, has sailed for Jamaica."

"Well!" he said, and then was silent. He had never spoken to anyone of his feelings. He had discussed the probable explanation of the tragedy with William, with some few of the doctors who were his friends; but of his suffering and bitterness and despair he had not said a word to a living creature. He had, indeed, a sense of communication; as he had said, there are those walking on the earth who have no need of the earth to walk upon. But this comfort belonged to the world of inner life. The outside world was there as well. Courageous as he was and willing to salvage what he could, there were times when the realization of his fate came over him like an arctic night. For the greater part of his life he had been so much accustomed to seeing interest and pleasure on other people's faces at the sight of him, to the consciousness that his presence was an advantage to any gathering—he had had so much appreciation and applause—he had forgotten how dependent he was on such an atmosphere for comfort and happiness. Now that he had to enter every public place with caution in case he were recognized, scan the face of every acquaintance to see whether he were to be acknowledged or cut dead, the treachery which had brought this on him had produced a cold, steady anger, like the burning coldness of liquid air.

In November he received a letter that caused him impatient disgust. The offer, published by Mrs. Bravo last May, of a five-hundred-pound reward to anyone who could prove the purchase of antimony by a member of The Priory household, had met with a belated response. A Mr. Ponsford Raymond wrote to say that he had supplied the late Mr. Bravo with six packets of Hayman's Remedy, a cure for dipsomania, each packet containing half a grain of antimony and some pink coloring matter. Mr. Bravo had obviously been trying to cure his wife of her fondness for wine. Mr. Raymond said he had hesitated to claim the reward earlier; he did not want to injure the sale of his remedy by connecting it in the public mind with a notorious death by poison. Now, he had decided to put in for it and he was offering this information to the people who had figured in the inquiry.

Dr. Gully sent the letter on to Mr. Kimber, who, on instructions, replied to Mr. Raymond that "Dr. Gully did not know Mrs. Bravo and was not interested in the case."

Autumn was now in the air, bringing dampness and chill at last, the skies daily losing some of their strength of light. He walked less now, for the old trouble was coming back. Sometimes pains in his legs and back obliged him to stay in all day. At these times Dr. Moore came to see him and to supervise the packing of him in wet sheets, of which he had to learn the method from the patient himself. At the beginning of December an arrangement was completed which gave great satisfaction to everyone. On a raw, gray afternoon, Pritchard stood beaming on the front doorsteps while a fly drove in at the gate, followed by another loaded with luggage. From the first one, Ann and Ellen descended, the latter taking her sister's arm and helping her up the stone steps.

Unlike what many manservants would have been who controlled a single gentleman's establishment, Pritchard was thoroughly in favor of the addition of his master's sisters to the household. He knew very well that they would not interfere. The large bedroom on the first floor overlooking the road and the smaller one beside it had been prepared for them. They did not stay to unpack but having taken off their outdoor clothes, came downstairs to the drawing room, to tea in the firelight. When Ann was sitting down, the look of uncertainty left her face and movements and she was her old self still. The doctor came into the room, telling her not to get up and kissing her where she sat; then he put his arm around Ellen's waist and kissed her too. Pritchard brought in the tea tray and put it down in front of Ellen.

"Quite like old times, ma'am," he said with immense approval.

Chapter 44

ONCE his sisters were under his roof again, he wondered how he had done without them for so long. Having lived with him nearly all their lives they knew how to be pleasant to him and how not to be in his way. When Ann had one of her good days, she was exactly the calm, intelligent, sympathetic companion she had always been, and Ellen was so vigilant in taking care of her that Ann's disabilities often passed more or less unnoticed.

Anything that made home more engaging was valuable to him. He did not go to the club or to lectures or conferences, nor did he go anymore to the meetings of the National Association of Spiritualists. References to him in the press, suggesting that a person of his debased nature was naturally a spiritualist, caused him agonies of compunction and dismay—he who had said that he was publishing the spirit drawings in the interests of purifying spiritualism! He continued to read the reports, but he felt he served the cause best by not attending their public meetings.

His increasing friendship with Charlotte Dyson was a small, precious consolation. Her family, of whom her brother was the head, would have objected to it; but gentle and retiring as she was, she was capable of deciding for herself and old enough, and sufficiently well to do, to claim her independence. She never introduced the matter of her own accord but when he occasionally spoke of the past, she listened with an intent, silent sympathy. He did once tell her what in his opinion was the explanation of Charles Bravo's death; she had said with a distraught face: "Poor, poor thing! One is so sorry." Then her eyes filled. "But *nothing* could excuse what was done to *you*." As a rule however they talked about books, pictures, matters of the day. He often went there to breakfast on a Sunday morning, eating simple, delicious food in a dining room whose walls were covered with William Morris' green willow branches.

On April 10, 1877, Willie took silk; his father got pleasure even from reading and rereading the announcement in the *Times*. He said to Ann and Ellen: "I have so wanted to meet him as a QC. It makes up for so much." Once, he would have had a dinner party for him at the Garrick. Now, well, a family dinner at Orwell Lodge was very pleasant too and gave enormous satisfaction to Pritchard, who told the doctor that champagne must be served as well as other wines, and that he would order what was required.

For that brief, glowing evening, with all his treasures of glass and silver and painted china on the table, the family faces around it, Pritchard filling the glasses with champagne to drink Willie's health, he could feel: "All losses are restored and sorrows end."

In August it was heard, as should perhaps have been expected, that Mrs. Bravo had left The Priory and a great sale of the effects was to take place at the auction rooms of Messers Bonham in Prince's Street. It was March, 1874, when all that furniture and upholstery and all the ornaments had been brought in—only three years and a half before! It seemed an unbelievably short time ago, when that vast ruin lay between.

He heard from the usual sources that Mrs. Bravo had gone

to her parents' home at Buscot, very far from well. No doubt
her condition was giving cause for anxiety; he heard of it with
the distant concern he would have felt for a case of sickness in
any stranger. He wondered, at this turn of events, what had
happened to Mrs. Cox; that she was in Jamaica managing her
aunt's business, while her boys remained here in the charitable
foundation where he, among others, had helped to put them,
that he assumed; but he also thought it probable that some
considerable sum must have been given to her. To pay her well
and get her out of the country on legitimate business of her
own would be a desirable end.

He thought, walking up and down the grass and on the sandy
shore of the great pond among the trees, how no one had been
allowed to stand in Florence's way once her comfort required
their removal.

He was not able to take many walks for the present; the
spinal affection was now causing him considerable pain. He used
a cab to take him as far as Charlotte Dyson's house on Streatham Common. One morning he was in the hall while Pritchard
brushed his low-crowned bowler with one of the little brushes
from the stand. Ann stood at the open hall door and saw the
fly drive in at the gate.

"Here is Griffith," she said.

He began to wonder if he ought to leave Ellen alone with her
while he went to Italy for the winter as Dr. Moore was urging
him to do; Ellen, however, supported Dr. Moore; Ann's condition had altered very little over the past two years; she was not
at all frightened by it.

He made up his mind to winter between Leghorn and Florence. There were family connections there now who would welcome him, and in Anglo-Italian society he would enjoy a return
to some of the past. He set out in November, returning at the
end of February and it had been so comfortable and pleasant

he felt he would repeat the winter visit as long as he could travel at all. He was thankful to find that in Leghorn the exquisite light and color enchanted him as they had the first time he ever saw them and that later memories had no power to harm. The hotel where they had stayed was so much altered he was hardly sure it was the one.

He came back much better and found that after this break he had more resolution to begin the ordeal of going about once more. He began to lunch at the Garrick again and though the first time was as keenly uncomfortable as he had known it would be, it was now easy. There was always somebody there who had a kind word for him.

It was in September that he suddenly received shocking news of her. The papers carried it as before. Last April she had settled herself and her staff of servants in a house at Southsea—was it one she'd remembered from 1874? Here she had refused all visits from relatives and acquaintances, except for her uncle, her mother's brother, who forced his way every so often. By September she had become so much addicted to drink, she could not bear to be kept off it; on Saturday, September 13, she had dismissed the woman Mrs. Everett who was looking after her in a nursing capacity and who had tried to restrain her; she was dead on the Tuesday afternoon. The inquest found that "the immediate cause of death was hemorrhage from the lining of the stomach, produced by alcoholic stimulants."

The *Standard* devoted a long article to the case: "How is it that Mrs. Bravo should have suddenly died under circumstances which, like those attending the decease of her first and second husbands, are compatible with delirium tremens but also consistent with slow poisoning? How has she been living since her second husband's death?" it demanded. "Has she been leading a secluded life or has she taken up again with her old companions and associates?" But the postmortem revealed no trace of irritant poison.

Her dreadful and pitiable end had aroused a general feeling of compassion, and part of this took the form of renewed vindictive attacks upon himself: "Dr. Gully at whose door in reality lies this second death, trots up and down in health and vigor. Serene and beautiful old man! How we envy his retrospections and, since he is an ardent spiritualist, the shining apparitions he is able to conjure up!"

For a few hours the horrors all came back; in his study they saw him sitting at his desk with a prolonged, unnatural stillness as if he'd been turned to stone; but time and determination had created defenses since the first attacks. He was shocked and distressed but with a sort of hopelessness, feeling that if he had been there, he could have done nothing. If he had answered her letter he would have plunged himself deeper into ruin without saving her.

One touching fact emerged. She had made her will last year and bequeathed her goddaughter Florence Julia a thousand pounds. As this beneficiary was only four years old, the copy of the will that would have been sent to her had been sent to her father. The latter showed it to him. Among generous bequests to her nephews and nieces she had left one hundred pounds each to the three sons of Mrs. Cox. Their mother was left nothing.

The bequests to the children brought her back to him. For a short while he found he could still suffer. Samuel Johnson had said: "In the decline of life, shame and grief are of short duration." But then, how does a man measure time? In 1879, he made his own will. Willie was his residuary legatee; the only people outside his family whom he mentioned were John Pritchard, "Who, for his long and upright service to me," was to have five hundred pounds and all his master's clothes, and "my old and dear friend Charlotte Dyson," to whom he left his copies of the Carlo Dolci and the two heads by Fra Angelico on a gold ground.

He made this will in August. In October, he received news which, if it had come seven years ago, would have transformed his life. On October 21, one year and one month after the death of Florence, Mrs. Gully died. When she had no longer been able to manage her own household, she had been moved to an establishment where she was taken care of, and where her last days were passed in comfort and kindness though she realized little of them. *Lacrimae rerum!*

Ellen's return to his house had thawed some of the ice floe that had closed around him. She had a great many correspondents in Malvern and when they knew that she was living with him they sent kind regards and messages to Dr. Gully. He realized that however fatally injured in reputation he was, there remained respect and affection for him still.

He was in Italy when on March 1, 1880, Ann died after being unconscious for several days with a stroke. Ellen, in sending him the news, told him that Dr. Moore was being everything that was kind and helpful and that he must not feel obliged to come home sooner than he had meant.

An impulse of love for his surviving sister brought him at once. He had some instinct now that at this age—he was seventy-two—and with the trouble in his spine, he was entering the last phase of his existence here. It made him more anxious and careful to keep to the routine which preserved his health and to waste none of the time which might remain.

One thing accomplished was an at least partial reconciliation with Susanna. When she was at Queensborough Terrace she wrote—no doubt at Willie's suggestion—to say that if her father would like to see her, she would be very glad to see him. He wrote a fatherly note in reply as if nothing had happened to part them. He lunched at Queensborough Terrace and the occasion went off well. Several times after that he saw her at intervals. Nothing could ever be the same for either of them, but the relationship was restored like some favorite piece of china that had been smashed and carefully riveted.

After a long pause, Lady Shelley had written to him. In his diary for 1881, he noted that in July he had been to see her in their London house, and had had a long talk with her about Field Place. They avoided by mutual consent any talk about the spirit drawings. He had said in his preface to them that if the public were interested in this series, he would publish more. It hadn't been open to him since then to approach the public again.

He was, however, putting together what he knew would be his final work, a treatise on "Fever and Its Treatment." The work was deeply imbued with his personality and experience. It showed his empirical approach—"The wise and conscientious physician will never reject any method that may aid his patient to recovery"—and the sympathy he had always felt for "the suffering sick, hanging between hope and fear." When he enumerated the causes which, carried to extremes, produced nervous fever, he included: "sorrow, disappointed affection, prolonged anger from prolonged cause." He managed to get the book finished and put by before his powers of mental concentration failed him. Even then, he was still able to get about; in August he went with his daughter-in-law to Joseph Jopling's studio to see the portrait the artist had made of Florence Julia. The child was sitting in an amber-colored frock, holding a violin. In the features of the little girl of seven, the promise of great beauty which he thought he had detected when she was three days old, was now unmistakable. "To Jopling, to see Florrie's picture," he wrote.

Gi-gi, still his favorite, "my small grand-girl," as he called her, sometimes visited Orwell Lodge. Grandpapa had to sit still in his chair most of the time but Pritchard, so kind and smiling, brought in delicious homemade lemonade and if it were summertime, strawberries and raspberries from the garden. Grandpapa gave her pieces of chocolate, *plain* chocolate; he thought chocolates full of brightly colored paste were unwholesome.

He could hardly walk now; he went for drives of an hour or so at a time over the common to Brixton or Clapham. Then came on the time of increasing helplessness and pain.

Chapter 45

ON a March afternoon of 1883, bright with east wind, Pritchard opened the hall door as William Gully came up the steps.

"A good deal weaker, sir," he said as he took William's coat and hat.

He went up the stairs to his father's room. The half-opened sash let in the keen spring air, a bright fire was burning. Between air and fire, the room was exquisitely fresh; the sheets and pillows were white as snow. His aunt Ellen, who had been sitting near the window in a shawl, got up and glided out.

He sat down by the bed. His father smiled but seemed too much fatigued to speak. He took his father's hand, whose square palm and strong, shapely fingers with their oval nails, had been familiar to him all his life, but now the color was altered; from buff it had become ivory.

As he sat, gently holding it, he saw a dark-green book lying on the counterpane; it was Moxon's edition of Tennyson, the volume *Guinevere*. His father followed his gaze and said in a faint voice: *"I must not dwell on this defeat of fame."*

There was a pause; he was going to speak but then his father went on: "Long ago, I was so anxious to make a name."

"You did make one, Father, a great name."

"But then, I lost—" There was another silence; it was so long this time he thought the meaning had escaped, but the words came at last: "I didn't lose one of the most precious things in my life: your love, Willie."

"No, Father, never." His father was smiling again, the bright, buoyant look he remembered from his earliest childhood. His father stretched out his free hand toward the book and Willie put it within reach.

"A very great poet," his father said softly.

"Yes, very, and he owed something to you, Father."

"I—we all—owe so much to him. This, it's *Guinevere,* isn't it?"

"Yes, it is."

"At the end, you know, those words—I've been saying to myself: *To where, beyond these voices—there is peace.*"

"I'm sure it will be so, Father."

"I wasn't thinking of myself; I was thinking of her."

Dr. Moore, sent for in the afternoon of the next day, was told by Pritchard: "I think he's going, sir." Pritchard followed him upstairs at a distance. The doctor went into the bedroom. The figure on the bed was flat and still. Sitting on the counterpane beside it, leaning over it, was a small child, her curls hanging, her skirt spread around her. Dr. Moore turned sharply to the landing.

"The little girl must be removed," he said. Pritchard on the stairs looked up in surprise.

"There's no little girl here, sir," he said. Dr. Moore entered the room again. He saw that it must have been a sudden effect of light. There was no one there except the dead man.

The news of the death was widely reported and variously received. Many respectable papers mentioned only Dr. Gully's great achievements, and many people who had benefited from his skill now wrote to say what they had always felt they owed to him.

In 1884, William Gully published "A Monograph on Fever and Its Treatment," saying in a brief foreword that he did so because it was known that so many of his father's friends and former patients would attach value to what he had written.

The Priory, Balha